THE
TWIN
CITIES

STEVEN HERZMAN

ISBN
978-1-964035-92-5 (Hardcover)
978-1-964035-91-8 (Paperback)
978-1-964035-90-1 (eBook)

Dedicated to my wife and children. Their continued support allowed this text to be created and for all of those who found a new character or two to love.

TABLE OF CONTENTS

PREFACE

MAGIC LESSONS

"I am going to be a great druid one day, Uncle Arty." said Almedda Thalin as she traced another magical form in the air. "I can be the greatest, don't you think?"

"Druids do not rate themselves. They strive for balance in their lives and enforcing balance on their environment. Without balance we have nothing." replied Artitous. "We strive for a perfect balance between the dark and the light. Slower with that form or it will not take. Balance in the trees and the streams. Simply perfect balance. Nature does not know good and evil, it simply is. That is how we should be. In tune with nature and with ourselves. No not like that, slower and with more feeling."

"This is impossible. Why would I ever want to produce an animal of light?" asked Almedda.

"This can be a great distraction to an enemy. Now try again. Slowly drawing deep within yourself. You can do it." said Artitous.

"Still teaching the little one illusion and worthless magic? She should be a wizard like me." said Torlin as he walked into the room.

"And what do wizards believe in, dear brother?" asked the younger sibling.

"Wizards believe in power. We believe in gaining it by any means possible and learning more magic. We believe learning more powers to be a vital part of our culture." said Torlin.

"In other words, you are power whores?" said Almedda.

"Not at all, we are scholars and teachers. Except for me, I just learn for learning's sake. I used to use my powers for selfish reasons, but I have learned a little of how to control my desires. Wouldn't you say Artitous?" said Torlin.

"Druids and wizards are different as night and day in philosophy but are similar in abilities. One is really no different than the other in battle, but in healing and life in other times the druid has the advantage." said Artitous.

"Coming from a druid. Without the wizard there would be no new knowledge. There would be limited education for the children. We are important in so many ways. Our knowledge is not just about nature; it is mathematics, science, and all manner of things." said Torlin as he started making the form she was trying to perform. "As you see, magic is magic. Your philosophy should be your own. We should not have the branches of magic user. There should be no more druid and wizard but that will never be the case. There will never be equality in magic." said Torlin as the form came together and a small dragon appeared before the three magic users.

"Why a dragon, brother? Surely you do not believe they will ever return. They left after that strange battle outside Tetra. They said they would not deal with the problems of man anymore." said Almedda.

"Why a dragon? Why not? They are majestic beasts with grace, power, and intelligence." replied Torlin.

"Kind of flashy, don't you think, young one? Something a little softer for your sister perhaps?" said Artitous as a rabbit danced around the amazed Almedda.

Torlin waved his hands and a majestic Phoenix of dazzling-colored lights appeared. Almedda looked at it in wonder for a moment and then asked, "You chose a Phoenix, why pick something that does not exist? Surely something that roams the world like a centaur, or a mermaid would be a better choice."

"Do you see the Creator? No, but you believe he is there. Do you see all the mystical creatures of our world? Of course not. Some beings are just not meant to be seen or heard. Have you ever seen a strange cloud flying overhead? It may look like a bird. But to you it is only a cloud because you believe it to be only a cloud. You must see wonder in all things to be a wizard or a druid. More so the wizard but I digress. Belief in a thing makes it real. With the power anything is possible. Even death can be left to stand on the door mat and never enter. Remember this and you will go far as a wizard or even as a druid." said Torlin, having one of his rare serious moments with his younger sister.

"Druids believe that nature should not be meddled with. You may be right about the world, wizard, but we druids keep the world in check. We tend the fields and the animals that you so wish to study and care for their ill and wounded. Stick with the druids that have begun your education and the world will be revealed in all kinds of ways no one else could possibly show you." said Artitous.

"I believe that I can be both, a wizard and a druid. Surely one can easily do both." said Almedda with a grin.

Artitous nearly choked on his tongue and Torlin nearly fell over himself as he tried to walk away. "No one can serve two masters." Torlin began as he recovered himself and resumed heading toward the door. "You have a choice to make and it is a serious one. Remember there are pros and cons to both sides of magic. Choose justly and there will be no regrets. Be well and I will see you for your lessons as a wizard." The door closing behind him as he walked through.

Artitous recovered himself as Torlin left the room. "Child, he is right. You can only serve one side of magic. Just as you cannot study the light and dark sides of magic. There is just no way to do both. You must choose your path. Keep in mind, there are no dark druids. At least as far as I am aware. If there are, they keep themselves well hidden. It is not so with wizards where temptations can take you all so easily."

"But what if I wanted to study the dark arts as well as the light? Maybe I could bring the balance that everyone so wishes. So many things to learn and a stupid title allows you to study one or the other. It makes no sense." said Almedda. "Surely the dark wizards have no problems. They do what they like."

"Yes, but they pay a terrible price. They lose all that makes them human. You do not want to go down the dark path. Please come to me regardless of your choice and do nothing until you have come to me." said Artitous.

The girl leaned over and touched the druid's leg and looked up into his face and smiled. Getting up she said nothing and walked from the room. The older man shook his head, these kids would be the death of him, he could tell.

As the girl left the room, she saw a dead bird near the pathway. She leaned over and whispered words of power and the grass and roses nearby wilted and the bird came back to life. She let the bird go and walked on smiling. She would find a way to do both.

CHAPTER ONE

SECRET MISSIONS

Twilight came upon the face of Thalinburg as the small caravan approached the gates. The coming darkness seemed to flow behind the small wagons and the accompanying riders. As the wagons and horses approached the gates a light appeared in the lead wagon and a Noom exited. He walked to the dwarven guards and bowed nearly to the ground. "Very formal, little one. What is your purpose in Thalinburg?" asked the sturdy dwarf.

"My lord, Formal is my way. I come solely for the sights and sounds of the great city. Surely a few Nooms with their goods are welcome. We traveled far to be here. All the way from the Mountains of Doric. We bring fine beers and tobacco from our villages to trade and hope to trade them for your fine weapons and ponies." replied the Noom.

"Of course, you have your papers, a bill of lading, something I can hand over to my officers. Surely you do not expect me to let you in just because you asked politely, now do you?" said the dwarf laughing heartily as he held out his hand.

"Of course, but why the security? I thought the region around Thalinburg was the safest in the world? Surely you do not expect trouble from a small band of traders, do you?" said the Noom bending once more in a formal bow.

"We have royal guests in the city. All of them are here for a summit of the cities. Thomas and Meka arrived this morning and Torlin and Roanda have been here for two. Tanis Thalin and his wife once more, Athinina, live in the city and the young ones have come as well from their studies with their brothers." said the dwarf as he once more held out his hand.

"Young ones? I was not aware of young ones. Who are they?" asked the now confused looking Noom.

"Why they are the Prince Garren and Princess Almedda. They came from the countryside just the other day. Now I will ask again where your papers are." His face suddenly growing darker and more menacing.

"Good sir I have your papers, was just looking for some information. You know travelers live on information. Just asking questions. Yes, well here they are, I hope these suffice." said the Noom as another of his species arrived at the gates from the wagons holding a sheath of papers.

Nooms were so named because in dragon tongue the name means half. They were roughly half the size of a man. Seen from afar they would resemble children with large ears and hairy arms and legs revealed by their coats and short pants. The boots they wear resembled low-cut shoes with long turn downs. Known more for their abilities at stealth and thievery, they were also known as being very talkative traders and farmers. The Nooms were known for their fine beers and tobacco as well as their invention of burning sticks. Burning sticks were tightly rolled tobacco leaves that one put in their mouths and puffed upon.

The dwarves were a small people as well. Not quite as small as the Nooms, they still stood a head smaller than a short man. Known for their large beards and big noses, they are best known for their forge work. They were known far and wide as the best smiths in the world and the second-best warriors. Only the elves rivaled the prowess of the dwarves in combat. That is only when asking someone other than a dwarf.

The Noom stood only up to the fierce dwarf's red beard, but his demeanor made him suddenly the larger being in the road. "I trust these will do?"

"I can't read these. I can only read the dwarven speech. Let me bring these to my officer." said the dwarf turning toward the shack by the gates.

As he turned, he felt the pinch of a blade entering his back between the plates of his suit of full plate armor. He tried to turn and face the Noom that had stabbed him, but he found he could not move. He managed one more step forward and then he fell to the ground, dead before he hit the soil. The Noom wiped his blade carefully in a rag then threw it down upon the dead dwarf. Leaning down he picked up his papers and handed them to his partner.

"Good thing he could not read Noom or we would have been in trouble. Our plans are all laid out in those documents. Open the gates and let us get to work. I wish this to be over as soon as possible. If they are all here that makes our lives so much easier. The only question I have is which one first."

He bent his small back and lifted the dwarf from the ground. He then set him up at his post and made him appear to be asleep. The strength of the Noom becoming apparent. Quickly the gates were opened and the Nooms moved through into Thalinburg. People passed them heading for the gates as they entered, and the other people paid the small beings no mind. Strange sights were common in Thalinburg and people were much more interested in their day-to-day activities.

The Noom leading the horses and wagons looked up at his partner and called out, "Hey Drummond, where do we go from here?"

"The Languid Dragon, Pommel." replied Drummond.

"Then let us go, I for one would like to have a pint of ale before we rest for the day." said Pommel.

They moved down the main avenue of Thalinburg surrounded by the stone-based buildings with their wooden upper stories. This was the new city, and many improvements were made to the rundown buildings here. As they progressed into the city the buildings were stone all the way to the top and were carved and gilded in a way that only the Ogier could do. It was still unknown who had built Thalinburg, but it was believed to be the work of the survivors of the war between the lizard-like Tetradons and Metradons. It was believed they abandoned their cities after the war and worked together to build a new one. The wizards and druids still could not find proof of this, but they still speculated.

The buildings were carved with frescos and scenes of hunts and wars fought and won, and lost, as well as scenes from the seas and the mountains. These made for a whirlwind of images bombarding the individual moving down the streets if you were not accustomed to them. To some it was overpowering, but to Pommel and Drummond the sights were lost as they ignored them looking for the inn.

At a large building, even for Thalinburg standards, decorated with a large dragon in a state of near sleep, the two Nooms stopped in front of the stable yard. The young man who came out was pleased to see the Nooms and their gold. He quickly put up their horses and had their wagons put into the storage area behind the stable. Before following the young man inside the Nooms tied shut the flaps of their wagons and cast weird spells over them. Knowing glances passed between the Nooms as they moved into the inn proper.

CHAPTER TWO

PLANNING

Inside the inn was lined with dark wood panels and a solid wood floor. The panels were covered with frescos of battles and of hunts. The floors shone with a dull glow from the reflected lamp light and the warm fireplaces set into both the north and south walls. The inn had two spiral stairways heading to the second floor and above. One on the east wall and one on the west wall. The door to the kitchens dominated the remainder of the west wall and the door they entered by was on the east wall. The inn had tables in the center of the floor in two neat rows, one row extremely low and had small benches for the dwarves and Nooms the other normal sized benches and tables for the men and the elves. It even had a small table and chair all alone the size for an Ogier. The landlord really accommodated everyone.

The Nooms were met at the door by a wide man in a dirty white apron. He was Heddie the innkeeper. He was not tall by the judgment of men, but he had a girth that would have made the kings of old swoon. Heddie was a jolly man with a quick joke for the Nooms as they entered. Laughing quite pleased with himself for his wit he led the young Nooms to the low tables and offered them ale and food, which they accepted most graciously. Pommel stared at Drummond and looked around the inn.

"Is this place really where we need to be? Kind of open and lack of privacy and all. Surely, we cannot be meeting our contact here. Why anyone sitting near us will be remarked at and we would not go unnoticed at the big tables. Please tell me you have a plan." said Pommel.

"Be still Pommel, we will have our rooms soon and then we will meet our friend. Look here comes the innkeeper with food and drink. I do not recall when the last time I ate was, but I am sure I missed luncheon and first dinner. Let us take our meat and then we will plan." said Drummond.

"We had lunch, Drummond, but you are right, we missed luncheon and first dinner, but now we have supper, and late dinner looks like it will be had as well. Who is our friend? I do not recall having been here before and I at least do not know anyone here. When will he come? Do we have to send for him? I really want to get on with our business." Pommel whined.

Drummond just bent his head to his plates and started eating. He continued as Pommel toyed with the food on his plate. Eventually both Nooms finished their meals and ale and put their heads together glaring at anyone who came close. Heddie came to them and led them to the second story and to a room that was two sizes too big for them. The beds required a step for them to get into them, though they were filled with goose down and the pillows were filled with the same. The chairs in the room were definitely not Noom sized. They struggled into them and their feet dangled from the edge. The table was well over their heads, but it would not be needed. The end tables were accessible from the beds and the pitchers and basins were located there for washing.

Drummond whispered something to the innkeeper and then closed the door. The two sat in silence as the day wore on and about an hour later a knock was heard at their door. Pommel opened the door and Drummond held a small crossbow in his hands. Seeing the man at the door, he put the bow down and embraced the man. Pommel soon did the same and they moved to the chairs and beds. The man spoke softly and detailed what he had planned. Dressed as one of the lords of the men, his rich cloak kept his face in shadow. Not that the Nooms needed to see the man's face to know who he was, but he thought he was being stealthy. The Nooms approved of his precautions but told him they were unnecessary. They would not reveal him to anyone, and when he was King, he could reward them.

The nobleman still left his cloak up and still spoke in whispers. "You know what you are to do, and when. People will be tired of the rule of the Thalin clan soon enough and I will be ready to take the throne as soon as it is vacant." The nobleman stood up walked out of the room not hearing the conversation behind him. "He will get his, he will, Pommel. He will get his."

CHAPTER THREE

WEIRD INCIDENCE

The day was growing long when Thomas and Meka came down from their rooms. Meka showed her pregnancy as she moved slowly down the stairs. Her small stature had never interfered in her role as a commander of the Tyris, women warriors from the Dark Lands who flaunted their weapons skill almost as much as they flaunted their bodies, but it did hamper her role as a wife and princess of the realm. She showed her pregnancy early, the bulge of the baby obvious to all very soon after the announcement. The woman was small as far as the Tyris were concerned. She stood shoulder height to her husband, but she ruled him with an iron will though and constant threats kept him in line. Thomas said nothing and glared at the man acting as his guard for the day. It was a sham anyway, who would dare try to harm him?

Meka on the other hand was glad to have the extra pair of hands around. Her condition had brought many desires with it and her husband had tired of satisfying them. Her physical desires were taken care of by Thomas; but all the foodstuffs she wanted or the cribs or toys or any other thing was put on the poor guard.

For what seemed the twentieth time that day, Meka was asking for ice chips. The druids carried ice down from the mountains and stored it in an enchanted building to keep it frozen. Torlin had offered to make her some ice using magic, but she preferred the mountain ice. Torlin's wife was also expecting a child and Torlin fawned over her completely unlike Thomas. Meka wondered at Thomas sometimes, he seemed happy to be a father, but sometimes the man seemed to be very cold and unfeeling. She knew he loved her but sometimes he just did not show it.

Thomas walked into the Throne room to find his mother and father waiting for him. It was strange to think of the man as his father as he had died in the first war of power, He was killed but was one of the Askanitowa and died at the hands of a goblin. Had the killing blow come from a demon he would have never come back. The Askanitowa were the race of immortals that oversaw the world of Dracos and kept it in balance. They were vulnerable only to demons and demon weapons. Otherwise, the Askanitowa would come back to life as soon as the wounds that had killed them had healed.

Thomas bowed slightly to his mother and ignored his father. He could not bring himself to respect the man. Tanis Thalin ignored the slight as he always did. The young man did have a right to be sore. Almost on his brother's heels in came Torlin and his slightly less showing wife. Roanda was also pregnant but she did not show her pregnancy as much as Meka. Roanda stood almost as tall as her husband, who was rather tall himself. She was also physically very well built so the pregnancy carried a little farther back. They joked that the children would share a birth date, as they had conceived them at about the same time.

The messenger arrived with the ice chips for Meka and Torlin produced a snow fall into a goblet for Roanda. She enjoyed the magical ice, seeing it produced as well as eating it. Torlin joked he had not used the spell before her pregnancy, and now it was the only one he used. Torlin was the head of the Mysteries of Magical Learning as it is now called. It had once been simply the Mysteries of Dracos but many in the magical community felt it needed a finer point. There were several forms of magical learning now and Torlin worked with each of them.

Thomas had been the head of the armies of Dracos until the Metradon/Tetradon incident. Thomas had ceded his city from the Lands of Dracos ruled by his mother and father and as such he was no longer the head of her armies; that had returned to Tanis on his return anyway.

Tanis looked at his wife and smiled. His children were all in the same city at least. He was happy with that. They would only be there a short while before returning to their respective cities, but at least they were all together. He thought that they may even be in the same building. His younger children had gone off for one reason or another, but he hoped they would be back soon. It would be nice to have all of them together at least once during the visit. The younger two children of Tanis had been conceived when he did not know who he was. The second wife, Claire, died shortly after the birth of the children. It was just as well for when he remembered who and what he was, he had no strings binding him to his new life. He was able to take his children and return to his old life. He was amazed that he had two sets of twins. Athinina had one set of twins and Claire another set. At least the younger twins he could tell apart.

Thomas and Torlin were identical twins except for a raspberry mark behind their ears. One was on one side the other was on the other side. Many a time Athinina had grabbed an offending child and checked those marks to tell which one needed punishment.

The younger twins were a mixed batch, one boy and one girl. The boy's name was Garren the girl was Almedda. They too had inherited separate talents. The boy was a soldier like Thomas. He would follow Torlin around though. The boy had latched onto the wizard, and Torlin enjoyed the company of the younger man. Almedda was a druid more than a wizard but had gravitated toward Thomas. Unlike his brother,

Thomas did not like the girl's attention. He would shoo her away after only a few minutes of talking. Meka thought it funny, but Thomas was always upset by it. The older boys were celebrating their nineteenth year while the younger twins were celebrating their twelfth. Despite the age difference, Torlin took to the younger ones and worked at their education. Thomas just ignored them figuring if he acknowledged them, he would have to acknowledge Tanis. He was not ready for that.

The elder boys were seated just below the dais top while the youngest at the bottom of the stairs leading to the dais. This was the first time they had been in the same place at the same time. Torlin created a full ceiling of birds and animals from around the world. He would make the birds to race around the room, first by themselves and later with dragons and phoenix. Thomas took no mind to it. His wife though, was entirely enraptured. She would jump at the dragons and clap merrily at the birds. Little Almedda would make the birds chase the dragons and caused much laughter. Torlin would just shake his head and set things to rights again.

As the dragon made the third lap around the room the door opened and in marched Duke Tobin Masters, Duke of the city state of McCryden, who would take the throne should the Royal family perish. "I hate to break up the festivities, My Lords and Ladies." He said as he dodged the bird that flew straight for his head. "But we have a problem." He said as he cleaned the residue of the spell from his cloak. "Our guards are being murdered. Four gate guards have died in as many nights. Each stabbed with a thin blade to the back. The city drunkard is accused and now awaits his trial. Justice must be swift, or our guards will not take their posts."

"Why the rush to try this man, do you have any evidence against him? The guard are the guard and will continue to man their posts, despite of our speed in trying this man. They know we will bring the killer to justice." Athinina stated from her throne. "Lord Nargus, as head of the guard go to your men and assure them, we are doing everything we can to find this killer."

"Certainly, my Queen, it will be as you say." Lord Nargus said as he bowed his way out of the throne room. Nargus was the head of the cavalry for Dracos as well as the head of the guard. His slightly bowed legs showed how much time the man had been in the saddle. He was also an expert with the lance and mace. His sword that rode low on his hip was his last resort as he did not possess the agility to be a good swordsman.

"But we caught the man leaving the scene of the crime. It is clear he is the killer. I need no other evidence." Lord Masters said as he worked his way toward the dais.

"Justice needs to be served as proven in a court. No man is guilty until a fair trial." said Athinina before her husband, Tanis, could speak. Tanis lifted his hand to speak and Lord Masters once more interrupted, "Then let us have a trial of might makes right. If he can beat one of our knights, then he is free. If not, he is obviously guilty and should be immediately hung."

"No one will be tried by might. We will have a civilized trial and hear all the evidence. The druids have been going over every inch of the man looking for means and evidence for or against him. Justice will be served." said Athinina.

Tanis once more began to speak when Lord Masters interrupted once more. "My lord and lady, the druids. They are healers what do they know of evidence. My men will torture the evidence from him." Squeaked Lord Masters.

"Why is this so important to you? Surely the death of four guards is not anything for the Governor of McCryden to worry about." said Tanis finally getting a word in.

"Just concerned with the opinion of the people and the letter of justice my liege." said Lord Masters as he bowed low and slid back from the dais. Tanis had that blasted elven magic in him. He could tell if there was anything amiss and Lord Masters did not want his plans sullied this quickly.

Lord Masters slid his way out of the door and looked around him. He had plans to make. He would have to see to this man himself.

CHAPTER FOUR

INJURY AND POISON

Meka was walking out in the gardens when she saw a pair of Noom running around. The little people fascinated her. They were so small, yet fierce warriors to be told. She did not know first-hand, but she had fellow Tyris who had faced them. These appeared to be looking into every bush in the garden. Meka cleared her throat and said to the little ones, "Is there something you are looking for? I will be happy to help you find it."

"Oh, you are standing there was not sure you were. Just pruning the bushes. They looked a little rough, so we decided to prune them. Nothing to see here." said Pommel as Drummond quickly slid the dagger from it sheath. The first of the royal family to go.

Still talking to the little ones, Meka almost missed the little one's blade. Turning to catch his hand she felt the pinch of the blade entering her side. Meka let out a scream and the guard came running but the would-be assassin was gone. She crumpled to the ground and was taken to her rooms by the guard screaming for druids as they ran her to her quarters.

Thomas was reviewing his troops before their show of military prowess later in the day when he heard the scream. He went running and saw the guard carrying her to their rooms. "Call Artitous and Torlin. They must save my wife and baby." Cried Thomas as he followed the now long procession to his rooms. He knew wounds from combat, but this was like nothing he had seen before. The wound though just inflicted was already festering. Meka was coming in and out of consciousness speaking repeatedly in her delirium of little people. There was no evidence of anyone else in the gardens. He ordered the guard to search the grounds for any sign of these little people, so that he could wreak his revenge.

The Nooms made it back to their rooms at the Languid Dragon as Meka was being first observed by the druids. "Well, the blade did not make it far enough. She twisted. How did she see the blade, I was sure it was hidden? We cannot make any more mistakes like that again. She may recover and report seeing Noom. Then our job becomes much more difficult." said Drummond. Pommel was sitting and whining. He was sure the guards were going to plow right into the room and take their heads right then and there. He was sure they left no signs, but you are never perfect. He hoped he left nothing major behind.

Drummond looked at his scabbard and asked Pommel, "Pommel, where is my dagger? If it is still in the garden, we must recover it. They will know the poison if they find it. And then they will know how to treat the princess. We have to go back."

Darkness was falling as the guard gave up the search of the garden. Thomas still searched for clues, but he found little. A smudged footprint, a bit of cloth, a few drops of blood. He was about to give up when from a bush he noticed the wires. *These bushes were not supported by wires,* thought Thomas. Walking over to the bush he investigated it and saw the device and the flame now moving down a fuse. Before he could react, he was blown backward into the garden wall. He tried to get up and found he could not. Faint cries from Thomas were not heard at first as everyone was looking for the source of the explosion.

Artitous looked into the next room where Almedda was practicing her magic and saw there was not an explosion in there, so he suddenly became concerned. Running to the hall he saw Meka's room door open and other druids working on the girl. Artitous walked over and looked in expecting to see a baby being born. Seeing the wound, he told the guards to go and search for the explosion and report back to him.

Pommel walked into the nearly empty garden and saw his booby trap had gotten one of his intended victims, laughing he quickly searched for and found the dagger left beneath one of the traps. He ran back to his rooms and excitedly told Drummond, "The prince has been taken down by one of the bombs. He will be dead soon too. I heard rumors of the princess's demise and saw the prince lying dead by the remains of one of the bushes. We are well on our way." Pommel was still immensely proud of himself as he felt the blade enter his back. "Why?" was all he could say as he fell to the ground.

"Because you are getting sloppy my dear brother. Nothing will prevent the destruction of the royal family."

It was Tanis that found Thomas on the ground against the garden wall. He slowly checked him over magically and saw the destruction in his back. The boy may yet live, but he would never walk again. Thomas would be crushed with that news. He ordered the guard to carefully bring the prince to Artitous. The old man should be able to do something about this and hopefully heal the injured back. No one was sure at this point, but he hoped.

Artitous came running around the corner and nearly ran into the guards bearing the now incapacitated prince. Artitous ordered the man brought into the other set of rooms near them. He checked the man over as Tanis had and found the back injury. "I will be back to him Tanis, but you already know we cannot heal that injury. Right now, I must save his wife and child. Stay with him and I will return when I can."

As he spoke, he left the room with druids flowing in with their assistants and students trailing behind. Tanis was about to leave the room to check on the princess when his son woke. He tried to move his legs to swing out of the bed and they refused to follow the command. Tanis moved to his side and Thomas looked at him. Thomas tried to lift his arm and again the limb refused to do as he wanted. "Can someone tell me why I cannot move. If Torlin is playing games I swear I will have my revenge."

"Will someone tell me the truth. What is wrong with me?"

"You sustained an awfully bad back injury. These druids have worked tirelessly to prevent your death, but the injury is beyond even my or Artitous's ability to correct. It will take time to heal and you may be able to do more with the aid of your druids. All we can do is wait and see."

"And how fairs my wife and child? Are they at least faring better than I am? She will never look at me the same after this. I just need a dagger and a few moments alone. It will all be over with then and she and my child will not be saddled with my condition." said Thomas.

"You will do no such thing. You are going to fight this like you fight everything else. At least you will be alive to see your child born. Right now, mother and child are still in bad condition. Artitous has pulled the druids from everywhere to correct the poison that she has been afflicted with. We still have no idea what it is, and she is still lucky to be alive. The wound spreads like a cancer and we are doing our best to stop it." replied Tanis

"How am I supposed to live like this? Tell me! You are supposedly so wise. Please share your wisdom." Screamed Thomas.

"One day at a time my son. One day at a time. Now let me check on your wife I have not been in there yet and am only going on what they are telling me. I want to see what is happening for myself. So, I will leave you for a few minutes and come back soon." said Tanis as he walked from the room.

Tanis walked into the room with the stricken princess. He looked at the wound and asked if they had checked for black magic. The druids did not even look up from their tasks and answered his question. Artitous stood tall and strong as an oak tree over the prone woman and continued to work on her as he spoke to Tanis. "We know it is not magic, but we cannot find any trace of poison. It is like the flesh is just rotting away. We do not have any clue how to treat this. We have never seen a wound like this."

As he spoke a wizened old druid walked in. "Why have you not rinsed the wound in spring water? The peach pit should get washed away and the wound will stop spreading." said the druid.

"What are you saying old one?" asked Artitous.

"Why you have a peach pit poison there. The druids once used it when we had the hidden warriors. God, I miss the old days. We could quietly dispose of people who attacked the groves." replied the old man. "But if you cut yourself, you rinsed it in water and then put a salve of rose petals and heal-all on the wound. It will heal up in a few days. After the wound is cleaned, she should wake."

"Are you certain? Can it be anything else? Quickly old man, speak." said Tanis.

"There is nothing else I believe it can be. I am the poison master for the groves and was coming at the request of the Arch druid Artitous to consult on a matter of close to death by poison. He should have known a peach pit poison by the look. So where is the patient? I am hoping it was not for a peach pit poison I was summoned." Sighed the old man.

"Your patient has already been diagnosed and by your extensive knowledge of all things poison. Thank you for your help." said Artitous.

"Move out of the way and let me do what I came here to do. Get me a basin of water and some clean cloths. You there fetch me some rose petals, and you there, fetch me some heal-all. You should be washing the wound with this like that." He trailed off as he started his work forgetting that everyone else was there until he spoke suddenly to the room. "She will be better soon. Just let the poor child rest. The poison should not have affected the little one but keep an eye on her for the next little while and when she wakes just make sure she is still until the wound has properly healed."

The old man was cheered as he left, and the attention made the old man blush. The old man looked flush as he left the room then he came back in. "Look for rogue druids or trained assassins for your culprit. This is not a commonly used poison and I fear things will get worse before they get better."

"Who still uses this poison? Just so we know where to begin looking for the assassin. They are used almost solely by the Guild of Blades or by Dark Druids anymore. It was once widely used by anyone who needed someone dead and in a painful way." said the old man as he once more turned to leave.

"One more question, sir. Who is the Guild of Blades? I have never heard of them."

"Ask the provincial governor. He knows more about them than he is letting on he does. I know the look of one of those and he has it. Now I am going to my hovel for a nap. Call me when she is awake and ready to be stitched." said the old man as he left the room.

"We can stitch her up ourselves, old one. We will call you again when we have need once more." said Tanis, "Artitous do you think Perrick has anything to do with this attack? He has been so loyal for so long with no instances of trouble from him or the Guild of Blades whoever they are."

"We can only ask him. Perrick should be open and forward with us." said the druid as the man they spoke of walked into the room. "Peach pit, huh? Who used it on her? Someone wanted her to die painfully." said Perrick.

"Perrick tell us of the Guild of Blades. Who are they? Where are they? Who belongs to them? We need answers Perrick." said Tanis.

"Wait one minute. How do you know of the Guild? No one inquiries about the guild and lives to tell the tale. They are assassins, thieves, and rogues. I was once a member as you recall at the gates of McCryden, but they look kind of funny at government officials poking around their affairs. Almost was killed by a pair of Noom, it seems like ten years ago. A peculiar pair named Pommel or Prommel or Gargemel, and Drommond or Drummond. The later was the knife while the other was the distraction. Cute little guys with hearts as black as coal. Needed a full month's wages to get them to finally leave. I wonder if they have come back to Thalinburg. If they have been hired for a job, then keep an eye out on the Hall of the Dead. The bodies will start to pile up." said Perrick.

"How do you know it is Noom?" asked Tanis.

"It is all over that she was speaking of little people in her delirium. If it is them then no one is safe. Not even you Tanis. But the good news is they travel together so we can rule out any Noom traveling alone. And the Noom always stay at Noom friendly hostels and rooming houses. The taverns will be in heaven because these guys eat like they have hollow legs. Keep a look out there." said the reformed rogue.

"Please inform Lord Nargus of this. He may find your little people. Noom were always considered fairy tales in the darker realms. They never traded with us and all their goods we attributed to the traders that brought them to us." said Athinina.

"Trust me, they are real. I will investigate the Noom angle myself. If they are here, I may get an audience with them faster than non-members of the Guild. They stand on formality. They call meetings audiences can you believe that?" said Perrick as he left the room.

"He is your friend remember that." said Athinina to Tanis as the thief left the room. Tanis just leaned over and kissed her and got a fist to the ribs for his trouble. "Not in front of the guests, My Dear."

CHAPTER FIVE

BIRTHDAYS

As the sun rose over the city, Torlin and Roanda were getting ready to go to the court for the morning audience with the entire family save his brother and his wife. They walked down the path through the garden and Torlin blinked at the sight he beheld before him.

The child had been hung by his feet on the garden wall with a strange language written around him. Pan Thor, the Catarel adoptive brother of Torlin, turned the path when he saw the two of them and jumped before them. Catarel are a cat like human species that was eliminated years before by the dragons in an ugly war. Pan Thor was the last of his species and was adopted by Torlin for saving his life. Pan Thor kept his back to the scene in front of the humans and cried out to them, "Avert your eyes! This is an extremely dangerous curse that only a few know how to reverse. We must keep this garden clear of anyone who may accidentally wander in until we can remove the attacking curse plastered here. Guards call for Tanis and Artitous and keep anyone else from coming into this garden. Under no circumstances is anyone to come into this garden except for Tanis, Artitous and myself. Not even the prince here and his wife. Now go furless ones, someone means your family great harm. Pan Thor is immune to this kind of magic so Pan Thor must be the one to destroy it. Go now. Please."

Torlin moved quickly and hurried his wife away from the display on the wall. If Pan Thor was that afraid of the magic, then he would not risk his wife and child by staring at it. Roanda walked on toward the great hall when she stopped suddenly grabbing her belly. She let out a scream and bent double, falling slowly to the floor. Torlin ran for the closest druid and had him come to his wife's side. "Sir, there is something wrong with my wife. Please help her. She has been cursed; I know it." Yelled Torlin.

"Your wife has not been cursed unless that is what they call it now a days. You began this ten months ago. Oliver, please get the midwife and you sir levitate her into your rooms. It is time for your child to arrive." said the druid as he grabbed a young boy running past.

Torlin immediately brought his wife into the air and floated her gently to their shared rooms. She let out a small scream every so often keeping Torlin on his feet. The midwife was quick to arrive and shooed the men from the room. "This is ladies' work now. Be still outside and we will see what happens. It will not be long now young prince. You will know of your offspring very soon."

Torlin was outside in a state of great concern. Every scream from his wife pulled him to try and enter the room. Guards and druids waited outside and prevented the prince from entering. Pan Thor came and sat with him in the sitting room as they waited. Pan Thor was offering Catarel names for his adoptive brother's child and Torlin rejected one after the other. He would admonish the Catarel that Roanda and he would decide on a name after the child was born.

A rushing of bodies made Torlin sit up as they approached. Was something wrong with his wife? He went to inquire about the crowd of people when they passed the door and hurried into the neighboring rooms of his brother and his wife. He caught a druid passing and asked what the hurry to Meka and Thomas was?

"The princess has awakened and now starts the pains of labor. You are not the only one to become a father this day. I must go, her wound will be needing tending as she works to bring forth her babe. It will not be long before you're both parents." replied the druid.

Torlin looked at Pan Thor and started pacing the floor. He was still waiting for Roanda to give birth and listening for his brother's wife to complete her labors. He was to become an uncle and a father at the same time. How was he to do this? He heard the cry from his rooms' just moments before he heard them from his brother's. They were literally moments apart. He moved to the door and was once more was forced from the room. "It is not over. Apparently, you also produce twins. She will be ready to finish soon and you will see your children. For now, just wait and be ready." said the midwife.

Torlin went into his brother's rooms as the team moved out. She lay there with a child in her arms and a smile upon her face. The wound looked much cleaner and less infected. She would be fine. "How is my niece or nephew?" Called out Torlin as he walked into the room. "And where is my lug of a brother? He should be here to see his child. I do not see him."

"He is in the other room. He is in a bad way. He will not see anyone. Torlin, you must go to him and see if you can heal him. His son is well and awaits his father. He is strong and full of life. Let his father see this." said Meka.

"What has happened to Thomas?" asked Torlin. "From what does he need healing that the druids cannot provide?"

"Thomas was caught in an explosion shortly after I was injured. His back is crushed. Surely you can do something. He needs to walk again to take care of his son." said Meka.

"Roanda is bearing her second babe. I am to be a father of twins. And now that is dimmed by the plight of my brother. I will do my best to alleviate my brother's pain and help him recover if possible. Go to see my wife when you are able. She will kill to see her nephew." Torlin said as he walked into his brother's rooms. He saw his brother on his back and druids all around him trying to heal his wound. Torlin fed magic into them and they pushed harder to heal the wound. A sharp hiss left his brother's lips as the spinal cord healed. Torlin looked again at the injury with a magical delving and saw all the shrapnel still in his back. "Your wounds will be healed soon, brother. You just have so much damage. It will take time."

"I don't care about time! You and your wizards and druids need to make me whole. What is the holdup, brother? Too weak to cure me. You still following those great new laws made by that man? Just remove all the shards and I will be whole again." Screamed Thomas at his brother.

"If I remove the shards all at once you will die. They will be removed when the wounds can be healed as they are removed. Until then there are other manners of movement for you. I will help you recover. It will be a long road and soon enough we will be teaching you to walk again. And then your recovery will be complete." said Torlin looking down at his brother with concern in his eyes.

"You foul wizard, Get out of here! You are not welcome. I will find a wizard that will heal me entirely or kill me. I do not want to live like this, I am worthless like this. I cannot be a father like this, what am I supposed to do? Make my child strong and powerful lying on my back. It will mock me." said a now desperate Thomas.

"You will be healed eventually. You child will love and respect you no matter how you are. That is what son's do for their fathers." said Torlin as he walked toward the door.

"A son. I have a son. God kill me now. I cannot have a son like this. Bring me my dagger, someone. I do not want to be seen as an invalid to my son. Torlin stop moving and kill me. I will send my troops to attack your city. I will hunt down your family. Just kill me. "Screamed Thomas.

"You will do what you will do. Guard, prevent my brother from being brought anything he can harm himself with. As for the dagger. If he wants it, he can come and get it." Torlin said as he plunged the blade deep into the stud holding up the doorway to his rooms. "Goodbye for now but I will return to assist on the healing process. You will be able to get your knife soon enough."

"You bastard. Come back here and it is a dagger. Not a knife," said Thomas as the wizard left the room. Torlin sent a wave over his shoulder and continued out into the outer room where the mother and new baby were sitting in a chair with Meka holding the baby boy wrapped snugly in a blanket.

"A picture from heaven. I must go see my children and wife now. What should we call the boy?" said Torlin as he walked from the room.

"Thomas and I will decide soon and let you know. Thank you for helping as much as you could. Thomas will come around soon. See you and your wife soon." said Meka.

CHAPTER SIX

PREPARING THE WAY

Torlin walked into his room to a scene of pandemonium. Druids and midwives were everywhere cleaning and putting things to right around the room. "Ladies and gentlemen, we have never had these rooms looking as neat as you have it now, Roanda and I enjoy a little chaos. Not a lot but chaos."

"You won't be wanting chaos anymore. Those babes of yours will keep the chaos going. Go and see your children and their mother now. They are all been cleaned and wrapped and fed. So, it is safe to enter." said the old man closest to the door. "I will not steal your wife's thunder. You will have to see her for the children's sex and weight and such."

"Thank you, good sir. I will be happy hearing it from her own lips." said Torlin as he walked toward his wife and his rooms. "I have arrived my dearest. What have I missed?"

"You have missed the arrival of Garath and Arlette. Your son is smaller than your daughter. He weighs seven pounds three ounces; your daughter is seven pounds four ounces. Though he eats more than she does. The little devils." said Roanda as she smiled at her husband as he entered the room. "How is your brother? Any more healing needed?"

"My brother hates all things and his life. He has threatened suicide. I do not know what to do for his mind. His body I will eventually heal, but his mind I can do nothing about. He only knows anger and pain. I will see him tomorrow. Maybe his mood will be better. He still does not want to see his wife or child. And she will not give the boy a name without him. She hopes that he will come around soon, but I believe it will be a long uphill battle. He may not ever be whole again." said Torlin.

"Surely, he is not that bad. Has he really threatened his own life? I feel so bad us having our joyous occasion while he lies injured." said Roanda.

"He has his own joyous note. His wife is safe and better, and he has a beautiful son. Meka gave birth, as you did. Within minutes of each other the children were born." said Torlin to his wife as he sat at the edge of the bed and gave his finger to his son. "He has a great grip like his mother."

"He does his father proud. She will be the apple of your eye, Torlin." said the new mother. She hissed as the girl latched onto her. The baby girl latched down hard on her mother and pulled her head back. "She has a bit of a mean streak to her though." As her mother spoke the child unlatched and drifted off to sleep.

"I sense that they will be a tribulation to us. We will do everything we can to raise them right and they will be our great pride as well as our great heartache, I fear. Before you ask no I have not seen the future, but I know what my mother used to say about me and my brother," sighed Torlin.

"I cannot wait to see my sister's son. You say he was born at the same time as our children? I will let the little ones' sleep for a while before handing them off to the nanny. Then I will walk over to see her child and check on her wound." Roanda said as she shifted herself a little bit to allow the babes to sleep a little softer. "Anything else of curiosity happen in the city? It seems strange that both Meka and Thomas suffered accidents at the same time."

"These were no accidents. I believe it to be a targeted attack against them. There was a strange spell that we almost were taken in by before Pan Thor saved us from its grip. I believe it may have been a deadly attack against us because of the dead child." said Torlin to his now drowsy wife.

"It was no child, Torlin. It was a Noom. One of the two that Perrick knew. His face once cleaned matched the posters from McCryden for the reward for their capture. We do not know if it is Pommel or Drummond, but we will know soon enough." said Tanis as he walked into the room. "So how are my grandchildren? And my other son, Torlin you get further with him than I do."

"Your grandchildren are well and cantankerous. And your sons are both going to be fine." said Roanda.

"Well, I see they sleep now so I will come back later to see them. I will let you know if Thomas is any better now. I head over there now." Tanis said as he left the room. "Your mother will be down soon she is holding court for now but will come when she can."

"We have seen more of them now then we have the whole trip." said Torlin as he closed the door and sat down next to his wife on the bed and looked down at his children.

INJURIES

Tanis moved into Thomas's room and saw Thomas lying on his side looking at a dagger. "What is so interesting over there? Your spine has been repaired except for the bone shards. Surely you can wait a few months to get back on your feet?"

"Your prized wizard son left it there for me to look at. If I had the dagger, I would plunge it deep into his breast before turning it on myself, father." said Thomas with a sneer on his face and mockery in his voice.

"I will allow you to do so as soon as you can walk over to it and take it from the wall. Until then it will remain there for you to see and work toward. Your brother is only trying to help you and between him and Artitous you can be under no better care," said Tanis.

"That would be fine except I leave soon for my city. It will not follow me there. So, I will have no incentive." said Thomas.

"It will travel with us, my love. It will be in the tent poles and in our walls. You will get that dagger. But you will only put it in your sheath and then walk to your son and give him everything he may need and want." said Meka as she walked into the room carrying the baby. "But now we need to give him a name."

"Call him what you will for all I care. It makes no matter to me." said Thomas. "Except naming him after your ex. He will not bear that name. And not after that dragon that came to our city and spied on us."

"How about Christoph? It was my father's name." said Meka

"Christoph will be fine. It would be nice to remember your family. Mine are a bunch of traitors. They are totally unable to be loyal." Thomas said. "Besides, they have their great hero again. Tanis, you have returned. What fatherly words of comfort do you bring me?"

"At least you used fatherly today instead of looking at me like a village idiot. You may acknowledge me as your father before the end of your ordeal." Sighed Tanis. "I grow weary of these constant battles we fight. I am sorry I missed most of your life, but your mother made sure you were well tended. How is Martin now days? I see him so rarely anymore. Word has it you spar with the men every morning. You will be healed and be able to go back to it, you just must have patience, it will not happen overnight. And now for you, young lady. Get you to your bed and get some rest. Childbearing is a hard business, and you need your rest."

"You are right. I will go to my bed. After it is moved in here with him. I will hear no objection, or I will give you your dagger in your ear. I will be near him and so will his child. Do not give me that hurt puppy look. Now sir, bring in my bed." said Meka looking like the biggest person in the room. Despite her small stature, Meka can rule a room with her presence alone. Being a commander of the Tyris unit located in the city of Tetra she could make herself the most opposing thing in the room. Thomas allowed these women only for his wife. She would let them in to the city anyway. There attire was eye catching to say the least looking like a single piece bathing suit with steel plates sewn into it. These women were deadly at the least and lethal when provoked. The Queen of Dracos was the ruler of the Tyris. Athinina came to Thalinburg to see the new ruler there. It was love at first site and she has been there ever since.

Roanda was also a Tyris though larger in stature she was the opposite of Meka. Roanda led the Tyris of Metra, the other of the twin cities. These cities are important because each of the sons of Tanis Thalin rule one. Thomas is at Tetra which is the Spartan and clean lines city. Torlin was the ruler of Metra which was the more ornate city with bridges spanning from building to building and fanciful carving on everything. They were compared only to those in Thalinburg. It was so ornate even the privies were decorated with fanciful beasts and plants.

CHAPTER EIGHT

ATTACKS

Roanda loved to walk the streets of the city and just look at the artistic skill and flair that she would now be sharing with her children. But that time was coming. She hugged her children close then allowed the midwife to take them to their little beds. She would visit her sister-in-law in a while after she got some rest and then play with her new babes.

A strange sound woke Roanda and she looked around. The babes slept soundly. A slight breeze ruffled the curtains. She looked around the room again and saw everything in order and no one else in the room. Torlin was probably still up talking magic with some new comer mage. It would not be the first time he had not come to bed for talking late into the night.

One more looking around the room showed still nothing then suddenly, her ears and eyes perked up. A barely visible shadow was cast by the window. She also realized that she had closed the window before going to bed. Now it sat open and the breeze floated in. Torlin was afraid of the windows here being open. He still saw giant spiders and other creatures around the grounds so he would close and secure the windows at night so they could not enter.

Roanda slid the dagger under her pillow slowly from its sheath. Still looking at the window she slowly made her way there with the dagger hidden in her night gown. As she approached the window the shadow slowly gained form and color. It looked like one of the children who worked with their parents in the castle had opened the window. She relaxed her guard and turned toward the child to see pointed teeth and a dagger coming right for her. She moved in what seemed like slow motion. She went to lift her dagger when the air around the two of them became thick and they were unable to move.

"Who are you?" yelled Torlin. "Why are you targeting us?"

The Noom just stood there frozen and said nothing. Torlin screamed again, "Who are you?"

"You already know the answer to that question." said the Noom. "As to why, it is just a job."

"You will perish this day after telling me what you know. There will be no pardon for you. Now tell me of this plan of yours. It is over." Screamed an even more irate magical man.

"But you do give me my escape, your majesty. Goodbye." said the Noom as he bit down hard with his back teeth. Moments later he was foaming at the mouth and lay dead.

"A gum paste tooth. And we learned nothing from him. Guard! Find where this creature was holed up and then tell me so I may investigate it. Do not tarry. I will want your report sooner than later." said to the guard as he turned to his wife and kissed her before releasing her from the spell. The dead Noom fell as well when the spell lifted. "I will get rid of that and allow you to put your dagger back in its sheath." said Torlin backing away a touch as the Noom's body fell.

"The assassin must have come in through the window. I told you to keep this closed and locked so nothing could get in." said Torlin as he helped his wife to their bed.

"But I did have it closed and locked. In fact, the breeze is what woke me. Had you not come when you had I probably would be dead next to the little guy there." said Roanda.

"Guard, did anything or anyone enter my rooms this evening? They left a window open and I wanted to ask them to close it." said Torlin closing the door behind him.

"Only the buxom maid, Margarette. She went in and then came out a moment or two later. Assumed she was just fulfilling a need of your wife." said the guard.

"Any idea where Margarette might be right now? I need her now." said Torlin.

"Why she is probably down in the garden by now. She goes there to clear her head some days and to entertain a new friend if you know what I mean down there amongst the bushes and lush grass." said the guard.

"Thank you, my good man. I will go down there myself and summon her. Just in case she is indisposed at that particular moment." said Torlin as he headed down the ramp to the garden.

The scene that greeted him in the garden was like a scene from a cheap horror play. Pieces of the maid were scattered everywhere and no knife or dagger were present. Her head was mounted on a post in the middle of the garden.

Torlin delved the garden looking for black magic and found it upon the area within the body parts. If anyone walked into it, they would meet the same fate as the maid. It was a nasty spell that took Torlin but a moment to remove. Slowly he gathered the parts of the woman magically and carried them down to the house of the dead. He would not lay a hand on the traitor.

Returning to their rooms, Torlin sat down on the edge of the bed and looked at his wife laying there just falling back to sleep. "They were careful. Using one of the staff to open the window was genius. Then killing her and laying another trap. Closed any sort of window to learn anything and opened the door for another chance at one of us. It should be over now. The Noom are both dead, and I hope not to find any other of their playthings lying around."

CHAPTER NINE

REPORTS AND
WAGONS

Torlin was just getting into his bed when the guard returned from his search. The guard cleared his throat and both wizard and Tyris were up and armed. The guard threw himself to his knees and begged "Please do not kill me good sir and miss. I have your report about their lodgings and such."

"Well please tell us, sir. What have you found?" asked Torlin.

"He and his brother were staying at the Languid Dragon. The innkeeper has not been seen in a few hours and the room the pair was assigned was locked tight and protected with spells. The same with their wagons kept in the inn's barn and storage field. No one can get into them. One man had his arm come off and turn into a viper that killed him dead, it did. So, I have guards protecting those things, so no one touches them until you get there." Cringed the guard.

"Rise young man." said Roanda. Pulling on her dress from earlier in the day.

"Let us go and check these creatures out. I for one want to make sure there is nothing left to harm anyone."

"I want this nightmare to be over." said Torlin. As he grabbed his box of magical items not to be monkeyed with. "Time to end this." Moving down toward the exit of the building. Roanda trailing just behind him and the guard in the lead they quickly arrived at the Languid Dragon. Torlin moved into the barn and then to the wagons.

Looking closely with magic and with vision, he slowly and craftily undid the traps around the cover of the first wagon. Lifting the cloth, he saw nothing at first but when he lit up the wagon with a ball of light his breath caught. In the bed of the wagon sat a cage that fit up to the ceiling of the wagon. Inside was what was left of the innkeeper and a giant spider almost too big for the cage.

"Hope he is full now. I do not relish the task of the man who has to kill that thing." said the guard.

Torlin turned to him and cast a spell incinerating the spider to ash. "I guess you are killing it. That looked like a dangerous spell. I am going to go over there and prepare the men to empty the wagon. Thank you, sir. Thank you." said the guard as he moved away from the royal couple as far as he could and still be in the storage yard. He just looked at the wizard with fear as he sat and talked to the other guards.

"The guards are not happy. They are afraid of both the magical traps and now me and all magical people. And to make it worse, he saw me incinerate the spider. We need to see what else is in the Noom's wagons then we can move on to the rooms."

"Of course, you are right. Let me check what else lies in the wagons." He said as he turned back to the spider wagon. Perrick came strutting in and leaned on the side of the wagon. Torlin opened the first chest in the wagon and found nothing but a change of clothes for both Noom.

The next chest showed some magical books and implements and Torlin ordered it brought to his laboratory in the tower. The third chest also had its own magical trap. Torlin waved his hands over the chest and delved again to find that the magic had not been undone. Perrick jumped into the wagon and looked at the chest. "That is a boomer that is. Touch your magic here and here to open it. I know because I have one. They are hiding something of great importance in there."

"What could be in there?" asked a now curious Roanda.

"We cannot tell yet. But we will know in a mad minute though." He said as he did as Perrick said and saw the magic go away. "It is gone. Now to open it. I will open it with magic just in case of any unforeseen magic that may or may not be there." Waving his arm and sending the magic to the chest. The lid lifted slowly and Torlin advanced to check the contents. Inside were stacks of pages and notes on the royal family. The problem was they incinerated themselves when touched. Torlin could find no reason for this. They did not have any magical spells on them and once more it was Perrick that saved the day. "Put your magic to work Torlin. Pick it up with magic but do not physically touch the paper. There is a mix of chemicals that causes the paper to burn at the touch of a person. There you go, now what do they say?"

"Your advice comes too late I am afraid the papers are all dust, and the costumes underneath are all that is left." said Torlin. He got up and went to the next wagon where a man lay in a cage. Once more the wagon was protected magically, and the shock of seeing a near naked man in a cage made Torlin step back.

"Who are you good sir?" Torlin asked as he opened the cage the man was in. Torlin at once realized his mistake because the man immediately turned into a tiger and leapt on to the shocked prince. As Torlin waited for the clamp down of the weretiger's bite on his throat, he looked up and closed his eyes. After a minute or two he opened his eyes. "Am I dead yet? Or did the kitty go attack someone else?"

"You are fine my love. You got pounced on a little, then the guards and I killed the foul creature. It lies right over there," said Roanda. Torlin looked where she pointed and saw nothing there.

"Are you sure that you killed it? The place you indicated is empty of any dead anything." Torlin said looking around quickly.

"I know I killed it. It should lie right there……. Oh, dear that could be a problem. I know I put it there with a spear in its guts." She said as Torlin launched a fireball right at her. She leapt away from the fireball and saw the weretiger, which had crept up behind her. She grabbed up a sword that was left on the ground by guards as they moved quickly from the storage yard. Torlin and Roanda stood shoulder to shoulder and faced the weretiger.

"You tried to kill it and me with that fireball, my love." said Roanda as she settled in beside her husband.

"Never to harm you. That cat will not die, how do we kill it? I have never seen the like. Maybe he Askanitowa. Then we will really have a problem." said Torlin as he launched another fireball. The weretiger leapt away from the fire and moved toward the now ready pair.

The weretiger moved closer to the pair and Torlin launched a lightning bolt into the cat. The cat was moved back a dozen feet and it fell over and ceased to move. "That finished him apparently. So, shall we get rid of sir cat?" said Torlin as Roanda pointed toward the cat. Torlin looked back and saw the weretiger getting up and shaking its head. He was in shock as he watched the feline move toward the pair once more. "Looking for suggestions from the peanut gallery. This thing is not dying," said Torlin.

"Freeze it so it cannot move." said Perrick. He came out of the wagon with a small silver dagger. "Then I will take care of our friend here. He is a big one, isn't he?"

Torlin wrapped the cat in magic so that it could not move and Perrick saw the man eyes coming from the tiger's face. "It is better this way. For you and us. You understand that, right?" Perrick said as he rammed the dagger into the creature's heart. The cat let out a scream as it slumped down in the magic that held it and turned back to the man. Torlin let the body fall and looked to the dagger.

"Poisoned I assume? It was their means of controlling the beast?" asked the prince.

"No, it is allergic to silver. As for control, not even they could control it. I fear these creatures were brought here for more malicious ends. The giant spider, now a weretiger. They were planning something big." said Perrick.

"Let us check out the last two wagons and see what lies in them. I am sure you found no valuable information in there. So, we will move on." said Torlin.

Once more he removed the spells that protected the wagons and went in. Using magic to illuminate he saw its occupant. "I think we have a problem." said Torlin. "It appears we have a Hydra in here. Anyone got a club and a torch?"

"For God's sake do not release the creature. Where is our back up? We cannot hope to take this thing alone. Your magic will not have any effect on this thing. And the guard are pretty much running away." said Roanda.

"I will summon help." said Torlin as he closed his eyes and whispered spells. "They come. We should have some help shortly. Until then he stays in his cage."

"Really, I thought we were going to play with it before they arrived?" said Roanda with a lilt of laughter in her voice.

"You may play with it, but I will stay out of it." Snickered Torlin. "I have no death wish. The rangers should be here shortly to deal with our snaky friend here. Too many heads for me."

A company of rangers came into the storage yard and began securing the yard. Their leader, an elf named Martin, came over and asked the situation. "We have a hydra in that wagon. I will float it out of the wagon and let you all deal with it. I grow weary from all the magic I have been using all day. I need to rest." said Torlin to the Ranger.

Martin looked at the prince and allowed him to sit on the hay bales. The cage holding the hydra slowly floated into the storage yard. Martin had his troops ready to go when Artitous arrived with Tanis on his heels. Artitous cast a spell and the hydra shrunk to the size of a small rabbit. Tanis grabbed it by the body and slid the Warmonger from his belt. The Warmonger was a magical sword that could be wielded by only one man, Tanis. It never lost in combat. The sword had a straight blade with its name etched along the center of the blade. It looked like any other blade to the casual observer but anyone who tried to wield the blade was inevitably cut or killed by the blade. Tanis drew back the blade and slid it through the hydra just below the heads and held it to the torch held by Martin. He then held the head side to the flames. Martin raised an eyebrow and Tanis explained, "They will become seven new hydras if not cauterized. And the body end would of course produce more heads. This little critter could have caused some major chaos here in the city."

"There were also a huge giant spider and weretiger in the other two wagons. I do not want to check the final wagon. Probably a captured dragon." said Torlin. "I know you cannot use magical fire on those critters. Each of these creatures can overcome any one of us. The hydra for me. They put a lot of thought into how to kill us."

Tanis said, "I will open the last wagon. It should be fun."

Torlin interrupted, "Watch touching the documents you might find in there. They are coated with a chemical that causes them to burn when touched. And for God's sake give me some warning before you open that thing."

Tanis said, "It is already open so let's take a look, shall we?"

Tanis and Torlin looked into the wagon to see a covered cage. Hissing could be heard coming from under the cover and you could hear a raspy voice saying "Let me out. And I will collect you first. The rest will join you soon enough. I am ready to control this city once more."

Torlin and Tanis looked at each other and closed the flap. "It looks like we have a medusa on our hands. Hey Martin, anyone got a mirror? I think I am going to need one sooner than later. No one enters this wagon. I must learn how to defeat a medusa. I have never come across one yet, so it is new to me." said Tanis as he walked away from the wagon. He moved quickly toward the library on the side of the palace. There were thousands of books there. One would hold the solution to the medusa problem.

Tanis disappeared into the palace and Torlin sat beside the wagon. Every so often a woman singing could be heard inside the wagon and several of the guard headed to it to inquire what was in the wagon. They would touch the fabric of the wagon just for the flap to magically seal itself closed once more. Torlin looked like a child who had just stolen a warm cookie. He was keeping the guard from a fate worse than death, but they would not believe him to tell them. He also did not feel like reversing a flesh to stone spell. So, he sat, and the flaps magically kept up their resistance to the guard. One guard was about to try and cut his way in on the side of the wagon when the singing stopped for a moment. He heard a woman saying, "Please save me from this cage. You have nothing to fear from me."

The guard ran to the front of the wagon and tried to enter from the wagon seat and found that way also blocked. "Prince Torlin, there is a beautiful woman in peril in there. Let me in so I can save her."

"You had better go back to your posts on the other side of the storage yard. What you are hearing is a medusa. She will kill you as soon as look at you. She will turn you to stone or eat you. Take your pick." said the prince.

"That cannot be the case. It must be a woman being held. Please let me in. She promises great rewards for her freedom. You just want them for yourself. Let the little guy get some of the action around here. I want the reward." said the guard.

"I assure you there is no reward. If there was a reward, I would give it to you. You have nothing to fear. And little to save. Except your life maybe. Now go." Torlin said as he sent a flow of magic to smack the guard on the back of the head. As he sat back down Torlin felt a smack across the bottom. He looked around and saw his father laughing like a little kid. "You will not use your powers wastefully, now, will you?" Laughed the older Thalin.

"I was just giving him a lesson. The helmet on his head protected him anyways. What did you find? Is this thing killable?" asked Torlin as he once more looked toward the wagon.

"Let us get cage and cover out of the wagon. Then we can worry about the snake head inside." said Tanis.

"Is it safe? The guards are liable to go and try to save the damsel in distress." said Torlin.

"They will meet a spell to keep them away. Now let us get this thing dead." said the older man.

"What should I do? Just give me my tasks and I will do them." said Torlin.

"Create blades of magic, two inches apart and as high and low as the cage. Make sure it will go through anything. Then we burn the remains. I will keep the cover up while you do the dirty work. I found another so you can cut the first one. Can you go fine-tuned as that? If not, I will trade tasks with you?" Tanis said to Torlin. As Tanis spoke the inner cover fell to the ground shredded and a loud cackle came from the cage. "Oh, dear wizard, you have missed me. Poor, poor wizard. Want to play again?"

Torlin straightened up and produced the magical blades all at the same time and shot them into the cage. He received a loud scream for his trouble and a sickening thud onto the ground. "I believe I got it that time. Who knew she would be able to squeeze into that small of a space? Now to incinerate the beast." Torlin said as he threw the cover down on the now sliced up cage and set it to magical fire. In moments, the fire was out and the last of the creature's remains were destroyed.

Looking into the wagon revealed a large sum of gold hidden in a chest right behind where the medusa cage was. Carefully he checked the coins and found them to be real gold and free of poisons and traps. This money was distributed amongst the guard and the two Thalins standing there. The men rejoiced and the Thalin men slipped coins from their shares into the buckets of the guard. They needed it more than they did.

One of the guardsmen looked up and shouted, "There are crows leaving here headed south." The rangers had their bows up and firing bringing down some of the crows. Torlin and Tanis captured the rest in a flow of magic.

"I would wager they were going to report what happened to someone. These ugly birds are just right for spying." said the guard as he looked proud of himself.

"These are ravens. They are allies of ours and the dragons. Nemeth, how are you? Sorry for the misunderstanding. Apparently, the guards here cannot distinguish between a crow and a raven. Please continue your journey and keep us informed of news." said Tanis as he released the ravens from the magical net. A ranger lifted his bow and aimed it at the flying ravens and Tanis softly lowered his bow.

"The messages they carry must be urgent. That a whole unkindness goes out with it. Here comes Nemeth again. What is your message, my dear friend?"

The raven gave a series of caws and crackles and Tanis listened intently. "Is this fact? Are your sources good on this? If it is true, we are in dire straits. We still have the problem of a pair of creature toting assassins. But I believe we killed them. We still have to check their rooms." said Tanis.

"What did the raven share with us? Surely it must only be something concerning the ravens." asked Torlin. "By the way, where is Artitous? I cannot imagine him being late for this."

"We have more problems than just a missing druid. The ravens have spotted a wagon train coming toward the city, loaded with Noom. And at least a hundred of their wagons. But if that is not the worst of it, we have trouble coming from the south. A raiding party was seen on the Fields of the Pheni. They were headed here. I believe them to be an advance party for one of the dark wizards or the Dread lords. The party bears no insignia which is strange. Usually, they march under a flag or shield ornament." said Tanis.

"Surely a dumb bird cannot tell you all of that, my Lord. Mercenary units from the Dark Lands. Are we to start listening to the deer next?" Stuttered an angry Duke Masters.

"Only if the deer wanted to chat. Nemeth is a valuable member of our team. He is the best scout around and can warn us days in advance of imminent attack. He and his brethren are a great boon to our cities." said Tanis as Torlin moved forward toward the now cremated medusa.

"There is something there. In the ash. It looks like a crest or pin. Shall I grab it father and bring it to the royal court?" said Torlin, moving to pick it up.

"I just dropped it, my Lords; it is nothing I assure you. Just a little piece of jewelry." said Duke Masters as he scooped up the object and stuffed it into his pocket. He quickly left the storage yard and headed toward the palace.

"What do you suppose it was? And when did he drop it? I for one do not remember seeing him when we killed the beast." said Torlin.

"It is probably nothing. Let us finish with the wagons and head up to the rooms. I grow weary and the night wanes." said Tanis through a yawn.

"Are you growing bored father?" asked Torlin. "Then let's check out the remaining content of the wagon." Torlin lifted the flap of the wagon and put his foot to the step. In what felt like slow motion the wagon exploded. Torlin was thrown back and caught by Martin. Tanis hit the ground running to check on the other people in the yard.

"It appears we will have to check the rooms. That was not a magical bomb. That had a trigger in the stair. We will have to look closer for more mundane traps." said Tanis to Perrick and the guards present. Torlin piped up his agreement quickly and Perrick made the commitment to check the rooms when they got there and Torlin would check for other traps of magical nature. With game plan in place, the group of men entered the inn. Moving quickly upstairs, they found the room that was rented by the Noom.

Perrick checked the door and found no sign of any mechanical device. Torlin went next and confirmed there was no magical threat. Tanis looked at the door and a frowned. Something was not right. It was too easy. Perrick reached for the knob and Tanis screamed out, "Don't open the door!" But he was too late. Perrick slowly opened the door a half inch and the door blew off its hinges and threw Perrick into Torlin who standing behind him. Tanis rushed over to the two men and then put the fire out. A couple of waves of his hands and water rained down on the burning room.

"It would appear you missed something, gentlemen. I do not think there is anything worth looking at here now. Torlin please go in and make sure nothing is left." said Tanis.

Torlin entered the room shared by the Nooms and waited for his eyes to adjust. He searched around the floor and found a small piece of parchment that had survived. On the paper was a name. One they had dealt with before. It would not be possible for her to return, but maybe some of her minions. The name on the paper was that of the necromancer, Elizarade. She had died in the last war.

"Why would the Noom be carrying her name with them?" said Torlin to Tanis as he stuck his head into the room.

"Whose name?" asked Tanis? "It is Elizarade. She died almost a year ago." said Torlin.

"I fear that there is more here than we thought. The cavalry is waiting for the Noom wagon train. They will surrender or die. The patrol moves closer with still no insignia. I hope the tribes down there have not reformed their joint army. Without the dragons and their allies, we are sitting ducks, waiting for the shot." said Tanis.

"We will survive. We have you, Thomas, and Garren to guide us all. With leaders like that who need worry?" said Torlin.

"You forget that you also have Artitous and yourself in that number. You two are formidable powers as well. You and Artitous are the most powerful of your kinds ever. I am relieved to have you at my back." said Tanis.

"Where is the patrol headed?" asked Torlin.

"For Tetra, Thomas will need help there, but we all have to defend our own cities. I hope the enemy is weakened spreading their armies over three fronts." said Tanis.

CHAPTER TEN

HOMECOMINGS

Torlin and Roanda left the next day with zero fanfare. It was decided that the royals had to return to their respective cities on their own and in a less conspicuous manner. Torlin and Roanda with the newborn twins were put into the back of a covered wagon and they headed home. Thomas and Meka left soon after quietly and with again the newborn. They traveled most of the day, not meeting any resistance when Thomas's wagon was attacked by Noom. The guards made quick work of them, even with Thomas begging them to flee and let the little ones come.

Meka silenced him quickly with a punch to the gut. "You are going to kill me one day like that. What did I do now?"

"You put yourself, our child, and me into harm's way. Do it again and it will be a dagger instead of my fist." Scolded Meka.

"My Lord and Lady, we have eliminated them all but a few. They took off with their ponies, but our horsemen will chase them down and kill them once and for all." said the guard.

"Good Sir," asked Thomas, "How many remain to defend the wagon?"

"Why, myself and another. Is there a problem?" asked the guard.

"Yes, there is a major problem. We are unarmed and defenseless. Get our horses moving and let us get out of here. It is a trap and we have sprung it." Thomas sighed.

Meka reached under Thomas and removed a long sword. She eased it from the scabbard and sat with it across her knees. "Just in case my love."

The guard scrambled out into the wagon train and ordered them to move quickly. He took control of the wagon that the royal couple was in and smacked the horses getting them going as fast as possible. Meka looked out under the cover and saw them moving extremely fast. "I will ask him to slow down or avoid the potholes. One or the other." Meka said as the wagon grew faster and faster.

Meka moved across the bed of the wagon to find the driver was not there. Looking behind the wagon showed the guard wiping his pants and hands off from the fall and saw him turn and walk away. Fury welled up in her, but she tried to climb out to the wagon seat instead of jumping from the wagon to kill the guardsman. She would deal with him later.

Getting into the seat was difficult, especially with her unhealed wound. She got up to the wagon to see that the reigns had been cut as well. The wagon was going out of control and she had no way to stop it. Looking ahead she saw several men in the garb of the druids. One of them saw them coming and raised his hand. The horses slowed and then stopped before the druids.

"Thank you. Thank you so much." said Meka. She leapt from the wagon just in time to see the fireball. "What are you doing? You saved us. Why try and kill us now?" She said as she leapt to avoid another attack. She looked at the garb once more. These druids were wearing a black ribbon on their arms. "You are dark druids, aren't you? You have been hired to kill us. You should have stayed in hiding." Meka screamed yet again she jumped from another attack. Reaching the wagon and the sword. She saw the druids moving quickly toward the wagon and grabbed the sword. Meka ran from the rear of the wagon sword held high and killed the first of the three druids standing there. The next turned only in time to see the sword bury itself into his belly. Meka hid behind the now screaming druid as the remaining druid let fly with a fireball. It hit the wounded druid and he fell to the ground burning. He did not move he just fell. Then Meka jumped to finish the last druid.

The druid had pulled his own weapon as they were now too close to one another to safely use his magic. He saw the new mother slowly fading and went to try to finish her off.

Meka's sword dipped a hair. She was exhausted. She would not be able to keep this up too much longer. The druid hit her square on the sword and drove Meka to her knees. Slowly she raised her sword and tried to rise. But again, the druid knocked her from her feet. She knew this was the end and started to cry. She would never see her son grow to a man. She tried once more to rise and again she was driven down and this time the sword was wrestled from her hands. Closing her eyes, she lowered her chin. He would not have the satisfaction of seeing the fear and pain in her eyes.

Just as the sword was wrested from the hands of Meka an arrow flew into the heart of the dark druid. Meka remained of the ground waiting for the druid's stroke and after a moment, she realized she was still alive. Looking around her she saw a group of elves coming from the wood. "Did you save me?" asked Meka. She tried to rise but could not. She was now out of adrenaline and she slumped were she sat.

"If we had realized that it was Thomas and his family we may not have. Thomas has killed more than a few of our brethren calling them spies. But the dark druids have over run this area. And the enemy of my enemy is my friend. Is not that the way it works. I am Gaitlyn and I am the head of the elves in this area. You are Meka. We will help you to your city but will not remain there." said the elf as he lifted Meka and set her on the wagon bench. Rigging up a set of reigns for the horses, they once more began moving and soon the spires of Tetra were seen.

Meka drove the wagon to the gates and a guard rapidly opened it when he saw Meka at the reigns. He was about to sound the call that they had returned when Meka urged the man to lower the horn. They would announce their return later. At least they had made it home. That was all that mattered. The elven escort turned and left at the gate as they had promised, waving fondly back to Meka. She would have to aid them and their people with troops to help them with the removal of the dark grove. *Some good allies around us right now would be a good idea.* She thought to herself as the wagon finally made it to the castle yard. Handing off the reigns she ordered the men to get Thomas to his rooms and place his son with him until she got back from an errand. She would not be gone long.

Meka went to the Tetradon that remained in the city. The resistance had risked much from their species to aid them and now she needed their aid. She spoke to their head and asked them to send a few men to guard the rooms of the royals. They hastily agreed and Meka slowly returned to her rooms which were also Thomas's. She was exhausted from the combat, but she would be better now. The Tetradon arrived and she was able to relax and sleep.

Thomas watched his wife sleep and reached under his pillow which was now shared by his newborn child. He smiled as he looked down on him but what will he be able to teach him as an invalid. He drew out the dagger but before he could do anything with it, he felt the pains of healing in his back. Looking around he saw only that he was being healed. He lay back knowing what pain he was about to feel as the healing took. But again, there was none. Slowly he attempted to move his foot.

First one foot then the other, he lowered them to the floor. He tried to rise to his feet and as he did, he saw all the bone shards fall from his body. Someone had helped him in his moment of despair, and he said a prayer of thanks to the creator. His son squirmed a little as he lay there and opened his eyes. He had his mother's eyes. The little child squirmed again and then the odor let his father know what was going on. He was not moving for him he was doing his business.

"Meka, wake up. Christoph has soiled himself. I do not know how to take care of this." said Thomas standing beside his wife's bed. Meka slowly woke and looked up at her husband. Her eyes were suddenly wide, and she had a smile you could not remove with magic.

"How? Thomas you are healed. How?" said Meka.

"You asked me that twice. And for an answer I must say, I do not know. One minute I felt the sting of the healing next thing I know; I am standing looking down at Christoph. The bone shards from my spine lying on the ground all around me." Thomas said.

"We should have Artitous or your father look you and Christoph over. He seems to be a little bit on the over soiling side. I mean having to change his diaper every hour or so is too much." said his smiling wife.

"Why should we bring them into this? I am healed and do not need them any longer. As for Christoph, let our local druid look him over. Why bring those men here?" asked Thomas.

"They are close to us and I would prefer them to anyone else when it comes to my child. So, you will send for them. Do you understand me? Get your father and Artitous here as soon as they can get here." said Meka raising her voice as she spoke.

Thomas knew that tone and he went out into the hallway and summoned his guard. After having him send a messenger to the two men, Thomas went to the balcony of his rooms. The cooler air of Tetra felt good on his face after the wagon and the city of Thalinburg. Thalinburg was too big and had a foul odor that he did not like. Torlin called it humanity and said it was a good thing but his city was not going to go that way. The new walls and defenses of this very Spartan city made him feel secure. True no one had ever breached the walls of Thalinburg and he had stopped build his walls when they were a third the size of Thalinburg's. He had enough.

Looking down he saw the Tetradon, the original builders of the city, down in front of the palace. He watched as they changed the guard and the men he had placed went home. His wife was at work again. She would do things like this without consulting him. After being out on the parapets for a while he went back to his bed. There would be plenty to do in the morning.

CHAPTER ELEVEN

ATTACKS FROM THE GRAVE

Torlin and Roanda had a similar story as Thomas except that the magical attacks were quickly thwarted. Shortly after having left Thalinburg, Torlin felt more that saw an increase in speed of the wagon. Not worrying about it at first, he continued to look at his children and his wife. How could he be so happy? Was it not a year ago that he was the most despised man on Dracos? He was pondering this when the wagon began to wobble and rock faster than it should.

He went to the front of the wagon and pulled the cover to the sides and gasped at what he saw. A reanimated dwarf sat on the wagon seat and swung a large mace at Torlin as he opened the curtain. The dwarf spurred the horses and turned to the couple and babes in the back of the wagon. Moving slowly, it moved into the back of the careening wagon and had just reached the wagon bed when a lick of fire set it on fire then air picked it up and hurled it out of the wagon. Torlin looked like he would destroy anyone who spoke and he turned to the horses. Casting a soothing spell to calm them and slow the wagon, Thomas found that he could be a protector as well as a soft-hearted person at the same time.

He was growing in his new found wisdom when the next attack came. The dwarf had a companion. The reanimated man reached Torlin and held him in a lock only possible from the dead. He could not move nor call out. He thought that this was the way he was going to die when a sword appeared in the head of the dead man. A sharp twist and the man went flying off the wagon seat. Roanda looked down at the sword in her hand and just shuddered. "How many times do I have to save your backside, my heart?" asked Roanda.

"Considering that I killed the first one, I would say we were even." said Torlin with a laugh on his lips.

The two hugged each other and heard the babies in the back of the wagon let out a scream. Torlin was there first and the scene that he saw before him was a scary one. The male child had his small hand up in the air and was causing a swirl of air above him and sister sending the men that had come into the wagon flying out the rear. Torlin was dumbfounded for just a moment before sealing the wagon with magical protections.

"Our son apparently already knows magic, my love. He was causing a whirlwind in here. Your daughter just looked on with appreciation. We may have to do something about him once we get them home." said an amazed Torlin.

Roanda looked down at her children as she stabbed a man entering the wagon without looking behind her. The man fell and she looked at her husband. "Who attacks us and why? Are we not the royal family?"

Torlin and Roanda jumped from the wagon leaving the babes wrapped and protected and looked around the wagon. He saw a small band of warriors that had seen better days and probably better lives as most of them were disintegrating corpses coming up the road toward the couple.

"The necromancer who did this must be close, these things would slowly lose their focus and animation. We must look for the dark wizard controlling them." said Torlin.

Roanda looked down the road and saw a druid approaching behind the group of undead. "Could a dark druid do this?"

"There are no dark druids. Ask Artitous. He will tell you. Why do you ask?" asked Torlin. He turned and looked at the approaching druid and saw the deep socketed eyes of a dark wizard. "You there, wizard, identify yourself. I am Torlin Thalin and demand to know your name."

"Trezur. The head of my coven of dark druids. You do know you will have to die for my employer to get his due. We come from hiding to show that we are indeed the stronger of our brethren. You unfortunately must die quickly. I would have loved to use you again and again. To learn all your secrets. But alas, I have no time. Now allow my minions to feast upon you both and your children so that only your brother's people remain. My fellows should have tended to them already."

"I have no intentions of allowing you to kill me or my family. You are the one who should be ready to die. Do you know who I am druid? I am the most powerful wizard on Dracos. Now stay where you are and destroy the shadin that you have created." said an irate Torlin.

"I stay where I am because if I am near you, I will not be able to use my magic. Look upon my pets and you shall see the Mandore Stones upon them. In the vicinity of these stones your magic is useless." Laughed the druid. "We found out by accident and several of my brothers were eaten. But now it is your turn. Have a nice afterlife."

Torlin raised his hands to launch a fireball at the druid and found his magic would not come. Panicking he tried to once more to attack the advancing monsters and Druid and again he failed. Realizing what he must do, he called out to Roanda and then ran back ten feet. Once he was farther from the shadin he found his magic again. With it he hit the shadin with a blast of fire and ice. They quickly blew to pieces and the druid was amazed at the destruction. An arrow through his eye stopped his amazement as he fell to the ground. Torlin looked back to see his wife and several of the Tyris standing prepared to fight just ahead of him with bows drawn.

"Are they all dead?" asked Roanda.

"Sorry dear. I did not leave much for you unfortunately. I am sure we will see more trouble before we arrive home. The things that the druid said gives me a pause. He was hired to kill the royal family. That means you, me, and the entire royal family. This could be a coup." said Torlin.

"Of course, it is a coup," said Roanda. "What else could it be? Just who is behind it? Could it be the Metradon returning again?"

"I am leery of any of the usual suspects. It could be a necromancer of great power. It could be one of those politically minded nobles that assume they would be named to the throne upon the royal family's deaths. It could be the Metradon. It may even be the Tetradon. We must use caution until we know for certain."

The two returned to the wagon with the Tyris bodyguard and again began the journey to their home in Metra. It was a few more hours travel when again the couple and their little party was attacked. Fireballs lashed out toward the wagon and the Tyris around it. The fireballs dissolved that touched the area around the wagons, but several of the Tyris fell having exploded with the fireball that hit them. The defenders quickly moved to the safety of the wagon's proximity looking for targets to attack with their bows.

Torlin watched in awe as the fireballs dissolved. Then they realized that the protections he had put up earlier in the day were still in place.

He began searching for targets when he saw the little hole in the air where fireballs were issuing from.

Torlin pointed quietly to the remaining Tyris and had the draw bow and wait for him to make the first attack. He quickly prepared his lightning and let it flow through the hole in the air. Arrows flew at nearly the exact same time.

The fireballs coming through the hole had stopped for a moment and some sounds of movement were heard from the other side of the hole. Quickly the Tyris moved to the sides of the hole and fired arrows into it. Torlin stood like an oak tree before the hole and placed a barrier on the hole repelling the fireballs.

The hole briefly disappeared and again came with the same barrage of fireballs. The difference this time was the hole was a bit larger and the magic user on the other side could be seen. Torlin placed magical protections around him and the Tyris warriors and the small group once more fired into the hole as the enemy's spells were dissolved.

A Tyris put an arrow through the magic user's surprised face as another of his kind moved into sight to attack. The hole was large enough for the women and Torlin to jump into. Torlin warned against it for the lack of knowledge of what lay on the other side and killing the wrong person could strand them there by causing the hole to close.

The Tyris fire more and more arrows into the hole and soon they ran out of arrows. Torlin made up for the lack of arrows with magical arrows and fireballs flying into the hole.

After what seemed and eternity the hole closed and did not reopen. The Tyris went and searched for more arrows as Torlin went to the wagon and lay down asking his wife to take the reins. He was nearly exhausted after the battle and need just a few minutes rest.

The Tyris returned quickly and had in tow a local druid. He went into the wagon and looked over the children and Torlin. The druid used a small amount of the power to relieve some of Torlin's fatigue, and asked what the problem was as he had felt the battle being fought. He was coming to investigate when the Tyris found him.

"It is a pleasure to meet you, good sir. I am Roanda and this is my husband, Torlin. We are traveling back to Metra and have had the bad luck of being attacked by a mage of some kind. What should we call you?" asked Roanda as Torlin slowly moved to a sitting position.

"I am called Sabre Hand. I am the druid for the local town. What can I do to assist? Are there any wounded?" asked the druid.

Torlin replied, "Our wounded are all dead. But those that survive are well and whole. You eased my fatigue and I thank you. Come with us to the city and we will see you justly rewarded. I will send one of my guards to inform your town that you have gone to the city. So, you can travel with us in the wagon."

"I will let them know and then come to the city. There is no need to trouble one of your guards. I will be there before the sun sets tomorrow." said Sabre Hand as he briskly headed toward the wood.

It would not be long before the city of Metra came into sight and the beauty of the city struck you. As ornate as Tetra is Spartan and bare, Metra was built in an age long forgotten by the race called the Metradon. They were highly advanced and had tried to take back rule of the city when they were awakened from stasis.

The city was eventually rid of the Metradon except the ones that had come to the city's aid during the battle. Now everyone, man, elf, dwarf and Metradon, lives in peace. Torlin still hoped to make peace with the rest of the Metradon but envoys sent to negotiate never returned.

Torlin now ruled with a just hand and his wife headed the army of Metra with the skill of a highly awarded general. In the most part life there was pleasant and quiet. It was a pity that his brother could not come to the same pattern, but it was not to be right now.

Torlin and his wife were met at the gates with fanfare and celebration. The royal babes were introduced to the expectant crowd and roars of approval met them. The little Garath and Arlette were overwhelmed with the attention and let out wails that were heard even above the din of the crowd. Roanda quickly put them back into the quiet wagon and returned to the crowd as the wagon moved toward the palace.

Many a building had frescos and images of animals that appeared to have grown on the side of the buildings and just froze into stone there. The palace was the crowning jewel of this city. The scenes on the palace were larger and grander than any other building and seemed to need the least repair.

The ruins had been cleared and now were being rebuilt and repaired by the new citizens of the city. The buildings were looking grander and stronger than ever. Even the wall that Torlin had not wanted looked like it had been remade better. The twin cities as they were called had housed a remnant of the population of the original builders of the city. Some remained but most had tried to overthrow Torlin and had been ejected from the city. The others lived in harmony with the new citizens. Though some sore looks did occur from some of those that had lived through the attempted coup. They would eventually get used to living with these creatures.

The Metradon are a people who look like large lizards standing on the hind legs. The Metradon are decorated from birth with tattoos on their faces and bodies. The more tattoos the higher the status amongst the Metradon.

The Tetradon were the polar opposites of the Metradon. Slaves were tattooed and only the slaves. Everyone else was marked by their strength and the number of horns on their head.

When the cities were found they were crumbling ruins and the twin boys cleaned them up.

The palace loomed ahead of Torlin and his family, when again a small man leapt at the magical man. Many of the guard had grabbed the man when he attacked and soon it was determined that it was another of the Noom. This Noom had a small crossbow with a poisoned dart. He almost loosed the arrow when he was stopped.

Torlin ordered the man to be brought to him as soon as he entered the throne room. Torlin arrived a few minutes before the Noom with Roanda at his side. She wore her mytan and had her sword ready. He had asked her not to dress this way at court but today he encouraged it.

"Noom, why did you attack me and my family? Who hired you to kill me? Tell me and I will forget your attempt on our lives and let you go." said Torlin.

"I must say good bye, good sir. My employers would kill me as soon as I left the hall. So good bye, and good health while you have it." said the Noom as he broke the little glass tooth that held enough poison to kill the Noom. He frothed at the mouth for just a moment and then lay still.

"We must check every prisoner from now on for these capsules. We cannot allow anyone else to commit suicide before we can question them." said Torlin as Roanda looked down at the little man's body.

"Who would set these things upon us? We have done nothing to hurt these people so why are they dying to kill us?" Roanda asked as she started moving from the throne room to their private rooms. She would not need her armor or sword today apparently.

CHAPTER TWELVE

WAR

Both of the royal men and their families were settling down in their respective cities when once more the attacks began. This time they were trying to eliminate Tanis from the scene. Tanis was believed by the mysterious architect of this coup to be the deadliest to his cause. He would bend when his wife and children were all dead.

Tanis was walking in the garden when the attack came. Three fireballs hurtled at the immortal warrior and Tanis fell to the earth without being hit, instead drawing his own blades and starting a rather nasty incantation. The wizard attacking saw his error too late as Tanis cut him in the arm and put the tip of his sword to the wizard's throat. Tanis had only a second to question him for as he was about to speak an arrow pierced the eye of the would-be assassin. The guards searched the parapets and walls of Thalinburg finding nothing. The archer had slipped away from the guards.

Tanis looked at the wizard and immediately recognized the face. It was Carson Reveal Hands. He was one of the wizards that had been set to McCryden to ensure a lasting peace there. This was troubling indeed if he had turned to the dark magic that seemed to be very prominent at the time.

Tanis was about to leave the garden and allow the guard to deal with the dead wizard when again he attacked. Tanis did not see the strike to his back but he felt it. Turning quickly, he had his sword out to see three men in the guards' tabards forming a small triangle around him. He asked the men, "Is everything alright my good men. You appear to have something you wish to reveal to me?"

"We only wish for you to die. Our employer is paying well for your head and we intend to bring it to him." said one of the fake guards.

Tanis moved like a snake striking its meal. He quickly killed the man who was speaking and was turning to number two when he saw his wife drop to one knee and fire the strange long bow that the Tyris used. Guard number three fell to the arrow that had suddenly appeared in his chest. Tanis quickly finished the last of them. "I believe we have a problem" said Tanis to his wife. "Someone has it out for us, I believe. Athinina, I think we may have to vet the guard again. As well as the wizards and druids. We want no more attempts by those close to us. Vet also the lords and ladies that have come to Thalinburg. We need to find all of the culprits behind these attacks. They are being careful but they will make a mistake. I will send Nemeth to the boys to warn them that there may be traitors amongst them."

"They probably already know. I believe they would have been attacked as they were sitting ducks in those wagons. Especially with Thomas wanting to die. Meka has her hands full with that boy. I will send out Tyris to back up the guards around the kids. I just hope they get there in time." said Athinina.

The Queen turned to leave when the giant spider fell from the ceiling and missed Athinina by a mere few inches. She went for her sword but was too slow as a magical arrow passed by her head and into the pinchers and head of the spider. Turning, it went into the spider's belly and out its forehead.

"Guess that one will have a headache for a while? I think we need to stick together for a while until these attacks end. The spider, I believe, was mere coincidence. We still have those buggers running around the palace and city. We just need to be careful." said Tanis. Looking down at the spider as he passed, he stopped in his tracks. Looking at the creature's fore arms he noticed something the local spiders did not have. This spider was a sword spider. They are common in the Mountains of Doric, but are rarely seen beyond them. Instead of the first set of legs, sword spiders had sword like appendages. They used these to hunt by falling upon its prey and stabbing with the swords.

"Sword spiders are not found this far south, are they? I think we have another problem. They have introduced sword spiders into the local environment. The two breeds could cause a super spider type of offspring. The ones we are used to are the smartest of the spiders. Sword spiders are the strongest. The two together would be devastating." said Tanis as he once more looked down on the dead spider. Looking into the spider's eyes he saw the one moving in above him and launched his magic arrow again and hit the spider right in the middle of its body.

Screaming in pain the spider launched itself down onto the couple below it. Tanis did not have time to move the arrow and took the brunt of the attack. Athinina quickly recovered and took the creature's head off. "Have we seen the end of these spiders for now, or are we going hunting?" she asked as she cleaned her blade. "These look like the hybrids we were concerned about, don't they?"

"Yes, they do. I will inform the guard that spiders are more dangerous and they may be falling from the ceilings. We do not want them taken by surprise. I will also let them know to kill all spiders on site." Looking up as he walked, Tanis moved to the throne room.

In the middle of the throne room was a weird scene even for the recent events. A large dog had two of the sword spiders held at bay in the center of the room. Tanis moved in to see that the large dog was indeed a wolf. Tanis moved closer and fired his magical arrow at the spiders. The wolf turned and started to approach the Queen.

Tanis did not know which way to look. If he attacked the wolf, he would be open for attack from the spiders. Attack the spiders and Athinina get attacked by the wolf. He was trying to figure out the best course of action when Artitous entered the room and blasted the spiders with a ball of fire.

Tanis sprang into action and swept his sword across the wolf's shoulders removing its head. *Even a werewolf would die if decapitated* thought Tanis. Tanis turned to his wife who was still trying to put her sword away and laughed. Her sword belt had somehow gotten twisted about her and she was having a terrible time fixing it. Artitous moved to assist her and the two began to get tangled and the Queen gave them both a scary glare. She finally straightened the sword belt and slammed her blade home. As the sword was put into its' scabbard, the Queen cursed and looked at her hands. "Broke a nail. I do this too often." Laughed the Queen of Dracos.

"It could have been your sweet head though, my love." said Tanis as he flinched at the fist sent flying at his gut. "I was just saying, my dear."

"Let us finish this dirty work. It will definitely be an interesting few days." said Athinina.

CHAPTER THIRTEEN

TRAITORS

The royal couple settled into the large gaudy thrones that had been found in the lower reaches of the city. It was time to vet the lords and ladies. They would be put out and pouty about it, but that was their problem. The traitor had to be caught.

The lords and ladies entered the throne room and all but two gasped at the carnage in the middle of the room. The lord of McCryden and the Elven Governor showed no interest or disgust at the corpses. The Elven Governor was expected to ignore the scene as he was an elf and had seen worse in his pantry being so close to the Mountains of Doric.

The lord of McCryden looked down and smiled. He quickly lost that smile and put on a worried face like the rest of the nobles in the room. He was too far along to give up now. Tanis noticed his slow reaction and noted it for later. He had been acting strangely the last few days.

Tanis looked over at Lord Masters and cleared his throat, "I am sure you are all wondering why we have sent for all of you. We have a serious problem. Dark wizards and treacherous guards have been attacking the royal family. There has also been a sword spider invasion in the palace. As you can see, they are getting brazen."

"My Lord Tanis. I will have these creatures eradicated as soon as my guards arrive from McCryden." said Tobin Masters. "They will no longer plague this palace or city."

Tanis interrupted and said, "Lord Masters, these things are hybrids. They have been blended from the sword spiders and or own giant spiders. Do not underestimate them. It will be a daunting task for anyone to go about their destruction."

"But my Lord, I can do it my wizards have been working tirelessly to eradicate these vermin from our own home. Their spells seem to work well. Let me give them a try. What is the worst that could happen?" the duke asked with a bit of command in his voice.

"Are you giving us orders, Tobin? Surely even with your great ambitions you would not think of ordering your rulers?" said Athinina loosening her sword in its scabbard.

As she spoke all the lords and ladies started with their own pleas to allow them to guard the royal family. Tobin took the opportunity to leave the very dangerous situation he almost created. As he walked from the room a sword spider fell in front of him. Pulling a rod from his pant pocket he pressed the button and the spider exploded.

"This will be easier than I thought," said Tobin to the wizard that started walking beside him. "Much easier."

CHAPTER FOURTEEN

TAKING OF THALINBURG

The guards and wizards, servants and staff were quickly checked for traitors. It proved a little slower than originally intended as some of the guard and staff had been informed of the search. In total twelve guardsman and seven staff members disappeared. As well as three wizards and nine servants also left.

The others that remained gave oaths that they were not traitors. Tanis checked each of them and found them telling the truth. Athinina thought for a moment that there were too few dwarves in that group. This was the city of the dwarves. She continued to follow Tanis and whispered her concerns into his ear.

Tanis turned and asked one of the remaining maids what was going on with the dwarves? Her answer surprised him. "They are all two-timing creatures; we should have purged them a long time ago."

"Explain yourself." said Tanis.

"Everyone knows the dwarves are evil. Just have to wait until they set upon you to realize they are just biding their time." said the maid.

"I appreciate your concern and it is duly noted. I will go now and review all of the documents that we have collected." said Tanis as he laid the papers next to his throne.

"I too smell a rat. Most of these people are men and women. Not dwarves and Elves. This is indeed strange, call for Martin. I have a task for him and his rangers." said Athinina.

The guards ran to get the elven ranger and while they awaited his arrival, they discussed what they had seen. Tobin Masters would have to be dealt with. He was going to be more trouble than he was worth, they agreed. He may or may not be the traitor but he was still acting very strangely. He would require watching. And the rangers are just the right group to watch him without his knowledge. They had all proven loyal and they would be a great asset to the royals.

Martin walked into the room at a brisk walk that he always used. He walked up and bowed to the royals and then made a strange request. "My Lord, please make us private. I need to tell you things that no one else need to hear."

Tanis created the ward to prevent listening in and sat closer to the elf. "What has gotten you so concerned that you would not speak to us unwarded?" asked Tanis.

"Let him speak, my darling. He has my curiosity up as well." said Athinina.

"I fear a problem. I only trust half of my rangers. Elves keep leaving or vanishing without word and these humans hardly look the part of rangers. They are being assigned by Sir Merrin Overmeyer. I do not know what he is doing but he replaced many of the guard as well. He was seen leaving that boarding house when the Noom arrived. The

Languid Dragon. I have also seen him with some of the wizards and other members of the nobility." said Martin.

"Sir Overmeyer? He is the first to have pledged fealty. I cannot believe he would be tangled in all of this. What about Duke Masters? Surely, he is the better suspect." said Tanis as he looked around the room. Several of the lords and ladies were speaking and moving closer to the throne. They knew they were speaking and hoped to catch a piece of the conversation.

"What about the Lady Brewster. She has been sticking to me and my escort like glue. Surely, she has a stake in this?" said Athinina.

"We have not worked out all of the enemies amongst us. We have also been monitoring for spies to the Dark Lords. Several birds left that way in last few days. We have stopped them at the borders, but some still make it through. We have tried to follow birds coming north but again they travel all over our side of the world. They have allies everywhere apparently. Even amongst the elves. The dwarves deny they have any people still loyal to the Dread Lords, but then we see birds leaving their quarter and going out. I do not know who is behind it but we will get a glimpse soon I fear." said Martin.

"Bring me Lord Masters and Lord Overmeyer. Should we include the Lady Brewster, my sweet?" asked Tanis looking over at the now enraged Athinina.

"We were assured by these people that they ruled in our name in their provinces. That they followed our commands to the letter. I fear our welcome would be a warm one in those counties. Let us hear what they have to say for themselves." said Athinina.

Martin moved swiftly at this and grabbed the Lady Brewster as she headed for the door. He pulled her kicking and screaming to the thrones. Curtsying deeply, she looked up at the royal couple. "How may I serve, my liege?"

"Please tell me about the coup you are planning. All the details. Were you the one that hired the two Noom? Did you set the magical attacks? What was your role in all of this? We are shielded from eavesdroppers. No one can hear us. Tell us your role or your will be executed and the others offered this deal. Tell us everything and you will be released to your men. They will hold you in prison for the rest of your days. But you will not be killed. This is the best I can offer you so speak and live." said Tanis.

"I know nothing about a coup. I was asked to follow her majesty by one of the wizards. He wanted to know her routine, I told him it is different every day. He became unhappy at this response and ordered me to follow her. That is all I know. I do not know the wizard's name nor any of his conspirators. He just told me to report by letter placed in a rat's hole near the center of the palace." said the shaken Lady Brewster.

"You are still a conspirator. Your fate will be the same as theirs. You will show me this hole and we will place a discreet watcher there to observe who comes to collect your latest missive. You will write in your code, as I am sure you have one, and tell him that we are suspicious of you. You will be watched as well. Any hint of aiding or abetting the conspiracy and you will be taken into custody and hanged." said Athinina

"Hanged? Like a commoner. I demand the headsman if it comes to that. I am of noble blood. I demand my due." Screamed the irate Brewster.

"You will be stripped of all of your titles. Formally after this affair is over. Then you will go to the gallows. That is the way this will go. Understand?" said Athinina.

"But I am not a conspirator. Just because I help a wizard and a few colleagues, that does not make me a traitor. Tell me my crimes." said the Lady Brewster as she started to curl up under the scrutiny of the Queen. "Have mercy on me, my lord. Tell her I am not a traitor. I can make it well worth your help. Please release me. I am your loyal woman, Lord Tanis."

"Two mistakes there. Number one is that I am not interested in rewards as you have nothing to give and I am not taking. Secondly, I am not your judge. That would be my wife. Telling me of your reward may have infuriated her even more than your treason. Be prepared for a bitter sentence." replied Tanis to the Lady's offer. A look from Athinina assured Tanis that there would be a discussion later about this encounter.

"Get up and go to my writing desk and write your code. Be careful what you reveal or you will be put to death sooner than later. Do you understand?" said Athinina.

The now much disheveled lady went to the desk and began to write. Half way through her task, she reached inside the desk and withdrew the small nib knife that was there to sharpen the pens and she quickly slit her wrists with it. Tanis reached out and tried to heal her but it was too little to aid her. As she slumped over onto the now blood-stained desk, Athinina roared.

"That filthy traitor. She got off to easily. Guard why were you not watching her? She should not have died that way. Tanis why did you not heal her? What went wrong here?" Fumed Athinina.

"I tried to heal her but her wrist was not her only wound; I believe. Let me examine the body. I think I know what happened." said Tanis moving from the throne. The guard jumped in front of Tanis and tried to move him the opposite direction of the body. "No need to go there, my sire. I will check the body for additional wounds. Martin loosened the dagger at his belt as Tanis moved around the guard. The guard moved quickly and attacked Tanis. Tanis felt more than saw the blade coming. Instinctually, he turned and thrust his own sword deep into the guard's body.

"What is happening here?" asked Athinina. "Why is this happening?"

"No one can tell you that. I just hope that this at least is over. Martin, have you tracked the others down? I suspect very similar stories. But we have to find that wizard. Triple the watch. I want no more surprises." said Tanis as he walked toward the body of the lady. Looking down at her he saw what he definitely did not want to see. The guard had stabbed her in the groin right about the femoral artery. It would have killed her in seconds. Had he known to look for it he could have saved her.

The guard was also dead and had nothing to alert the royals of his place in the coup. Tanis had vetted the man not a day ago. How could he have missed this?

CHAPTER FIFTEEN

MORE TRAPS

As the attack at the palace in Thalinburg was taking place, Torlin was enjoying his wife and children. He looked about as happy as he could possibly be. Torlin moved closer to his children and that was when he saw the trap. Quickly lifting the children, he handed them to his wife and searched the area. Every five feet he found interconnected traps. Had Roanda stepped wrong one time she would have set off the trap killing them all.

He was not sure if immortality was passed along family lines and did not wish to test the theory. He carefully moved his family and looked closer at the traps. His wife had the children in the palace proper, when a guard came running into the patch of grass. He kicked one of the traps setting them all off. Torlin fell to the ground wounded by the flying shrapnel from the devices. He tried to move and felt his strength betray him. He looked around and saw the guard dead a few inches from him. Why had the guard betrayed him?

His wife came running and called for the druids to meet her immediately in their rooms. Lifting Torlin into her arms she lovingly moved her husband to the rooms and laid him upon the bed. "You better not die on me or I will rip you from your rest and force you to take your own share of dirty diapers. It is only fair. Please Torlin hold on. The druids are coming. They will aide you." said Roanda.

Torlin slowly closed his eyes and lay back. Roanda kept talking to him but he felt himself slowly fading. He would not see his children grow and become the friends and colleagues they should be. He would not be able to hold his wife again. He was not ready when the flash of light filled his vision and he was once more looking at the face of his wife and children looking distressed and worried.

"It was a close thing, My Lady." said the old gnarled man sitting at his head. "We almost lost him. But he should be just fine after a few days. How was he injured? It would not do with what happened to the garden would it. Apparently one of the guards was killed when a series of explosives went off. I was with him when you summoned me. Had I been in my usual haunts, Torlin would have perished. He had many wounds that needed to be healed and many of them alone would have been fatal. It is a good thing I got to him when I did."

He stood up and started to leave the room when Artitous ran into the room. Looking around at the people in the room he looked at the druid and asked, "Good sir, what is your name? I do not recall ever seeing you before. I appreciate the healing you have given Torlin. It would have been a dear thing to have lost him."

"I have just arrived with my grove. We will be taking this city for ourselves now. It is now our rule and you will all leave it." said the man as he morphed from old man to a young man in wizard's garb. "I had hoped this would come without bloodshed but that stupid man set off my traps. Now leave or die."

"You do realize that you are surrounded and unable to escape?" asked Roanda.

"Oh, you will find the case to be just the opposite. Guards take these three into custody. Put them on the wagon leaving this morning send them back to his parents with his wounds and let them know that Metra has fallen to the new crop of dark lords. We have taken the city and its inhabitants as our own without a struggle. If you noticed all your normal guards and associates are either gone back to Thalinburg or dead? You have no alternative but to leave. Artitous, I made sure we added some of the Mandore Stones around. I wear the counter stone but you two would not be able to use it. It is tuned to dark magic." Laughed the young wizard.

"Who are you?" asked Roanda.

"No harm giving the exiles my name. I am Asher and I now rule Metra." said the wizard. "Now guards take them and eliminate the loyal guards to them. We don't want a civil war now do we?" giggled the wizard.

The wizard and his family were roughly shoved down the hall. The elven rangers that had come with them as well as the Tyris that had followed saw the situation and attempted to save the royal family but there were just too many of those loyal to Asher. The elves moved back a step at a time until the guard came up behind the elves and the killing began in earnest. They fought bravely but in the end the number proved too great for them.

A few yards beyond the now elves came the Tyris. The small battle once again began in earnest and the Tyris were pushing back the guard when all of a sudden three of the Tyris turned and attacked their sisters. Pulling a black lace form their mytan, they wrapped them about their arms and continued to fight their colleagues. The remaining Tyris saw too late the treachery and were again slain by the followers of Asher.

"Why my sisters have you attacked your sisters and failed to protect the royal family? You are Tyris, not the common rabble that these guards consist of. These men and that wizard do not deserve your loyalty. Return to our side and slay these usurpers. The Tyris looked at the princess and smiled. One lifted her sword and looked at it and turned to face the guards. "Shall I gut them now, or wait till they get to the wagons?" asked the Tyris.

As she asked the question the sword pierced her heart. Slowly looking around as she died, she saw all the Tyris lying dead. The guards had turned on the lady warriors. The head of the new guard smiled and looked at the royal family and smiled. "They turned once why would we believe they would not turn again? No loose ends and now here we are at the wagons. Who will go first? You see you will all be dead going back to the capitol just to show that we are serious. So, which one dies first?"

Torlin leaned up from his litter and smiled himself. They were outside the effects of the Mandore Stones. He raised his hand and one of the guards tried to cut it off but was met by Roanda's sword. Torlin raised his body and fired a fireball right into the middle of the group of new guardsmen. The sounds of battle followed them as they tried to get to an empty wagon and leave to warn their parents.

As they finally found a wagon, several Tyris jumped into it and Torlin turned to face them. "Hold we are on your side we got through the line to assist you in your escape. Now go. The others are sacrificing themselves to save all of you. Let's go. Roanda better that we drive. They will not stop a couple of women in a wagon but they would kill you on sight."

"Thank you, my sisters. Let us away" said Roanda as two of the Tyris shed their armor and donned dresses. Torlin went beet red as the armor hit the floor. Roanda gave Torlin an elbow to the ribs and he settled down. They quickly dressed as the other few Tyris jumped into the seat of the wagon and got it rolling.

Torlin looked out the back looking for signs of pursuit but saw only a couple of horsemen following with swords drawn. The Tyris fell them quickly with their bows and continued the slow run from the city.

"Should we be going a bit faster? This speed they will be on us in a moment." said Torlin.

"Be still. If we go to fast, they will realize that we are the wagon hauling you and your family. Right now, our sisters in the dresses drive the wagon and we are closing all of the curtains and falling into a column of other wagons headed for the capitol. With luck the capitol has not fallen." said the Tyris.

The wagon moved on in silence for a while and the hiding worked. The wagon passed a little village and most of the wagons stopped. Guards stopped those that were continuing and searched them before letting them move on. Looking around the Tyris on the seat of wagon spoke with the three Tyris still concealed within the wagon. "There are only three of the new guards here. The village looks terrified of them. I think this town needs to be liberated. Shall we?"

Torlin opened the back of the wagon dressed in a pair of pants and a peasant shirt and moved behind the three guards that stood there. The three Tyris in the wagon and Roanda waited for Torlin's sign. Torlin quickly sounded a bell in the air and fired a fireball into the three men looking around for any more guards lurking about. The Tyris jumped from the wagon and searched the town. The only other guards were in the tavern, and appeared to have drunk half the beer in the barrel they were sitting in front of. The Tyris quickly dispensed with them and moved back to the village center where the citizens were holding a rousing hurray for the Tyris and Torlin and Roanda.

"Welcome to Landsdale. We are formally and completely loyal to the Queen and the city of Metra. Those men came in the dark of night and slew our regular guard and took over. They laughed as they raped a young woman and then killed her. The parents were killed when they tried to intervene. We are so proud of our leader, Torlin Thalin and his party." said the rotund mayor. The mayor looking at the bodies of the guards and scoffed. "Should have known who they were dealing with. Dump those six where the vultures can feast on them."

"Mayor, let them be buried with the respect of a man. We are all men and should not treat another human like waste. We will assist in digging the graves." said Torlin as he looked down at the men laying at his feet. They would not have done it for them but it should be done. It is the right and proper thing to do.

They went out to the grave yard and Torlin used his power to create the holes in the earth for the men. The Tyris lay them into the graves and were laying their weapons upon their chest as was the Tyris way, when they were stopped by the mayor.

"We could use those weapons in the event more of these people come. Let us collect these arms and armor for our own defenses." said the mayor.

The Tyris looked at him and their leader came over to the mayor and said, "The souls of these men will look for their weapons and the one using them will perish by them. These weapons have seen poor conduct and false bravado. They have been used for misconduct and must be left with these men so it can never perform these actions again. We have extra weapons and armor. We will happily share it with you, good dwarves."

"Well, if you put it that way, I guess they can remain there. Just looking out for my people you see." said the mayor.

"Well meant and all we are happy to help you in any way we can. I would like some help burying these creatures and their ill-used weapons that now bear their curse to be vile and evil." said the Tyris. Several of the men came over and started helping throw dirt onto the corpses below. As they covered the corpses, an arrow flew from out of the surrounding forest, imbedding itself deep into one of the wooden shovels. The Tyris had their weapons up in a flash of eye and the dwarves with their new weapons just a smidge slower advanced toward the archer.

"Be still all of you or you will all die. This village is now property of the wizard, Asher. Anyone trying to challenge that will be thrown to the very hungry grey lions in the palace for the entertainment of the wizard. Now lay down your arms and die properly. Said a voice in the woods.

Torlin let loose with a round of fireballs into the surrounding trees. As the trees were touched by the fire, they dissolved so the fire would not spread. Torlin let loose another volley of the fireballs and several men came into view dancing and screaming about their burning bodies. As the Tyris and the dwarves surrounded them they realized that they had no clothes on. Torlin had not burned the men. Just their clothing, weapons, and armor.

Torlin apologized for the state of the men to the dwarves and Tyris saying, "Sorry, the spell burns all non-organic material including cloth. I hope we have enough blankets to give them as they rot in the village prison."

"My Lord, we have no prison. Never needed one. We always sent the people who required jailing to the city of Metra to be dealt with." said the dwarven leader.

"Then we shall continue the tradition. Move back all of you. Not you. Now watch closely village wizard." said Torlin. Slowly moving his hands, he showed the spell to the local wizard and the men shot from in front of them into the basement of the prison bound and gagged. The jailors there were surprised at the appearance of the men and Torlin closed the hole to the basement. "That should slow down any more attempts at harassing your people. They will move on to easier targets. You have to get to the other villages locally and warn, liberate if necessary, and arm them. This way we can take back our city."

"It will be as you say, sire. But even with the elves? I am sure they have plenty of bows and have no need of being liberated." said the mayor.

"Yes, good sir. Every one of them. They are your neighbors and all will be needed in the end. Roanda, we will be staying here and using it as our base of operations. My family will see our defense and retrieval of our city and we will be a spotlight for the others. Tyris make these people more comfortable and assist them in making some kind of palisade. They will need it before too long. The wizard will go looking for his people, and find out what we have done and where."

Roanda got the children put down with the local midwife and went out to help with the battle preparations. The dwarven smiths had already begun working on weapons and gadgets for the coming battles and Torlin assisted by making them magical. The people here may be out numbered but they will have the best weapons ever created. Dwarven weapons mixed with the magic of the greatest of sorcerers. It did not get better than that.

A smith walked to the Tyris with shirts he had just made of mytheral, a silver steel that when worn protected them from harm by physical or magical means. He blushed as the women took his gift and kissed him for his gift. Roanda went to join her sisters when a look at Torlin changed her mind and she just shook his hand. The dwarf raced away to the forge and peeked around the corner at the women who had moved on to other things. They laughed amongst themselves as the dwarf would turn red as soon as one of them looked at him. The poor dwarf would probably die of embarrassment was the common bet amongst the Tyris.

Torlin laughed at the comment and went to reassure the dwarf that all was well. They continued to make and don weapons made by the dwarves. Even Torlin bore a shirt of mytheral. "I look the fool in this, Roanda." said Torlin.

"Now dear, do not offend our hosts. They wish you to have it and you will wear it. And the robes that you and the wizard created. You may need them by the time all this is through. You never know." said Roanda. "Now do you think you can kill this other wizard? Asher has made a neat trick of putting the Mandore Stones in your way." asked Roanda.

"His stones will not hinder me." said Torlin. "After all, he forgets that I invented the things. I will figure out the weaknesses and make them work for me."

"Then I guess we have to get to work." said Roanda as she moved toward the smithy in the middle of the town.

CHAPTER SIXTEEN

LANDSDALE

Torlin worked hard in the village, preparing for the wizard's response to the loss of his troops. The wooden palisade would hold for a while, but it would fall to wizards and other magical attacks all too quickly. Torlin fused with magic the wall that had sprung up, it seemed like overnight. Torlin made his way to the smithy where he found his wife and other Tyris follow the commands of the smith as they made weapons. To keep peace amongst all the parties involved, Torlin had his mytheral shirt on. It was under the robes that he had decided to don again. He just did not like trousers. His wife looked up and smiled at her husband. They would make this the center of their resistance.

Torlin had sent a raven to Tanis to alert Thalinburg of the present situation. Metra may have fallen into evil hands but they were fine and about to fight back. Torlin also asked for aide in defending the little village.

The raven returned quickly with Thalinburg's response. There could be no aide as they were unable to determine who was loyal and who they could not trust. They would not send an army that may turn on them. Torlin was disappointed but he understood his father's position. He would not send troops either if he did not know that they would do as directed. Letting the raven go its own way. He asked that it stay close in case of emergency.

Torlin knew one would come, but when he did not know. The woods were quiet as he walked the top of the palisade just thinking and trying to figure out how to destroy those stones. As he moved around toward the road side, an arrow hit him square in the chest. As it hit, he was flung back to the ground about ten feet down. Groaning he pushed himself up. Roanda was already there as Torlin pulled the arrow from his chest and lay it down.

The dwarf smith came out and was jumping up and down with joy. His mytheral worked. It did not kill the wearer when the arrow hit. He was beaming and strutting about when the rest of the arrows started falling.

Torlin reacted quickly and put a shield up around the village to block the arrows. Several of the dwarven warriors went up to the top of the palisade and mooned the soldiers firing at them. They stopped their sport and grew serious as the barrage continued. Tyris replaced the dwarves on the wall and fired their weird bows. They looked like that had been dried in the summer air. The bend was so subtle that it could be easily missed and the notches for the string were concealed amongst what looked like roots on both sides. The center of the bow was twisted in what appeared to be a spiral. These weapons were more that serious though.

The Tyris fired these bows with skill and accuracy. They let fly several volleys of arrows before the startled attackers realized they were firing. The whole thing was over in minutes as the attackers fled into the forest. Roanda was about to order a pursuit when Torlin stopped her. "My darling, it may be dangerous to your people to follow these enemies into the forest. Something does not feel right in there."

It became apparent why it felt wrong in moments as the trees started to move toward the palisade. Torlin fired blasts of magic into them and the trees fell fast. "That is druid magic. Why the druids would be fighting for our enemy. Artitous will want to hear of this."

As he lifted his hand to call in the raven when a blast struck the shield. Turning he saw the druids moving into view with magic flying. Warriors moved below the palisade even though they were already safe behind the magical shield. The village druid came to the front and looked at the men at the foot of the palisade.

"These are dark men. We must destroy them. I will unleash the trees upon them." She said as she turned to see that the trees were already fallen and unable to be used.

"Oh. I did not see that before." said the druid as Torlin fired fireballs down into the druid below. Within minutes the druids were all dead and the small fire extinguished.

"Dark druids. Rogue guards and wizards. What else has been sent after us?" asked Torlin turning and seeing the hybrid sword spiders from Thalinburg falling from the overhanging trees. "I did ask, didn't I?"

The sword spider was quickly dispatched by the Tyris as Torlin could not raise his hands fast enough to beat the speed of the women warriors. He would like to see more of them in his is mother had set up a camp to teach young women to become Tyris. It was always full and people waited for years to get into it. But the quality of warrior was never less than the ones that had come from their homeland deep within the Dark Lands.

Several more of the spiders appeared around the village and all were quickly dispatched. The dwarves were not going to be outdone. Several of the dwarves had suffered wounds from the sword appendages but no one had died. Thank the creator for small miracles.

The wounds were not serious so the druid just bandaged them. No need to use magic and drain the wizard and druid's strength. The village wizard came up after he finished enchanting the weapons. Looking around he just looked at Torlin and shook his head. "Looks like I missed all the fun." said the wizard.

"Not all of it. There are more coming." said Torlin. "In fact, I am sure we will be taking turns while the others rest. One of us should be enchanting arrows, one resting and one on the front lines. We follow this rotation. The wizard on the walls goes to rest, from rest they go to enchanting arrows, and after enchanting arrows they move to the walls. We must maintain this shield. It will be hard once the wizard arrives but we can do it. I noticed that Asher's hand was filthy. I realized the stones do not affect him because he covered the hands from exposure to the stones. So, wizard and druid, if you see stones being placed around the village, cover your hands with mud. Then give the wizard a bath. Then he will be helpless."

"Do you think that will work?" asked Roanda. "After all, the stones are powerful and he has created more. You had only created one and this man has many. Could he have changed the formula?"

"If he did then we will find out fast. But for now, it is the best we have." said Torlin. "I will take the wall first. The druid will enchant arrows and you will be resting good wizard."

"As you say, sire." replied the wizard and druid.

Turning to the mayor he leaned over and asked him, "What are their names again?"

The mayor let out a jovial laugh and said, "Saundera is the druid, Rexon is the wizard."

"And now you, sir. What is your name?" asked the prince.

"Kind of you to ask, sire. My name be Tamron, sire. Tamron Flatfeet." replied the dwarf.

"Mister Flatfeet, it is very good to work with you. We should be safe here for a while. But if he unleashes the full might of the Metra Army, we may have a problem. He only has command of a few of the men and generals as of yet. I may be able to signal the loyalists to us to fight for us here." said Torlin as he raised his arms once more and a silver-grey bar shot into the sky and headed to Metra. "It is only visible to a few people and they will know where to find us now. They will hopefully come to our aid."

"People are coming!" Shouted the dwarf in the newly made tower.

"Could it have worked already?" asked Mayor Flatfeet.

"No Tameron, I did not work that fast. My good dwarf are they men, elves, or dwarves?" asked Torlin.

"These be elves and dwarves, sire. Many of them are armed. Shall I sound the alarm?" asked the dwarf.

"No. I shall speak to them when they approach." said Torlin.

It took the people a short while before they were at the gates. Torlin stood on the palisade looking down at the new arrivals. He called down to them to produce a spokesman and an older elf stepped forward. "Good sire, we are glad to see you thus alive. The rumor was that you were murdered when Asher took control of Metra. Asher claimed to have your bodies and had burned them. The army follows him now and peasants and elves and dwarves are being forced out of the city or they disappear, never to be seen again. It may be a small thing but my bow and my service are yours."

The rest of the people in the group quickly repeated that they too were for the cause of the prince. Torlin waved a hand and the gate opened. Since the attacks had come the gates were sealed by magic so none could enter nor leave without Torlin knowing. He even made it so the other magic users could not open them, just in case.

The people walked into the town square and were quickly offered food and ale. Torlin saw the dust cloud first. "Please hurry and enter. I fear we have some company coming soon. They are moving fast so I need to ask you all to move quickly."

The people had just finished coming in when the cloud of dust manifested into several of the mounted knights. Around them strode the royal archer brigade. Before an alarm could be arranged the elves with the newcomers were on the walls with bows drawn.

"Hold your fire. No one lets an arrow fly yet." said Torlin. "You there, reveal your faces to me."

"And if we refuse?" came the sarcastic response from inside the helmet. Torlin waved his hand and the helmets sprung from the enemies' heads and crawled away.

"Sir Bradfield. Do you speak for all of these men? Or are the parties independent of each other?" asked Torlin. "Surely, we did not put too hard a yoke upon your shoulders with the royal archers, did we?"

"I work for Asher and you will do well to bend knee to him as well. All the dwarves and elves that your family coddle and protect are being forced from our cities or are being executed. We were told that you were dead. But this man has powers you do not have now nor will you ever possess. Lay down your arms and we will let the village alone. They will have to tear down the walls and let us in, but they will be left alone for the most part. Now you cannot hope to beat the new royal archers."

Torlin looked out into the crowd of archers and saw only men and smiled. They had removed every elf and dwarf from the ranks and now the men were poorly trained mercenaries from the Dark Lands.

Torlin looked at the elf in charge of the group and nodded. A volley of arrows sprung from their bows and dropped a large number of the archers below.

"I am sorry but I think the people here have another plan. You may not want to press further." said Torlin.

"Do you think he sent only archers? We have engineers that will figure a way into the city and we have axe and mace men eager to attack those cheap wooden walls of yours." said the knight.

As he spoke another cloud of dust approach the city. More armed men came into view and Torlin called for his wife. "How many Tyris do we have here in town?" asked the prince disregarding the men's words.

"About seventy, my love. They have been sneaking out of the city and coming here. There are rumors of other problems out into the kingdom." said Roanda.

"First things first, my love, first things first." said Torlin.

CHAPTER SEVENTEEN

THE SIEGE OF LANDSDALE

The army from Metra set up camp outside the walls of the city. They camped close to the palisade without fear of the enemy inside. Tyris were working day and night with the smith and his apprentice. Rotating shifts, the groups made all kinds of arrowheads and weapons to aid in the defense of the town and its new residents, the Torlin family. All those in the town had sworn oath to protect the royal family to the death. The small children were moved into the storm cellars the night the enemy set camp. No use in taking chances. Three women and two Tyris guarded the children hidden in the depths of the earth. The royal children interacted well with the other children and the small ones were content playing as much as their age would allow.

The night had fallen and once more the elves took to the battlements of the town. Dwarves also took to the walls, this time with molten steel in the crucibles. The fires below them were monitored by the dwarves and no harm came to the walls. Torlin fired a single firework into the air and a rain of fire arrows and molten steel poured down on the closest tents and occupants. Some were missed by the first wave of attacks from the town but were quickly taken down by the elves on the wall.

Torlin once more sent a firework into the air and the firing stopped. Slowly the enemy outside the town moved closer to the village to find that now the town's wooden walls were now steel. Torlin used his powers to cool the metal before it could cause them major problems. A few small fires proved easily extinguished and the dwarves hammered out the arrow notches on the lower levels of the walls.

Elves took places at those notches with their longbows and the Tyris took still others with their weird looking bows. The dwarves not to be out done set next to all of the notches with crossbows at the ready. The people of the town were ready to fight to defend themselves.

The people of the town stood awaiting the next command. While they stood there a flicker of a firework shot up into the sky. Instead of the assumed reaction by the people of the town, no attack ever came. The people upon the wall stood there like statues. The enemy once more sent up a flare and again the people of Landsdale stood by and did nothing.

Torlin let off a series of two fireworks and then one firework. The elves once more fired down into the unexpecting crowds below them. The notches were opened and arrows and bolts flew from them, the covers being replaced after each shot. The elves had assisted in making the armor as well as the dwarves and Tyris and many of the elves stepped to the gate. The elves were in full armor and the dwarves in full dwarven armor. They all bore weapons created with the magic of the three magic users as well as the elfish and dwarfish styles of construction. They had the appearance of an army ready to march off to battle not a guard to protect the city upon the breech of the walls.

Torlin had the armored elves and dwarves hidden inside the town ringing the walls so that where ever the wall was breached the armored warriors would be there. The elves and dwarves were trained warriors and those that were not were quickly taught the basics.

The wall was still full of elven archers. They still held their arrows ready for battle awaiting the next signal. A strong breeze swept across those on the ground outside the town. As the breeze quieted the archers released another barrage of arrows. Arrows came from what seemed like everywhere.

An enemy looked into one of the arrow notches looking at the elf reloading his bow and he slowly drew his sword to stab the unaware elf. As he slowly inserted the blade into the notch, he saw the smiling dwarf. The enemy turned to strike the closer person when he felt more than saw the bolt crash into him. Looking through the hole as he fell, he swore he saw a laughing dwarf inside the town.

The murder holes made into the wall were doing just what they were supposed to. The elf and dwarf working that particular notch were reprimanded due to keeping the notch open while loading. Their locations should not be revealed to the enemy. Torlin looked down and saw an enemy soldier approaching the wall. He stood at the wall and relieved himself on the now solid metal. Looking up he saw the arrow headed right for him. Once more the man fell and the elves and dwarves on the battlements hollered and celebrated.

A giant voice swept through the town saying, "How dare you all, resisting me? These lands are now mine and you will comply. Failure to comply will result in the death of every one of you. Send out the royal family so they will finally die properly and not just come back to face me. Torlin your powers are nothing compared to me. You do not stand a chance. So why are you sentencing your followers to death for you? Look around you, these things are animals not people. Rid them from the land and everything will be perfect for my rule."

The mayor looked at Torlin with worry in his eyes. Torlin thought back to the battle at the gates of Thalinburg that Tanis had told the story of. Tanis said he won that battle by deceit and trickery. He told of the laughter he started and the warriors gained a great boost to the morale.

Torlin listened until the voice stopped and then let out a peal of laughter. As he laughed so did the mayor, then one trooper then the next and soon the entire village was laughing. The enemy down below looked at the scene on the wall and did not know what to think. Suddenly another magical flare hit the sky and the laughter stopped and arrows flew. The enchanted arrows when fired would burst into flame. It burned with a magical fire that burned until it touched ground. This prevented damage to the surrounding forests and to the town.

Again, and again the arrows rained down and soon the army at the gates left to find shelter in the trees. Archers had tried to fire into the city but were thwarted by the magic shield that Torlin had built. Those archers also fell to the enchanted arrows and soon the small clearing became a slaughterhouse. Small fires burned everywhere and were swiftly extinguished by Torlin.

Smoke covered the area when the wizards appeared. Torlin looked down at the wizards and smiled. Asher had inadvertently given him the traitors amongst the wizards. He cast a spell and let it descend upon the wizards below. It appeared the wizards were trying to link their powers and it failed. Again and again, they tried to use powers that were no longer apparent they had.

Torlin sent a sleep spell down onto the entire enemy army and ordered that the wizards be brought into the town. Torlin warned them to be wary and sent elves and Tyris as they had dealt with magical folk before. Soon the entire group of wizards was kneeling, chained with magical chain that prevented their use of magic, before Torlin who looked down at the traitors. "Why did you turn to the dark magic?"

"Because we were promised great power and maybe a new dread lord position. Asher has the power to bring back human rule and have the other races subjugated like they deserve." said the wizard kneeling in the first spot. The racist slurs passed over Torlin but was angering the dwarves and elves who cried for their immediate deaths. "They must receive fair trials and sentencing. This is not a dictatorship it is a free land. Just because these men would have slain you does not mean that we must also sink to their nasty and ridiculous standards. Do you not agree?"

The mayor was first to speak, "These are enemy combatants and we have every right to end their lives right now. They know it too."

"But what might we learn from them? The gags of air I have put into place should prevent them from using the glass teeth that they have in their mouths. You may remove them now," he said to the elves sitting in wait for orders.

The elves went to work and quickly all of the wizards had no teeth in their mouths. The head of the elves looked and apologized. "We seemed to be a little over zealous in our work. Many apologies my lord."

"It may have softened them a touch for answering questions." said Torlin as he began grilling the wizards for information. After what seemed like hours of interrogation one of the wizards began to speak of Asher's plans. "He is seeking to rule all three kingdoms. From sea to the Mountains of Doric. He has collaborators all over and each have careful laid plans to take each city. Yours being the weakest we took it first. Asher's army is very depleted thanks to your efforts here. He is amassing a large number of mercenaries to fight for his cause. He promises them great rewards but has yet to deliver. Most of them believe the gold and loot all reside in Thalinburg. Asher knows there is a vault in Metra, containing a large collection of small figures and shapes. He swears that they can enhance our magic by one hundred-fold. I am looking so forward to him finding that vault." Laughed the wizard as the gag was replaced.

"Do you remember the day we fell for each other? I had surely been obsessed with you before the incident in the library, but it was there that we became inseparable. Remember the little figures that I had gone back for after the incident for study?" Torlin asked his wife.

"But of course, I remember them. I had to help you collect most of them. What of them?" responded Roanda?

"Asher still does not know where to look. This may be the break we need. Let us sit and make plans to recover the magical enhancers and take back what is ours." said Torlin.

CHAPTER EIGHTEEN

BINDING

As Torlin conspired with Roanda and his new found allies, Thomas was experiencing some similar problems. Thomas walked around the nursery waiting for Artitous who was checking the little one. Christoph was smiling and waving his little arms around and around as the druid looked down upon him. "He has very strong magic. I have bound him for the time being. I learned a lot from your brother so long ago. The block will slowly fade away as he is instructed in magic. Congratulations, Thomas. The magic of the crystal cave is in your son as it is in your father."

"Don't compare the two. The man you all have claimed is my father is a powerful wizard and warrior. My boy will be a warrior. None of this magic stuff. Meka, do you hear this? Apparently, our son healed me. He has also done many other magical things and Artitous says that is why he is soiling himself. The residue of magic. He is an infant. That is what they do. Eat and poop. Telling me that he is so powerful a magic user that he must be bound. You do what you must Artitous but the boy comes to no harm." said Thomas.

"My husband, our child's talents must be trained and honed so he can grow happy and content." said Meka.

"The magic missed me. It went to my brother. Is this child his? I have no magic and you are also bare of magic. So how do we produce a magical child?" asked Thomas?

"You had better not say such things again or you may get your dagger after all. The child is ours and no one else. Do not let the paranoia take over again." said Meka.

"Magic can skip generations. It can skip for a thousand years and suddenly pop up out of nowhere." Artitous said trying to calm the situation.

"No one asked you, old man. I am having a quiet discussion with my wife. Leave us and go back to Thalinburg where you belong." said Thomas. As Thomas spoke a raven landed on Artitous's shoulder. The raven spoke to the druid in the language of the ravens and the druid went pale.

"I have to go and you have got to get back to Thalinburg. Torlin and Metra has fallen. There are rumors of him in a forest town. But the wizard that took over claimed that he killed the entire royal family there. I must go and see for myself." said the Grand Druid as he proceeded out the door.

"Fear mongers. That is all wizards are. Torlin is probably doing one of his outside inspections to see that his people have all they need. That is worthless. They need something they apply to the throne." said Thomas, "That could never happen here. I have my own hand-picked guard and army here." said Thomas.

"My dear, I saw no one that I knew except Tetradon guards. There are none of the elves or dwarves and Noom fighters that you have gathered along with your men." said Meka. "I am not being paranoid now when I say we may be in danger."

"My people would never turn on me. Where is your friend, Yangzom? Surely his people will help protect us." said Thomas. Hearing someone come into the room Thomas turned to see the druid in the doorway. "There he is now. How are you planning on protecting us? Hey wait why can't I move my arms and legs? Meka are you likewise entangled?"

"My sire, you miss my intentions. I do not mean to protect you but to imprison you with the rest of your loyalists. My people now run Tetra and you my good sir, must die along with your entire family. But it will be done publicly so the people can see that they now belong to me." Smiled Yangzom.

Meka whistled harshly and the sounds of combat were quickly heard and subdued. Meka waited for the Tetradon to come and release them by killing the traitor that now stood before them. But no one came. The druid laughed as his guardsman came in and reported that the Tetradon would not be of any concern to him any longer. They were either dead or captured. Meka began to cry as they took Christoph and the two of them down to the dungeons below the palace. All around them Thomas's soldiers and allies sat contained in the cells as well as the political prisoners of Thomas's.

One of the prisoners looked at Thomas and smiled, "Well look what we have here. His majesty is imprisoned in his own jail. What an opportunity to once more beg my innocence. That is as we have our way with your woman, and all the ladies that have joined us down here as of late."

"I would not suggest it. These women can kill without thought. You would find yourselves in a bit of a pickle. But please try. Do not let me deter you from your plans. Anyone have any ideas about getting out of here? I do not believe I have a tunnel here." said Thomas as he looked at the walls of the dungeon.

"You would forget your feet if they were not screwed on, you buffoon. Over here in the back corner." said Meka as she walked over and pressed a combination of bricks and a door slid open. The open door revealed a strange giant spider with swords on its front appendages guarding what looked like a nest. "Oh my. It would appear we have found another problem. Tyris, let's kill this thing and gain its appendages as weapons. Then we can take our city back."

"I do not think two sword-like appendages would suffice to get back our city. We must look for my brother and see if the rumors are true. If so, we are all doomed as it is a wizard we must be facing. We have this tunnel and several connect with this one. Let us go and see what the situation in Metra is." Suggested Thomas.

"At very least we must find weapons and supplies. Let these prisoners loose. They can follow us out and go whatever way they choose. The rest of us move west toward Metra." said Thomas. "Children are kept in the center just in case of attack. They will be less vulnerable there."

Thomas moved the women with the children to the center of the party of men and women and they began their travels. He moved as silently as one could with children. The little ones would act up at the worst moments and the older would complain of boredom. Thomas was at his wits end when they moved into a large storeroom in the tunnel. "Where did this come from, Meka?"

Meka smiled and simply replied, "A gift in case of emergency."

"Well placed as the exit should be just another small way forward." said Thomas as he picked up his armor and sword. I am ready to go and take them on now."

"Or we can continue to your brother and parents. The children need to be in a place of safety." said Meka.

"Of course, my dearest." said Thomas as he moved toward the exit of the tunnel. Slowly opening the door, he found it clear. He had hoped they had not found it yet. Moving out into the sun the people now armed and ready moved hurriedly toward the west and Metra. Looking back showed magical combat in the high towers. He wished the wizards and druids still loyal to him good luck as he walked away.

In the towers of Tetra, a battle was ensuing. Artitous was collecting his things when the coup below had occurred. People were running this way and that and at first Artitous ignored the bustle. The servants must be getting things ready for Christoph.

He jumped when the door burst open and several maids ran into his study and cowered behind a chair. "What is wrong, dear ladies?"

Before anyone could speak three of the guard rushed in. One grabbed the druid and the others went for the girls. "Wait one minute" said Artitous. The guard holding him looked him in the eye and demanded that he be still and no one would get hurt.

Artitous began to chant a sleeping spell on the guards when a flash filled the room. The druid looked around and saw the druid, Yangzom, staring at him. "So, we meet again, druid. I have not seen those robes for quite a while. That is since I destroyed the ancients. You did not know they were gone did you? The look upon your face gives you away. It is the time of the dark druids now. I will be pleased to have finished my task and kill the brat of a man that I just threw in the dungeon with his wife and offspring."

Artitous thought for a moment. He held the family and the others. They had probably figured a way out of the dungeon by now so all he needed to do was get the innocents in the palace out and then out of the city. Artitous feigned to produce a fireball and instead struck with a lightning strike through the flames. Yangzom barely dived out of harm's way when he was hit with the shatter senses spell. Screaming Yangzom grabbed at his eyes and ears. The spell had done what Artitous had hoped and temporarily blinded and deafened the dark druid. It would not last long so he took the ladies and headed for the lower levels of the palace and the exit.

Guards moved to prevent his passing down the corridor three floors down and the druid just wiped them away with gusts of wind. The guards fought to stand but were thrown hard against the walls and fell to the ground knocked out. Artitous continued moving gaining servants and other people visiting the palace as he moved. Again and again, he was attacked by magical folk or by armed men. Every time they were thwarted and the now large group of people headed for the door.

Artitous blew the doors off their hinges and moved everyone through. Pushing the people verbally to make haste they headed for the gates. Once more Artitous was caused to pause. The gates were already closed and filled with archers. All of them aimed at the refugees and a Lord of the land was telling them to fire. "Kill them all you idiots do not let the man in brown and white have a change to raise his hands. If you do, we are all toast. Now fire. Now fire into that mob of people."

Artitous had already prepared a spell and launched a great fireball to hit the gates, blowing them open. He told them to move through while the guards were busy putting themselves out but they just stood in awe. Once more he told them to move and they finally did. Arrows followed the mob and several of the people in the rear fell to them.

Artitous continued to fire upon the walls and the gates with fireballs to keep them from firing but soon even his great strength was exhausted. He was supported by several men as he moved toward the west and Metra. He prayed that the prince and his wife and child had escaped. Hoped beyond hope.

They had not traveled far when they saw the cloud of dirt before them. Artitous tiredly moved to the front of the column and raised his arms to fire when he saw it was wagons moving toward them with Thomas at the head. Meka rode next to him and waved at the now very unsteady Artitous.

"What is your father's name?" asked Artitous of Thomas. "Speak or I will attack."

"The man's name is Tanis Thalin. Happy now, you old kook." said Thomas.

"Yes, the man in the tower was disguised by magic. I had to make sure you were not his people. It is good to see you free." said the old druid.

"Load up everyone and let's head toward Metra. I found these wagons abandoned not far into the wood. The owners were nowhere to be found." said Meka.

"I believe I know where they are. We have been infested with a new kind of spider." Began Artitous.

"Yes, with swords for forelegs. We have met them in our tunnels. Do you think they are the cause of the owners' disappearance?" asked Meka.

"I would wager on it. The others probably stopped to search for them and was trapped by a colony of them. We need to find your brother before we attempt to clear them. I am too tired to attempt it now." said Artitous.

"Good thing we showed up. Huh, old man?" said Thomas.

"Indeed, but I am still active enough to teach a spoiled prince to sit straight and lose his sarcastic tongue." said Artitous.

"He is sorry, Artitous. Just cranky. He has not had his nap yet." Smiled Meka.

CHAPTER NINETEEN

REFUGEES

The town of heard the coming wagons before they saw them and were armed and ready upon their steel walls when they came into view. Torlin looked down at the wagons and saw his brother and his family. "Open the gates." Torlin called out as the wagons moved toward them. The shining steel of the gates almost blinded the refugees.

The warriors of Asher had left hours before and the appearance of his brother made Torlin much happier. As the wagons came in and the people and new found goods were unloaded and put where they needed to go, Torlin rushed to his brother. "Happy tidings. How is it that you are able to walk? Tanis and Artitous find a way to heal you? "

"No," said Meka, "Our son did. Apparently, he will need to choose between the druids and the wizards. His father wants him to grow to be a warrior. I just do not know what to do with him."

"Well for now let me introduce you to our mayor here, Master Tamron Flatfeet. His counterpart amongst the elves here is Chappel Eisner. I have been calling the shots here and I fear that I have been making a dog's dinner of it. Look at the walls. I told them to use the steel they produce here to pour over the walls and then pour boiling water down. Now our walls and gate are covered in a thick layer of impregnable steel. The murder holes even have tight steel covers. I have defended the town by luck more than skill three times and soon I fear we will have to do it again. At least this time we will have a proper leader." said Torlin.

"That was brilliant." Meka exclaimed. "We should be safe here for a long time. As long as they do not try to fire over the walls. The sky looks hazy are we expecting rain?"

"A shield covers the town from the walls and above. The skies are as safe as the walls. Do you bring other magic users with you? We could really use the help. We have an enchantry set up to enchant arrows and weapons. We need help maintaining the shield. And of course, we need warriors. How many have you brought with you from Tetra? Metra has fallen and I am in exile in my own lands. We need all the help we can get to reclaim the city. I am afraid." said Torlin.

"We have only twelve magical folks. Artitous is sleeping in the back of the lead wagon. He fought a major battle out of Tetra. Now he is exhausted and resting. When he is ready, he will emerge. Do you have places for all of us?" asked Meka as Thomas admired the walls.

"We have for this group but not for the rest of your host I am afraid." replied Torlin.

"This is really steel? Dwarven steel? We will only have to abandon the walls in a thunderstorm or wizards hurling lightning…" said Thomas trailing off as his wife elbowed him in the gut. "You really will kill me like that one day. Then what'll you do?"

"Marry an infantryman to replace you." She said as she looked at the worn man before her. "We have no reinforcements coming I am afraid. Tetra has also fallen. We now hope beyond hope that Thalinburg remains. Your parents will have to save the day I am afraid."

"It has not fallen," sulked Thomas, "I am just not in charge of it right now."

"I know, my dear. Why don't you go for a tour with Mayor Flatfeet and Lord Eisner? They can show you the shiny wall while they take you around." Quipped Meka.

Looking at Roanda, she simply said "Men."

The ladies around them smiled and some burst into laughter. They moved around and made introductions as were needed and they began to plan for the long run of staying where they were. Plans were discussed about food and drink as well as for caring for and protecting the children in an attack.

Meanwhile the men discussed the types and makes of weapons and armor the dwarves had made with the elves, wizards, and druids help. He looked over the armor and weapons with a discerning eye and asked questions and gave suggestions about improving them. Taking from this style and adding from that style and how they were enchanted. Before long a new set of armor in three sizes sat upon the racks. Looking like full plate but as light and supple as mytheral.

The smith and wizards got to work and soon every person capable of fighting was furnished with the new armor. The Fletcher came in with a new bow design and once more they were enchanted and distributed to the waiting warriors. The weapon smith saw to the swords, axes, and war hammers that the dwarves favored. Once more the weapons were adjusted and then enchanted.

The little village now looked like an army and the enemy should be afraid. Horns bellowed as the look outs spotted dust coming from the east and west. Torlin had the elves line up on the walls and the shield was draped all the way down to the walls' base.

The horns sounded once more as the southern look out had reported an incoming cloud of dust. Torlin sent Nemeth up into the air to scout and returned with word of three enemy armies approaching. He also warned of enemy ravens reporting to the other side, messages meant for the King and Queen or the boys in their respective cities. The younger Thalins were fine and Thalinburg still stood. It would be a challenge losing the ravens but he at least will be loyal.

Artitous heard most of the conversations and suggested that Nemeth be kept at the town and be allowed to remain in safety as the other raven who turned to the other side may try to cause him harm. Artitous stretched and looked at the situation.

The army, such as it was, were circling Landsdale and showed a good front as the archers mounted the walls and murder holes. They were ready for anything. The wizards on the walls that were able to fight, and were not maintaining the shield, loosened the arms and legs as if they were athletes and the druids just laughed. The people were in great moods and helped boost the morale of the new comers in their lines.

Thomas looked around and went to Torlin. "Is this how you defend your town? From inside these steel walls? Your warriors should be outside the walls not inside. What is wrong with you?"

"My people remain inside in the event of a wall breech. They then can go and fight for our town. If they do not get in, we do not lose any men and women."

Said Torlin.

"In other words, they are cowards." replied Thomas.

'I for one think it is genius. Do not change a thing. Your brother is just jealous you thought of it first." said Meka.

Torlin smiled as he walked away and Meka elbowed Thomas in the ribs yet again. Thomas just looked down and went to the ramparts of the town's wall. Archers lined the wall in their new armor with their new bows and arrows. They had chased off three attacks thus far. Now they would have to do a fourth. The elves stood calm and ready focused like a laser beam. Just waiting for the order to fire.

Dwarven crossbowmen were ready at the murder holes with three extra bows and a man to reset used bows so the fire would never stop. Thomas grabbed an arrow and threw it down into the amassing army. It stuck into one of the men below and he burst into flame killing him as well as two of the men unlucky enough to have been near him. Thomas grinned. A great weapon after all.

The archers readied their bows and the tunnel the enemy was digging was seen coming. Torlin settled the earth there and caused the tunnel to collapse. Right now, he did not concern himself with survivors. The elves stood awaiting his command to fire and the enemy brought forward large tubs of water. The enemy must have figured that they could put out the fires without a problem. They were in for a rude awakening.

Engineers brought forth large catapult and trebuchets to attack the walls. The ground troops all had their ladders. Though not high, the walls would take a bit of doing to get over. The top edge was as sharp as a sword and the elves avoided it. The enemy thought this a sign of fear and proceeded to move to the walls as their commander ordered them to hold.

Torlin nodded his head and the arrows flew. After what seemed like forever the enemy fell back to the safety of the forest. The next wave came swiftly on the back of the first. The second wave had tamed some of the elephants that were native to the Dark Lands and had brought them for the attack. The elephants would run as the elves killed the enemy riding them. They all seemed to be going back where they came from. The few that remained were soon chased off by well-placed arrows by the elves. Miraculously not one elephant was injured or killed.

Thomas became the hero because the third wave made it to the walls. The dwarves at the wall went up quickly and smashed the ropes on the sharp top of the walls. Thomas drew the first wave to him and killed them rapidly. Again and again, he fought and killed men by the tens. The dwarves would assist were necessary but were in awe of the human prince. He surely was as skilled with a weapon as his brother was with magic.

Meka watched and soon joined them on top of the walls. She was fighting her way to her husband when the man who had gotten up on the wall behind her thrust his blade toward her back. She felt the tip of the blade enter her body and then everything started going black. The last thing she remembered was Thomas thrusting his sword deep into the man's throat.

CHAPTER TWENTY

THE FALL OF THALINBURG

Tanis was watching the city from the walls when the raven arrived from Metra. "The city had fallen. Lord Torlin and his family are unaccounted for. It is believed they died in the fall of the city. A wizard by the name of Asher now ruled Metra."

Tanis jumped up and headed for the door when yet another raven landed on his arm. "Tetra has fallen and the druid, Yangzom, has taken control of the city. Artitous injured the man severely with a shatter senses spell, but it did not total disable the man as he can now semi-see and semi-hear. The nose and feeling still worked."

Tanis hit the door and was nearly knocked over by a guardsman. "Sorry my good man. I have to get to the Queen with some terrible news."

"You will be joining her in a moment. I am taking you to Lord Overmeyer. For execution." said the guard. Drawing his blade, he looked at Tanis and charged. Tanis moved over and the guard missed his charge. Tanis reached for his weapon and found that he had not worn them out onto the wall.

Tanis waved his arm and the guard froze where he stood. It was sad to lose a man that way, but he had to defend himself. Looking at the man he realized he did not know him. Looking closely, he saw the death's head tattoo on the man's wrist. He was a mercenary. Since when had Thalinburg needed mercenaries? Tanis ran from the wall and into the store room he had been in earlier in the day. Looking around he saw the Warmonger sitting in the corner. The Warmonger was a plain looking sword with the name Warmonger etched onto the blade in a hand that was as harsh as the magic that had endowed it. Tanis also saw the Holy Avenger. This blade was as abnormal as the Warmonger was normal. The blade appeared to have the look of a snake without head nor tail. In a hand that could have copied a bible the same day, said Holy Avenger. These two blades fit into Tanis's hands and he ran to his apartments where he found his wife covered in the blood of the men around her. She snorted at the fallen men as Tanis came into the rooms.

"I see you already know of the coup going on. Where are Garren and Almedda? Surely, they are around here somewhere." said Tanis as a huge fireball flew down the corridor. "I think I found them."

Tanis ran out of the rooms and saw Garren attacking a group of men with his sword and dagger in a classic Florentine stance. Almedda stood with arms folded and again throwing a fireball at the advancing column of men. Tanis jumped in beside the boy and Athinina jumped in next to the girl. They attacked the men and as were about to attack the third group when Athinina saw Martin and Perrick.

"The men are marshalled on the second floor, Highness." said Martin. Perrick spun his head around looking for trouble as Martin spoke.

"Then let us get to them and defend our city." said Athinina.

"Miss, the throne room and command chambers are taken by the Lord Overmeyer. He claims to rule in your stead now." said Perrick.

"Well, we shall see how well he rules with my sword through his throat." said Athinina.

"I would have thought that it would have been Lord Masters. He seemed more the type." said Tanis.

"Lord Masters is the second in command in this affair. He is supposed to be the ruler of the elves and McCryden. While Overmeyer rules the rest." said Martin.

They had no sooner mentioned his name when the Lord Masters came around the corner. Several of the sword spiders fell in front of him and he lifted a strange rod at them. "Should I send them to attack you or should I just destroy them. I think I will send them after you."

Tanis prepared to fight when the spiders did not move as Masters dramatically hit the buttons upon the rod. Shaking the rod, he hit them again. The spiders started to advance at the Lord and he smiled. "Stupid bugs. Too bad would have liked to see them tear you apart. Oh well. Stop you imbeciles." said Masters as he hit the red button on his rod and again nothing happened. Looking at the rod he realized he had been betrayed. The rod should have lit up when he pressed the buttons. Overmeyer had promised him. The last thing Masters saw was the weird spiders ram home their swords into his body and begin to feed.

"It would appear that the betrayers have themselves been betrayed." said Tanis as he raised his weapons to attack the now approaching spiders. The spiders got within ten feet of the party when they exploded. Perrick looked around and whistled as Tanis held out his hand. "Sir, would I have had something to do with that? Seriously, you still do not trust me?" said Perrick

"The real rod, Perrick. Now." said Athinina, "And as to your question. I know you so no. I do not, you thief."

Perrick feigned hurt feelings and smiled brightly, "Yeah, I would not trust me either." The group continued to the second floor where several hundred of the ranger guard stood in waiting. Armed to the teeth, they were ready to go. Tanis took command and they all marched down the hall. Spiders exploded as they continued down the corridor. Perrick pressing the button when they were close. The rangers fought off the men who attacked from some of the hidden tunnels and passages around the palace.

The group finally got to the throne room and Tanis blew the doors off the hinges and walked into the room. The throne was occupied by Lord Overmeyer, screaming at what appeared to be a game keeper. "I need more spiders and I need them today. There are three hundred elves and a very pissed off immortal headed here and I need to be defended…."

The doors stopped him his tirade in its tracks. "My Lord and Lady. I have kept your kingdom safe. There are several lords and ladies that have betrayed the throne. I will bring them all here for your justice."

"You have proven that you are the mind behind this situation and if we kill you the rest will flee to the Dark Lands. How does that sound?" said Tanis raising his hands.

"Your children have already perished and two very powerful wizards and druids now hold the cities for themselves. Kill me and you will never get your children's bodies back. They may even allow you to keep Thalinburg. Wouldn't that be nice? Kill me and you get nothing but a cold, hard death yourselves." Tanis looked at the man and nodded. He looked up at the man and launched one of his daggers into his eye. Athinina was shocked until she saw the rods of the spider keeper and the lord being raised. The spider keeper set the rod down and kneeled before the royal couple. "I just did as I was told, my Lords and Lady. I only did as I was told." He smiled as he looked down and Perrick pressed the button on his rod. The spiders they had not seen coming exploded right behind their back splattering them with the insects' remains.

"Damn things were closer than I thought. Must have been trying to protect the farmer here. How do you destroy all of them?" asked Perrick

"They require a dose of dragon's blood every twenty-four hours. Without it they die. What's left of them will be coming here in a few hours for the dragon's blood. We captured several dragons and they have been feeding the colony."

"Where do they go? Where are the dragons?" Demanded Tanis.

"My life for the dragons. That is a small cost is it not?" said the farmer as Tanis yanked him up and held him in the air by his neck. "Or I can just tell you that they are in the forest due east of here. The people of Tetra could almost see the farm from the parapets of the city wall."

Tanis threw the man to the side and headed for the door. The dragons had abandoned men because of their lack of decorum and protocol. Now he would have to explain this. What else could they do but go to the forest and free the dragons. It would be a minute, as the enemy guardsman came stumbling in and they had to be taken care of before they could mount a rescue.

The rangers aimed the bows they carried as the soldiers moved in. They moved rapidly for the door when the saw the dead spiders and the Lord Overmeyer dead with Tanis's dagger still in his eye. The group tripped over themselves trying to escape until an officer pushed them in the opposite direction. Tanis looked at Martin and laughed as he gave the order to fire into the mass of bodies now tripping over each other.

These warriors were not the cream of the enemies' army. That was for sure. Soon they all lay dead at the door and the rangers and the rest of the royal party left the throne room. Looking down corridors as they progressed, Tanis made for the dungeon deep beneath the palace. As he had suspected the bulk of his supporters and those of the Queen were here. Also, most of the army of Thalinburg and the army of Tyris.

Releasing them from the dark, damp dungeon appeared to be the best thing to ever happen to them. Quickly reclaiming armor and weapons the men and women raced to the surface and began the battle for Thalinburg in earnest.

Fighting progressed street by street until the enemy was forced beyond the gates and they were locked closed as fast as they could fasten them. Tanis climbed the wall and sent tornados of fire after them. The enemy ran as fast as their legs would take them and more of them approached the gate as the battle progressed. They would see the gates closed and cry. These same men were defiling women and killing children just hours before. Now they cried for mercy that was not coming.

Arrows would rain down upon the soldiers as they tried like mad to reach the safety of the gates. None made it but they tried. Hardened mercenaries cried as the portcullis was lowered. The men slowly sat down and dropped their weapons. The battles were still going in drabs and dribbles as the night started falling.

Tanis had already left the city with Martin headed to the spider farm. When he got there the site that beheld him was like a scene from a horror film. There were two dead dragons lying on their sides with the bodies bursting with spiders. Seven other dragons were tied to the earth with great chains. The spiders were advancing toward the dragons when Martin hit the red button on the rod in his hands. Spiders exploded in every direction. Tanis moved amongst the spiders killing as he walked until he reached a dragon he knew well.

The dragon was injured by many swords strikes but was still just alive. Mastol was the leader of the dragons of Dracos. The largest of the great wyrms, Tanis looked at the others that had been brought the ones that had died and the ones that still awaited the torture and death. The great wyrms were all there. All nine of the ruling dragons lie trapped by chains. Tanis made the chains about them disintegrate and

Mastol looked at his human friend. "I am spent, Tanis. I am unable to recuperate from the wounds and draining the vicious men lay upon me and I know several others about to succumb to their wounds."

"We have several healers here that will help you. Do not worry my old friend. You will be soaring again before you know." said Tanis as he flooded the dragon with healing magic. The dragon before him shuddered and then lay back again.

"Are you going to lie to my face, old friend? I know what I am feeling and you do not know enough of us to heal us. This appears to be the end of our friendship. Just know that I will always be with you, Tanis. The youngster that tried to steal a scale." said Mastol

"You, old lizard, you are not going to die. I had the foresight to send Nemeth to the dragons. Healers from your own people also are coming. We will have you all patched us as soon as they get here." said Tanis sending yet more healing magic into the dragon. The dragon still looked pale but at least the bleeding had stopped. Tanis stroked the face of the giant lizard and spoke softly to him. Soon many druids and wizards came into the clearing and began the long process of healing the dragons.

At first all of the dragons were wary of the druids and wizards, but they slowly allowed the magic users close. It had appeared that the farmers here had magical help to capture the dragons. Mastol was coming in and out of consciousness and was unable to add to what they knew.

The dragon arrived shortly after the druids and wizards. Tanis went to greet them and noticed that only younger dragons replied to his call. "Why so few of you? You are all very young. Where are the other elders? Surely you have others with you."

"We are all that is left after your humans came. Only you knew our location. Except other dragons and no dragon would allow this to be done to another. Unlike your people, we have no dark dragons. We all fly in the light and agree as to what is best for our people. Even the young ones." replied the dragon. "I am Ridley and I speak for the dragons until our elders are all found and returned to us."

"Are there really no other elders? This must really be upsetting to you. But I can assure you, I have not betrayed your trust and revealed the location of your dens. I would continue to look for your culprit." said Tanis "You have already found him." Came a booming voice from behind him.

Turning around quickly Tanis saw the great black dragon behind him. "Did you think that our location was so easily found? Certain arrangements were made and now I am eldest as the rest of these are about to die by my claw. Thank you, humans, for keeping them alive long enough for me to finish them. Now move and prepare to be subjected by the dragons."

Tanis called out to him and the dragon laughed. "You should at least know who had caused all of this. I am called Marious. And I will now conquer my people as well as yours."

"You have better think twice. You are outnumbered by the dragons here and I have many magic users here. Not to mention archers and soldiers ready to rain pain on you the moment you attempt an attack. You have no chance of victory. Give up now and let your people deal with you." said Tanis.

"You miss understand me, I have two hundred strong dragons and hundreds of men heading this way. You are the ones that will not survive the day. Good bye, little man." said Marious.

Mastol was released from his chains as the healing had finally finished and looked at the discussion happening. Enraged he made a decision. And he hoped it worked.

CHAPTER TWENTY-ONE

THE ARRIVAL OF DRAGONS

The dragon raised his head to attack Tanis when Mastol arrived. "Now what? Does anyone one else want to interfere with this? Everyone will have to wait their turns to die." said Marious.

"It will not be them that dies this day," said Mastol, "My son. Stand down and discuss this. It is not normal to attack and try to take over the world. Call all of your armies and people off. They have no chance of success as long as these elders survive."

"Your elders are barely alive because of me. They will not have the strength to fight and they will be slain. As for you, once I kill you all the dragons will fall in behind me. Now old man, prepare to die." said the black dragon.

"My son forgets his manners, Tanis. I fear I must reprimand him. Erect a shield around you and your people. Include the elders in that shield. That should protect you from the fire and acid of this fight." said Mastol.

Tanis created the shield and watched as the black dragon and the green dragon surrounded each other. Before a strike from either side could be made the dragons that Marious had recruited and the mercenaries in his army arrived. Smiling as he looked around, he said, "You look like you are all in a bit of a jam. Don't worry we have plenty of time to kill you all. Just do not resist, it will hurt less. Hear that, old one, or shall I say it louder?"

"I guess you have forgotten who taught you to fight and to be civil. It looks like you need a refresher course in both. Let's get this charade over with. Your people will need to be great, because they will soon fight without their leader." said Mastol.

"The only thing they will do is show how great we are. Will you truly kill your own flesh and blood? Or will you try to beat me into submission? Can you kill me, old man?" said Marious.

"With current events being taken into account, you are no longer my son but a creature I do not recognize. Will I strike a killing blow? I have friends that can do that for me." said Mastol.

"Where are they? You speaking of your pet human? Tanis? He is too soft and gentle to do such things. You have said as much. He would rather talk things out." Laughed Marious as from out of nowhere he felt the sting of a sword enter his belly. Looking at his belly he saw Tanis with one of his blades deep inside his belly. Marious took to the sky and flew away to the south leaving his army to fight. The men and dragons looked a little confused until the rangers and troops came out from the wood.

The dragons landed and allowed men onto their backs as they flew away after Marious. Soon only a few men from the enemy stood alone on the field, and they surrendered without incident.

"I fear we will see more of him." said Tanis. "I am sorry for attacking your son. I didn't even know you had a son."

"He will indeed try again. He is one of those that does not know when he is beat. Now I really need rest. The show I put on was just that so you could get close. I would not last a moment in the fight with him. I am getting old, old friend." Mastol said softly as if a huge bellows could be called soft.

"You have been through a long, strange ordeal. We had figured all of you had just disappeared as you said you were. I had no idea that this was happening right under our noses. We have become lackadaisical in our patrols; things have been going so well for so long. We just felt that we were safe now. But now we know we were wrong. We know who we are facing now. But we do not know his numbers and how much territory we have lost. Rest old friend and regain your strength. We will have guards watching for the spiders coming and destroy the ones that are still here. See you soon old friend." said Tanis as he walked away headed for the head of the column of warriors. Looking at the commander of the men he asked, "Has Athinina had any problems getting the enemy army out of Thalinburg? I am sure they must have tried all sorts of mischief. Good to see loyal men at my side once more. Three of our most trusted lords went to the dark side of our world. And trying to attack Athinina and the kids? They must have been a little drunk to perk up their confidence."

"The Queen has cleared the city of the rabble that they had called guards and dwarves and elves mixed with loyal men now guard all the gates and the palace. I was Masters' student you know, sire. I find it difficult to think that he was involved in this, but I guess there were signs and tips of what he was going to do. I chose to ignore them. I deserve a disciplinary hearing at the least and execution at the worst." said the young knight.

"You are no more complacent in this as I am. Believe me, I should have seen this coming. After all magic user, and warrior, and royalty. If anyone deserves to be ousted it is me." Laughed Tanis Thalin. "No young man, you are not at fault for wanting to see the best of your hero. The difference is that when the times came, you kept your loyalty to the throne right… I have forgotten your name." Tanis said blushing a touch as he laughed.

"My name is Sir Monreal DuMont. And I am serious in this matter I should have known before I was clasped in chains and thrown into the depths of the dungeon with the rest of your mounted guard and loyal soldiers. It was Martin that got us thinking how to escape. Garren and Almedda had a great deal to do with our rescue. They had burst into the dungeons and took out the guards that watched us. They opened the cells and we ran to the armory to get weapons and armor. I am afraid I lost track of them shortly thereafter." said the young knight.

"We are glad we could be of assistance. Now let's see what the situation in Metra is. I hear it has fallen to the enemy and I want to see for myself. Torlin had prepared for the people of Metra, a year's worth of food and water in the event of assault or siege. If the enemy has figured out a way to access that, we are in trouble. Hopefully we will be seeing the same situation. Releasing the men from the prisons and dungeons should get our army back to strength. But first find my sons." said Tanis as he walked his horse toward the East and Metra.

CHAPTER TWENTY-TWO

AIDE AT LAST

The trip was uneventful as they moved toward Metra. Moving in from the North, they saw a glint in the distance and decided to see what it was. As they advanced, they saw the glint getting bigger and bigger. After a time, they had to avert their eyes from the glint as it became painful to their eyes. Before long, a village under siege came into view. Seeing Torlin and Thomas both on the walls, Tanis turned his force and attacked the army directly to the east.

The horsemen split and charged the eastern army with the full force of two hundred mounted knights. The men on the field to the east never saw the attack coming as they were so focused on gaining entry to the town. Men started flying in different directions as horses knocked them out of the way or brought them to the ground.

The men on the ground did not take long to turn and face the horsemen. Many of the men on the ground had halberds, pikes, and spears and created armadillos to protect them from the incoming forces. This was working well until the arrows rained down from the town's walls.

But again, they adjusted to the attacks. They soon had shields over their heads and spears sticking out in every direction. They started to move their formations into the horsemen when the pikes and war hammer bearing dwarves came into the battle. The formations attempted to retreat but found themselves incapable of getting away as the newcomer foot troops had surround them all. The formations slowly surrendered to the city's defenders.

Tanis led his men to the other two sides of the town where different armies were attacking the walls. The army from the south had mounted knights and foot troops. Tanis's larger force swept through them without hesitation, leaving only the carnage of battle behind them.

Moving to the final side of town. The west was overrun by mountain wolves and creatures of the Dark Lands. Including some greater demons. Tanis charged into the fray headed for the demons when he saw her sitting in a basket on one of the greater demons back. Looking closely, he recognized his mother-in-law from his first marriage. The woman yet lived to torment him.

His first marriage was a blissful time for him until his mother-in-law intervened and forced them to go through the tortures of the elven people to wed. Before the ceremony the woman was supposedly destroyed by being thrown into an active volcano.

He was plagued again after the Dark Knight had killed his first wife and his children. She once more followed and killed many of his soldiers. Again, it was thought that she was destroyed but once more she has shown her face in the lands of the light.

For some reason Tanis was not surprised to see her. She seemed to have a million lives. Tanis fought hard to get to the demon and his passenger but it was another knight that pierced the heart of the demon. As it fell Tanis saw the heat waves form around the basket and once more, she was gone. He knew somehow that she would not be gone long. It would only be a matter of time before she reared up again and this time Tanis would kill her.

As the enemy here was subdued and destroyed, the gates opened and a horn sounded. Out of the gates strode his sons and Artitous. "Thought you were the army that had taken Thalinburg coming to finish the job here. Had you not come when you did, we would have had a problem." said Torlin as he hugged his father and looked at the army Tanis led. "Kind of low numbers, aren't they?"

"Like you, most of our armies are scattered to the winds." said Tanis as he hugged his boys. Thomas accepted the hug begrudgingly but accept it he did. He looked lost and confused. Tanis had never seen him without his normal sarcasm and bluster. Seeing the man in shock really concerned Tanis.

"Thomas, are you well? You seem to be not yourself. I am concerned." said Tanis.

"I believe my brother has had a terrible moment and it will soon pass." said Torlin.

"Where is Meka?" asked Tanis. "Surely, she is not going to miss our celebration on defeating the dark lords once more. Why the sad faces all of a sudden? Roanda go and collect your sister."

Torlin pulled his father aside and whispered "Meka was severely wounded in the battle. She may not survive the night. We have all of our wizards and druids working on her, but she was severely weakened from the peach pit poison still and should not have been in the parapets. We may have to have my brother restrained before the day ends."

"My god. Come show me the wound. Maybe I can help. She is strong and a fighter. She will survive just to take care of Christoph. Let us hope we are not too late."

Tanis and Torlin rushed to the wounded and found Meka in the center of the group. Tanis ordered the wizards and druids to get to the rest of the wounded. He looked down at Meka and frowned. The sword had gone in her back and came out a small bit from the front. Flowing magic into her and started trying to heal the wound. Ever so slowly the sword was magically pushed from the wound onto the floor. The flesh looked like it had come back together but infection still seeped from the wound.

Tanis ordered a pitcher of river water and used it to bathe the wound. Still the dark ooze came from the wound. Tanis had Artitous look at the wound and all he could do is shake his head. They were both at a loss. The infection resisted their magic and still oozed a dark green.

An old gnarled looking druid the Artitous knew well came over and looked at the wound. He took clothes of fresh river water and bathed the wound with it. The more he bathed the wound the more Meka would squirm. It seemed almost like a living thing. Still lore and more the old druid bathed the wound. As she moved the druid would cease his cleaning and see if she was finished with the infection.

The old druid examined the sword and had a glint in his eye. Looking at Artitous, totally ignoring Tanis, he said, "Your man did not clean his blade often. It has the rot on it. All we can do is keep cleaning the wound until it is clear of the rot. Who left the blade inside the poor girl so long? Did they not know of this before I was sent for?"

"Then it is an infection caused by the blade? Why was the blade not removed? Who was in charge?" Hollered Artitous.

"I made the decision to leave the blade in place. I had hoped it would keep the bleeding staunched and she would heal faster. I never looked at the blade itself. I just have not seen a case of rot in over thirty years. It is like someone intentionally soaked the blade in stagnant water." said Tanis.

Repeating Tanis almost verbatim the old druid spoke to Artitous. When Artitous asked him about why he did not address Tanis, the old druid and laughed that he was not a druid, and druid stuff should not be told directly to a wizard.

Tanis began to protest but the old druid never let him start. "All we can do now is wait. If she is strong enough, she will survive. If not, she will die very quickly. The show she put on while I cleaned the wound tells me she may not make it through the day tomorrow. Have her spouse and son say their good byes, I think."

"So, there is nothing we can do? Is that what you're telling me? Look at me old man and listen to my questions. Damn the old rules about druid/ wizard interaction. Just tell me what she needs." said Tanis looking at Thomas. His son looked over at the men arguing and would just walk away. He knew what the debate was. Thomas was even starting to like Tanis as he continued to try and pry information from the old druid.

Looking closer, Artitous found what the problem might be. He asked the old Druid if he had seen the small insects on the blade. The old druid looked closer and exclaimed, "Of course. Let me by. Once more the power began to be used and this time a small bundle of insects came from the wound and the wound almost sealed.

"Dead eaters," the druid said. "These are nasty bugs. Must have gotten in to her on the sword that pierced her. These things eat a person from the inside out. Watch her closely for the next twenty-four hours until her bleeding subsides. I will speak to you then."

The man sauntered off while Tanis took the first turn watching and cleaning the wound. Artitous was cleaning her wound when she finally awoke. "I feel as cold as ice. Did we win the battle? How many did we lose?"

"We lost some. But every man or woman lost is a great loss. We almost lost you. But now you are nearly healed and we can all rest easy. Many of the wounded have come around. As for your feeling cold, I will have them bring you a vessel of hot coals. It should take the chill away. But we did win. Thanks to the efforts of you and your husband. We could not have won without his prowess in battle and having you there just doubled everyone's determination." said Artitous. "Now rest, young lady. You are not out of the woods yet. We still need to make sure you don't still have any of the bugs inside you and that the infection has died."

Thomas looked over with delight when he saw his wife sit up. He was concerned but happy she was awake. A couple of times, Meka coughed up blood or the ooze of the infection. Thomas would sit at her bedside and stroke her hair and hold the basin they brought for her to use. After a few days the coughing stopped and soon the wound was closed and healed. Meka was able to get out of bed but was weak and tired.

The druids tried to give her meals heavy with meat to build up her strength. She politely ate some but gave most of it to Thomas. Her stomach was not up to such heavy foods right now. They also feed her grains and greenery. Spinach and oats were given to her quite often and again she would eat some of it and send the rest back to be given to others. Thomas did not like the healthy stuff.

Four days after she had been injured another assault came at the town of Landsdale. This time it was merely horseman and archers. The archers were protected by the pole weapons. Halberds and pikes, spears and pole maces all stood sentinel in front of the archers as they tried again and again to fire into the town. Torlin had warped his shield so that the arrows slid down a funnel and landed in the enchantry. The arrows were enchanted and used against the people who had fired them.

Torlin thought himself clever. The flow of arrows was almost constant. Canisters and quivers of arrows flowed from the enchantry to the walls and from the archers to the enchantry. The enemy could not see where the arrows went but they assumed they were getting through and fired more and more of them. The arrows lasted for hours until the enemy supply had run empty. The enchanted arrows had put down at least half of the enemy army, and they were frustrated by the lack of weapons. The pole arms attacked the steel walls and their weapons were damaged or destroyed as frustration continued.

The enemy commander left and soon the army too had moved back toward Metra. The town was once more excited by the victory. Looking around Torlin noticed huge bundles of arrows. "Ready for next time, I guess." Sighed Torlin to Tanis as they looked at the enchantry bringing out yet another bundle of weapons and arrows. Tanis looked at them and smiled. "I believe we may just be ready to try and move against the wizard in Metra. Our army may be just what he won't expect."

"I don't understand. Why would the dregs of the old army be of concern to him? The wizard captured dragons and bred spiders on them. Are the elders even back to their normal selves yet? I know the remaining seven elders were rather sore with the human race. Except Mastol who barely survived his treatment. The fight with Marious was exhausting to him as well. But the dragons will not aide us while he is alive. They search for his lair even as we speak. We have only the personal bodyguard of each of us, and a lot of the citizens of Metra. But they were only used to give the illusion of might, they should not be used to really fight." Torlin said.

"I believe it is up to the citizens of Metra and its surroundings whether we fight or not is that not so, my sire?" said Mayor Flatfeet. "Just saying I believe we do a say in this, right?"

"Of course, you do." Responded Tanis before his son could put a word in. "We will prepare you all on how to use and handle the armor we have given you. That will include the weapons. I have the world's best commander of troops here as well as the most powerful wizards and druids. We will train you all. Pay the wizard here no mind whatsoever." said Tanis

"Uh, isn't that my call? It is Metra after all? And Thomas would not be happy to be roped into teaching peasants to fight. Just saying, it may be a challenge." said Torlin.

"No," said Tanis, "You have no power here until you are placed back on your throne. And Thomas better be cooperative or I send him back to Tetra with only the clothes on his back. That will wake him up."

"What do you need of us?" asked Meka as she and Roanda walked into the clearing.

"Meka, I need you to rest and Roanda I need you to train the women. They fight differently than men and you are the best we have. Meka may supervise but no heavy work, understand, young lady?" said Tanis.

"Is it because I am a woman that you make me rest?" Meka said.

"No, it is because you were severely wounded. I would tell Torlin or Thomas the same." Tanis said as he strode away giving orders to the fighters as to accepting so many of each people to their squad.

Tanis promoted all the regular soldiers to squad leaders and assigned the new officers' troops from the peasant ranks. Soon all the peasants that chose to fight were in a squad. The old squad leaders were promoted to section commanders and section commanders set as regimental officers. The regimental officer, Martin, was promoted to supreme commander. The army was set as soon as they could finish training the peasants.

CHAPTER TWENTY-THREE

THE BATTLE OF THREE ARMIES

The ragtag army was almost ready from training when the assault came. Tanis ordered that the squads be rotated from the walls. Each of the squads would gain a little experience today. Each of the squads had bows and melee weapons. The arrows rained down with deadly accuracy as the arrows flowed from the newly trained troops' bows. Each squad would cheer as it was removed from the walls. The army had quite the size. Torlin had taken in everyone from Metra and Tetra that had fled. The tent city that sprung up around the steel walls of the town was impressive and slowed down the attackers.

People from all over were now part of his army. Elves, dwarves, noom, and men fought shoulder to shoulder. The elves rained down arrows along with the men. Dwarves were firing down with crossbows. Even the noom were firing off their slings. Everyone had a ranged weapon and a melee weapon. A first squad would fire from the walls while a second would prepare to repel any attacker that made the walls. Hammers, swords and daggers were shaken at the enemy as they cheered every squad.

Once more the assault was halfhearted and soon the enemy would retreat to the city nearby. The squads cheered as the assailants turned and ran. They had won and it felt wonderful. The ground they found to be littered with useful items abandoned by the retreating army. But it also had the ghastly burned bodies, dead piled up everywhere that the enemy stacked to protect themselves from the arrows. The carnage was everywhere and many of the squads were shaken until Tanis told them, "It is better we bury their dead than ours."

The villagers who had decided not to join the army went out every day and buried the dead from its previous battle. Many of the piles were incinerated magically were they sat. This way there was no smoke and no problems with the smell attracting other deadly creatures. People still reported some spiders of the giant variety near the town walls but the attacks by the creatures had for the most part stopped.

The assaults on Landsdale had stopped for the time being and the army was starting to relax. The training was put back into being by Tanis saying the real battles would begin soon. He warned them once more that they could lose their lives. When they attack the city proper it will be the enemy with the advantage. "Hopefully they do not take a page from our play book," said Tanis. "Otherwise, we are going to be in trouble."

The army all agreed that it was acceptable odds to defend their homes. Or to get them back. The elves began packing their wagons with the dwarves following suit. Rumor had it that the gates were still wide open in Metra. Either they did not know how to close them otherwise they were waiting for the Landsdale peoples' attack.

It would not come in the way they expected though.

CHAPTER
TWENTY-FOUR

RECLAIMING METRA

The wagons moved off from Landsdale with the covers tightly closed. The knights and other soldiers that accompanied Tanis rode at the far back of the wagon train and then stopped entirely just beyond the view of the city. Torlin churned up a dust cloud to travel between the two columns. The squad leaders were with each of their squads in the wagons while the rest of the troops followed the dust cloud. Tanis hoped that this would work.

The gates remained open and surprisingly unguarded. Entering the city, the people of Metra looked in amazement as the men driving the wagons entered the city. As soon as the wagons reached the center of the square, the troops began to pile out. The citizens of Metra cheered at the appearance of the men and women at arms. Forming ranks the ragtag-no-longer army moved toward the palace and into the city.

Tanis rode at the head of the ranks and Torlin took a large contingent toward the tunnels that littered the city. Roanda rode with the Tyris and the rest of the soldiers that came in behind the dust. Soon sounds of fighting rang through the city streets as the army of Landsdale found the guards. The guards were fighting half-heartedly as Asher had taken away their pay. He had promised them a large reward for attacking and taking the city. Now they could not even loot it. Asher had soured a lot of the guard but he at least had them with promises of wealth elsewhere.

Tanis rushed the palace as fireballs erupted in his ranks. Torlin and Tanis put up shields to protect the people below as Asher and his people had no care where the fireballs hit. As the army moved closer to the palace, the resistance from Asher's guards increased. There came at the smaller force from Landsdale a concentrated assault from the guards. Tanis fired a small fireball into the air and soon the Tyris and other troops came charging up behind the army. As they approached the guards, the rear guard of the army was caught relaxing. The armies of Asher came pouring from the houses and surrounded the smaller forces of Landsdale.

Laughing the soldiers approached the very nervous Landsdale army. Shouts of pigs and fairy folk rained down upon the army as the guard moved forward. Tanis prepared to attack the incoming attackers when the guard found themselves surrounded. The citizens of Metra came pouring out of the streets and attacked the surrounding force.

They were really a strange army armed with kitchen knives and swords so rusty you knew that they lay dormant for years in an old chest. Every so often you would see an old guardsman with his weapon and armor, but they were rare. Soon a hole opened amongst the guard as they now had to fight on two fronts.

Tanis sent the elven archers up to the walls. Torlin showed them the way to gain the parapets and fire down onto the guards below. The enemy had been too confident it would appear and left the high ground unguarded. Soon arrows filled the air as the elves fired down at their foes. Each arrow bursting into flame as it hit a guardsman. Small fires started here and there as the men fell to the arrows. The well-placed arrows did not allow the men to run as men would do when on fire. The men fell as soon as they were hit.

Torlin had once more disappeared and Roanda and her lot were nowhere to be seen. The mages above redoubled their efforts but Tanis and the few wizards and druids kept the shield intact. Every once and again a magic user from the palace would cease with their attacks and not restart them. Some of the noom looked up from the rails and smiled.

Tanis did like those little guys when they were not trying to kill him. The noom moved slowly and with purpose as they attacked the various magical personnel of Asher. Many of them appeared to be caught off guard as the noom attacked from the rear.

It was over quickly as the noom finished clearing out the magical folk on the walls. The battle raged and soon the guard were kneeling without weapons. The army of Tanis and the city folk had been hurt badly with wounded and the losses to death were just as bad.

"You have removed the guard from the city. Now we have to remove these invaders from our palace. I asked so much from you already. But we need one more push to remove the monster that started this whole mess. Those who are able to lift weapon and armor please follow me once more, the wounded please remain behind with the druids. Mayor Flatfeet, please lower the sword and get yourself patched up. I need only those who are uninjured from this point. Once more I say take back your city. Follow me once more." said Tanis as he walked the lines and observed the men and women that had come to his aide and those he led here. So many injured, so many dead. The sight enraged Tanis to the point of kicking a helmet lying on the ground. It would be ok. The owner of the helmet lay not far from where it had started. He would have no more need of it.

Once more the army advanced and easily gained the gates to the palace. The guardsmen that stood watch there had seen the incoming troops and lay down their arms. These prisoners were escorted to the holding area where the other prisoners were held. The guardsmen that were held first were abusive to the new comers until the elves and dwarves threatened to kill both groups.

Tanis left the prisoners with their guards and left once more for the palace. His troops had set up a base camp at the gates and prepared for the siege of the palace as the doors were tightly secured. The dwarves and elves had both tried to force the doors open but they never moved. Magic users tried attacking the doors and found that they too could not open them. Secret spells and fireballs rained down on the doors and scorch marks were all that showed they had tried.

Torlin once more approached the army. He was covered in dust but he had returned. Looking at the doors and at Tanis, he went to the doors and produced a long skeleton key. "You all did this and all you needed was the key. Why did you not try yours, Father? I sent you one when I had the locks made. The tunnel to the throne room is destroyed. Asher must have found it."

Tanis looked in his pouch and gave a sheepish grin. He reached into it and produced the key. "Thought Asher had changed the locks." His face now cherry red with embarrassment.

"No one is perfect, Father. Sometimes a door is just a door." Torlin said as he put the key into the lock. Torlin tried to turn it and the key would not turn. He smiled and tried again. "May need a little oil." said Torlin as he waved his father to come up and turn the key. Tanis grasped the key and tried to turn it. Again, the key refused to move.

"Try your key, Father" Torlin said removing his key. "I fear I have the wrong key."

Tanis took his key and again the key refused to turn. Tanis looked into the keyhole and saw the wood stuffed into the key's receiver. It was only covering the pins, letting the key in but not allowing it to turn. Tanis suggested burning it out, but Torlin said no.

"If you cannot go through the door then you must go under it. Roanda keep watch here with half our forces. The rest come with me. Father, you as well I may need your skills here before we are done. Artitous has stayed behind with the druids healing the wounded." said Torlin.

"But I recall us speaking about the dust on you. Is not the tunnel collapsed?" asked Tanis.

"The tunnel to the throne room is collapsed. But no one has found the one to the courtyard behind the waiting guardsmen. They stand waiting for the doors to open. Roanda just keep trying to get through the door. I will send up a flare of fire when I am in position to attack." said Torlin.

So, the troops following Torlin and Tanis move with stealth and speed through the tunnel. Torlin was just getting to the entrance when he heard the sounds of fighting. Figuring they had turned on each other, Torlin burst out of the entrance to see Roanda standing there with the enemy commander's head and sword. The last resistance was finally being quelled as the rest of the army exited the tunnel.

"Figured you could use the help. Did you not check the latch? They did not lock the doors before they disabled the locks." Laughed Roanda as a fireball fell from above.

"Asher is getting scared. He is still not using all the might that he has. It may be a harder fight then I figured once up there." said Torlin as he swatted the fireball into nonexistence.

"Well let's find out, shall we?" asked Roanda as she headed for the palace proper.

CHAPTER TWENTY-FIVE

THE RETURN TO METRA

The palace was once more moving into friendly hands when Thomas, Meka, and the other half of the army left Landsdale for Tetra. He was unaware of his brother's great work, but he sensed that it was just about over. Meka was watching the flood of people moving toward Landsdale, concerned for Torlin and Roanda. "If they are stupid enough to let people leave the city, then they are stupid enough to get their rear assaulted. Besides these are refugees not soldiers.

Look at them most have seen too many summers." said Thomas.

"Or too few. There are infants and children here. Looks like anyone who is eleven years to sixty-five years has remained. That could be good news or bad. Who is fighting in the city?" Meka asked an old woman passing by.

"Everyone, my lady. Absolutely everyone. The people of Metra that remain are all fighting for Lord Torlin. The guard are fighting the army that Lord Tanis brought in. Lord Torlin is a bastion by himself, firing fireballs everywhere. Even my grandson fights there. He has made us all proud. He started the resistance in Metra. Said no one would suspect him, as he was only ten years old. They took out the guardsmen that watched the dwarven section and the elven section and everybody gathered all the weapons and armor they could find or make. They then went straight after Lord Tanis and his wonderful people, some come now to keep us safe as we left. My husband went to the smithy and stole a sword. The people here want to help too." said the elderly lady dwarf.

Meka looked at Thomas and did not even say a word as Thomas turned around and roared orders to head for Metra, complaining under his breath of weak brothers and strong wives. He even mentioned stupid fathers. His mother would be so pleased. Meka moved to the front of the army and explained the situation in Landsdale. "Yeah, Yeah, I am familiar. My idiot father and idiot brother have gotten themselves into hot water and now I need to save their bacon. Use the tunnels to get into the city and we fight from there. At least it was not magical fighting as I sent all the magic users with him and I have kept the real soldiers to fight at Tetra." said Thomas as he moved toward the city of Metra. "Should just conquer it now, so this does not happen again."

Meka threw a punch at his head that hit him in the bread basket and he was rubbing his side and smiling. She was still the strongest woman he had ever seen.

Thomas's army started moving toward Metra and was met at the gate and welcomed in. The Mayor of Landsdale was waiting for them and took the opportunity to deliver the news in a speech that took longer than the journey the army had just undertaken. Thomas moved to continue to the palace when the wizard's full force came at them. Meka tried to draw her sword but her injuries prevented it. Thomas stayed in a guard mode for Meka as he sent soldiers to different locations and he even put in the non-combatants as he called them amongst the army.

The mayor being interrupted from his speech, drew his hammer and dived into the fray from the wall. A small expanse opened around him as he killed the men who attacked the city. Thomas left a pathway behind him as he cut his way to safety for Meka.

Meka still held her sword but realized she was safe. She shook her head and Thomas left to fight the invaders. Soon the wizard's men turned into goblins and orcs. The goblins, small but wiry warriors, were usually allies of the cities. To see them fighting for the other side gave the defenders pause. They had helped to rebuild these cities.

The orcs drove the goblins with whips and chains and fought with huge swords and halberds. These beasts never left the Dark Lands. Why they were here confused the defenders but still they fought. Thomas seeing the weapons being used shifted his attacks and soon the wizard's orcs and goblins were put to flight. Archers from the elven kingdom had arrived just in time to destroy the remainders as they fled. The monsters could not be allowed to escape.

Thomas saw the elves and ordered the army to press the enemy into the teeth of the death trap set up by the defenders. Two opened triangles were created and as they closed with each other the enemy was trapped in a huge diamond shape that there was no escape from. The defenders pressed in on the enemy and soon all had surrendered or died. None of the orcs had surrendered but quite a few goblins did. The goblins claimed that they were forced to fight by the orcs that lived nearby. They came in the night and stole wives and children with promises of death if they were not obeyed.

Thomas searched the body of the orcs and found a major problem. These were contracted to destroy the ancient cities. They could have the personnel they found within it but they were to destroy both cities and their populations. Thalinburg was to be left alone as Marious had taken care of that. The nobles that thought they were in charge there, would be sorely corrected when the dragons came and took over.

It was an ingenious plan, but the dragon needed warriors and they were leaving in droves. The money and power they were promised was just not delivered. Marious killed several of the guardsmen to show he was serious about them trying to leave. They stayed now afraid of the dragon's wrath. Some still talked of leaving since the elder dragon, Mastol, had almost defeated the medium sized black dragon.

The warriors of the enemy looked down in defeat as the smaller force quickly defeated the larger. Thomas's skill once more shone as the last of the enemy lay down his arms. Looking at the goblins, Thomas shook his head. They had been allies for a long time. He gave the order to move the prisoners to the prison camp and moved closer to the palace.

A magical storm of flame and lightning flew around the throne room's balcony. Again, Thomas thought it would be best to take over from both of them at once. Meka must have been reading his mind as he looked up at the balcony because she came and smacked him in the head.

"What was that for?" Muttered Thomas as she approached again.

"Keeping you on your toes, my dear." Smiled Meka knowingly. "We have to allow them to finish their battle meanwhile, I suggest start acting as a rear guard and help your brother by keeping Asher's troops from coming to assist him and taking care of anyone assisting that evil man."

"Well, what are we waiting for, deploy the troops and let's get this done." said Thomas. "I will set them proper." Thomas was true to his word as he set up guards at every gate and door, and selected a patrol of Tyris and infantrymen from his soldiers and the locals.

Thomas remarked at the locals, "They fight better than any army I have ever seen. And they know the pathways."

"They are well trained and skilled, but they have something worth fighting for. They fight for their homes. That is a big thing. Now let's liberate the throne room and take this city back." said Meka.

The selected warriors left and walked into the now unguarded doors and headed toward the throne room. Several times they ran into enemies that were quickly captured or killed. Noom roamed the corridors and waved friendly to the advancing party. Soon they saw patrols of men and elves and dwarves. They too were friendly and some joined the small army.

Deeper they entered the palace the more they began seeing the damage and the dead. Meka was still behind Thomas as he would not allow her near the combat. To keep her out he reasoned meant staying out of it himself. They also observed parties of men, goblins, and orcs headed for the throne room. They picked up their pace hoping to beat the incoming troops to the throne room.

Torlin entered the throne room and saw nothing there but smoke and clouds. He conjured a bit of a wind to clear the smoke as the Tyris with him and the rest of his party scouted out the pillars of the room. They did not find anyone in the room. It appeared to be deserted.

"You can drop the hiding spell now, Asher. I can sense you and see you." said Tanis. "Now let us finish this." Tanis launched a fireball right at the front of the throne just as one flew from the throne of Torlin. Tanis deflected the fireball as the wizard in hiding deflected his.

The air shimmered and there stood Asher looking a bit perturbed. "This city is mine! How dare you come in here and try to oust me?! Give me one good reason not to blow the two of you to kingdom come." Screamed Asher.

"It is over Asher. You are out-numbered and out powered. The two of us are too much for you. Just give up and you will not be harmed." said Tanis as Torlin prepared a spell.

As a response Asher fired a lightning bolt at Tanis's head. Torlin responded with a shield defending both men. "I think he may want to fight it out, Father. What do you think?"

"No, he is just stretching his powers. Give him a second, he will come around." said Tanis as he sent another fireball at the wizard. Torlin sent a spread of lightning into the wizard and again they all dissolved before hitting him. Torlin walked slowly closer and closer to the wizard. The stones in the wall were slowing down his powers and Torlin was getting concerned until he saw the Necklace of Mantra around his neck. Using a flow of air Torlin snuck into the other wizard's shield and snapped the necklace.

Feeling the necklace fall Asher started to attack the walls where the stones were hidden. The attack progressed until the stones were no more. Tanis and Torlin just watched as the hated stones were blasted into non-being. Power surged back into them and the attacks renewed with a fervor. Asher was showing his lack of strength now as Tanis and Torlin came to their full potentials.

Asher once more employed the hiding spell and ran quickly toward the open doors. Fireballs followed him as he ran. He would return with lightning and continue to run.

Thomas nearly ran into the man as he fled the wizards and Meka knocked Thomas over as a fireball nearly missed his head. "Hey! Watch it with the magic. Where is this little sneak? We will make him pay."

"You just missed him." said Torlin, as he ran up beside his brother.

"When did he leave?" asked Thomas.

"Just this second, you literally just missed him with your sword. He was hidden." said Torlin.

"Damn wizards. Why don't you fight like normal people? Hiding behind a magical barrier because I ought to just stab the living daylights out of him. Where is he? I will get him…." Thomas stopped suddenly as he felt his sword hit something. The hiding spell that hid the wizard fell as the wizard collapsed at Thomas's feet with a dagger in his hand. Thomas's sword was buried in the wizard's abdomen. Thomas looked down and started to laugh. Tanis and Torlin joined him as did Meka and Roanda thinking of the irony. He could have run but had come back to assassinate the royal family.

Thomas just said, "That was convenient."

"Try not swinging your sword around as you speak, Darling. It was pure luck that got you the kill that time." said Meka.

The whole corridor roared with laughter as the royals led the way back to the throne room.

CHAPTER TWENTY-SIX

THE ARRIVAL OF THE PHOENIX

As Roanda cleared the tunnels and entered the palace proper she saw the stones that Torlin had said was impossible to feel the power when they were present. She took her sword and tapped the new mortar and knocked the stone clear of it. Holding it in her hand she felt nothing. She thought the stone would be hot or electrified or something. But it sat in her hand and did nothing. If fact as she squeezed the stone it broke and crushed to dirt.

The dust looked shiny so she took it to the brazier near her and threw it into the fire. Once more there was a little fizzling and popping, but again no major reaction. The sand, as that was all she could call it, was slowing shifting in the brazier like a living thing. Looking down at it she could hardly believe her eyes.

A small bird like shape emerged from the stones remains in the fire. Slowly opening it eyes it looked upon Roanda and cooed. Roanda slowly put the fire out and reached cautiously for the bird. It has sprouted feathers in the time it took for the embers to cool. The bird spread its wings and beautiful colors swam up and down each wing. Jumping from the brazier to Roanda's hand the bird cooed once more and then settled down. In a moment it was asleep and Roanda was in love with it.

Calling for the stones to be taken down and thrown into the fires, Roanda went to find her husband. He would know what to do with this bird. She moved down the corridor and a large pack of guardsmen headed her way.

She drew her sword and prepared to fight. The bird she shielded with one arm and her body as she prepared to fight with the other. She lifted her sword to fight and the bird popped up in front of her and screeched. Buffeting the men with a hot wind, the bird turned to flame and dived at the men in front of her. She entered the fray as the phoenix made a second run. The men were trained well though and tried to bring down the larger than Roanda remembered bird.

Swinging at a large guard that had been missed in the two runs by the phoenix, Roanda felt the sting of a sword entering her shoulder. Roanda still had her sword arm but this guard was well trained. He laughed as again she felt the sword enter her other shoulder. She was about to collapse when she felt yet another stab, this time in the leg just above the knee.

She did not let a sob exit her lips as she continued to attempt to fight and maneuver. Slowly she was wearing down. The sword entering her other leg brought her to the ground. This time a sob entered the air. Seeing the shadow of the large man leaning over her, she saw the shadow of the man reaching down for her head. His rough hands caught her moving hair and pulled tight stopping Roanda in her tracks.

He pulled back her neck and reached for a dagger he had in his belt. The man had faced the Tyris before she laughed. He was about to kill her with a Tyris weapon. She closed her eyes and resigned herself to the fact she was about to die when she heard the bird screech again and the hand in her hair release her.

Opening her eyes, she saw the firebird beating the man with its wings. It screeched and a barbed like tail raised to attack the man. Seeing the tail, he ran for the corridor with the bird settling down beside her. "Hello mother." said the phoenix and leaned over her crying. Well known legends of the phoenix told of tears having healing powers but this one placed its wings upon her and cooed once more. The song caused her to fall to sleep and when she woke the bird stood next to her. The wounds that she had received were healed and she could move her arms and legs again.

"Did you do this?" asked Roanda.

The bird let out a little coo, remaining at her side.

"I do not suppose that you can talk. You are a bird after all." said Roanda as she came back to her feet.

"Some of us speak the human languages. Some hide the fact, like me. You are welcome by the way." said the firebird, "And I am not a bird, I am a phoenix. I hope as we continue to travel together you will remember that."

"What should I call you? Obviously, you would not like to be called phoenix all of the time." replied an astonished Roanda, "And thank you. Thank you so much."

"It was nothing my mother. My name is Janell, and I am now your companion and guardian. You have done something that few have done in our history. Saved the lives of all the phoenix stuck in those terrible stones. All Tyris will be gifted our companionship. We need to go back and release the others."

Roanda moved back down the hall pulling down the offensive stones and the firebird burned them to nothing but ashes and firebirds arose from them. This bird would start growing as soon as they were free of the ash and they flew down the hall.

Roanda ordered all the Tyris to accept their travel companions and to strip the walls of the stones and have them burned by the firebird. Soon every one of the Tyris in the city had a phoenix on her shoulder. Roanda thought the flames would burn her but Janell sat there quiet and serene with no harm to her. Now Janell was the size of a small eagle. Janell assured Roanda that she would get no larger.

Now that the firebirds were settled on the Tyris they proceed down the corridors of the palace looking for guards. They met with other groups of freedom fighters and waved as they passed. In one group, Almedda Thalin was fighting. The youngest of the Thalin children were both in this party. Garren lowered his blade as Roanda approached with the phoenix on her shoulder. The wings kept changing colors like a fine made kaleidoscope, as the younger Thalins came to see it on her as well as the other Tyris.

"These birds are gorgeous. How did you capture them? Are they dangerous? What did you name him?" asked the excited Prince.

"I did not capture them we released them and they imprinted on us. A slight squeeze by Janell's claws reminded her not to reveal too much. Her name is Janell. They are exceptionally dangerous." replied Roanda.

Almedda looked at the birds and walked off. *They are real.* She thought. "How do I go about getting one?" asked Almedda as she continued to walk away.

"You don't," responded Tanis as he cut her off from her walk. "The phoenix are rare creatures and they are a knowledgeable race. They decide who they partner with. Are you ok, Almedda? You look pale and gray."

"I am fine. You are mistaken. I am neither pale nor gray. I am tired from having exerted myself all morning protecting Garren. He tries to fight those he knows nothing of. Going after wizards and mages. What is he thinking?" said Almedda.

"You need to rest then. You will feel better in the morn…." said Tanis as a large group of the wizard's guards came swarming them. The Tyris were on their feet in just a moment and their birds took off right behind them. The Tyris fought as they always do, like tigers, and the phoenix just attacked and attacked killing more than the Tyris.

Several of the phoenix fell in the short battle and the Tyris that carried them felt woozy and angry. It was like they were possessed. It was Janell that explained the bond between bird and companion. She also explained that burning the body of the phoenix will save those who were bonded to them. They did so and the phoenix burned their companions only to have new phoenix rise from the ashes and fly back to their companions.

Those who had lost their bird, or the birds that had lost companions all returned to normal. The rage and upset were over and done. The companionless birds bid the rest farewell and left in search of other Tyris. The new bond between the Tyris and the phoenix was strong. The Tyris were to be the phoenix handlers for the rest of their existence. The birds would be passed from Mother to Daughter as the phoenix were immortal, unlike the Tyris that they had bonded to.

CHAPTER
TWENTY-SEVEN

DARKNESS FALLS

As the companionless phoenix left, Almedda looked around at the area she was in. It was some kind of armory. Looking around she heard a weird sound behind her. Turning quickly, she saw the black phoenix standing there. "Looking for the Tyris?" asked Almedda.

"No. I searched for you. I have found you now. I am to bond with you. The Queen's order. Just as my normal brethren connect to the Tyris, I attach to wizards. We must not be seen. Let us head to the dark tower in the Dark Lands. There I will teach you magics you have never heard off. They are great. Powerful, dark, and beautiful. I will explain everything once we are alone." said the midnight colored and moving phoenix.

Almedda moved quickly past the winning army, headed toward a tunnel that would bring them outside the walls. She moved stealth fully and kept her head down looking like another wizard leaving the palace with a raven on her shoulder. Slipping quickly into the tunnel, she followed it to its terminus.

The brightness of the sunshine burned at her eyes. The great phoenix that rode on her shoulder shivered in the daylight. They moved quickly to catch a trader headed south. Settling in she rode the wagon in darkness until nightfall. The trader had stopped the wagon for the evening and was cooking the evening meal.

Smelling the food, Almedda came out of the wagon and sat on the ground watching it cook. The phoenix helped it along with flaps of her wings. The fire roared into a bonfire instead of a cooking fire. The trader was vulgar and rude and hinted at what he wanted for passage. She was curious that he would accept no gold for passage south.

The man moved closer to Almedda and she smiled. They finished eating and she stood up. The man thought that certain relations were going to happen. She went into the wagon and lay down. The man came into the wagon and started to undress.

Almedda looked on in horror as the man approached her. As he closed the gap with the now cornered Almedda, the phoenix burst in. Getting in front of the man it blasted him with the fire from its wings. The man turned and ran but the phoenix pursued and hit him again with the power in her wings. The man fell and the phoenix descended landed on him. She fed on the charred human being and her colors once more made her wings look like the night sky. Even the stars and the white moon shape appeared on her wings.

Almedda went out and saw the phoenix eating. A little concerned, Almedda asked the phoenix, "Is that what you have in mind for me? Am I to be your dinner?"

"No child. As I said I am bonded to you now. I eat what I kill. It is nature's way. Go inside and get a little bit of rest before we continue our journey. It is going to be a long ride so keep yourself ready. Where we go, the creatures do not like interlopers, spies, and new people. They will get to know you soon enough but for now, implement caution. Use extreme caution." said the black phoenix.

She had eaten as they spoke and now, she flew above him and burned the remains to ash. Flying over to Almedda, Almedda looked on in wonder at the brutal efficiency of the phoenix and her power. She watched the phoenix, in awe of the beautiful creature and its magic.

"What shall I call you? You must have a name." asked the youngest Thalin.

"I am Carlee. The head of a division of phoenix. I am not connected in any way to those fools that bond with the Tyris. We share a species and I am embarrassed to say that." said the phoenix as she settled onto Almedda's shoulder. "They believe that they have power, but I have power that they could only dream of and you shall have it too."

"I cannot wait. Can you show me anything now? I am eager to learn." said Almedda.

"Patience. The world was not made in a day, and we have some traveling to do." said Carlee.

The next morning Almedda and the phoenix started off with the trader's wagon. As she headed south it seemed that the air was getting lighter and the sounds and colors were all more vibrant than those near the cities. Carlee directed her to drive well away from the wizard's tower as they traveled south. "That is Marzioa's Tower. He is a friend." said Almedda.

"He is no friend to where we go." replied Carlee. "We do not need the questions."

So, the wagon moved further to the west and south just missing the view of the tower. It seemed to grow warm and damp as they entered the forest on the border of the Dark Lands. Giant webs were everywhere and giant spiders watched from the trees. Carlee sat on the wagon seat and the spiders moved away from the wagon.

Looking back, Almedda saw the spiders close the road they had just traveled with thick webs. It would take someone a long time to penetrate that web even with magic. The spiders stood watch on either side of the block. "I have never seen spiders act like that before. Usually, they are very stupid and aggressive." said Almedda.

"These are wild Andromeda Spiders. They protect us here in the Dark Lands from outside attack. Not even Tanis Thalin or Marzioa can pierce their webs. Not even the great druid Artitous can bring the webs down, and the spiders are immune to magic. They will be wary of you for a while, but soon enough they will be like big dogs to you." Carlee explained.

Further into the forest, Almedda saw the largest web she had ever seen. She was about to move to it and Carlee stopped her. "There is where the Queen of these spiders resides. Do not go there for the Queen is a dangerous, greedy being unlike her minions. We sealed her in there and the others have followed us ever since."

"That is one huge web. How does she not escape?" asked Almedda.

"Once a year the web fails. It is then that we seal the web again for another year and her minions create a larger web to cover the breach. Over time it has gotten to be a rather large prison. Over time we have sent several others to reside inside with the Queen. We never see those people and beasts again." said Carlee. "Now let us move on. We are almost there."

Looking through the trees Almedda saw the largest tower she had ever seen in her life. Centaurs and firedrakes moved around its base and bowed to Carlee as they passed into the courtyard. The creatures closed the gate and Almedda stopped the wagon in the middle. A strange looking groom came out and collected the horses and took them to the empty stables. The wagon Carlee ordered be burned.

"Why burn it? No one here knows of its origins. And I strongly doubt we will have guests from the outside." Almedda said.

"We do not want a clue to your location revealed until we are ready for you to be found." Carlee smiled as she ordered it destroyed. "Before they destroy it, take anything from the inventory that you would desire. He has nice fabrics and fancy jewels. They will aide you here. Plus, he has contraband magical items. These are fine here but illegal in your father's realm."

Almedda grabbed out everything from the wagon as far as the trader's inventory and used magic to bring it with her as Carlee showed her to her new rooms. Almedda gasped at the size of the room and set everything down. "This must be the Queen's rooms. I cannot stay here she will be angry."

"No, she won't. You are the Queen now. Your commitment to knowledge will help you here. You have the maids begin on making your dresses and robes while I begin your training. In time you will rival your brother and Tanis Thalin in power and you will hold life and death in your hand." Carlee said.

Almedda explained the robes she wanted and the maids took the fabric away. Looking back at Carlee, she said, "A girl can get to liking this. I told them I would be the greatest of all time and now they will see. They will all see." She let out a cackle as she sat down in the large chair in the center of the room and Carlee sat on the perch next to it and began her lessons.

CHAPTER TWENTY-EIGHT

BUDDING ROMANCE

As the darkness filled his sister, Garren looked around the parts of the palace at Metra that were now liberated from Asher. The battles raged above them and Garren longed to be beside his father in the combat. The guards were surrendering to the servants and fighters. The battle was over determined the young prince as many of Asher's guard lay down their arms and were taken to the prison camp.

He wondered at where his sister had gone. It was not like her to wander away when trouble was brewing. Usually, she would be in the thick of things and was shocked she was not there. He looked for a little longer then was distracted by a young Tyris petting a phoenix. The girl was a bit older than him and a beauty with bright blonde hair and warm tanned skin.

He walked over to her and sat down next to her. "That is a beautiful bird. Did you give it a name yet?"

"Excuse me, boy. But I already have a name. And I am not a bird I am a phoenix." said the firebird.

"My apologies but I did not know you already had one. Nor did I realize that you were a phoenix. Please forgive me." said Garren.

"Its name is Hetrick. And mine is Gardell. So how may I assist you, my prince?" asked the Tyris.

"Just wanted to talk to you. You are a beautiful creature and I wanted to get to know you better." said Garren.

"I know the bird is beautiful. As for getting to know me better, well we will see what the King and Queen have to say." said Gardell.

They both laughed and continued talking until Tanis turned the corner. "You bothering this young lady? I apologize if he is bothering you. He just does not have a sense of bother and decorum."

"My liege, I was just getting to know him and find him to be a perfect gentleman. I would like to get to know him better." said Gardell.

Tanis's jaw hit the floor as she spoke. His little ones were growing up. It figured someone would find them attractive. "As long as he remains a gentleman and does not become a nuisance you two have my leave. Be gentle with him."

Tanis laughed as he continued down the corridor. As soon as his father passed Garren smiled and kissed Gardell square on the lips which she returned and then punched him square in the ribs. She smiled at him as he rubbed his ribs and looked at her. "Ask first. Do not take liberties." Gardell said as she pulled him into her and absorbed him with another kiss.

She smacked his cheek and then went to the training grounds. Garren went with and watched the training of the women with the phoenix. He was mesmerized by the whole scene. The birds flying in unison as the Tyris moved in unison. Gardell smiled at him from time to time and Garren was in heaven.

Several hours had past and Garren had forgotten his search for his sister. Enraptured with his new girlfriend, he was brought down to earth when his father asked about his sister. Garren had not been able to find her and a trader had gone missing. He assumed they had regrouped at Landsdale and was awaiting them there.

Later that day, the Tyris and royals were back in the saddle and headed toward the city of Tetra. To find Almedda, the family had taken an aside and moved toward the town of Landsdale. When they arrived, they received a hero's welcome. They had heard of the liberation and many were returning to the city. Tanis inquired as to where Almedda was. The mayor moved forward and said to Tanis, "I am Mayor Flatfeet. It is so good to see you all well and moving freely. No one here has seen Almedda, my liege. Has she come to Landsdale?"

"That was what I was hoping to find here. The answer to your question. Since she did not come here than she is probably in Thalinburg by now. We will check when we return from Tetra." said Tanis Thalin as he moved toward the horses.

"Someone reported seeing a small fire and a trader headed south. They may know where the princess was headed." Reported Mayor Flatfeet.

"Artitous send Nemeth to search for the trader and let me know what he finds please sir." said Tanis. It would not be the first time the child had tried to run away with the circus."

Nemeth flew toward the wizard's tower for that was the direction the wagon had appeared to take. He soon overtook the wagon and was flying around it when Carlee saw him and flew up to the old raven.

Nemeth laid about him with his claws and wings but the phoenix was too powerful.

Nemeth tried to fly back to Artitous in Landsdale and the phoenix pursued him. Nemeth landed in a tree and tried to hide behind the branches, but the phoenix looked at him and smiled as the spider snuck up behind Nemeth. Laughing Carlee returned to the wagon as the spider latched jaws on the raven's wing.

Nemeth fought the spider and the giant arachnid let go. Nemeth once more headed for Landsdale burned and poisoned. He barely made it to Artitous before he started falling into and out of consciousness. He made his report with the last of his strength. The trader was headed south and had a dark phoenix with him. Nemeth could not see the face as the phoenix had attacked as soon as spotted. He apologized for his failure as he took his last breath.

Looking down at his faithful friend, Artitous said to him, "You have done well my friend. You will be missed."

The unkindness of ravens that Nemeth had belonged collected his remains and took them away with them. They would return soon after taking care of the old bird's remains.

The attack on Nemeth had seemed strange and where did a dark phoenix come from? Surely when the race of phoenix was captured and pushed near extinction, they had also captured the dark phoenix. There had to be an explanation for this.

While Nemeth had been investigating the wagon, Torlin had sent a raven to the wizard's tower in Thalinburg. Almedda was not there either. They had just turned eleven. They needed to be under parental supervision.

Tanis began to get worried, until one of the prisoners said that he had seen her in the tunnels. She seemed to be having a great adventure.

The mercenaries were warned to return to the places they had come from and not to come back. Many of them picked up arms and followed the princes and Tanis. They would turn no one away as they were now to face the next fiend in this war.

CHAPTER
TWENTY-NINE

THE SIEGE OF TETRA

Yangzom was standing in the tower as the army approached. It was a futile effort to try and take the city. Other more powerful enemies had broken their will on these walls. It was impregnable. He ordered his magic users and archers to line the walls and prepare to fire on his word. These people were useless peasants that could not breach a trench let alone the walls of Tetra. Thomas had done well in his construction.

The tunnels he had the engineers destroy so they could not be used against him. This army would be helpless and defeated in mere moments and the royal family would be dead. He would be greatly rewarded for his efforts. If these demons and dragons kept their word and immortality and riches were to be his. It made him laugh as he thought of the rewards.

A small band broke from the approaching army and rode to the gate. They were flying the flag of truce but Yangzom was in no mood to speak to them today so he ordered the magic users and archers to fire on the group at the gates.

They remained where they stood for a few moments and waited for a response. Not a single one of them had perished. How was that possible? The shields they could weave may protect over them but they did need to breathe. Arrows aimed toward their lower body also hit shield. They needed a hole to breathe. Where was it?

Torlin sent a barrage of lightning up into the towers and wall tops. Thomas complained about his walls being damaged but did not order his brother to stop firing. The people on the walls backed up a hair and leaned on the metal grate that Thomas had put on the internal edge of the wall to prevent falls. This once more proved dangerous as the lightning hitting the wall was aimed at those grates. Soon the whole city round cackled with the sound of electricity on those rails. People were on their knees praying it did not attack them.

Yangzom watched without a thought. He knew when to open the gates. The wizards and druids on the walls were the first to fall as the lightning passed between the grates and the spikes of metal on the wall. The leather armor and wooden weapons protected the archers. As long as they did not touch the steel tips, they were fine.

The archers on the wall lit great braziers and set fire to the arrows before firing to cause panic as well as to destroy the arrows they realized were being collected and fired back at their archers. The collection continued for another short while and then Torlin destroyed all of the missile weapons launched at them as well. The archers up there were joined by younger men with slings and crossbows.

The missiles were again destroyed before they hit the earth or archers. They had just readied another volley when the rails stopped cackling. Moments later the wall was filled with Tyris and their phoenix. Yangzom screamed. The tunnels were supposed to have been destroyed. Apparently, one had been missed. If he had not killed the dwarves that had constructed them to keep them secret, he would have killed them again. Yangzom guessed they knew he would kill them when done and left one or two operable.

He would now have to do something about this. Asher hid behind his stupid stones. The Tyris use phoenix. It could not have gone well for him if they were now at his walls and sneaking in. He sent a strange cloud out into the city and it filled the streets. It did not harm anyone but it revealed the locations of all the tunnels. Guards were immediately sent to check the tunnels to ensure they were all destroyed. Yangzom went back to his rooms and lay down. He had such a headache.

A moment or two later as he attempted to lay down, he realized the reason for the headache. A phoenix dark as night was attacking his head. Sending out magic to chase it away, the bird simply looked at him. "There is a new Queen of the Darkness. Do not let it be known who or I will return and destroy you and let you watch as I eat your brain in front of you." Whispered the bird.

The phoenix had flown away by the time the druid came at it with magic ready. The bird was fast. It was also stronger and bigger than most of the firebirds. What was up with the black feathers? This bird was strange and terrifying, especially when she mentioned the new Queen. If he was not loyal now, he would be killed.

When did a new Queen get selected? I was not summoned for the vote. Thought Yangzom. Asher's failure may be the cause of the emergency vote for the Queen of Darkness. A wizard arrived at his bedside as he attempted to rise. The wizard carried two severed heads. Two Tyris with the mark of darkness on their necks.

"These people were just as ruthless as the Queen. The marks were hidden under all their hair, how did they find them?" They did not show in the light of the sun and they only showed when said warrior was dead. He knew they had allies in every camp in the world as did the fighters for the light. They would know of some of the plans before they happened or they would be assisted from within. This was ideal for now. But how did the Queen order people into this particular mess.

Yangzom was nervous indeed. The signs and signal from the dark agents should be obvious to those who know how to look. These women showed no sign. This could be a danger later, but he had to plan for the use of said troops.

"How did they die? Was it the Thalins or was it our people? And where were they found?" asked Yangzom in a slightly concerned voice.

"They were sneaking into the palace and the phoenix on their shoulders reared up and killed them. Somehow the phoenix can sense evil intentions. These two were all we found so far. The Queen of the phoenix arrived earlier and now sits upon the shoulder of Athinina. She joined her husband earlier today. As far as I can tell most of our mercenaries are working for the right master. They have the marks. We could blackmail them later if the need arises. Right now, they have all fallen back to the palace. The city is once more in Thomas's control. But he does not hold the palace." said the wizard.

"This is so?" asked Yangzom.

The wizard nodded and as soon as he nodded Yangzom fried him with a fireball. He did not need bad news. He had to figure out the new Queen of the Dark. Would she send troops to aide them or would she just ignore them here and hatch another plan for taking over? Yangzom called someone to clean up the mess as he started pacing around the throne room. His magic had made it impregnable by anyone not bearing the mark, He had his safety to tend to.

As he was pacing, he saw the enemy at the throne room doors. HIs troops passed freely through the barrier. Soon once more the battle turned for them and soon, they were once again in control of the palace. He continued to pace until he heard a sound from outside the main windows. *Some bird or other I would suppose.* Thought Yangzom. He started pacing once more when the window imploded right into him. Elven rangers with ropes around their bodies fell into the throne room drawing their bows. The evil druid obliterated the first wave of troops to pass through the window. The second came quickly on the heels of the first and Yangzom had cooked up a particularly dangerous spell for them until he realized that he could not feel his power.

He called for his troops to attack the enemy at the windows. As the elves continued to pour in from the broken window a rumble from above turned out to be the collapse of some of the roof and dwarves pouring into the battle.

"You, Fools, kill them! Kill them all!" Screeched the now very worried druid. Looking toward the battle he tried once more to work magic and still found himself bound. The wizard and druid he feared most walked into the room glowing with the power, they were holding so much. He must have his people attack them to take down the barrier so he can kill all of them.

Torlin and Artitous walked into the room holding the barrier in place. Torlin looked at his old mentor and remarked on the enemy's strength. Artitous explained as they walked those dark powers seem to build a stronger magic user but one that quickly loses their ability to do the good works that we perform.

Yangzom was screaming to his troops. The two magical beings ignored him until the weapons started being aimed at them. A fast barrier went up as Tanis stepped into the room. "What a mess. Thomas will be swallowing his tongue seeing this."

"We had to do what we had to do." Laughed Artitous as Tanis launched a lightning bolt at the approaching horde.

"Allow me to get a little more intimate with these braggarts and I will return in a moment." said Tanis as he drew the Warmonger and charged into the fray. The enemy seeing it lost their nerve and the ones that tried to surrender were killed immediately by their peers at the order of the officers.

"We fight to the last man. No one stops fighting unless you're dead." said the officer. Tanis squared up with him and he notice the heron mark on his blade. Tanis attacked and the man limberly moved away from the attack and caught Tanis in the arm.

"Is that the best you have, old man?" sneered the officer, "I was hoping for a better fight. All well. Prepare to die at my sword and I will receive the greatest of rewards."

Tanis struck hard at the officer again and again he moved and sliced a cut on the back of Tanis this time. Tanis slowed down his movements and began to fight like a blade master, instead of the powerhouses that had arisen lately.

Form after form flowed from each of them and soon, they were both bleeding from a half dozen wounds a piece. The heron mark moved like lightning smiling the entire way. A quick feint and the man thrust his sword right below the Warmonger. Tanis took the hit right to the chest, just as Warmonger came crashing down onto the head of the heron mark weapons master. Both men fell. Neither had noticed that the battle had ceased while they were fighting. Side by side the enemies stood watching their leaders fight it out.

The wound to Tanis was dressed quickly and the officer was hauled from the room by superstitious dwarves. They believed that the dead who died fighting great battles would awaken and kill the soldiers around him when he died. They did not want this one coming back to life.

Artitous walked to Yangzom. "It is time to end this. What is your name before I make this barrier permanent? I would like to know whom I am placing on trial."

"You will not have my name!" screeched the dark druid. As Meka entered the room.

"Why did you do this Yangzom? What have we ever done to you? Why did you throw this temporary coup?" asked Meka.

"So, it is Yangzom. Thank you Meka, he was not sharing. I suppose that I should cut him off from his abilities with a barrier that none will ever break. Then I will exile him to the Dark Lands with an escort to make sure he arrives there promptly." said Artitous as he slammed the barrier in place.

"You woman why did you do that? He could not have forced it from me. Now I will come back here and kill you. You have the black mark now Meka Thalin. You and your entire family will never be safe again." said Yangzom as they hauled him to the stables. The barrier that he had produced fell with his powers cut off. It was strange. He was using multiple powers at the same time. That should not have been possible.

"You know, before we exile him, maybe he can tell me how to use multiple types of powers at once. I am at a loss as to how to do that." said Torlin.

"Forget it. It is a product of the dark arts if you noticed his attacks were sloppy and the barrier weakened as he attacked. It is over extending yourself and could result in burning out your powers." replied Artitous. "Now, let us get him to the Dark Lands. He should be very unwelcome there."

CHAPTER THIRTY

THE LOST CHILD

Searches around the three cities and Landsdale had come up with little to no sign of Almedda's passing there was found. They checked her rooms and nothing there was amiss. They were slowly moving the search farther and farther from the cities.

Tanis was getting concerned. She and Garren were his youngest children. They were only eleven. She was still deep into learning magic. She was in a place where she was dangerous as she did not know the extent of her powers. She also did not know how to control that power. She would be ripe pickings for a charismatic magic user trying to turn her to the dark side of the power.

Tanis asked the dragons for help searching. Nemeth had reported a trader headed for the Dark Lands and had died trying to find out about him or her. Then the wagon is found burned down to the wheels and the horses roaming just far enough from the wizard's tower that Marzioa would not notice it.

These events have to have a common factor. Even the dragons do not fight with phoenix. They say they do not have a death wish. The only way to kill a phoenix proper is to freeze it and then destroy it before it thaws. That is easier said than done as the phoenix's heart is made of fire. You can freeze the whole animal and still not freeze it entirely. Then its heart thaws it as fast as you freeze it. The only way is to freeze the heart and then the rest of it.

A Tyris had the first real hint as to what had happened to Almedda. She reported that a trader had taken a girl with a dark bird like midnight on her shoulder, and was in negotiations over something. The Tyris could not hear and was not certain if this meant anything. She could not see the girl well, but she thought it might still be Almedda. "She was probably buying some fabric to make her bird a sweater," mocked the Tyris.

Almedda had a reputation for taking in strays and trying to nurse them to health. She had chosen the wizard's path but she was so much into protecting and helping the injured that her teachers said she should have been a druid. That was just who she was.

The dragons would not enter the Dark Lands as they had people that were skilled in killing them. So, the Rocs made a search there from a mile above them. They would be safe there. Looking over the Dark Lands the Rocs saw a flock of dark phoenix and turned back to the lands of the Thalins. This was of great importance as the dark phoenix could not be killed. They absorbed everything thrown at it magic, weapons, missiles, spears, and pellets from the slings all absorbed and turned into a larger Phoenix for a time. Then it would shrink safely back to itself. They could be over loaded and killed like that but took a lot of power and weapons.

The dark phoenix was known to follow the dark ways. They were a threat to anyone. If they had looked up the Rocs would not be here to give the news. They would have destroyed them to the feather of the last of them. There were too many for them to try and kill one or two. If they took one the rest would follow and destroy them.

The tempers of the birds were also a bit tangled. Very pleasant until they get what they want and then they kill those that they got what they wanted from. It was a tangled web.

Almedda looked around and saw a strange culture about her. The servants were of the race of orcs named Skulle. The Skulle were not warriors, they lived to serve the royalty of the Dark Lands and that was her. The phoenix had left her for a moment as he had to accomplish a simple matter. While he was gone, she got the guided tour of the tower. The wizard's alchemy tables were upstairs in the top of the tower.

Below the alchemy rooms were the rooms for the torture of prisoners and people who turned against her. These rooms were capable of torturing even Artitous himself. The magical barriers that went onto any magic user entering the rooms would be found to be useless. It was a question of the proper runes. It was large enough to hold many a prisoner and the equipment looked like it was frequently used.

The next floor was the warriors' mess. It was there that the warriors who stayed across the lands to come when there was an operation up coming. This room was massive. Rows of tables stretched as far as she could see. The lamps were not lit as some of her troops sat and ate something she did not know what it was, and hoped never to find out.

Moving down the tower she came to armories and magic weapon creation. Even the creation of the dangerous hellstone. With that a magic user could destroy an entire army. But the wizard would be drawn into the stone and have to reside there forever if they were not strong enough. A strong wizard would be able to use it as many times as they wished in relative safety. The stone worked by destroying the living flesh around the user.

The magic user using the hellstone would be forced to create a shield at the same time as they activated the stone. A bit tricky but doable. That is why it took so strong a wizard. It also created the power stones.

With these smoked by the magic user, the magical person would gain a great deal of power, but it turned their very personalities to the darkest black. Almedda was offered the stones and at first, she refused not knowing what they were. Carlee explained that they boosted her powers and she decided to use them.

Slowly her temperament changed. Carlee smiled at the strength she possessed now. Not only could she use a hellstone, but she could lay waste to the humans, dwarves, elves and the other races of the light world. She was still not one hundred percent evil but she was changing as her power grew.

A Skulle had spilled a goblet of wine at her feet and she made the poor creature lick up the spilled wine. As it did as she instructed it, she stepped on the poor creature's head and shoved it down into the wine. She held it there until the creature stopped moving. She made a sharp inhale and then savored the air.

This new behavior will be fun, she thought. "Bring one of the human peddlers we caught in the wood to the torture chambers." She said as she headed up to them.

The peddlers were all sitting naked on the side of the room and Almedda just looked past them. Sitting in the observer's chair she called for the first one to be brought before her. "Why are you in our lands?" she asked as regally as she could.

"I am a simple trader. I have no other intentions. I am only a small merchant." said the now terrified man.

Almedda looked at him and then ordered the torture to begin. Again and again, he was struck with the whips and irons of the torturer. The whole time Almedda just sucked the air as if it contained a juice or substance she could drink. She ordered the torturer to do more ungodly things to the poor man as she continued to savor his pain.

Just as he thought he could take no more, Almedda stopped the torture. "Let him be healed and be brought back in the next day."

The next man was dragged before her and looked down the skimpy dress she was wearing. "Burn out this man's eyes out for ogling me. He will learn proper decorum." said Almedda as she took another power stone from between her breasts and put in the brazier. The smoke filled the chamber above it and she drew a breath from it and threw her head back in ecstasy. She was so addicted to the stones she used them often. Each use made her want more of it.

Taking another breath full of the smoke she wriggled in pleasure as the power filled her. She groaned in the rapture it brought her. Again, she ordered the man tortured. This time she, herself, cut the man's throat. She got blood on her hands and she licked at the fluid. This also brought burst of delight and she wiped the blood from her hands on the poor man's body. "Bring me more." She whispered to Carlee.

"As you say, your majesty." said the firebird as she flew away. Things were working out perfectly.

CHAPTER THIRTY-ONE

LITTLE GIRL LOST

A severely tortured man was found in his wagon moving aimlessly around the wizard's tower. Tanis had come to see Marzioa and had spotted the wagon as he rode. Marzioa was able to heal some of the man's wounds and Tanis worked on the poor horses that had been branded several times before being released. The poor animals needed expert healing and there were no druids nearby. Tanis did his best and the horses settled down.

Marzioa told Tanis that there was a new Queen of the Dark. The man had been tortured by her for coming into the Dark Lands without her leave. He described the little he remembered of her and the two wizards tried to think of who she maybe.

Tanis had the man brought to Thalinburg, and he continued to the tower. It was unsettling that there was a new Queen of the Dark, but it was more so that his daughter was missing. Marzioa tried to scry for the missing girl and all he found was nothing. It was as if the princess had just disappeared. Tanis was even more concerned now. The days of searching had turned to months and Athinina suggested that the funeral services be held without the body. It would bring closure to the family. If the scry had not found her than her energy was spent and her life over.

Tanis hated to think that but had to agree. It was time to give up the search and move on with his and his family's life. The boys and their wives and the grandchildren all came to the service. Garren sat in despair as the ceremony progressed. There was nothing there. His sister was gone and he had not even had the chance to say good bye.

Tanis officiated and then there was a quiet celebration of life afterwards. The stories of Almedda were told and laughed at and the people there were both slowly relieved of their grief and had joy back into their life. The celebration lasted most of the day and night.

As they prepared to depart to their various cities of abode, a flaming figure appeared before them. The figure spoke in a loud voice that rattled the room, "The Dark Queen demands that the border of the Dark Lands be no longer past. Any of your people who ignore this will be executed and it will be considered an act of war. Then she will bring down the full weight of her army and power down upon them. What you have faced heretofore will be nothing compared with that will be unleashed upon your lands. The armies of the Dark are led now and they are ready to destroy everything and everyone in their way."

"Who are you? What do you want from us? Speak Queen of the Dark before we start with threats and innuendos." said Tanis

"You will find all your answers when we come in ten years. That is as long as you have to exist. Enjoy it" said the figure as it wavered and then collapsed into nothingness.

"Everyone, I believe we have a problem on the horizon. And I believe it is not going to be a pleasant turn of events." said Artitous.

"Everything is going to change, isn't it?" asked Garren.

It would be a few weeks later while hunting that Garren found the remains of a girl about his age that had been ravaged by the animals and insects of the forest. There was no way to identify her except from the scraps of cloth that surrounded it. They were the clothes that Almedda had been wearing when she had disappeared. It would appear that his sister had been found.

Garren escorted the remains to the family crypt, and sat in review of the remains for the designated time. He then closed the crypt and lay a wreath at the door. Garren looked down and a tear escaped his eye. *At least she is home now.* Thought the prince. He continued to walk toward the palace and thought that something was just not right.

He talked to his step mother and asked if she knew that his father had lived after she buried him? She made soothing sounds and hugged the boy close. It had hit him hardest and it was going to take an awhile for it to sink in and he stop the mourning and grieving.

He trained harder than ever to improve his skills. He would spend a lot of time with his brother, Thomas. The two would spar and discuss strategy for the coming battle. It was very strange the timeframe the Dark Queen had given them. Why ten years? The boy could not wrap his mind around it.

CHAPTER THIRTY-TWO

PREPARATIONS

Strange things began five years after the loss of Almedda. People spoke of the Dark Queen in whispers. They would always give the protection from the evil eye when her name was brought up. Peasants had strange superstitions. Tanis walked amongst them and listened to the whispers.

Some said that she was building the largest army the world had ever seen. Some said that the Dark Queen would have the Metradon and Tetradon at her disposal. All of what was whispered seemed to be accurate at the time it was spoken, but soon other darker rumors would take over. People disappearing near the border. Giant spiders twice the size of the general ones near the cities had been spotted traveling up and down the border. It was said that these spiders killed anything in the air or on the ground that passed them.

The most troubling was the talk of how a covert group of nobles had sent an envoy to the Dark Queen and they were destroyed with one exception who was returned insane with the words "you were warned" on his forehead. The man screamed of the torture and destruction of the envoy and of his own torture by none other than Almedda Thalin.

Tanis asked the man be brought to the palace at Thalinburg where the druids and Tanis himself worked to fix his broken will. There was no helping his mind though, the man spoke of dark creatures and demons surrounding Almedda and how they all responded to her and her whims. She had giant beasts bite of chunks of some of the envoy's members feet. She had demons burn marks and sigils into the skin of them all and she herself cut the throat of several of them.

All the while she had a breather mask on with a strange blue smoke coming from it. She tortured torturers that were not going fast or slow enough for her. She wore scandalous dresses and attacked with magic as well as the mundane tools of torture.

How could the child of Tanis Thalin have been so corrupted? Tanis felt that these were the ramblings of a madman and disregarded them. It troubled him that the nobles had violated his orders not to approach the Dark Queen. He would find out who had sent the envoy. When he did, he would have them all stripped of lands and titles and executed.

The instructions of the Dark Queen were explicit. No one passes the border. Now they may have to deal with war sooner than later.

In the Dark Lands, Almedda got curious. She had been given permission to see and do as she pleased with whomever she pleased. But they still warned her of the Queen of the Spiders.

Almedda one day approached the prison of the Spider Queen. She climbed to the entrance used to feed her the prisoners. She had so savored hearing her kill her victims. She pushed open the door and looked in. It was dark and quiet inside and many that had joined her asked her to leave. They grew more and more fearful as she looked into the prison. Suddenly Almedda created a bright light and something inside the prison screeched with pain.

"Be still now. And I will lower the intensity of the light. Agreed?" Slithered Almedda.

"Who are you?" asked a voice from inside the prison.

"I am your Queen. Come up where I can see you." said Almedda.

Almost human hands reached out and tried to grab the child Queen and all the arms got was a flash of fire. Again, the arms appeared and again they were pushed back with bursts of fire. Finally, the Queen of Spiders moved into the light. She looked like a normal woman. She turned her lower body into a spider shape and moved toward Almedda.

"No one has caused me that much pain in a long time. I am a drow. Capable of being fully human or fully spider or half and half as you see here. As for who rules who, I will teach you manners now." said the drow.

"I think I will be the one teaching here today." said Almedda as the drow approached the door. Almedda let loose a large attack of ice at the drow and she stopped short. Again, she attempted to attack and was once more defeated by the power of Almedda. Carlee stood on her shoulder as Almedda worked and soon the drow was begging for mercy and forgiveness.

"Tell me drow, do you know Tanis Thalin?" asked Almedda.

"Of course, he married my half elven daughter. What of him?"

"We are to seek revenge on him and all the lands of the light. We will have all of our forces united to take care of these confrontations. No one will remain and darkness will cover the land. And I will rule it all." said Almedda.

The little chit will learn manners, thought the Drow Queen. *She will learn manners.* "It will be as you say, my Queen." She said as she sent a web flying toward the Dark Queen. The web disintegrated as it approached the Queen. Almedda sent a lance of fire at the drow and hit her in the shoulder pushing her to the other side of the web prison.

"That was not polite." Almedda purred as she prepared another nasty spell to destroy the drow when Carlee stepped in. "Yes, Carlee. What can I do for you?"

"The spiders grow restless. Remember she is connected to them. She has an army to attack us from." Carlee said.

"She cannot contact them right this moment because I have her abilities blocked. And when I choose to release her, she will do as I order. She should have learned her lesson. Right?" said Almedda.

"I am your humble servant, my Queen." said the drow. "Please your majesty, call me Morreal."

"I will call you whatever I want, whenever I want, and you will respond. But Morreal is nice for now." said Almedda with a smile. She leaned over and made the lance a little thicker and the drow screamed in pain, "Now isn't that right, Morreal?"

Through gritted teeth she said, "Yes, my Queen."

"Release her and settle her in the castle. You will be a woman or half and half while in the tower, or I will allow the other creatures already there to destroy you." Whispered Almedda to the drow.

"Yes, majesty" whispered the wounded drow.

A dark druid approached to heal her wounds and Almedda stopped him. "It is cauterized and will not kill her. Leave it as a reminder to her what can happen to a rebel. And as a warning to others who may try to rebel."

CHAPTER THIRTY-THREE

DAYS OF PEACE

Garren found that when he was not studying or planning and sparing that he was with Gardell. The two would be found talking about the new bond between the phoenix and the Tyris, or military strategy or some other thing that had nothing to do with anything.

Garren's mood improved when he was around her and she seemed to enjoy his visits as well. The two of them almost always were together, and after a while being apart only when they absolutely had to be.

Christof was getting big as he grew and learned to be a warrior like his dad and a wizard like his uncle. The warrior part was required but the magical was a luxury that the young prince leapt on.

His cousins were growing as well. Garath was turning into quite the magical being while the early signs of magic faded from Arlette. Torlin worked with both children but it was obvious after a time that she would be like her mother. Roanda had no problems with that but the little princess wanted to be like his hefty brother. While Arlette was a very average to small girl, Garath was a large boy. At three he had been four foot high and at least fifty pounds. The young boy was a bruiser.

But between the two Arlette possessed the temper and the ability to make someone hurt, while her brother was more a talker than a fighter and landed him many a bruise as they grew.

Garren was teaching Christof, Garath, and Arlette strategy while the arch druid, Artitous, and their grandfather, Tanis, taught them magic. Arlette joined in these lessons even though there was no spark. The adults doing the teaching humored her and Christof picked on her.

One day as they were practicing lifting things into the air, Christof and Garath were doing well as Arlette tried herself again and again. Christof pick up the item that Arlette was trying to lift and held it up while she had her focus on it and lowered it when she stopped. Crying out to Tanis she said, "Come look Grandpa, I did it."

Christof giggled as she tried to repeat the feat and could not. Christof told Tanis, "I must admit that I did that to cheer up Arlette, I made it seem as if she were performing her task. I am sorry if this hurt your feelings, Arlette, but it was done in good cheer and good fun."

As the grand children grew, they were housed at the palace in Thalinburg under twenty-four-hour guard. Several times a raven arrived in their rooms and flew toward the Dark Lands to make a report. The raven was being hunted by the rest of the ravens but they still had not found him.

More and more bodies came from the Dark Lands. Scouts and patrols would disappear and be found a week or month later. Some wrapped in web, some wrapped in a weird film, and some just laid out. These people were all burned beyond recognition and many had smaller bite marks as if it came from a bird while other marks almost looked human. These were the disturbing ones.

The man found alive several years before, was still mad as a hatter. He was not able to say anything about his captivity, except that the

Dark Queen herself performed his torture. When asked to describe her or what happened he would go into convulsions and nearly choked on his own tongue. After a time talk of his captivity ceased. He was getting worse when pushed and even a minor question about the Dark Queen caused him great discomfort.

Artitous looked him over and determined magic had attached spells to the man's brain. He tried to dismiss the spell but found himself unable to. The magic was so strong set that even Artitous and Tanis together were unable to remove it. Tanis fed the spell with a small amount of additional magic to enlarge it so he could see who cast it. The pattern used looked familiar but Tanis could not place it. Even Artitous could not identify the wizard or wizards involved in this magic.

"It is definitely dark magic. The pattern looks familiar though. I just cannot place it. I know who it is but I am drawing a blank. Besides, how would I know a dark wizard?" said Tanis as he continued to look at the magic in the man's head. *There had to be a way*, Tanis supposed to himself. *After all magic is magic.*

He fed the pattern a little more magic and the pattern shifted. It was a minor shift but it moved. He added a little more of the power and again it shifted. "Artitous, add power to each of the nodes. I have almost removed one." said Tanis as he fed more power into the man's brain. After a few moments the man started screaming again. Looking at the nodes again, Tanis saw that the magic had changed and not for the better. Now it appeared to be severing the nerves of the man. After a few moments the man lay dead.

"How did it change like that? It was a trap. This should not have happened." said Tanis. Artitous just looked at the residual power and an epiphany occurred.

"I know the weave that was used and I know the wizard that created it. It was created by the necromancer, Elizarade. But who cast it being that she is dead? It is strange that the necromancer's powers are suddenly back. There must be another necromancer in charge in the Dark Lands. I really miss Nemeth now." said Artitous.

"You mean someone has her grimoire. I thought we collected that when we found her lair in Thalinburg. Could it have been stolen?" asked a confused Tanis.

"There may be more than one copy. After all she was paranoid. It was rumored that she kept the grimoire in three pieces. This way no one person would be as powerful as she was. They could not all be found by an enemy, because she went through the challenges of hiding the pieces until she needed it. If the three pieces combine there will be no stopping the wizard with it. It may be wise to double the guard on the piece in our possession." said Artitous.

"We would know if the grimoire was coming together. There would be shockwaves as it restored itself." said Tanis.

"This is true. I hope that the wizard using it is unaware there is more than one section." replied Artitous.

CHAPTER THIRTY-FOUR

THE GRIMOIRE

Almedda was in the main library when she came across it. The grimoire was heavy and thick without a back cover or a front cover. She picked it up and the book opened to the slaying spell she had used on the prisoner they returned. Reading about it from the book she got a new idea for the next victim to come to the Dark Lands. She flipped through the pages and studied some of the spells in this great book.

Carlee came into the building and saw the grimoire open. "It likes you. It does not open for anyone. Do you feel anything?"

"I feel the need to go to Thalinburg and to the wizard's tower. I feel the remaining pieces of the book are there. Prepare our armies to march. We head to the wizard's tower tonight." said the wickedly smiling face of Almedda.

Morning came to the Wizard's Tower and the army of the Dark Lands stood around it. No one was allowed to leave and ravens were all killed as they tried to send them. Almedda put a non-magical sphere around the tower while putting on a dome of magic around her and her companion, the Queen drow.

Moving into the tower proper the two moved up the tower, slaying wizards and apprentices as they climbed. They had reached the wizard's tower's secret library. The drow Queen, seeing Marzioa rumbling through the library, ran to and attacked the now defenseless wizard. Marzioa drew a sword and attacked the woman that was now a gargantuan tarantula. The more he struck at her the more the creature laughed. After a few moments a familiar voice told the tarantula to just kill him. The spider attacked him and he went down. His mind projecting to Artitous the attack on the Tower. It would be too late by the time help arrived.

It would not matter if they rushed for all inside the tower were dead. The vision to Artitous faded into darkness as the wizard used his last strength to move himself over the small door in the floor that hid the grimoire. He had assumed that it was what they were looking for.

The young wizard looked around the tower room and saw all the blood on the floor. Reaching down she removed her shoes and played in the dark puddles. The blood flowing between her toes and under her feet sent thrills up and down her body. Around the room she danced until she stood beside the fallen wizard. Sending magic into the air she lifted his corpse and danced with it and set it down in his chair.

The door on the floor was magically sealed but a little magic popped door and frame from the floor leaving just the basin in which the piece of the grimoire was resting. Almedda picked it up and a dark shadow came over her. She opened the book and cast the first listed spell at the orc leading her war party.

The orc was stretched to the ceiling and you heard rather than saw his bones shatter. The creature was dropped and it collapsed into a pile of bone shards and flesh. "Let us go. I have had enough of this place. Burn it." Almedda said.

Carrying her prize, she entered the wagon that had been made up just for her and she closed the sides. Sitting down on the floor of the wagon she took the second piece of the grimoire and lay it upon the first. A shaking and rumbling began outside. She looked outside and laughed as everything got buffeted by wind and stones. She ducked back inside and pushed the edges together and a shock wave moved across the land.

Dark clouds moved across the skies and the area around the tower went dark. Almedda ordered the return to the Dark Lands and had all entrances strongly guarded by the spiders. No one was getting through by magical or any other means. She was certain that this would prevent anything from going wrong and the plans she had laid destroyed. She had a meeting later with the Metradon. Two Horns was an intimidating figure but he would know his place. The big Metradon had beautiful tattoos all over his visible body. They were builders that revered arts and nature. Unlike the very Spartan look of the Tetradon. They would be here too.

The Metradon and Tetradon were a lizard like people that her brothers had encountered at the recovery of the Twin cities. Some were evil and some very beneficent. The kind ones remained in the cities. The evil wished to have them back so they could take over the entire world of Dracos.

Dagmar, the leader of the Tetradon, entered the room and stared at the Metradon already there. "If they are here, we are leaving. You said that the Tetradon would be the only city represented here. We don't need the painted freaks."

The two lizard-men attacked each other and soon both where breathing heavy and all had cuts and wounds. Almedda let them indulge themselves of trying to dictate who would lead their combined forces. The winner leads, the loser is sent to the spiders for dinner. She need only deal with the strongest of these people.

After a few minutes, Dagmar raised his head in victory as he held the head of Two Horns in his hands. "They were always weak. Now I rule them all."

Contests between the leaders had almost always ended with the Metradon leader falling and the Tetradon moving the whole of both armies where they would go. Dagmar was looking around at the other wizards and druids and generals of the peoples of the Dark Lands and spoke loud and angry. "I am leader of the slaves now. All bow before me and I will spare your Queen."

"Now let's not get too hasty here. As far as who rules here, that would be me. You are the one who will bow if I have to force you to do so. Do not be so simple as to think that you can take over. I let you win your little battle there. I could have helped one side or the other, but I love a good bloodshed. I also can destroy you where you stand. So now you will bow." said Almedda.

"You are a slave, now, bow to your master." replied Dagmar.

Almedda smiled as she cast her spell and watched the agony of the large lizard man's long demise. It would take him some time for his head to explode, but it would. As she watched his suffering, she magnified her words with magic. "All of the Metradon and Tetradon now belong to me. Your leaders are dead. You will do as instructed or you will all feel your demise. Now form ranks all of you, we move on Metra."

CHAPTER THIRTY-FIVE

THE ATTACKS IN THE TOWER

As the years past Tanis became more and more worried. Who was the new necromancer and how could it not be identified? Tanis moved from room to room and stared at the chambers that used to house his daughter. The boys came every so often and sought to comfort the man. Tanis had lost a child before and it nearly destroyed him. Now it was happening again. Artitous would take Tanis out to the sparing grounds and the wizard loft in Thalinburg to learn even more of the magic he possessed. It was during one of these sessions that Tanis felt the shockwave. Artitous saw the message from Marzioa and called for a council of magical individuals.

The council convened in the throne room and Artitous broke the sad news. "Marzioa has been slain. And his piece of the necromancer's grimoire has been stolen. Tanis what is your proposed course of action?"

"I believe that we have to go to the Wizard's Tower. We must see if we can rescue any of the others. Then we can collect all that is left and bring it back to Thalinburg until we get more magical folk to teach in the Tower." Whispered Tanis. Another friend taken by this necromancer. They would have to pay for their actions.

Tanis got to the tower to see that it had been razed to the ground. The fire and magical powers used were so powerful that not one stone stood upon another. It was terrible to see. The sky was empty when they arrived and saw the carnage. Artitous searched the wreckage to find nothing. Anything of import, including the grimoire was missing. Only ash remained.

Tanis called out to his long-time friend and said, "The tower is gone, old friend. The necromancer did their work well. There are not even bodies to bury. The evil has won a major victory. Many of our top wizards and druids were in that tower to discuss how to deal with the Dark Lands inching its way further and further into our lands."

"I will have them put a memorial here. We will not rebuild here, but we will rebuild the tower. I know a safer place for the new tower. It will serve the same purpose as this one. To watch the Dark Lands and to teach our young wizards and druids." said Artitous as he lifted a small stone and moved as if he were incased in a jelly or thick honey, around the site and looked for anything he could find.

"As for a victory, it is not complete. There are still wizards and druids capable of assisting in the destruction of those who would do us evil." said Tanis.

Artitous did not speak but continued to circle the site of the tower. He cast a spell over the ruins and nothing appeared to happen. He performed the sigil again and again and seemed content with what is power had done.

"I have found the necromancer." said Artitous. "She made a very amateur mistake. I can now tell that she is a she. And that she confines herself in the Dark Tower in the Dark Lands. Everything else is a blur. But she left us a breadcrumb."

"It may not be a mistake but a trap. We are still very emotional right now." said Tanis as the shockwave from the joining of the grimoire knocked them to their knees. Tanis recovered first, saying, "What was that?"

"That was the grimoire being reunited. She has two pieces. Hopefully she does not have the third." said Artitous watching as the skies darkened. "That would not be very pleasant, I believe."

CHAPTER THIRTY-SIX

GRAVE POWERS

Almedda felt the delving and left the old druid a little bit of crumbs. Let them think I had finally made a mistake. It has been ten years and she was now more powerful and even stronger than her father. The phoenix that was her companion was talking to a small group of men when she turned and asked, "My lady, when do we go for the third piece of the grimoire hidden in Thalinburg. It is the final piece of it and will make you invincible. We have the troops. Let us go and get it."

"No need, dear friend. We already possess it. I may have liberated it when I was much younger trying to learn both sides of magic. But who needs the goody two shoes magic when I can have power over even death? Come with me." said Almedda as she walked from the room to a small alcove in the wall near the throne room. Reaching into the alcove and turning the statue a small compartment opened before her and the last piece of the grimoire was seen sitting there.

Almedda reached in and gingerly lifted the last piece of the grimoire. Taking it to the throne room she sat upon her throne that was now made with skulls and bones of her enemies. She took the two pieces of the book and brought the third to them. The first two pieces had melded immediately. She hoped for a similar performance. Picking up the third piece she set it upon the other two and the whole grimoire lit up like a sun in Almedda's hands.

The shockwave from the second joining nearly cleared out the fields near the Dark Lands. Fire was falling from the sky and the air started swirling. It had the feel of a tornado before it formed. The air was moving quickly in every direction and the people headed back to Thalinburg had front row seats. The shockwave knocked the riders to the ground and maimed the horses. Seeing the flames raining down Artitous cast a shield around the party. He hoped this did not mean what he thought it meant.

Tanis spoke first, "I suppose this means they somehow have all three pieces of the grimoire. It was last looked upon in the vault under the library where all of the texts of dark magic are stored."

"Apparently it has somehow made it to the new Dark Lord. God help us. We may not be able to fight it. We would need all of our allies' armies and all our forces and we may still come up short. I fear not even dragons will save us now." said Artitous.

A familiar voice spoke from behind them, "We have some new allies. The Tyris all have phoenix. The dragons don't even play with them. They are dangerous at best and deadly when provoked. But they are fierce friends and will do anything to protect your warrior women. I have gotten an old friend to come to us to aid in this coming war. You do remember Ruark, he sends his best and the faerimouth will be joining the battle if necessary."

"Mastol, you should be resting not preparing for war. How did you find the faerimouth? I thought they had left us to our own devices." said Tanis.

"We know where to find everyone. And they did swear fealty to you. So, they will come." said the old dragon. "Besides some of the dragons have gone over to the darkness. So, we too have a stake in this."

"Sounds like we are getting ready for war." said Tanis.

Almedda had all of the dread lords before her. She addressed them about the coming battle. "My brother and half-brother have both taught me the ways of battle so naturally we will use different plans. There are twelve of the dread lord men and women. There are six dwarf and three elven. Obviously, the elves will get as high as possible and fire down onto our enemy. The dragons with us will face their dragons. Now here are the plans for the rest of you." said Almedda as she pulled them close and explained her plans. Many of the dread lords laughed in appreciation some laughed at her for her quick wit. And some looked at her with fear. The woman was a threat to their rule. True she was the Dark Queen and had even conquered the Spider Queen. But their lands were theirs. She would take them from the dread lords.

"Fear not about your lands. I will not seize them unless you anger me. And if you do then there is no need to worry about them anyway. You will have no more use of them." She purred. "Besides I am your Queen and you will bow before me." She waved her hand and all of the dread lords folded in the middle bowing low. "That is better."

All of the dread lords made rapid vows of fealty to the new Queen and waited for her orders. She finally removed the spell and the dread lords went to their peoples. There they drafted their armies and marshalled them at the border of the Dark Lands directly behind the webs of the giant spiders.

Meanwhile a small bird flew over the black tower. The darkness emanating from the tower was scary to the young bird but he had to continue. After a time, it felt that it had accomplished its mission and turned to leave. It flew about a mile when it saw the murder of crows approaching.

Quickly trying to send the message to another bird so it could relay it to Tanis and Artitous. The bird tried for about a minute when the murder descended and killed the smaller bird. One of the murders flew off to notify the Queen of the Darkness, the message did not go through.

A day later a bird flew onto Artitous's shoulder and began speaking to him in his native bird language. Artitous looked at the bird and looked at Tanis. "The message that got through before the poor bird died was simple. They come."

CHAPTER
THIRTY-SEVEN

THE FIRST STIRRINGS

Tanis and Artitous decided that sending any other creatures would be a waste of their lives. The Dark Lands were active and marshalling for an attack. The warriors of the light began gathering at the site where the old Tower had stood. Artitous and Tanis felt the missing wizard. Marzioa would have known how to find and destroy the grimoire. Tanis made another prayer to see the old wizard, but knew that it would never come true.

The armies of the lights set camp and prepared for the coming battle. Torlin and the armies of Metra were present as were Thomas and his armies. The faerimouth had arrived earlier in the day and the dragons stood watching the Dark Lands for signs of movement. The Elves of the elven kingdom had arrived in the night and the dwarves surrounding Thalinburg had arrived that morning.

The massive army was sitting watching for the attack that was supposed to occur. Hours went by with no attacks. Birds and dragons patrolled the angry sky above the area looking for anything out of place. It was a young dragon named Walton that found the problems. Getting near enough to the border the dragon reported seeing an army leaving the dark land and headed toward the cities.

He also reported another smaller force headed toward the amassed defenders. They were either going to surround them or the dark was going to attack the cities again. All of the cities had a defensive force left behind to protect them, but were few and mostly older veterans and younger recruits.

The potential threat to the cities worried the peoples of the defense but Tanis calmed them down with a rousing speech about how this army would defeat the coming enemy, then defeat the siege that was looking like was possible. He was thinking that he hoped it was so.

Several hours later the smaller assault of the amassed defenders began. It started with giant spiders the size of horses and a drow at their head. The drow looked familiar as she approached with her minions. Artitous looked at the drow as well and the two looked at each other. Tanis spoke first, "Does she look familiar?"

"I see it but I don't believe it. It can't be." said Artitous.

"Hello gentleman," she cried as she approached. "Remember me? Ahh, my old son-in-law. How's the new family? They will all join your old one soon enough."

"And what would you know of family?" said Tanis as the drow approached, "Surely even your husband has been trying to kill you since the last battle for Dracos. He was a good man. Too bad."

"He was a stupid elf. He deserved what he got. Could not even tell he was married to a drow." said Morreal. "It was almost too easy to infiltrate those light blinded fools."

"They helped you and helped your daughter you should be grateful. After all, they brought you the object of your search. Don't think I did not know. You would be very foolish to think that little of my power." said Artitous.

"You know nothing of power. Now you will watch as your world burns and is destroyed." said Morreal as she lifted her arm and the spiders attacked.

Artitous and Tanis battled the drow while the other fought the spiders. Mastol blasted the front line of spiders with fire, while a white dragon elder fired ice down the other side. Tanis paused in his battle to watch the two dragons fire their breaths. It was magnificent. Tanis returned to his battle with a bit of inspiration. The drow had backed off for a moment and the two magical folks talked.

"We can win this quickly and for good. You attack her with ice storms freeze her to her core. I will cause air and earth hammers to hit her causing her to break into a million pieces. See the rest of our army. The dragons freeze the spiders and the troops smash them to pieces. Clever and working." said Tanis to Artitous.

"Sounds good," said a voice behind them. They turned to see the drow Queen standing almost on top of them. Artitous let loose a barrage of ice into her which she blocked with a fire shield. Tanis attempted the same and again it was blocked. Artitous started attacking with the ice and changed it to a sleeping spell. The drow had planned for the ice but did not expect the sleep spell.

"That should keep her out of the fight for now. How goes it with the rest of our armies?" asked Artitous.

"Her spiders and small troops are retreating. I am assuming they attacked as long as she does. Now she is in our custody and her army takes flight. We will soon learn the new Dark Queen's identity if it is not her. She may be the Dark Queen." said Tanis.

"Walton came with another report," said Artitous as he turned from speaking to the dragon. "The armies of the dark still move but cannot be sure to where they go."

"Keep a safe distance and follow their armies, Walton. Thank you for your help." said Tanis. Walton stood for a moment more and then took back to the sky. "I hope I did not just send him to his death." said Tanis.

The battle slowly ended as the last of the Dark Queen's troops withdrew from the field. The allies roared in victory the sound shaking the ground and the trees. Many of them had attempted to follow them to make their victory complete when Tanis stopped them. "You may be walking into trouble. They will regroup and return to save the Spider Queen. They are at their most dangerous now being without rule. We must be ready as we move the spider to our dungeon at…." said Tanis.

Mayor Flatfeet interrupted and said, "Landsdale is closest and now being in steel, the dungeon will hold her well."

"To Landsdale then and the dungeon to confine this monster in. It should be alright to bring her there. They have no idea of where Landsdale is. The latest of the great cities." said Tanis as he turned his horse, letting Artitous and Thomas leave a rear guard to ensure no one follows and the attack is not renewed in their absence.

CHAPTER
THIRTY-EIGHT

• • • • • • • ● ● ● • • • • • •

THE DROW QUEEN

The travel down to Landsdale was pleasant and no enemies were spotted behind them. Tanis had figured that they could deal with an ambush if it was set but a large group following could be trouble. The larger force ahead would probably be going to one of the major cities so he did not need to worry about what was ahead.

He walked his horse casually along with Artitous keeping the drow woman asleep by magical means. Tanis laughed as they walked looking down at his mother-in-law and said to Artitous, "She is going to have one hell of a hangover after she wakes, won't she?"

"Definitely after being under the influence of this magic so long. I hope the trial is brought quickly and that she is executed just as fast. I fear that she was taken too easily. Something just is not right." said Artitous.

"Relax Artitous. Not every victory has to be dragged from the clutches of defeat. It was a quick battle and it went in our favor for a change. That is all we need to worry about." said Tanis. "What is that in the distance?"

Artitous sent out a raven to check the smoke plume they were seeing and continued toward Landsdale. The raven returned quickly saying that Landsdale was aflame and none remained alive there. The population of the town now hung from the walls of steel. The gates were wide open and anything not steel was destroyed.

Tanis picked up his pace as did Artitous and the army behind moved a little faster. Mayor Flatfeet moved fast to the front of the army after being told of what had happened. "What are we to do? Our town is destroyed."

"We do not know that for certain. What a raven calls complete destruction may mean only partial damage. We will not know until we arrive. We need to go cautiously right now to make sure it is not a trap." said Tanis.

"Trap or not we need to bury our dead. Let us arrive sooner than later." Cried the mayor.

"We will get there. We must use due care though so more bodies do not end up on the walls." said Artitous.

"Ask the drow how they found our town. Ask her what awaits us. I would have her head as soon as we arrive. She is behind this. She is the Queen of the Dark. Let us end this now." Cried out again the dwarven mayor.

"We must have a fair trial. She has many crimes to answer for. Not the least what has happened to Landsdale." Tanis explained.

"I want to see some justice. I do not want to hear about trials. I just want it dead. And the rest of its army as well." said Tamron Flatfeet.

"Tamron, we will see justice done. But we will do no good if we are dead as well. Please give us the time we will need. A fair trial can be composed quickly with the people we have here with us. It just needs to be arranged. Come let us begin the recovery of your town." said Tanis.

"Tanis, you have until we bury our dead or you will face us to protect that thing." said the mayor.

"Do not let it come to that. We have no desire to see her free any more than you want to see it live." said Artitous. "Tanis, may I speak to you alone for a moment."

The two moved apart from every one and Artitous whispered to Tanis, "I have a concern. If she is indeed the Dark Queen, where is the grimoire? She would not let that kind of power out of her sight. We are missing something here. She would not have been so easy to capture either. I think we may have to keep her alive until we can figure all this out."

"Artitous you need not whisper; we are protected from eavesdroppers and we are speaking of a subject that all should have a say in. As for not having the grimoire, she may have it under lock and key in her tower or castle or whatever it is. It could be a spider's nest for all we know and it is woven into its threads. I believe we have caught the Dark Queen and now we need to try and execute her." said Tanis.

"As you say, Tanis. But I think you are wrong in this. You see only the woman that caused the death of your wife and two of your children. Athinina loves you and you still have three children and three grandchildren. Think of them. We want all of them to be happy and healthy and not concerned over a Dark Queen that we have yet to find." said Artitous.

The Queen Spider was taken down to the steel dungeon and lock away waiting for trial. Above she heard the sounds of rebuilding. *They are falling right into her hands.* She thought. "I wish to speak to Tanis and Artitous." She said to her guard.

"They left to scout out the enemy and will not be returning for several days. You will have to talk to Mayor Tamron Flatfeet. He will hear what you have to say. Then we can execute you." said the guard.

"Do not think of execution so quickly. I can bring you to the grimoire and you can see it destroyed. You can see the power of the grimoire. It is intoxicating." said the Spider Queen. An officer saw her speaking to the guard and came over and rapped on the cage door.

"Be silent, prisoner. We know you speak only falsehoods and trouble. You will not enchant any of our dwarves with your speech. We are wary of you." said the officer. As he watched the drow transformed into a giant spider. It attacked the bars and walls and got nowhere. Again, she tried and failed to free herself from the prison that they had constructed.

As she attacked for the third time she wavered again and became the full human drow. She walked to the bars and attempted to squeeze between the bars and found them magically sealed. Screaming in frustration she attacked the bars with fire spells the dwarves had never seen before. The dwarves jumped away from the flames and saw that they did not leave the cell. The magical barrier was holding.

"Come and let me out. I will not hurt you. I will give you whatever reward you may desire." Whispered the drow. "Come and open the door."

The officer made as if to obey her commands and stopped short of the door and smacked the bars again with the large staff he held. "I told you to stay back and be silent."

The guard was laughing at the drow who just gotten chased down the side of the cell. "Now I will inform the lords when they return of your request for and audience with them. I must go upstairs but will see you again later."

The guard was placed a few cells down so no one would be tempted to speak to each other. As time progressed, the guard grew weary and fell asleep. A prick to his back woke him briefly before the drow poison had taken effect. He had looked around and saw nothing at first then turning as his body started to fail, he saw her come flying into him from the darkness.

The guard was found dead several hours later at shift change. He was wrapped in a cocoon of webbing except for his severed head that looked like it had been bitten off. Looking at the gate to the cell it had been messed with. Only someone outside could have done this. They had a saboteur and an angry spider Queen around.

The officer that had set the guard was nervous. Tanis and Mayor Flatfeet will have his head if it was known he did not remain in the dungeon. He was going back up to the newly finished guard house, he passed a place that was deep in shadow. He looked around nervously feeling eyes on him.

He turned his head to the shadow and a glint of light reflected off a shiny object. He realized what it was too late as the spider form drow, attacked him. It had him wrapped in his own cocoon in just a few seconds and then the mandibles of the giant spider moved toward his still exposed head. The jaws dripped saliva as she moved to kill her prey.

She felt the first arrow attack her exposed flank turning quickly she saw those foul rangers coming after her. She had taken too much time with the officer but he had annoyed her. They would find the saboteur soon enough in the little corner in which she had hidden. The Lady Flatfeet was a loyal servant but she was also a loose end which needed to be tied up.

She moved quickly away from the rangers with arrows flying at her and left the building. Moving into a dark space in the wood she changed to woman form and walked toward Metra. The ranger raced by her without looking trying to find her spider form. She waltzed away with almost no one noticing. A small boy cried when he had seen the spider run by and was now crying because he did not understand shape shifting. The woman walked a little more and stole a loose horse. She needed to get back to Almedda. She would have to pay for her torment.

CHAPTER THIRTY-NINE

BATTLES IN TETRA

As the Spider Queen and her minions were being routed in the smaller battle the main army approached Landsdale. Almedda knew that there were followers hidden amongst the people of the town. She approached the gates and giant spiders flew up the walls with speeds even the Dark Queen could still not comprehend. But the spiders were in the town in moments and the followers opened the gates. The people depending on the gates to hold, were quickly over run by the minions of evil. Soon everyone left in the town was dead, and the army left them a calling card.

The bodies on the wall were a nice touch. Something for them to enjoy as they came home. She quickly marshalled all of her minions and ordered her followers in Landsdale to be killed. "You are no longer hidden. Your use is at an end."

She started the short march toward Metra and stopped her army. They would expect that her first target would be Metra. It had the shortest of the three walls and the least defensive capabilities. She thought a while and then turned the army toward Tetra.

As the army moved toward Tetra an elf was spotted up ahead in the distance. Almedda tried to grab it with magic but it had ridden away as soon as it had seen them coming. She sent the spiders and dragons to find and kill the elf. No one could warn the city before she arrived. Surprise had to be her ally.

Gaitlyn saw the force coming toward the city of Thomas Thalin and smiled. There appeared to be a day of reckoning coming for him. The elf rode quickly to get the elves out of the way of the large force coming into the area. He noticed a shadow fly over him and assumed it was just one of her spells trying to capture him. He moved his horse and continued on. He heard a crunch near behind him and saw the first of the giant spiders sent after him. Quickly loading and firing his bow he took the first spider in the eye. He had six arrows and a sword. He was in serious trouble. He sent one of his arrows straight up with fire laced on it. He hoped someone had seen it and was sending help.

Meka was standing on the walls of Tetra. She still fumed at having to remain in the city while her husband played police man of the world. How many of these raids was she supposed to see? She looked out over the land and saw the distress signal from the forest.

Quickly she ordered a war party and headed out toward the arrows launch. Her rangers and Tyris were well armed and heavily endowed with arrows.

Gaitlyn took his third arrow and aimed at the following spiders and let fly. Two more of the wicked creatures died and fell where they had stood. A shadow over head caused him to fire his fourth arrow prematurely. His people probably were not looking for the arrow. He was growing desperate as he saw the following dragon directing the spiders to him. He loaded the fifth arrow into his bow and turned to face the pursuing spiders and fired again. This time the spider was hit in the abdomen. The wound would not even slow the creature down.

He was now getting frantic. He once more saw the dragon leading the spiders and got an idea.

Looking above him, he loaded his last arrow and aimed carefully at the dragon. He drew to fire when he saw the dragon burst into flame as a hundred arrows peppered its skin. The spiders still followed and he fired his sixth and last arrow into the lead spider. The wound was in the eye and the spider fell. Gaitlyn removed his sword from is scabbard and jumped from the horse. He stood as several of the lead spiders passed and finally realized he was on the ground. Spiders a small bit behind saw him though and attacked almost immediately. As he braced to feel the arachnids' bite, he heard arrows fly past him. Opening his eyes, he saw some of his people and people from the city in a great battle surrounding them.

Meka went to Gaitlyn and asked, "You done? I would have thought you would have helped finish the stragglers."

"These are the forerunners. An army follows and a great many more things than spiders are with them. I think we have a problem." said Gaitlyn.

"Fall back to Tetra now! Thank you for the information. Now join me upon my horse as yours was taken down by one of those monsters. We need to prepare for this battle." said Meka.

"How are you going to summon help? This army is huge and the few warriors we have here will not last long." said Gaitlyn.

"Then we send up a flaming arrow." Smiled Meka as she spurred her horse toward the city.

Almedda cursed and looked at the man who was in charge of the spiders. He raised his hands in defeat and said, "The animals are just that, animals. They do what they will. Once the dragon fell, they just went crazy, then disappeared."

"Yes, they did. It displeases me to see that you do have control over them. Well, there is nothing we can do at this point is there?" said the Dark Queen.

"Yes, of course. Nothing to do for it. Hehe." said the animal trainer.

"Wrong!" Screamed Almedda as she waved her hand and the man began to scream as light flooded into him and came pouring out of every pore on his body. His eyes shot out light as his eyes dissolved in the power flowing through him. Light fell from his mouth and nose. Ears flamed as the light shot out of them. Slowly the man fell to his knees, then to the ground. "Now, there is nothing you can do for it. Someone, get in here and clean up this mess. I don't want my horse's hooves soiled with failure."

Two orcs came running up and buried the liquidated man. They made sure that nothing remained and bowed away. Almedda stroked the binding of the grimoire. The terrible power of the book now resided inside her and desired after all these years of confinement to be used and Almedda indulged it. She caused the skies above Tetra to turn dark as night as she approached with her army. Dense fog proceeded them, keeping their numbers hidden.

Almedda cloaked herself in dark magic to keep her identity hidden. As her army approached the defenders of Tetra, the few that they were, fire arrows down onto the oncoming army. She waved her hands and the arrows stopped and reversed flight. They attacked the defenders and the defenders stopped firing. Magical folk would fire lightning and fire down on the enemy and they would burst into flame as the Dark Queen cast her spells toward them. Some melted on the spot, some just burst into fire, and others suffered from the dissolving light.

Looking up at the walls, she made her voice loud enough to be heard inside, "Give up now or feel the wrath of the Dark Queen. I will let your citizens live, but all of its leaders must perish in sacrifice to me. So, send them out and prepare for your new master."

The gates opened and armed warriors flowed from the gates. Old veterans and new untested troops ran from the city to defend it. Meka and her Tyris were also there as was the druids and elves of the local forest. Many of them seeing not enough summers to be a steady soldier while others have seen too many to be able to fight any longer. But fight they did.

Almedda turned and led most of her troops away. The ones staying would be able to defeat this meager force. She engorged the spiders and trolls making them twice their normal size and turned and left. She did not need to be there to see this rabble wiped off the face of the map.

Too bad, thought Almedda. She had hoped for more resistance. It was way too easy to take over this world. She must find others to conquer. Her army marched toward Metra and would be passing Landsdale again. They would not be ready to defend again yet. But she would melt their giant walls of steel and laugh as the town folk fed her army this time. The thought of it made her giddy.

CHAPTER FORTY

THE WALKING DEAD

Tanis was waiting for the other shoe to drop. They had seen the coming army from miles away due to the darkness and fog surrounding it. It would not be long before it returned to Landsdale. They had figured it would have been coming from Metra, but it was coming from the direction of Tetra. In the direction of Tetra, Tanis saw the wizards send up the pillar of flame. Tetra was still in danger but that massive army stood between them and Tetra. It would have to be the remaining forces of Thalinburg that went to the aid of Tetra.

Tanis sent a dragon to Athinina, asking to assist the warriors of Tetra. Athinina would know what she needed to protect Thalinburg and know who she could send to Meka at Tetra.

Thomas asked what he was talking to the dragon about. Tanis just said it was a message for his mother. Best to leave the problem of Tetra to them and not worry and involve Thomas. After all, he was the loose cannon of the bunch.

A voice sounding like thunder came from all around the defenders at Landsdale. "Give up now. You do not stand a chance against the Dark Queen. Thomas Thalin, take your family and bend knee to me and I will give you what was once yours. The rest of you, send me your other leaders as sacrifices and I will allow you all to live as peasants under me. Deliver them to the fog line before we reach the wood line or all of you will be destroyed. I hope personally that you will not send them. I need more blood to dance in."

Tanis listened and caught a familiar twang in the words. But it could not be her. It must be a twisting of the grimoire. He knew that Elizarade was dead. She could not be back. And definitely not so powerful. The necromancer was long dead now.

It was the undead that emerged from the fog first. The skeletons and zombie warriors came from the mist like a nightmare. The defenders saw that the enemy was their dead. They had buried all of their dead out at the wood line due to the sheer number of them. Now the necromancer used them to fight their families.

Tanis dispelled the coming attack with a counter spell that released them back to death. He then cremated the remains so they would no longer be able be made to serve the Dark Queen. Artitous tried without great success to dismiss the fog and cloud cover. It was just set in its current state. Tanis finished his work and came to assist Artitous when the faerimouth landed at the edge of the fog. Two of them entered the fog and immediately turned into stone and were smashed by unseen hands.

Tanis warned all of his army not to enter the mists. "Let them come to us. They must really fear us if they hide in a killer mist." Laughed Tanis. He stopped laughing as the giants came from the mist. They swept the front lines to the side and were bearing down on the commanders. As they moved, the phoenix took flight. All of the phoenix lifted off at the same time and a blast of flame enveloped and destroyed the giants where they stood. The phoenix went back to the Tyris and put their heads under their wings in sleep.

"I guess we wore them out." said Thomas. "What next? Harpies?"

"Don't ask lest we find out." said Tanis, and if he were a prophet the next wave arrived. In it was harpies and dark elves. Noom and Dwarves also poured from the mist toward their light side counterparts. Men followed with the whips and spears pushing the under races to fight.

Tanis attacked the men and left the other races be. Harpies attacked the defenders and each other. The dark elves slipped back into the mists and fired their bows from there. The noom and dwarves and other races of Dracos turned and faced their tormentors. Soon the defenders had another line and a half of those that had turned on the Dark Queen.

The defending army heard laughter from the mists as a line of fire and exploding earth went from the men pushing her troops to the lines of the defenders destroying the earth as well as the creatures standing upon it. Artitous and Tanis together was able to dispel the dark magic, but as they did another wave came behind the first. Two became three, four, and finally a fifth wave before the Dark Queen moved on.

The grimoire opened in hands of Almedda and a smile crossed her face. This was even better than she could have dreamed. Grabbing one of her people she cast a spell and sent them into the fray. These warriors fought harder than any of the others on the field. And as they fell, they exploded with a magic so strong it evaporated the people around the soldiers. Tanis began grabbing those warriors and sending them flying back to the Dark Lands' forces.

Soon the warriors were erasing warriors on both sides of the conflict. These creatures were juggernauts and heavily armored. They were not killed easily and the victors found themselves dying with them. Tanis redoubled his efforts and soon the warriors were no longer coming from the mists.

The orcs and goblins came from the mist next. They clashed with the gnomes and faerimouth and again were soon pushed back to the mists. It seemed like for now at least the sides were equal. The dragons faced their counterparts above the battle and men and other races were killed as one side's dragon or the other's hit the ground in their fights. The dragons were fighting as hard as they could but neither side was killing the other. It seemed like they were just too evenly matched. The battle below seemed to ebb and flow as the battle above them did. As the dragons for the light pushed forward the forces of the light below pushed back the attackers. But when it was reversed the dark armies surged forward.

Tanis threw his aide to the dragons and Artitous attacked the creatures in front of them. After what seemed like an eternity the dark forces began to withdraw from the field of battle. Not far, but they moved back allowing for a lull in the fighting. Looking at the faces of the men and dwarves and elves and faerimouth around him, Tanis ordered a return to Landsdale. Many of those that had come with him were no longer there.

Looking to west he saw a cloud as another army came toward them. The exhausted warriors strapped on their armor, ready for the next battle to begin when it became a bit clearer that it was the men and women of Tetra and Thalinburg. Cheers rose from both the advancing parties. Meka rode at the head of the defenders of Tetra and Athinina in front of the defenders of Thalinburg.

Thomas nearly swallowed his tongue seeing Meka and ran to her screaming how she should be in Tetra. Troops also arrived from Metra as the troops of Tetra arrived. Now all of the remaining children of Tanis and their significant others were present. Tanis was getting ready to order them back to their cities when the grand children came out as well. Tanis smiled and sent the youngest Thalins into the city of Landsdale.

Christof was walking around the city and cast spells to redo some of the steelwork. It was made harder and stronger and the little one felt like he was contributing. His cousins watched his back as he worked and soon, they made it all around the town. The cousins would point out areas that required more help than others and Christof fixed them. He wore no sword like his cousins. When a pair of orcs tried to attack a magical blade formed in Christof's hands and he slew them with the forms of the warriors his father so loved.

Apparently, the army would not fit into the town so horses and other beasts were sent toward Metra. Food stuffs and animals were sent toward Thalinburg where they could be seen and monitored. People entered the safety of the town in shifts to sleep and be healed. Every six hours a new group got to rest. The warriors who were refreshed left the town and formed up new front lines while those on the shift before fell back to the middle and the third shift was allowed into the city to rest.

Christof was working overtime apparently as when they entered the steel coated walls, he had magical defenses spread all over the city. Tanis could see the nets of protection if the others could not. His grandson had done well. He would hate to be a follower of the Dark Queen coming into the town.

The two magical folks were talking when someone screamed. Christof and Tanis both moved to see Saundera squirming on the ground and screaming in agony. Tanis tried to undo the weaving which had already killed the druid and lifted back into its place of protection.

"Christof take this off the town apparently it does not work. Druids do not come in the dark variety. So why did it kill the poor woman?" said Tanis.

"It should not have been able to do so, Grandfather. Only followers of the Dark Queen should have been able to be harmed by the magic. I was quite specific with the magics." replied Christof.

"Do not remove anything right this moment. There was a traitor amongst the people of Landsdale and I think I know who now." said

Artitous. "Let everyone know that followers of the Dark Queen will die if the enter Landsdale. It is what I most feared. There are dark druids. We just need to weed them out."

"What in the name of all that is good is that?!" exclaimed the mayor. "Was that our druid by chance?"

"Apparently, she was a dark practitioner of druid magic. The rumors were there, I just did not heed them. Then there was Meka's accounts of dark druids. Both the kids seemed to run into the dark magical folk on their way back to their cities. I should have followed up with them more. Now we see it with our own eyes. This is a major discovery and may answer a few questions." said Artitous.

"You beat yourself up over nothing. We could not have known and now our trap has caught us one. Let's see who else falls to our trap." said Tanis.

"We got lucky today. They pulled back too quickly. They had us dead to rights. We should have all perished in that battle. Why back off?" Ask Thomas as he walked up to the older Thalin and Artitous. "Their general is either stupid or unskilled or we have a major problem coming."

Tanis was a little shocked the young man had come to him, but replied quickly, "I do not know our enemy's mind but he or she has sacrificed large numbers of men and women and other creatures. There is always a reason for that." Together the three men went to walk the battle field. There were many enemy dead and crews worked to remove their dead from amongst the creatures. Tanis leaned down and noticed a brand on the enemy troops burned into their skins. He had seen this brand before but he had no idea where he had seen it. "This symbol means something but I do not know what it is. Artitous, do you recognize the brand?"

"I have seen it somewhere but I cannot place the image. It was not a brand at that time either. I just don't remember the device." said the Druid.

Thomas spoke up and said to the others, "Well, let us just wipe the brand off the face of the world of Dracos, shall we? I think we can surprise them with a night raid. It would catch them flat footed. That is for sure."

"They would not expect it that is for sure but with that cloud cover over us I don't really know what time it is. It is going to be a long day. We have to assume that they are nocturnal and they are going to plan their own night attacks. What we need is a surgical strike to destroy the grimoire and the Dark Queen all at once. Then we will be able to route this army. She summons more and more so we may see all of our enemies yet." said Tanis.

"Cutting off the head of the snake is not going to work. They become less organized but the attack more and more and harder and harder to destroy. We need that magical person alive until we defeat its army." said Thomas.

"Are you sure, my son? Don't you think killing the Dark Queen would end this? What is your plan?" asked Tanis.

Thomas led a small group headed out away from the combat appearing to be headed to Tetra. She had offered him a place in her armies. He should have taken it. She sent a small regiment of noom out after him with orders to destroy them to the man, and woman. They would carry out the task faster and easier than men would.

As they crested the hill and went around toward Tetra. Their view of the party was obscured by the hill and now she had to depend upon the skills of the noom.

The noom approached the retreating party, moving quickly. Thomas ordered a halt and waited to see their intentions. Surely there could be no trouble from these creatures. Thomas climbed down and loosened the sword on his hip. Meka loosened her bow upon her back and even the phoenix on Meka's back stretched out its huge wings.

"Oh, it is big people. We have trade goods for you. Tobacco and whiskey. Beer and spirits of all kinds and flavors, please allow us to show you, our wares." said the lead Noom. "Old Johnathon here will keep you right and on the slim and narrow."

"I believe I can do that for myself. You do realize that these goods are no good for most of the general population. Few people use the week of prayers and necessary prep to partake of your goods." said Thomas. "Now bugger off."

The noom rapidly made a show of cleaning the path when the first one turned and fired at Thomas. Tanis steamed up to the field as the first noom let bolt fly. Meka slashed the bolt down, and prepared for the onslaught. But the noom cowered around their wagon and lay down their weapons when Tanis drew Warmonger. He roared into the noom and swung his blade like a farmer cutting wheat.

The noom that had lay down their weapons were spared while those that chose to try and fight ended up laying on the dry dust of the road. The wounded and dead were looked after by their companions and Tanis allowed this. Christof had built a barrier around his family to prevent arrows from hitting them and many stood stuck in mid-air. Christof waved his arm and the bolts fell to the now blood-stained ground.

"Having that kid around is a good thing. He is very good at what he does and seems to have been born like Torlin and had a large benefit of the crystal cave I was born in. He is almost as powerful as a full circle of wizards. That is insane. He makes me look a little dull myself." said Tanis.

Christof looked at his grandfather and grinned. He walked toward him and then conjured his magical blade and ran toward his grandfather.

CHAPTER FORTY-ONE

DARK PLANS

Almedda was perplexed. Her legions of monsters and men and women of all races should be doing better. They are being defeated in every attack they made. Almedda consulted her grimoire. The book seemed to know what Almedda needed for as she went to open the book, the book opened for her. She scanned the page and looked closely at the spells. A large grin crossed her face as she cast her new spell.

The creatures around her fell into a kind of trance and she linked them to the best warrior of their type. All of a sudden, all the creatures fought with the skill of the linked officer. This could work out well for her.

She went down the ranks of warriors casting the spell and watching her army become the greatest army in the world. Carlee went to her and whispered in her ear, "You do realize that if the lead creature is killed then the group attached to him will also die immediately."

"Carlee, you worry wart. I am not linking that many to each officer. But the whole army is a thousand times more powerful than it was. These magic users here are pulling twice what they were and by the time they burn themselves to a cinder, the job they needed to do will be complete." Laughed Almedda.

Carlee was still concerned but she did not care. Almedda seemed to have everything in hand and if she were to die too bad. She suddenly found it hard for her to think. The black phoenix turned around and saw Almedda smile as she completed her spell. Slowly the phoenix felt the power of the grimoire. It had been linked to the Queen. This could not have been a worse thing. Her cognizance started fading and all she saw was white. The plan had failed terribly.

Almedda smiled as the phoenix finished the link. Oh yes, she was the most powerful being in the world of Dracos with the exception of her nephew. He had somehow inherited the power of the ancients. She did not know how he had gotten the full powers and she had gained but a small sampling. He would have to be dealt with first.

Looking at her squad of assassins she had a small woman that looked like she was a young woman. She could pass as an eleven- or twelve-year-old. And she could get close enough to the prince and see him dead. It was a perfect plan.

Almedda called the woman to her, "What is your name, child? I have a special mission for you."

"I am Sasha, and child? I have almost twice the number of summers as you have seen. So, who is it you call child, milady?" said the assassin.

"Nice, nice. You are going to get close to my nephew and kill him. He cannot be allowed to face me. Not now, not ever." said Almedda, "and remember I am your Queen and I will call you as I wish."

Her other niece and nephew were safely housed in Landsdale. Arlette was trying to get the forge put together so she could get to work. She had studied the art of smithing in the city as she grew up and had become quite the little blacksmith. Getting the smithy running would be a good thing. Arlette was at home in the heat and with a hammer in her hand.

Garath would enchant the items his sister made with properties to assist and improve the materials of her constructions. The two were not much for the combat that had been happening in the past few years. Garath would move between the city of Metra and the now city of Landsdale. It had grown well since the wall upgrade his father had caused. He sent waves of air over the surface polishing the wall to a sheen. They should be clean.

Arlette was not making anything today due to fixing what was left of the forge. Garath came in and helped strengthen the forge so that she could use it at hotter temperatures. This would allow armor and swords to be forged. He had used a sword for the first time in Metra taking back their homes. He was not able to use magic at that point inside the palace but he felt the weakness in the spell and almost exploited that. It had been a kill or be killed kind of day. It seemed like so long ago. But it was just ten years ago. He was only five in the battle of Metra. Now he was almost a man. So long ago.

He looked up from his ponderings and saw the young woman coming toward him. She had a smile on her face as she looked at the seated prince. "Hi, can I help you?" asked Garath softly. He was a painfully shy boy. And the attentions of a girl were always an embarrassment to him. His face grew red when she spoke to him.

"Hi, I am Sasha. You look like you are imitating a crab with that red face, calm down I am just looking for work and you looked like someone who can lead me to it." said Sasha.

"I am Garath, son of Torlin and Roanda Thalin of Metra. And a kind of magic user. Christof is much more powerful than I am. Everyone is more everything than me. I am just a middle of the road guy." said Garath.

"Oh, you're not Christof? Your Cousin has quite the looks. Not as nice as your mind but nice. Middle is a great place to begin. People can always grow from medium to high and extra high. Are you a wizard or druid? Tell me more about you."

"You do not want to hear about me. I am like I have said. Ordinary. I am an ordinary wizard, an ordinary warrior, an ordinary thief, ordinary looks, ordinary as ordinary can be. The only one who thought me more than ordinary is dead. My aunt thought me better than I am too." said Garath.

"She sounds smart. I am sorry to hear of your loss. Surely you are noticed by your parents and family? You seem to be a good man." said Sasha as she tried to move a little closer to the young man and he scooted a bit farther away.

"Ordinary people are not noticed. Family does not count. Members of the opposite sex around here are more interested in the other guys and I am left alone." said Garath.

Sasha was intrigued by the young man. She could not tell why but something about him was just right. "You do not have to scoot away from me, I won't bite you. Not hard at least." The boy jerked back in fear causing the girl to laugh, "Just kidding. You are a little tense. Just try to settle your nerves."

She moved closer again and this time the boy did not move away from her. He looked her in the eye and again moved back slightly. He was so unsure. No one had paid this much attention to him before. Except his mother and father. Even his sister did not pay him a whole lot of attention unless they were in the forge. The girl moved closer to him again and he stayed put this time. She moved her hand and placed it on his arm. "See, that did not hurt anything. You are relaxing now. I am not going to hurt you." said Sasha.

"I am just not used too this," he said as she moved in and tried to kiss him. He leapt to his feet almost knocking her to the ground. She laughed and tried to get him sit down next to her again and he politely declined.

What was he supposed to do? He had never kissed a girl. He would make a fool of himself and she would lose interest. He just knew it.

"I am embarrassed. How do I say this? I have never…" said Garath as she cut him off.

"Kissed a girl. Well, let's see if that is true. Look over there." She said pointing to a group of people off to the side. He turned to look at where she pointed and ended up with her lips planted squarely upon his. The kiss lasted mere seconds but to him it lasted a thousand years. When she took her lips away, he looked at her sheepishly.

"Sorry, I did not see you there. I should not have gotten so close. Oh my, I hope I did not offend you. I am so sorry." Garath stuttered.

"You did nothing wrong and I liked it. I would like to see you again, if I can. I have to go right now." She remarked.

"Of course, I would love to. I mean if you would like. I mean if you really…." Stuttered Garath, even more than before. Not sure what to say.

"I do and I mean it. I will meet you right here tomorrow." said Sasha as she sauntered away. Arlette had watched the encounter and laughed as she approached her brother.

"It is not a crime. Kiss her if you want as long as she is willing. You just need some confidence." said Arlette.

"What do you know of it, now? You do not have a boyfriend. Do you?" asked Garath.

"I will never kiss and tell." Smiled Arlette and ran from her brother. Garath went after her hoping she did not go to their mother. How would he explain this one to her?

CHAPTER FORTY-TWO

WERERATS AND GRANDCHILDREN

Christof looked like and avenging angel with his magical sword bearing down on his grandfather, when he jumped over the scared and confused Tanis. The sound of a sword hitting flesh caused him to turn, expecting half his body to come apart when he saw the poor creature on the ground split into three pieces. Looking closer, Tanis told Christof, "Quickly, have your cousin make me a dagger of silver. No questions just run. Looking down on the wererat, Tanis cast a spell to freeze the pieces from reconnecting, as they had been slithering to do.

Christof raced back and said that Arlette and Garath were on the case and he would have something soon. Christof looked into its face and said, "It looks almost human. Why are we going to kill it? And why the silver dagger?"

"These creatures were once human. But they were bitten and turned into the abomination you see before you. It is a mercy that you are giving the people confined to these forms. As for the dagger, silver is toxic to them. It is the only way to kill them." Explained Tanis to the younger man.

Looking at the squirming pieces of the creature trying to come loose from the spell, Arlette and Garath came running up with the cast silver dagger. Arlette said that she was not a silversmith but it was the best she could do. Garath in turn made the silver smooth and sharp. Enchanting the edge so it would not go dull.

Tanis released the spell on the first piece of the wererat and it worked its way to the center piece and reattached itself. Tanis released the center piece of the wererat and it once more wiggled and squirmed its way to the head section. As it reconnected the wererat suddenly sprung back at Tanis only to find itself still trapped by Tanis's spell. Tanis walked carefully to the wererat and plunged the dagger deep into the beast's heart. The creature closed its eyes and fell to the ground. The silver dagger sent the appearance of gangrene flowing through its body.

The process took less than a minute. The hair and tusks and teeth all fell back to the size and shape of a man. The kids seem to think that the process was slow and painful. The gangrene flowed to every portion of the wererat and finally a man lay were the monster stood. The man lay dead and Tanis removed the dagger. "It has to be this way. There is no cure for the curse. Some of these creatures are several hundred years old. They cannot die unless killed by a silver weapon. This is truly a mercy that we can grant to them."

The law enforcement arm of the elven army approached the now naked dead man and the children and Tanis. "What happened here? My Liege, did you kill this man?"

"The man was a wererat. He was attacking and we had to stop him. There may be more. We need to make search for them." said Tanis as he started to walk away.

"Wait. Even the king of the Elves is susceptible to murder charges. We must investigate what has happened here. If your story is the truth, then we hunt these creatures. If you are in fact wrong, you will be executed as per elven law." said the Elven officer.

"You do not believe me? Were you there for the weretiger? Same situation. Just different creature." said Tanis.

"We have a job to do. Do not interfere or you will be found guilty and it is the gallows for you." said the officer.

"I may get to show you. Turn and fight for another of the vermin is coming." said Tanis as he let loose with a magical dart. It hit the wererat in the breast and it fell. The elves turned their backs to it just in time to see Tanis hurling a fireball in their general direction.

The elves dived from the ball and saw why it was cast. The wererat was on its feet again. Once more the elves were able to bring down the wererat but Tanis came right behind and stabbed the wererat in the heart with the silver dagger. Once more the fur and tail fell to earth. The teeth went back to the same as they were whenever the man was transformed. The tusks falling from his mouth. Again, when the transformation was complete a man lay where the wererat once was.

"We see, there was no murder here. But watch your movements for you are being watched. It is not me or my companions, but someone has engineered this and is waiting to bring you down." said the officer as he turned and went looking for more of the wererats.

"Arlette. I fear we will need many of your mytheral daggers. Silver forged into weapons, who would have guessed it." said Tanis.

CHAPTER FORTY-THREE

ANOTHER ATTACKER

Almedda had a new plan. Her armies were thwarted for now by her big brothers. She sat thinking and fondling the grimoire when an elf entered the room. "My lady, when did we start watching their movements? There are creatures spying on your old family. What should we do?"

"Those creatures were not sent by us but we can still use them. Gather up one or two of them and I will question them." said Almedda.

"Would it not be better for me to interrogate them, my lady? After all I am a bird, they will speak to me." said Carlee.

"I will interrogate them as I said I would. If they refuse to answer to me, I know a thousand ways to torture a creature to death and then resurrect them as mindless workers for us and then they will tell us all they know. One way or the other they will talk." said Almedda.

"I forget you have the full grimoire. It gives you unstoppable power. Only one close to you can take it from you. So now I will take it from you for now and let you sleep." said Carlee.

"Forget about it." said Almedda as she sent a wave of air toward the bird blowing it into the side of her command tent. "Don't you have something to do? Like finding these spies and seeing to whom they belong. Now be gone. I do not wish your counsel now."

"As you say, my lady." said Carlee as she flew from the tent.

Almedda looked into the grimoire and found the summoning spell. It would bring the undead to her. She may need that one before this is over. Her step-mother would not be alive forever. She could take the throne the right way, or she could kill all the competition and take the throne by force. She liked that thought the more blood to dance through the better. That wizard's, Marzioa, blood had stained her feet as she had danced through it. She did that now whenever she killed a person or an animal. She had people killed so she could dance and play in their blood.

Continuing to read the grimoire she figured something out that would change the course of this conflict for now. She summoned Morreal and began to plan. They would never know what hit them.

After what seemed to be hours, they took their heads from one another and laughed critically. This was going to be great and even Tanis the brave would not survive. It was perfect.

Almedda sent out Morreal to go and start preparing for the offensive. This would be epic.

Tanis watched as the cloud of dust that was the armies of evil headed over the horizon. They were retreating and that would give them a much-needed time to rest and rebuild their facilities. The healers had complained that they were unable to really work for their center had been burned in Landsdale. Wounded that could not make the trip to one or another of the cities where being kept in the most intolerable conditions.

They tried to clean an area but the temple needed to be rebuilt. And the constant fighting had kept it from being built. The druids tried but they were not stone workers.

Torlin came into the town and started to rebuild it with magic. He caused the stones and wood to go back to the way it had been before with a wave of his hand. He worked awhile and continued to build all of the structures of the town with the exception of the smithy. It had already been rebuilt. Looking around Torlin smiled. Just like before he made subtle improvements to the structures as he continued.

He did not use mortar to repair the brick, he fused it with magic. Literally melted the stones together. He set the wood to grow in these places to fill in open spaces. He again worked it so the branches were intertwined and they were not coming apart. The people's homes would be stronger than they ever were.

He did not really expect the problems about to occur.

CHAPTER FORTY-FOUR

NEW FRIENDS

Things seemed to be getting back to normal. The army of the light had separated and headed to each of their cities or towns and many a person offered to write or visit. The war felt over to many of them and they had made new companions that would last for the rest of their lives.

It was illusion though. Back on the battle field a dragon that had switched sides was murdered. It was blasted to death and its hide and meat was sent to feed the army. If anything remained when she animated this dragon and sent it forth, that would make things so much better. Carlee was concerned as they were watched by several smaller animals. Swooping down she snagged a rabbit from the field and was about to fry it when the Queen came over and grabbed the rabbit.

"That was my lunch, My Lady." said Carlee.

"He is cute. I think I know what to do with him." She said as she used her teeth to kill the rabbit. Throwing the carcass to the phoenix as blood dripped from her mouth she said, "All yours now. I just wanted a bite." Smiling she strode away. Almedda licked her lips and cleaned her face then moved to the dried dead dragon. She waved her hand over the dragon and it magically reassembled and stood before her. It slowly moved its head, turning it from side to side. Almedda cast a spell pulling the dead dragon to her. It looked in her eyes and told it, "You will do my will, traitor, or next time your death will be permanent. Understand me? I control you now."

The dragon looked horrified if bones and sinew could look horrified. It was trying to run or fly away, but found it could do nothing but look at the small person in front of him. The Queen looked in his eyes and once more taunted the dragon, "Keep trying. You will not succeed any more than that rabbit had. Now we need to get to work. Your breath will no longer bring fire but death. Let's test it shall we. Orc! Get your miserable hide over here." She screamed. The older female orc came over and Almedda set her in front of the dragon. Almedda ordered the orc to remain where she was and Almedda went around behind the dragon. Its breath should not harm her but why take chances.

"I order you to use your breath. Now!" screamed Almedda. The dragon reared back and let loose a black cloud from its mouth. The cloud surrounded the orc and she began to scream as the cloud slowly removed her flesh. When it had finished the soft parts, it dissolved the bones. Almedda walked up to the now small pile of bone shards and goo and smiled.

"This is going to work. Bring me all of our dragons. We must make them loyal. This traitor will be followed by others. We cannot have that now can we." She said as the dragon handlers went to get their charges. "We needed to feed our armies anyway."

The dragons that had been left after the battle lined up in front of Almedda. The handlers prodding them and hitting them to keep them in line. It was a bit intriguing to the young woman as she watched the great beasts being bested by little goads and men. She walked up to the first dragon and cast a spell around it. The spell settled on the dragon and its heart flew from its chest. A couple of minutes was all it took for the spell to strip the dragon of all its hide and meat leaving only skeleton and sinew.

The handler was a good-looking man, by all accounts of the women in camp. He started to cry as he watched his dragon die. Almedda went to the crying handler and enveloped him in a deep kiss. "I will make you forget your dragon. Come to my tent in thirty minutes." Smiled the Queen. She was twenty-one years old now and she wanted a child. She was accorded to be a very sexy woman. None would say so to her face, but most thought it. She tended to read minds when bored and saw several of her high generals thinking some interesting thoughts.

Things to try out. Moving down the line she murdered than reanimated all of the dragons. She had an army of death causing undead dragons. This would definitely give them the advantage in the next battle. Tanis and Torlin would be dead by the time they arrived with their new army. The dead on the field began to reanimate and moved to join the dragons. A fine army she had now. But other distractions awaited her in her tent.

She entered the tent and the handler stood waiting for her. A small tear still lingered in his eye. Almedda saw the tear and wiped it from his eye. "Still not going on about that dragon, are you?" asked the Queen.

"It was a special animal, my liege." said the handler as he turned to face a now very naked Almedda. Almedda pulled out a dagger and then blew out the lantern.

An hour later, Almedda came out of the tent and ordered the orcs to go and clean it. They walked in to find the man in pieces and blood splattered everywhere. Almedda had not only mated with the man but had utterly killed him.

"Thus, I deal with the weak." said Almedda as she entered the dragon handlers' pitch.

"What has happened to Shamill?" asked a dragon handler.

"He will no longer be a blemish on this army." said Almedda. "Now let's go to war."

CHAPTER FORTY-FIVE

BURROWING ENEMIES

Peace seemed to be fleeting as they saw the cloud of the enemy army coming over the horizon. Sasha looked at the cloud and swallowed hard. Garath came up to her and put his arm around her waist. Looking at him, she smiled. The army would wipe them out, but she would at least have died having known love. Garath squeezed gently and asked what was on the horizon.

"The enemy approaches. They are coming slowly though. They severely outnumber us. I would have expected that they would be moving faster." said Sasha.

"I would agree with you. They are not using their whole force either. I do not see the dragons with them." said Tanis as he walked up behind the two. "Garath, they need help enchanting some items, would you do so? I will keep your lady here company for a while."

Garath squeezed her once more and she let her smile slip. Tanis knew. That was the whole of it. "So, did you come here looking to kill him or me or Torlin? I realized you were an assassin sent by the Dark

Queen shortly after you arrived. I have not ousted you because you genuinely care for the boy. And he does for you. That cannot be faked. But I would know, who is the Dark Queen?"

"I will gladly share any information I have, but I was hired by one of her colleagues. They did not give names simply gold and a list of names to end the lives of. I was sent to the wizards only by chance. I felt weird when I touched one of the coins though like a jolt of lightning hits me." said Sasha.

"Allow me to see the coins." said Tanis, examining the coins closely. "I fear this is Gareth's area of expertise. We will find a way to get him to examine these without him finding out your little secret."

Tanis walked away with the coins and she suddenly felt happier and stronger. It was no longer like the coins weighed her down. Thoughts brought shocks. Now she thought of the boy and no shocks came. She was bolstered and climbed the tower of steel to look upon the approaching army.

Garath found her on the tower, his face downcast. "What bothers you, my sweet?" asked Sasha as he finished his climb to the tower.

"Someone has been monitoring you through these coins. The shocks to force you to do something you may not want to do. What were these given to you for? Why would someone want to monitor you? I have disabled the spells. They are very dark magic. As dark as it comes. They would have killed you after the job was performed. I know you would bring us no harm now, but what were you sent here to do?" asked Garath.

"I guess you know it all now. I was originally sent here to kill you by the enemy. These coins were my payment. I was to kill all of the wizards in this town so that the enemy could wipe it from the face of

Dracos. Now that it is obvious, I failed, another will be sent to finish the job. And I will be added to the list." said Sasha.

"You couldn't have told me. I like you a lot. I even think I may be in love with you. But I do not know now. You should have told me. I could have protected us. My cousin could have protected us. Christof is even more powerful than my grandfather. We could do this." said Garath.

"I feared this very thing. That you would be angry. But I am eager to fight by your side. Not your family's, yours. We will work together with all of our allies, not just the Thalins. We will make this work. I am quite skilled at infiltration. Maybe I can get to the Queen. Cut off the head and kill the snake." said Sasha.

"Then we fight together. I will go with you to kill the Queen. We will do this." said Garath.

"Neither of you are going anywhere. Artitous is feeling a weird rumbling under the town. That cloud out there gets closer and closer. I can make out different giants and other larger followers of the Dark Queen. I do not sense the grimoire which means the Queen is not there. There is definitely something wrong." Tanis said as he looked toward the advancing cloud of dust.

"She would have to be there to guide her fewer living minions would she not?" asked Sasha. "Her undead monsters would need to have her nearby unless she has the Elizarade grimoire. If she has that then we are lost anyway."

"She does have the grimoire. As of this point, she does not know how to master it. The grimoire controls her. And when it can it will consume her and her power and she will forever be a slave to the book. She will not be separated from it at this point. It will get worse. The more she finds she can do the more it will take control until she is Elizarade. It was the same with the previous owner. I researched the grimoire and found out that the first person to claim it was a magical person named Sarah several centuries ago. She was ordinary in skill but was also ambitious and prone to the darker magics. She became entranced with the grimoire and used it to fell several enemies she had. Soon anyone who came to her was to call her Elizarade. The more she used it the worse it became. She would use the powers of the book for everything. Soon all that was left was the poor girl's shell with the spirit of the grimoire living in her. She was killed by a magic user and the grimoire was split into three pieces. The previous Elizarade had only one third of the book and she was still totally and completely corrupted. This poor creature has the full effect of the grimoire. I pity her." said Tanis.

"She has control over it though. I saw her opening it to certain pages and selecting the magic she wanted. She is a very strong-willed woman. She murdered one of the assassins by enveloping them in a disintegrating cloud and then danced in and drank his blood. She is as dark as you can get and she has not changed her name as of yet." said Sasha.

"Hopefully we will see just what is in store soon. I have sent for your parents and your Uncle Thomas. We will need them all soon enough." said Tanis.

"The vibrations from the earth have stopped. I fear what is to happen, be about to." said Artitous. "There is strange magic in the air."

"I sense it too, old friend. At this point anything can happen. Look to the west. The cloud of her armies comes ever closer. We may have to leave these walls to face her. Ready the armies to march forth. It is going to be a hard battle." said Tanis.

Garath left the wall and tripped on the path. Looking down he thought he saw bone but shook his head. That could not be. There was no way it could be. Ignoring it he continued to run and help enchant weapons. Sasha stayed right by his side, nervously fingering her dagger.

CHAPTER FORTY-SIX

DEFENDING THE SMITHY

The enemy stopped about half a mile from the town. Tanis looked out toward them and saw them pounding shields and spears together. If they were closer the sound would have been deafening. Sasha followed Garath and suddenly pulled him back. Looking back at her he saw the dagger in her hand and went to protect himself when she flew past him and killed the man he had barely even seen. Looking up from the dead man, "They are called glass men. They are assassins that have given up their very souls to be the best killers they can be. They cannot be sensed by magical folk and can barely be seen by anyone. This one moved too quickly or we would have both died just now. I hope he is alone. I don't want to end up being stabbed through."

"Can you as an assassin sense these men? They do follow your own trade." asked Garath looking down at the man that had finally been revealed in the sleep of death. Several Tyris came flying down the street nearly knocking the young people to the earth. "I wonder what the hurry is."

"I would rather find out amongst many people than in this quiet lane." said Sasha, moving toward the walls.

"Not that way!" Screamed a Tyris, her phoenix flying over her head protectively. "The rear walls have fallen. It is only a matter of time before they make it into the town proper. We will force them to earn their advance though. The Phoenix can sense the evil all around us. They are extremely nervous. Now get to the smithy and remain there, young prince."

"Where are they fallen? Christof and I may be of some help." asked Garath, but the Tyris turned him toward the smithy again.

"Christof and your sister and now you will be in the smithy. Your lady will join the Tyris, I hope." said the woman warrior.

"I must be where Garath is. I am his personal protector." said Sasha.

"A loyal woman, young prince. Treat her well and protect her well. Be well and survive the battle." said the Tyris.

Only a Tyris could say good bye by wishing you were not killed. Garath arrived at the smithy and formed his sword like his cousin did. They watched the streets north, south, east, and west. Sasha looked South with her daggers ready, while Arlette had her hammer ready and watched the North. Christof had his magical blade ready facing the East and Garath insisted on the West. Garath turned his magical blade into a long spear. Christof looked over in appreciation. The young ones were not going to allow anything past them.

They had only a small wait before the first of the enemy arrived. The orcs had somehow pushed their way deep into the town. Warriors tried to keep them at bay, when Christof and Arlette let loose with their own attacks on the foe. Arlette lay about her with her hammer with the skill of a seasoned blacksmith. Christof swung his sword like the great swordsman he was, killing some of the enemy. Garath let loose a blast from his magically produced spear and drilled a hole through eight or nine of the attackers. They fell rapidly to be replaced with many more. The magical kids and the warrior women cast about them with weapons and magic killing and wounding all around them.

Garath felt a warm spot on his back. He turned his head ready to kill the enemy there and found it to be Sasha. He erected a shield of magic to protect her and continued his fight. Arlette and Christof ended with their backs together and the woman warriors fought with great skill and their phoenix killing as fast as their wings could move them.

Before they knew it the battle was over. The Tyris leader there smiled coyly at Christof, causing Arlette to laugh until her sides were sore. "These boys are all getting in with all these women. What will happen to them if they continued to flirt like this? One of these women will end up marrying them." She said as she continued laughing. Christof had placed a shield around most of the women they fought with and Arlette suddenly stiffened as an arrow pierced her shoulder. He had missed his cousin and now she lay in the dirt with an arrow in her shoulder. Christof ran to her side and removed the arrow. The dirt of the road had gotten into the wound track and the dirt on the arrow seemed to cause the wound to swell and turn unhealthy quick. Christof called to a Tyris, "Go rapidly to Artitous and have him come here. I am unable to clean this wound. Find him and some of their brethren to come and heal this wound."

"That will not be. The druids followed the main army to the field. There are none left here." said the Tyris. "In fact, the only two magical folks left in the town are you and your cousin."

"This cannot be! Why would they all leave? I am afraid. I do not know what to do from here. They cannot be gone. Not all of them." Cried Christof.

A rain of arrows bounced from the shielded woman and from the two magical folks. The rain of arrows continued as the magical boys continued to throw magic at the enemies. Direct magic was not hurting the creatures and Garath figured out that the magic was useless against the enemy, but thrown items with magic hurt them just as fast and badly as being shot from the bows around them. Garath and Christof picked up hundreds of arrows at once and let them fly into their attackers. The attackers looked for the archers and found themselves unable to find them as another wave of arrows came up and killed many of them with their own weapons. Soon the enemy rained down more and more of the arrows, hoping to kill the archers. The boys continued to throw arrows and the sky darkened by the flights of arrows either way.

Christof was about to let fly another volley of his arrows when suddenly the ground opened below him. Christof fell into a hole under the town and sensing evil there, Garath leaped down into the hole. The Tyris and assassin jumped down after them and found a strange stalemate. In the center of this subterranean chamber the two wizards were back-to-back. Orcs and undead approached from all sides and the two boys fought with the power and magically formed weapons.

Garath was fighting with his spear, creating piles of the dead and dying. Christof was letting loose a barrage of magical projectiles in circles just beyond his cousin. The two fought with fervor and the enemy stayed back from the magical folk. The ladies joined in the fight and looked at what appeared to be endless waves and waves of enemies coming from all sides. The two magical men stood like an ancient oak tree against the winds of a storm, just pushing back the enemy as fast as they approached. The enemy officers drove the creatures forward with whips, chains, and flails. The dead from the driving force was just as large as the casualties from the boys. As the two fought and the women looked for places to fight, Arlette was moaning from above.

She was moaning now instead of crying which was not a good sign. But the two magical folks could not break free from the combat. Finally,

Sasha went to her and tried cleaning her wound. The wound was deep and the barbs on the end of the enemy arrows would prevent the arrow from being removed the way it went in. The barbs were faced in multiple directions and impossible to pull out of Arlette's shoulder. Sasha picked up a large stone and Garath was about to fire a bolt of magic into her when she smashed the arrow and shoved it through Arlette's shoulder.

Sasha looked around for water and finally asked Christof if he could produce any water for cleaning the wound. Christof looked at her and said, "A little busy here. Do any of you have a drinking horn?"

A Tyris ran forward and set down next to Arlette and Sasha. Sasha took the flask from the woman and poured a small amount of the water in the flask into the wound where it boiled instead of rinse away the refuse. From her pouch, the Tyris produced another flask. This one was loaded with a creamy caramel colored drink.

"I will ask later where you found that but for now, let us hope it works." said Sasha as she poured the liquor into the wound. Arlette screamed for what seemed like an hour but was only a few seconds and the refuse was indeed being cleaned. The Tyris was taking a small sip as she would pour it onto the wound. Soon the wound was clean but the woman and her phoenix were completely snookered. It seemed that the phoenix reflected the Tyris. As the Tyris tried to wade back into the battle, the phoenix was flying around and around in circles. Every time she striked, it hit nothing and the phoenix was nearly as bad.

The two danced around and around tried to find an enemy to fight and they still were unable to find any. The enemies were in full retreat killing the officers driving them. They were running from anything in a mytan or throwing magical energies around. Soon the small group remained alone in the dark cavern. The magical weapons and phoenix in fire mode had lit up the cavern. Now it was a dark hole. Christof fired up a ball of light and they looked around the cavern.

There were several passages leading further underground and other leading from the surface what seemed like a mile away. Christof and Garath launched explosive balls of fire into the far ends of the passages and sealed them. It would take them a while but the enemy would eventually get back through. Garath ran to his sister's side and looked down at her. Now he wished he had paid more attention in the healing classes. His sister lay there with her eyes closed and appeared to be peacefully sleeping.

Christof leaned over her and checked her for breath and felt the soft whisper of breath on his hand. She was alive but not responsive. This worried both the young men until Sasha explained that they had used alcohol to cleanse the wound and she seemed to absorb the liquor quite quickly.

Garath laughed. His sister was going to be fine but she was drunk as a skunk. He could not wait to relate the tale to their mother. She would be furious at them but at least her daughter was alive. The small group slowly made their way to the surface by Christof cutting stairs into the side of the cavern and using those to escape.

Roanda and Meka waited at the top of the cavern looking decidedly concerned, when they finally reached the surface. Roanda grabbed up Garath and checked him over. Seeing no wounds or hurts she quickly went to the prone Arlette. Seeing the terrible wound on her shoulder, she picked up her drunken daughter and carried her to the smithy. Inside was his grandfather and Artitous working on the wounded with the other druids.

Roanda set her daughter down and she called out to Tanis. "Come quick my daughter was hit with a draught of sleep arrow."

Tanis came over and looked at the wound and smiled. Waving his hands above her the wound slowly looked better, then it seemed to seal itself. Looking at Roanda he said, "Do not fear. She was hit with a barbed arrow that was left too long. They were smart to drive it through instead of pulling or she would be dead by now. She will be fine though."

"Then why does she still sleep? If she is fine, why does she still sleep?" asked Roanda looking decidedly upset at that particular moment.

"My guess is that she is drunk. The amount of liquor used to cleanse the wound was a bit excessive now she must sleep it off." said Tanis with a laugh.

"Who would use liquor to cleanse a wound anyway? Isn't that the stuff of myth and legend? You, Tyris, come in here and explain yourself." said Roanda.

"I am Sasha and am not a Tyris. You and Meka should be proud parents. Your children acquitted themselves well. I poured the liquor because there was nothing else to use. As you can see, she will be just fine as soon as her hangover is over." said Sasha putting her back up and looking Roanda in the face eye to eye.

Tanis noticed the escalating situation and called out to the women, "Arlette appears to be coming to. She will tell you she is fine and then we all can get back to work."

"Where am I?" asked the groggy young smith. Looking around she looked at her brother and whispered to him loud enough that the whole room heard, "You got a girlfriend. I'm a going to tell Mom." Patting his face as he began blushing, she plopped back down into a deep sleep.

"Well, be wary of women with weapons." said Roanda as she walked away.

From behind her as she walked away, she heard, "What about you and Grandma and Aunt Meka? You all carry weapons."

Waving over her shoulder she went into the street and out to the walls.

CHAPTER FORTY-SEVEN

DARK THINGS COMING

Almedda sat on the back of a giant demon, watching as they marched toward the city of Metra and the town of Landsdale. She was hoping that the new strategy she was going to try was going to work. It was a close thing their last battle. Now that she could create the death dragons and the undead, she should be in good shape to defeat the stubborn peoples of the land of the light. She was asked to return to the tower by all of the dread lords hoping to get command of the army.

Almedda looked at the surrounding dread lords and she decided to teach them all a lesson. "I will return to the Dark Tower as you have all asked. I leave Morreal in charge until I decide that I need to return. As for the rest of you, you will hold to our battle plan. It will work at the steel town and will work at Metra. When both have fallen, I will return to enter into the cities and announce my presence."

Looking at the Lord Knight that had defected from the land of light, she smiled at him. "Someone please come and erect a tent for me. And you, Lord Knight, join me in the tent as soon as it is erected."

The other dread lords headed to their varying armies as the cries began from the tent. First in ecstasy and later in pain and ecstasy. The Dark Queen left the tent, climbed up on the waiting demon and called down. "Clean up that mess."

With that she was gone and Morreal looked at the dread lords remaining. "Get to work or you will all end like that man. Do you understand?"

Morreal was thinking how the woman had become the darkest soul she had ever met and was so proud. That woman was going to take over the lands of the light. She was aware of how powerful she was and of how to use that book. If Morreal could just get her hands on it for a moment she could graft it to her. As it was it only opened for the Queen, but if she could just get it for five minutes, she would be Queen and show them all a black heart.

She ordered the first wave of the army to begin its attack. She also ordered the engineers to build the tunnels under the town so that they could attack them from three sides at once. The whole thing was based on them not finding the tunnels and chamber being dug beneath them. She smiled just thinking of it.

The first wave of attack was the goblins, orcs, and spiders. It was a slaughter for the defenders at first until the Calvary and archers arrived. The horsemen were tearing through the creatures so badly that she almost felt sorry for them. The humans, elves, and dwarves were good. They had more troops coming to reinforce the people's army and Morreal smiled, it was working.

She was about to launch the second wave of the attack when she got word that the chambers below the town were revealed by the engineers and attacked the royal family. One was injured but the others had found a way around their magical protection. None were killed but their own. Morreal killed the messenger that had been forced to report this failure.

She reveled in the blood of the messenger and drank deeply of its corpse. She would be strong enough to fight the war ahead of her.

Morreal called the army back as she readied the second wave to attack. Looking at the mix of men and snakes and Metradon as well as Tetradon, she was sure this run would work better. These creatures had minds of their own and would follow orders and adapt if necessary. Sending the engineers again was worthless. The enemy was listening for the sounds of a tunnel being made so they would not be surprised again.

Morreal called for the goblins, orcs, spiders, men, Metradon, Tetradon, and snakes and sent them all forth. The armies of the light had quit the field for the night so they should be caught unawares. The men and orcs were killing the scouts that they found and no coded messages were getting through. They would find out about this wave when they lit their torches.

The army of the light had quit the field and was treating their wounded when word came that there was a lot of movement from the enemy army. Tanis went forth and checked the situation magically and smiled. They had sent creatures of the night to come and attack. Tanis ordered all of the archers to their posts without the fires going and stationed them all around the town.

The creatures of the dark moved closer and were about to light their torches when the bonfires of the armies of the light came on and arrows loosed into the enemy approaching. The armies of the light had prepared for this and now it showed as the archers came to bear and fired at point blank range killing many of their enemy at first blow.

The battle was brief but the blood shed by the armies of the dark showed that the armies of the light were ready. Tanis once more chased the remaining small band that was left back to the fields.

He got to the fields and called for a halt. Something was not right. Tanis sent out his magical vision and froze were he stood. The armies of the dark had been assembled around the army routing the smaller force.

Tanis ordered an immediate fall back. "Do not pursue them any farther. It is a trap! Back to the city now before they can spring it." But his words were too late. The trap was sprung as soon as they had touched the borders of the Fields of the Pheni. Demons and dragons that appeared to be undead surrounded them. Tanis let fly a large magical blast that killed many of the demons but more continued to come.

The dragons were unaffected by the blast and Tanis tried to attack them individually. With magical blade they were vulnerable, by magic alone they were immune. So many of the enemy's peoples were immune to magic. The shielding she was using was definitely being found by the grimoire. They had to destroy the book this time. Before another innocent young girl is turned into a necromancer.

Tanis was aided by the horsemen that had come to bear on the army of darkness and was lying about killing the undead dragons. It seemed to be going well when the dragons pulled their pieces back together. They looked at their attackers again and let loose their death magic. The few that had not been resuscitated were found to have been broken bones in the skulls and necks of the dragons. Many of the dragons tried to feed on the men and elves fighting against them after using their death stream, but all it did was cause the dead to fall to the floor and build up in piles.

Tanis noticed the trend and ordered the men, elves, and dwarves to go for the heads of their enemies. Soon the first wave of the undead was exhausted and the people of the light fell back to the castles and walls. The town was waiting for them and Tanis wanted to check and make sure he was clear on what was happening at the town.

Tanis was tired from the battle that had ensued and headed back to the town with the rest of the armies and saw that the town had lit a bonfire for them to follow. Maybe things were not as bad as it seemed.

CHAPTER FORTY-EIGHT

LYONSDALE

As Tanis came closer to Landsdale, he sensed that something was not right. He looked to each of his colleagues riding with him and looked again at the town. At his side was Artitous and a new lord just appointed by his wife. The young man had introduced himself as Roland Pikeman. Artitous took to him quick enough but, the man made Tanis nervous. They had ridden talking of meals and beer, but something was gnawing at the back of Tanis's skull. He called the column to a halt and looked at Artitous who was just speaking of a great venison or beef steak and had not been paying anyone any mind.

"Artitous, I feel something is not right. Those fires to welcome us for one. Torches I could see but bonfires. They look like watch fires. Lord Pikeman, this is your chance to show what you have. Go and inspect the town. Be discreet." said Tanis as he turned to the town once more. "We need no more heroes today."

Tanis watched the man ride away and summoned Martin. "Follow our friend. Make sure he does not get himself into mischief. Bring two hundred rangers with you just in case."

Martin bowed and ran off to collect his rangers and left, staying well behind Lord Pikeman. Tanis followed them for as long as his eyes could see, then he turned to Artitous who was disgruntled about not getting his dinner. "Old friend, something is not right here. It is too easy. Something should be happening out here. A party from the town should have come to greet us. Torlin setting off his fireworks. Something. I am getting worried."

"Worry not old friend. The town is probably fine. They are probably busy rebuilding from the attack. We left and they were hard at work maybe they still are." replied Artitous.

"That remains to be seen." said Tanis as he called the column to advance as slowly as they could. He would not be running into trouble again. The last time nearly left the army destroyed.

Martin came running back to Tanis. He was out of breath and wounded on the right arm. "The town has been razed. The people are all missing. Even the royals have been taken. Christof was not capable enough to have handled their defense this is all the rangers and my fault." Tanis came out of the saddle and walked to his friend and healed his arm.

"This is not on anyone but the Dark Queen. When I find out who she is she will suffer for her atrocities and those done in her name. We just have to capture her." said Tanis.

"The drow Queen sits at the top of the town's hill with all manner of creatures and men waiting for our army to return. We have runners checking Metra. We are hoping beyond hope that the people of Landsdale have found safety there." replied Martin.

"Then let her have that empty shell. She will not be able to raze the town to the ground with that magically endowed steel. We just have to get to Metra and hope for the best. Have your rangers break off the engagement and return to Metra immediately, we will do the same." said Tanis.

Before Martin could respond a ranger ran up to Tanis and Martin. Standing beside his commander, the ranger stood waiting for his commander to walk away from the rest to hear the report. "Tell us what you have found." said Martin to the man as he seemed to be anxious to get it off his chest.

"Metra is still ours they have not attacked it yet. And all of the people from Landsdale are safely inside. We just have to get to the city." said the guard.

"Make haste to Metra get the column moving again to Metra using the Lyonsdale road. It will steer us away from the enemy and allow us to collect and protect their people as well." said Tanis.

The army moved slowly as to not attract attention as they approached the town of Lyonsdale. They found the city was surrounded and they did not have a wall. Dwarves and elves were lined up around the town to keep the elderly and children safe. The giant spiders were snapping their jaws and the men of the enemy army were calling out insults and threats.

Tanis moved stealthily around the town with his much larger army and gave the order to light the torches and have the archers with arrows drawn. The enemy looked around them and saw the light. This gave them a little pause as they started moving toward the citizens of Lyonsdale.

Tanis gave the order to attack and the creatures were being killed quickly and efficiently by the men, dwarves, and elves. They caused a great rift as the people around the town fired their hunting bows and used their pitchforks to kill the enemy coming toward them. Tanis and Artitous began throwing magic around and found it strangely ineffective. Artitous started lifting rocks and tree branches and had them attack the enemy.

They had pretty well won the battle, when the trees started moving. Slowly like the wind had gotten a hold of the upper branches and then more and more the trees started to take steps with their roots. Artitous tried to stop the trees advance without damage to them but they were being controlled by someone in the town.

Artitous had called out to the druids in town and one came out to him. His eyes looking like that of a raccoon, and the dark robes he wore were covered in blood. "Best leave now, old man. We have the town well under control. Nothing to worry about but your own hides." He said as he shifted the trees closer. "Let's just say there is nothing to see here."

Artitous looked up at the advancing trees and muttered a spell under his breath. Slowly the trees stopped their advance. The druid in front of Artitous fell first to his knees and then to his face. Artitous smiled as the druid fell. Artitous looked the druid in the face. In sleep, he was no different than anyone else. He was tapping into evil and that was what was destroying him. With a wave of his hand the druid before him was severed from the power. They could not tolerate what Artitous thought merely legend, a dark druid, to remain a threat.

The power induced sleep wore off quickly and the man was back to his feet. He raised his hands and tried a fireball spell. The fact that the fireball never formed filled the druid with wonder. "What kind of shield is this? Neither of you hold the power yet magic cannot flow."

Several of his followers slowly backed away from the fight that was ensuing in the center of the town. Villagers grabbed them though and dragged them to Artitous. "These men too. They followed him, they did. The things they did were anything but beneficial to our town. Let them know your justice. For all of us." said a burly man who wore a leather apron and carried a hammer the size of Tanis's head.

"I think I can help there. Gentlemen, do you admit to us that you are followers of the man trying like mad to cast a spell? And if you do, you will show us where to find the rest of your evil brethren. We cannot have evil druids and wizards going in behind us to destroy the peace we are spreading. Speak men and I may allow you to keep your abilities." said Tanis.

"Why do we need to speak? You are going to condemn us anyway. Look what you did to Shan. Why should we do anything better than he did?" replied one of the captive druids.

"Do you speak for all of you? For if you do, then you will all end up severed from the power forever." asked Tanis.

Several of the druids started to discuss in the back of the circle that formed around them. Whispering and pointing here and there at several people and areas the druids came forward and lashed out with the power. The aim was at the people of the town and structures here and there. The spells formed then slowly fizzled. The druids tried and tried and soon realized that they had indeed been severed from the power. Some of them wept. Some tried suicide with the knives at their belts and yet others sat down and rocked on the floor.

The blacksmith that had spoken before looked at them and said, "These are broken men. What are we to do with them? It is inhumane to force them to live with this, do you agree?"

"Treat them as prisoners until I can arrange to have them come with us to be incarcerated in a deeper prison. You seem to be capable enough to keep seven prisoners." said Tanis.

"We have many prisoners and many more added after your rescue. We will find places for all of them and you will find them well-nourished and well cared for. That's our way. Your coming was indeed a blessing and we appreciate being out from under those men. The weaker in the power, the nastier they were. Several had forced our young women to couple with them. It was horrible. Now we are free." said the big man.

"You will hear from us soon. We move to Metra with all speed I would suggest grabbing your prisoners and follow us. They have already sacked Landsdale, and we do not want a repeat of that. So, get your important items and follow us." said Tanis.

"There may be nothing to return to but we will follow you, Tanis Thalin." said the blacksmith and as he turned, he lifted his hammer and aimed at the knight's chest. "I know this crest. He is as dark as these are. He hides it well though he is not a magical warrior so he cannot be told by his magic. But I have watched the extreme beatings and tortures he has inflicted on the people of this town."

Tanis magically pulled the man's helmet off his head and tossed it to the ground. "Is this the case, sir. Are you truly the commander of this group of magical folks?"

"I do not know what he is referring to, my lord." said the knight. "In fact, last time I was here I spent some quality time with some of the locals. Hehe, they have me confused with someone else. Do you not agree or do we need to have another chat after they leave you? I would hate for any of you to be falsely accused of things and executed at my word."

"Executions are handled by the throne, not the province. That should have been explained to you, Sir Pikeman. You have no real power here. Continue to Metra. I will work with the locals." said Tanis.

"He is a little over zealous don't you agree." said Artitous. "He must have felt that the man had done some very bad things."

"Nobleman are prone to over react to perceived threats and insults. Maybe the man did not bow deep enough for him. I do not know. But the man bears watching." said Tanis. *The spy you know becomes your agent.* Thought Tanis. He would remember that later. But for now, he would let him hang himself.

CHAPTER FORTY-NINE

TRIUMPHANT RETURNS

Lord Pikeman rode at full strut as they approached the city of Metra. He waved at the locals as they cheered for the incoming army. Christof was at the gates with Torlin, magically setting off fireworks and Garath was busy with Sasha. Arlette was standing on the walls laughing and waving. She was doing as much as her wounds would allow her.

Tanis noticed all this and fired off a few sparks off from his fingers. Everyone laughed at the sparks and Tanis kept them up for over an hour as they approached. When Lord Pikeman saw he was no longer center of attention he began doing tricks on his horse. Tanis quickly had him stopped but he would sneak one in every so often.

They had reached the palace when Lord Pikeman demanded a spot in the palace. "Torlin, this is your home. Will you take this man into it? Or shall I find him some room and board in the city. The inns of the town and the barracks available should house the entire army as well as the horses and supply wagons. Many a person has fled here it would appear trying to avoid the war. Roanda, how goes the stores of food and protective projectile weapons?" Tanis inquired.

"We look good at this time we will call the farmers from their fields when the enemy is coming. We have a resource for them to enter even under lockdown." She replied.

This statement perked up Lord Roland Pikeman's ears. If he could find this secret entrance, he could escape if he needed too. It could be a long siege. He did not want to have to starve to death with the peasants if he did not have too. He was nobility after all.

Peace ruled the city for several days and farmers came in bearing their food stuffs and tradesmen were hard at work producing the items to help in case of siege. Baskets were woven and steel weapons and utensils made. Armor was being made as well as all manner and form of clothing and buckets for the fire brigades. They were leaving nothing to chance.

The prisoners stood in their cells. Tanis had blindfolded them entering the city to ensure that anyone looking through the prisoners" eyes would not see anything. This would be a bit of a problem to the Dark Queen and her subordinates.

The blindfolds were released as soon as they had placed them into a dark and walled cell. It had only one opening toward the wall and it was sealed by a large iron door. The small window was all they could see out of their cells and it faced a wall. No reason to give them anyway to enter or find their colleagues.

Torlin looked at the cells and frowned. He had not used this room ever. He had hoped he would never have had too. This room was designed to hold the magical folk amongst the Tetradon. It had no other purpose than to contain the magical threat. The room had four cells built into it and they put all the magical folk from the village of Lyonsdale into the biggest on the west wall. They could be there comfortably until their fate was decided and they were sure there was no chance of them causing mischief.

Torlin turned on the lamps with a wave of his hand. He was not a butcher nor was he a torturer. He would allow them light and regular meals. He turned to the stairs and nearly ran over Sir Pikeman coming down. When Torlin saw him, he asked, "Why are you down here? We made sure that this place was secret. How did you find it?"

"I am to interrogate the prisoners. Tanis's orders. Hard interrogation to find out how much they knew of the enemy." said Roland.

"I am sure that is not true. It was him that ordered the secrecy in the first place and you were not privy to that conversation. You followed me, did you not?" asked Torlin.

"I am telling you I am to torture the prisoners into telling us all they know. No one else has the stomach for it. Tanis told me to do what I had to do." said Sir Pikeman.

"I think you are out of place, sir. I will not ask you again, join me to the palace where we can discuss why you are here." said Torlin turning his back on the knight. Torlin was about to turn around to see if he was following when he felt the dagger pierce his lower back. A moment later Torlin lost consciousness.

The last thing he remembered was the sounds of screaming.

Several hours later Torlin was discovered amongst a scene that horrified and sickened. Torlin showed a small amount of breath but he grew weaker the longer they sat there trying to get him off the floor and onto a stretcher. Tanis finally got him up and had him sent immediately to Artitous and the druids.

Tanis looked in the cell to see filleted men. They were totally removed from skin and bone. The magical folk had been ruthlessly and quite messily dissected and thrown all over the place. In the back corner of the cell lay Sir Roland. He rushed to him to check for wounds and found the man had his throat cut from behind. Tanis tried to find a pulse and felt none he was no longer breathing.

Tanis looked around for signs of who was responsible for these atrocities and finally gave up leaving the filth where it was. He could not take the smell any longer. His son needed him now. Ordering the druids to clean and examine the crime scene, he slowly marched his way to the Druid hospital and searched for Torlin.

Torlin, it turned out was back in the private suite behind the building. This was a retreat for the druids usually, but when royalty comes to them, they are treated there. Tanis and Torlin had tried to keep them from doing this, but apparently, it still was not working. The place was packed to the gills with Roanda and kids, Roanda's phoenix, Artitous, the druids, Athinina, and Tanis. Tanis looked down at the young man and asked for a status report. "My liege, he is still holding on. Barely, but he is. He is a fighter and we will bring him back. He has lost a lot of blood but I think we can save him. Good young man there. He is sleeping and we have put a half bottle of the local liquor in him so that should help too."

At the words liquor Arlette turned almost as red as her shirt was. She was still self-conscious about the incident in the smithy in Landsdale. She watched as her father was given glass after glass of the liquor and was embarrassed when he opened his eyes and looked at her for a brief moment. He knew what had happened and he had a laugh about it. Now he was going to be snookered and she could not help but laugh as he sipped the liquor.

Her dad was a caring man and she was afraid for him. The phoenix only cried for its user not for family it would appear from Roanda's constant argument with Janell, her phoenix. The family was going nuts and no one could believe any of it. Torlin woke for a moment and said one word, "Traitors."

Tanis left the room wondering who he meant. He would have to wait until the man was totally healed and on his feet. Artitous came out of the room and approached Tanis. A worry crossed his face as he went to him and started to explain that Torlin had been severely stabbed by a kris dagger. It was thrust deep almost penetrating all the way through Torlin. "Torlin is strong," said Artitous, "If anyone can pull out of this it is him. Especially with his wife standing there making all kinds of threats if he were to die. Christof is trying to knit the wound closed with magic and doing quite well. I told him he needed to be a druid."

"Christof is strong. He will do well by his uncle. The wound was that deep? Surely the assailant must have had his hand penetrate with the dagger. We find a bloody gauntlet or glove and we have our suspect." Tanis said looking down and worried. He felt a lot less confident than he was showing. Christof was a young man after all.

"What do you make of his word, Traitors? Do we know of any traitors?" asked Artitous and looked at Tanis as he slowly broke down and cried. "Is this my fault? Artitous please say that it was not hatred for me that leaves my son all but a corpse. I cannot suffer the loss of another family."

Artitous held Tanis as he broke down. The most powerful man on Dracos and he felt totally powerless. He would find the men that threatened him and his family and he would destroy them one at a time. Artitous tried speaking to Tanis but Tanis was not listening. Tanis could only think of the scene down in the dungeon and how his son could have been one of those filleted. Tanis was so grateful that his son was spared and he hoped they could cleanse and heal his wound.

Roanda came out and held Tanis, her phoenix resting on her shoulder. The phoenix saw the pain in Tanis and rubbed against him in a soothing manner. Tanis slowly gained his composure and asked Roanda if there was any news. "He seems to have cheated death yet again. We have got to keep a better eye on him. If he keeps up at this rate, he will be dead before he has grandchildren. He has no concern for his own safety. He does not travel with Tyris or any other guard. If he did this would not have happened. He will from now on and he will not complain about it." said Roanda as she too broke down to tears.

Seeing his daughter-in-law breaking down caused Tanis to break down again. The two sat together in their misery for a short while. The two people absorbed in their perceived loss. Christof came out and hugged his grandfather and aunt. "I have finished cleaning the wound of debris. The little pieces took forever. He is being finished by Artitous. We did not have any of the beetles or poisons this time at least. My mom had a bad case of those beetles, but Artitous got it cleaned up. Uncle Torlin is up and speaking as we finished our work on him."

Both of the grieving people ran to the room and pushed their way inside. Torlin looked still frail and weak, but at least he was awake. Tanis gingerly hugged the man and his wife kissed him deeply. "We have traitors amongst us." said Torlin. "We need to discuss this. For they killed the druids we had in custody as well as Sir Roland. It was Sir Roland that stabbed me. He was quite proud of his handiwork as the others followed him in. They noticed that my eyes were open and I was still breathing. They decided to leave me there and continued with their dirty work. After what seemed an eternity, they left. But before they did, they reprimanded the Lord Roland and grabbed him, dragging him into a cell and there I heard the sound of a gurgle and Lord Roland did not emerge with the others." said Torlin.

"Sir Roland is dead, is he not? I know that he was a traitor wanting to release the magical folk. But he still did not deserve this. The others' faces I do not recall. I was pretty much blacked out visually but I do remember their voices. That I will never forget. I need rest now. But we will solve this mystery." Finished Torlin.

"Set a watch around this house and especially on Torlin. If he does not do as instructed tie him down. He will remain a good patient or I will have words for him." said Roanda.

"I promise I will behave," said Torlin, "We will find the traitors."

"Be sure of that. Let us continue from here. You have done well." said Tanis, as he headed for the door. He told all the warriors there not to allow anyone into this building unless they are the druids tending him with Artitous, or they are of the royal family. "Do you understand your orders?"

The soldiers quickly agreed and Tanis headed into the building with Roanda at his side. "My Lord, I must be the one to avenge my husband's attack. When we find them, it will be me that takes them down."

"It is Tanis, and as for that you have a large army of people who would argue for that spot. I for one would allow you to have the trial and punishment, but your mother-in-law, she may have other plans." Laughed Tanis as he made a monster face at Roanda.

They walked on for a while longer headed back to the dungeon when they heard an alarm bell toll once. "That sounded like the alarm at the Healing House. But why did it stop so suddenly?" said Roanda, "If there was a problem it should continue to ring."

"Then let's go and see what the issue was. Hopefully a false alarm. I am not even sure I heard the bell." said Tanis as they headed back to the health hut. A second peal of the bell rang out and Tanis and Roanda went from a walk to a run. Running down the corridors to the entrance of the palace showed all of the guards gone from the entrance. Tanis said, "Roanda, stay here you and Janell should be able to hold the entrance until reinforcements arrive. I will go and check the health house and see what is going on."

Roanda drew her weapons and stood in the great door way with her phoenix in flight hovering above her. The image was one of no-nonsense and inspiration. Tanis continued to run and finally made it to the house. It seemed to take forever to get there but he finally arrived to see two dead druids on the porch. The first lay on his back with a dagger in his chest the other had the cord to the bell wrapped around his neck, he and the bell were solidly planted into the ground.

Tanis jumped over the rail and ran into the building. Several guards and Christof, Garath, Arlette, Garren and Meka all stood fighting a large party of what appeared to be black robed soldiers. Meka called out just as Tanis was about to strike that the creatures were Mardocks. Not quite alive anymore, but not quite dead, the Mardocks were called wizard killers due to the fact that magic had no effect on them. Soldiers touching them found themselves burned or the limb frozen.

The Mardocks attacked again and Meka blocked the advance. Looking to his side he saw Sasha come and hand him a vial of black liqueur. Tanis look at her quizzically and she pointed to throw the liquor onto the Mardocks. Tanis getting the hint threw the bottle onto the advancing monsters and Sasha shot a fire arrow into the liquor. Instantly, the Mardocks burst into flame and turned to face their new attackers. Two stripped the robes they wore and came at them in just their black armor and helmets. Tanis lifted a half dozen discarded arrows upon a wave of air and flung them into the advancing creatures. The creatures went down and Tanis drew the Warmonger. "We are not done. There is more coming." said Tanis as a large fireball erupted from the palace gate. "Stay here. Christof did you see what I did? Do it again if they try another attack."

Tanis ran as fast as he could to the gates of the palace to find a large group of green armored creatures at the gates attacking Roanda. Janell was burning them to death a wave at a time and those that are missed by the fire came to face Roanda. Tanis lay into them with

Warmonger from behind and Janell readjusted her aim after setting fire to Tanis's cloak.

"Hey! Pay attention there, Janell." said Tanis stomping on his cloak. Seconds later the two were attacking the green armored creatures again. One finally turned and sent the back wave up against Tanis. He looked at them and recognized Metradon and Tetradon firing their beam weapons and Roanda dodging back and forth. She had miraculously avoided injury but was getting tired as was Janell.

Tanis let fly a spell that acted like a filament that went around most of the necks in the gates except Roanda and Janell. Tanis pulled the spell taut and the heads of the creatures popped off. Several lifted their weapons not yet aware that they were dead, but fell as they did.

"Alright Roanda? That should do for these creatures. What happened? Where did they come from? They would have had to pass the healing house to get here but I did not see them." said Tanis as Meka ran up to Tanis. "What are you doing here? Are you not watching your brother-in-law?"

"That is why I am here. Torlin is acting weird and it was requested by Artitous that you return to the healing house. I will remain with Roanda. We and our Phoenix will stand guard here. You must help Torlin." said Meka. As Tanis turned to return to the health house, he noticed the shimmer in Meka's cloak. Turning again quickly he struck down the figure before him. Roanda screamed at him as the woman before her fell.

Roanda stopped screaming when she saw the snake tail grow from beneath the cloak. "It was a Naga." Tanis said. "It would have tried to kill us both when I turned but I saw its illusion shift when she turned."

The creature finally stopped moving. Looking like a scaled woman with a snake's tail instead of legs, the Naga could take on the forms of other creatures and people. Tanis looked down at the creature and wondered where she had gotten into the city. As Meka, she could have gone anywhere in the city. This was troubling.

Tanis walked back to the health House to check on the situation there. Christof was sitting down nursing his arm, while Meka tried to soothe him and get him to let her look at it. All present there were either wounded or dead. The guards had been laid out in state as it were and Arlette looked like a bloody mess. She smiled at her grandfather and let the druid before her continue their work. She had suffered some leg wounds. All of the defenders that lived had minor bumps and cuts. The rest were dead laid out on the porch. The attackers had fought to the last man. That was if you could call them men. The phoenix attached to Meka floated around the room, watching the people below and ready to attack should the need arise.

Tanis saw Torlin laying there on the bed and he appeared to have fallen back to unconsciousness. Tanis rushed to his bedside and felt his hands. Torlin opened his eyes and smiled at his father. "My father. I am well was just taking a nap as I was not allowed to assist in the destruction of the attackers. I honestly would have been in the way anyway. Someone has a book of the darkest magic. Only they contain the means of creating these creatures. Some call them the soulless. I call them misunderstood prisoners turned assassins by an extremely evil necromancer. The Dark Queen should suit that particular benchmark, wouldn't you say."

"The Dark Queen has started using the full power of the grimoire. It will soon consume her and cause the necromancer to mentally change forever to Elizarade. Then we will not have the ability to defeat the armies she will send at us. First, we have to find the tunnels the enemy has used to enter the city. Their engineers have worked fast and hard to produce these tunnels, I am sure." said Tanis.

"The tunnels are of my doing, Father. As I was rebuilding, I had several of them made to act as last-ditch efforts to leave the city." said Torlin.

"How many of these tunnels are there, son? You do realize they work both ways." said a nervous Tanis.

"Only a few I assure you." replied Torlin as he looked down at his feet. "How many are a few?" asked Tanis.

"Two hundred from the various sections of the city and thirty from the palace. Not that many." said Torlin with a smile.

"Two hundred and thirty tunnels. How are we going to stop two hundred and thirty tunnels?" asked Tanis.

"Father, they have all got one-way doors and false starts and endings. They would drive anything that may have gotten in that way mad. It is a major labyrinth down there." said Torlin.

"We are getting attacked by groups that are just popping up. They have to be using the tunnels below our feet." said Tanis. And if to punctuate his point a dark dressed head peeked up from an area near the door. He was still in the tunnel but his head was sticking out. Tanis just pointed and shrugged his shoulders.

"We can fix that. I swear. Someone, please kill the wizard killer there. I do not wish to deal with another run of them." Torlin said as he tried to get out of his bed and was put right back with just a look from his wife. Tanis swung the Warmonger and the man's head came right off and landed in the bucket next to the door.

The others prepared for the onslaught but it never came. Looking at one another, they crept to the top of the tunnel. Looking down the defenders saw a sight that lightened the mood for them all. The man that had died at the top of the ladder had fallen on the rest of his colleagues and cause many to fall on swords or daggers. Others were accidentally skewered by falling companions. One survived and he went to the ladder to make his attempt and the ladder started rising from the base of the tunnel.

Christof looked around and around and whistled as the ladder landed on the floor. The man at the bottom of the tunnel jumped and scraped air and dirt trying to climb to the tunnel entrance. He kept attempting until Martin came in and shot the man in the forehead with his bow.

"About time you got here, Martin. Where is my wife?" asked Tanis.

"Behind you, my love. I swear you could be snuck up on by a herd of elephants. Next time try and pay better attention." said Athinina.

"But my dear that is what I have him for." said Tanis, looking at Martin who just shrugged his shoulders.

"Well, I have a child to bed and his wife ready to skin him, we are missing one child, but his wife is here. We have the young ones both here and it would appear at least one boy and one grandchild have found pretty little things for their arms. Of course, ladies, if anyone else calls you that, you have my permission to skin them alive and stake them over anthills. We have quite the family tree here. Now where is my wayward son?" said the Queen of Dracos.

As if on cue, Thomas smashed through the door swinging wildly at the men in front of him killing one and barely dodging another. The rest of them jumped in to assist and soon the enemy all lay dead at the Thalin family's feet.

"What took you so long?" was all Thomas said as he went to his wife and son.

CHAPTER FIFTY

THE DREAD QUEEN

Almedda looked out the tower window looking at her realm. She was liking more and more the things she saw. The orcs and goblins working together to build the weapons of war she would soon need. The newest member of her crew was the Mardocks. Mardocks the souls sucked from their bodies and the body left to be used by the power she possessed. She enjoyed the process because of the utter pain her captives went through.

As Almedda she could never have this kind of pleasure. But as the Dark Queen she was free to use whatever powers she saw fit. She went into the chambers used for the creation of the Mardocks. In the room several prisoners sat huddled in a group in the corner. *Her orcs had done well,* Sighed Almedda. These prisoners were the best batch yet. The orcs had captured a family. The man and his wife were perfect. The children gave her an unscrupulous idea. No one would suspect them as being assassins. She would have to ponder on how she would use the children.

Almedda went to the man and grabbed him in a flow of air. As she floated him to the table, she would use to work on the family she taunted the man. "This will be excruciating. Feel free to scream and holler." said Almedda as she sat him down on the operating table. Her orcs and goblins quickly bound the man's hands and feet and left the rest free to move.

Almedda went to the head of the man and looked at the family in the corner. "Come watch this woman, or I will make you watch your entire family go through this. You will all be immune to magic and with the new armor and weapons we have produced you will be safe until you start to fall apart. That can take several months even a year or two. Now get over here and watch your husband."

As the woman approach Almedda began to pull the soul from the man. The man tried to resist the urge to cry out but soon he was screaming and yelling. He was not screaming at Almedda though. He was screaming to his wife and children how much he loved them. These words seemed to perk up his family and once more he went silent. Though his body convulsed, he would not give her the screams of pain and the begging for it to be over.

Almedda completed the process and the woman collapsed in fear and grief. The woman's pain was almost intoxicating to Almedda. It was so deep and despairing that she almost fell onto a chair and just drank it in. After a while the woman regained her composure and went to her children.

Almedda had the orcs bring the oldest of the three children, a boy of thirteen, and had him replace his father on the table. Once more the woman begged and pleaded for her son. Almedda drank in the pain the woman was feeling and was again forced to sit until the wave of pleasure she was receiving past.

The woman sat at the foot of the table with her hands on her boy's bound hands. She was inconsolable, every look at the table and at her husband's soulless body made her tears that more intense. Almedda had the boy released from the table and brought the husband back to the table. He would be converted entirely and see the response then.

Almedda passed her hands over the husband's body uttering necromancy so vile it almost dripped from Almedda's mouth. After a moment the body began to move, and the man looked around. Almedda pushed the necromancy and he once more went into a state of pain. The wife screamed at her to make it stop.

"You do not get to tell me when to stop. Nor when and how you will all be transformed. That is in my hands. See your husband lives but he knows none of you and will do exactly as I tell him. Let me show you. Mardock, bring me the youngest of the children. See he is a good soldier and does as he is told. Mardock lay her out on the table and restrain this woman." said Almedda.

The Mardock that was once her husband set the child on the table and grabbed the woman into his arms. The arms were stronger now the woman noticed but the eyes were empty. Her husband was no more yet she tried to speak to the thing holding her, "Please, my husband. Save the children and me from this fate. I am sure you can. Just do not let this thing happen to all of us."

The tears and begging fell on deaf ears and the woman collapsed from the grief and pain. She barely heard the screams from the child as she had been begging him to help. She finally heard the screaming and saw the youngest, a six-year-old boy, sitting on the edge of the table with the same blank look of his father. The boy was gone and she had missed it. The mother wept for her son and Almedda felt the heart of the mother break in her.

"Boy Mardock, get your oldest brother." said Almedda.

The young man was waiting for the youngest boy, and tried to fight him off. The older boy seemed to be winning until the younger boy slipped from his brother's grasp and wrestled him to the ground. The two boys rolled around on the ground each trying to outfight and out wrestle the other. The middle girl jumped into the pile again trying to help the oldest son. The weight of the ten-year-old hit the oldest brother and he collapsed with a groan.

Looking up he smiled at his sister and the two ganged up on the Mardock boy. It looked again as if the two elder siblings had gotten the upper hand when the boy again slipped from their grasp and grabbed the girl by the neck. "Kill them, Mardock. Bring them to me." said Almedda.

Almedda thought that the woman would die of grief when first her oldest and then her daughter joined the ranks of her mindless, soulless and pitiless murders. The woman was then stretched out onto the table and looked down at the mother. "I have something even better for you. This is going to be good."

CHAPTER FIFTY-ONE

THE UNQUESTIONABLE

Once more peace was ruling the three cities. The armies of the dark had retired back to the locked gates of the Dark Lands. Tanis wished they would never see them again, but he knew this was merely a recovery time for both armies. The Dark Queen had to be found and her powers bound. The assaults were getting more targeted and more deadly. He spent days wondering what the woman was going to send next.

They had tried to interrogate some of the creatures of human or near human intelligence and all perished rather messily when they tried to reveal anything. Even human officers who tried not to speak of her but write it down found themselves again deceased in a rather sticky manner.

Tanis checked the prisoners for the spells that might cause this and found nothing. Looking around he saw nothing environmentally that could be sending signals to the Queen of the Dark Lands. It was a mystery. Even when they were told to simply shake their heads if the information was correct, the punishment was the same when they tried to reveal anything from the Dark Lands.

One prisoner got the gumption and said a few words before the curses destroyed him. "Check the royals…" was all he got out before he was dead and in a mess on the floor.

Tanis asked Artitous, "What does he mean, check the royals? Does he suspect one of the kids of being an agent of the Dark Lands? I know that I for one have not even been in the Dark Lands. Neither has my wife. The oldest two have their hands full as it is with their children. The youngest batch of the children was now only Garren. He was still upset about the loss of his sister to that group and would not have anything to do with them."

"The grandchildren would have nothing to gain by such an alliance, so who is our traitor?" Finished Tanis.

"We shall see, my old friend we shall see." said Artitous.

Tanis was pondering the man's words when the next prisoner was brought in to be interrogated. Tanis was out behind the building and saw Oswalt, the druid, looking into the window behind the building. "I wish I could find out what is happening to our prisoners. It is driving me crazy. We have to be able to find out something."

"Did you say something, my liege? I was delving the prisoner. I cannot find the string that she has placed in them. It has to be there. It is maddening." said Oswalt as he started to walk away. Tanis stopped him and asked him what he was referring to.

"Majesty, I have found a dark thread from the prisoners going somewhere close. It is a magical thread so it jumps and twists. I have followed it as far as I can but cannot find the origin. It would have to be a magical being that controls the thread." said Oswalt.

"You have made a great discovery then. But why not track it from within the dungeon? Why linger at windows?" asked Tanis.

"The thread does not show up inside for some reason delve the prisoner and you will see the thread from here. Apparently, the threads do not need to be managed, they can be set and left." Answered Oswalt as he once more attempted to leave.

Tanis delved the man in the middle of the room in front of him and saw the fine filament coming off his head. Tanis turned around to ask more questions of Oswalt but could not see the man. He was tired of having people do that. He looked around and followed the string right to the healing houses in the middle of Metra.

Thomas, Meka, and Christof had left two weeks ago to tend to Tetra and his wife was gone back to Thalinburg. She had taken Garren with her and his new lady friend went along. Gardell had asked to be assigned to the man's protective detail. Garren's mother was ever so happy to comply with the request. So, he headed home with Gardell at his side and the phoenix floating above them. Hetrick had yet to say anything to Garren but was in constant conversation with Gardell.

Hetrick was alone one day on a section of the wall and Garren was sitting there with him waiting for the return of Gardell. Hetrick looked the man in the eyes and said, "She wants you to kiss her you know."

"Have you met her? If I try, I will have a dagger in my ribs." said Garren.

"Maybe. But I know Gardell. She may stab but she will return the kiss." said Hetrick.

"But how do you, I mean, how do I, I have no experience how. I mean." Rambled Garren and Hetrick moved to be behind the prince as Gardell returned.

"You will thank me later." said the phoenix as he shoved them together and his lips landed on those of Gardell in front of him. He let it linger a moment then pulled back looking ashamed and startled. Gardell walked up to him and said, "This is how you do it."

She reached up and pulled the man to her and kissed him deeply. Garren felt the passions rising in him and pressed back into the kiss. Neither of them noticed that Athinina had walked up to the pair. "So should I prepare for another wedding?"

Garren jumped and tried to set his clothes back to right and she just grinned like a Cheshire cat. "My lady, I would very glad to have you plan our nuptials. That is if the groom can stop blushing long enough to agree." said Gardell. Hetrick was sitting on a roof nearby laughing.

"What are you laughing at you oversized turkey?" smiled Garren as he went to his mother and Gardell, his face slowly becoming less red and more normal.

"Told you." Laughed as the phoenix took off and landed on Gardell's shoulder.

"And what did you tell him?" asked Gardell.

Hetrick just smiled and snuggled into Gardell's neck where the phoenix was accustomed to sleeping. All eyes turned onto Garren who just said, "I do not kiss and tell." And walked away with Gardell hand in hand.

CHAPTER FIFTY-TWO

ANOTHER ROYAL WEDDING

Athinina thought that waiting for the entire family to be told of the wedding and waiting for them all to arrive at Thalinburg was a bit unrealistic but Gardell insisted. She was an only child and her parents long dead.

Garren on the other hand, had sisters and brothers and parents who should be there. She even left a chair at the main table for his long dead sister. Garren laughed that Almedda would have been laughing at Garren's difficulty with public displays of affection. He would take Gardell into a private space to kiss her. He just was not into showing what he had and being watched.

All too soon the family was together, and the wedding progressed. Athinina laughed at the dumbfounded Pan Thor when asked to walk Gardell down the aisle. Garren enjoyed the attention from his nephews and brothers. Garren received his first broadsword as he prepared for his wedding. Tanis came in and presented the man a sword he had made by the local smith. It was made of elvish steel and forged by a dwarven smith. The combination was a sword of such nicety and such craftsmanship that it even seemed able to slice the air around him. He swung it and put it through its paces and sheathed the blade.

Garren hugged his father and he hugged him back. All of his children were now old enough and competent enough to be on their own and married. How did that happen? He could not help but think back to Charina and Paul. The young man would have been about forty by now. He could not help but wonder what path he would have taken.

Paul was as affectionate as Garren was. Garren would be a great father. It was strange to think of the boy as a twenty-two-year-old when just yesterday he was helping him on to his first horse. The children had grown up quick. Torlin was complaining at thirty-eight that he was getting grey hair in his beard and on his head. Thomas just grumbled when Meka would tease him about his premature grey. Tanis still had no grey hair. He looked the same as he did when he was twenty. His wife would laugh and ask him to dye his hair for her so she would not look like a gold digger.

Garren set the sword into the scabbard and headed for the door with head held high. He was definitely ready. Tanis went and sat on the dais next to his wife and kissed her hand. Not that much later came Gardell. She was wearing a dress of dwarven lace coupled with elven jewels. The mix of cultures due to Tanis's rule had brought about some of the best work of all kinds. Metalwork was at a premium and the best ever done. Magical items were the strongest in memory and jewelry and clothing styles had no match.

The white deep ruffles on the shirt and delicate lace upon her breast were enough to stop a man's heart and Garren's jaw had dropped. Tanis lifted his son's lower jaw and told him, "Stay focused. You do not want to drool on her dress now do you?"

"I never imagined this. This cannot be happening to me, can it?" asked Garren.

"Be silent now, love. Let's get this finished so we can retire for the wedding night." said Gardell with a wink.

Garren turned beet red as he turned to his mother and the ceremony began. The ceremony had just begun when a dark cloud formed over the crowd in the audience and a voice said, "We come for you all." And lightning dropped from the cloud. Tanis, Garath, and Christof cleaned up the cloud and saved the day once more.

Gardell looked amazed and Garren just stood there his head down. Tanis came back and told them, "This is mild compared to most of our weddings in this family. Remind me to tell you all about them"

Garren just groaned and Gardell laughed as the Queen pronounced them man and wife and directed them to kiss one another. The Queen looked over at Tanis and handed the newlyweds a whistle. "Let's just say that things get interesting on wedding nights around here. Use this if you need help with any dangers. And I mean dangers other than your wife. Now let us feast and embarrass the newlyweds as much as we can."

Once more Garren groaned.

CHAPTER FIFTY-THREE

MORE INTERRUPTED NUPTIALS

Garren headed to the suite set aside for him and his new bride with Hetrick and Gardell in tow. The two laughed at each other and together. They reached the door and a perch had been arranged for Hetrick. "I suppose I get to stay out here?" said the phoenix as the two lovers went inside and closed the door.

At a little past midnight, the whistle blast sent all of the guard into the room with swords drawn and Hetrick with her powers swelling. Garren lay on the ground grasping his arm and rolling in pain on the ground. The head of the guard was Paul Alon the son of Perrick and good friend of Garren. Seeing his friend on the floor naked and in desperate pain, Paul covered both of the newlyweds and brought them quickly to Artitous.

"What happened? You stab him already?" asked Artitous.

"Not yet, but he was with me and then he flung from the bed and landed on the floor screaming as if he had been stabbed. Of course, he had no wound as you can see, but he complains it is a knife through the arm." said Gardell.

"The pain seems to have dissipated. I am sorry. I do not know what happened. One moment I was fine the next I was in excruciating pain, then once more, fine. I must be going mental." said Garren.

Artitous looked him over and delved him for magic. It was then he saw the two cables coming from him. Magically he was connected to an evil that had turned its life force black. The life source from him was purest white and he seemed to be the life end of the connection. Artitous tried to remove the two life forces and failed with Garren suddenly going into convulsions. "Whatever you are doing stop. I do not wish to be a widow on my wedding night." said Gardell.

"I agree we must watch this. The cords of this life force are so thick I do not know how we missed it before. He is the life force behind a link with a dark evil character a necromancer or dark wizard. They will not be able to be harmed and definitely unkillable. Not with Garren alive." said Artitous.

"Can we reverse this? Surely, we do not want anyone connected in any way to us, right?" asked Gardell. She looked down at her husband and smiled as he struggled to dress himself. Garren was blushing from ear to ear. He looked around and his face flushed even more if that was possible. The convulsions had stopped and he said he was feeling fine.

"We can see if we can find this thing that has latched itself to your husband but you will have to trust me. Do you trust me, Garren?" asked Artitous.

"With my life, sir. Do what you must." said Garren feeling a lot less courageous than he showed.

"Then let us begin. I will try to get the other party to pull the attachment." said Artitous.

"How?" asked Gardell, looking kind of skeptically at the druid.

"Why we are going to kill him, of course." said Artitous

Artitous drew his dagger and set it on the bedside and took hold of Garren. He once more delved the cables of power flowing to him and he gently slipped the dagger between the cable and Garren's skin. "The dagger is magically warded to affect all magical flows and creatures. I just making it to the other being as if Garren is being killed. It should cause them to withdraw the bond between them."

"So, this is supposed to make the other person believe he is dying and withdraw their connection. What if it does not work?" asked Gardell.

"We can only hope that this works." said Artitous as he once more delved the man before him and saw that the white flow was gone and the dark side was almost totally severed. "It is working. The flows are reversing. We can only hope to hold on to the life force."

Delving again he found the connections both gone. "He is free of the connections but we will have to watch to make sure they do not try again. I fear that the connection can be used to spy upon us if it is reconnected. For now, we wait and watch."

A druid walked into the room and whispered that a druid named Barrish had been stabbed in the arm earlier in the evening and had just fainted. He needed the arch druid to heal him.

Artitous left quickly followed by Tanis and Gardell. Hetrick followed quickly after the pair and the end of the line was Garren trying to get his clothes on as he ran. He begged from behind to wait for him but the others had gotten way out of view of the prince.

After standing and waiting for someone to poke their heads around the corner looking for him, Garren moved to the cross path and the scene that he beheld was one of chaos. Druids ran around looking at the man, Barrish, while others assisted Artitous. The rest had started to form the magical circle to bind the powers of the man, for he had obviously been the one connected to Garren.

No one noticed the druid slinking away from the scene holding a wounded arm and was visibly shaken. Garren spotted him and followed slowly behind. He saw the man enter the houses of healing and he watched from the window as he was treated for his wounds and he heard the phrase killing the royal family repeated multiple times.

Garren had heard enough and headed back to the corridor to let his father and Artitous know of the plot by the group of druids there. As he stepped slowly away from the healing house, he stepped on the tail of one of the cats that frequented the area. The cat let out a howl and Garren ran for all he was worth.

Fear held the boy as he returned to the corridors. He grabbed his father and was practically shouting at him the scene that he has seen in the house. Tanis tried to calm the man but he would not listen, he was determined to get that hive of evil magical folk. He was about to run back to the hut but found that he had forgotten his sword. Running back to his suite he recovered the blade just as a dark cloaked figure entered the room and locked the door.

"You have made a very grave mistake. You should not have been eavesdropping at the window. You realize that we are going to have to silence you. But before we do, how many men did you see in the hut? Tell me true and I may leave one of your family alive. Lie to me and they all die." said the dark cloaked figure.

"You know what I saw and as for killing my family, you have no intentions of leaving any of us alive." said Garren, as he eased the sword in its scabbard.

"You do not amuse me. Tell me how much you heard and what you told your meddlesome father and his friend. Do so now or I will destroy you where you stand." said the figure. The figure turned to check on the lock and turned to see Garren's new blade aimed at his throat.

"Now it is I who will have answers. Such as who linked to me and why?" said Garren.

"Look he has a training pig stick…" the figure was saying as Garren pushed a little and the blade went through the dark figure's neck. He was oblivious of the pounding at the door as he tried to place the man. Hearing the door, he pulled it open just as two guards were about to knock it down.

Gardell walked in and saw the figure on the floor and Tanis rushed in and drew Warmonger. They were all prepared to defend Garren when they saw he had taken care of his own problem. Tanis looked at the sword Garren had across his shoulders and smiled. It had served him well.

"Do you have any calm weddings in your family?" laughed Gardell as she looked down at the mess on the floor. Garath and Sasha came in and Sasha gasped. Leaning over she pulled back the creatures' cloak to reveal a creature that looked like a black colored bear faced man.

"That is a Bearman. I have seen these at the meeting that hired the assassins. Garren you are lucky to be alive. These things are amongst the deadliest of the assassins. They are usually reserved for assassins that have failed in their missions. That Bearman was probably sent for me. For I have joined you instead of following my orders." said Sasha, "And I regret nothing Garath. Especially not meeting you."

"So, when will we be hearing your wedding bells Sasha?" asked Gardell as if the assassin laying on the floor was nothing but a rug.

"When he is old enough to shave, I would wager." said Sasha laughing as Garath sputtered.

"I shave." said Garath almost pouting, "Well, I do."

The room exploded in laughter and the people searched for tunnels and other means of entrance to the city. Chatting about weddings and wedding nights. Tanis let it be known that his first marriage started the ball rolling on bad luck. Everyone laughed as he gave over details from his own disastrous weddings. Stories of spiders wrecking the night or Torlin saying that the Metradon had done for his, and yet Thomas spoke of his wife trying to kill him. No one had seen Thomas come in, but he seemed to be in a talkative mood. Meka asked, "How long have you known?"

"How could I not know? I was trying to sleep when you drew that dagger of yours." Smiled Thomas.

Meka walked over and gave him a short punch to the ribs, smiling as he grunted. "Guess I deserved that one." said Thomas as the people again became engrossed in the Bearman.

Meka opened the cloak and check his pockets and pouches. In the pouches they found black powder that Artitous took and set on the window sill. "I'll deal with these." said Artitous.

"I have got his correspondence," said little Arlette. She sat on the bed and began to read. "These are descriptions and summaries of our skills and lack thereof. This one appears to have come from the Dark Queen herself.

She wiped her eyes and a bloody tear rested on her hand. Artitous grabbed the letter and waved a sigil over the girl. Just as fast as it had started it was gone. Arlette asked what that was. Artitous answered, "A cursed document meant to kill those that read it. If it was not intended for you. Such as you reading the Bearman's mail."

"I have really got to keep all of you near me. I am my own worst enemy. I can finally forge again, and I nearly kill myself with a letter. Sheesh." said Arlette.

"We all need to work together. And help each other. Christof, we will teach you the magic dismissal sigil as well as to your uncle. Arlette we will need your expertise on weapons and armor. And Torlin and Thomas you have cities to run and I fear this is a precursor to what is to come. We all need to go to our separate cities and prepare for the coming storm. Garren and Gardell, you will be ruling in Landsdale now. Help them and guide their rebuilding efforts and then build up your defenses. You are the first avenue of defense. All of you be well. We will plan on your departures in the morning. Many of you have only a day's ride some have half a day. Let us get some rest and go to our homes to prepare." said Tanis.

"Could not have said it better myself, my husband. But when were you going to tell me of the threat to our family in general and our lands as a whole?" asked the just arriving Athinina. "Looks like a Bearman snuck in. Who killed it?"

"Your son, your majesty." said Tanis, "My new sword for him has worked wonders. He should be ready for the next time now."

"There should be no next time would you not agree." said a concerned Garren. "Our family and our lands will hold, my lady."

"Let us hope. Let us hope." said Athinina.

CHAPTER FIFTY-FOUR

THOUGHTS OF WAR AND MURDER

Almedda reeled from the spell snapping back at her. The boy was smarter than he looked. Several of her druids had set the bond in place and had suffered from her test, but that was fine. They would get over it. She knew the magic worked but her brother was clever and had Artitous to check him over.

She would have to destroy Tanis and Artitous if this was to succeed. The Bearman sent after the traitor, Sasha, had not returned with her head yet, which told her that they too had failed in their quests. Her druids reported back that the Bearman were all dead.

Again, it was Tanis and Garren. Garren turned into some sort of swordsman since she had seen him last. She sat and pondered for a moment or two and then summoned two of the best swordsmen in her army. They both were heron marked weapons masters. Heron marked weapons masters were the best of the best. These two had earned it and then thought they should rule instead of the current royal family. The battle when they joined her was fierce. No one would have noticed that they had disappeared. The rest of the army of the light were withdrawing. The dark land army continued to lose despite the larger and stronger warriors.

True the land of the light had more heron marked weapons masters, and they were leading the great army of the Thalins. She should have the herons teach the rest to fight. That would even the odds. The weapons masters came in and sauntered up to the dais. "You two have a special mission. You are to hunt down my brother and destroy him." said the Queen of the Dark Lands.

"Which one?" asked the nearest weapons master?

"Garren. If you can kill Torlin and Thomas while there have at it. But kill Garren and return. I need you for another task after you have completed this." said Almedda.

"It will only take one of us let one of us stay and start your other project, while the other goes and does the butcher's work. It would be a waste to send both of us." said the man.

"I said both of you. Do not underestimate these people. My brother moves to Landsdale. Kill him quickly and return. His wife is a Tyris. You may have to deal with a phoenix as well. Do not take this task lightly." said Athinina.

"We apologize but a Tyris. We deal with them every day in the fields. They are but a nuisance. The phoenix will be a challenge if it gets involved but the man can be caught alone." said one of the assassins.

"They are newlyweds. How many times will they leave each other to do much of anything? You will have to kill them both. But just get it done. Now go." said Almedda. Turning she ordered another of the prisoners be brought to her chambers. She was turning into a great praying mantis. She would soon be with child and her succession will be complete. She liked to kill those she copulated with, which made it difficult to find potential mates. The prisoners made great lovers for as long as they lasted anyway.

She had her fun and the bloody mess that remained of her current mate was being removed from her rooms. She looked at the mess and wondered why she could not become with child. She must have had at least twenty lovers so far and none of them got her pregnant. She would have one of the druids check her over. Make sure she was doing things right.

She walked out onto the parapet and Carlee flew to her. "How is my Queen today?"

"Trying to become pregnant. And it is not working. What am I doing wrong?" asked Almedda.

"Have you asked the druids about this?" said Carlee.

"Not yet but what will they say? That I am barren? If they do, I will lash out and probably kill one or two. I do not have enough men and druids left to randomly kill one or two. I need them for my army." said Almedda.

"Self-control is sometimes the best avenue a ruler may have. You look at your predecessor. She would not control herself and the grimoire destroyed her. You are different. You are using your power well. Continue and you will have the people bringing you children to pick from if you do not have one of your own. Keep the faith and keep trying." Carlee said as she flew away to do whatever it was, she did.

Almedda wondered what the bird did when it flew from her. It had a tendency to say something intriguing and then disappearing on her. She usually came back with blood on her wings so she must be eating. *She never shares with me*, thought Almedda. The phoenix would be gone for an hour or two, and then come back and roost on her shoulder. The bird usually fell asleep when she returned.

Almedda went inside the tower to ponder the situation while Carlee hunted.

Carlee flew from the Queen and headed to the army. Three men had deserted from the light's army and now Carlee was checking them over. "What do you want? We can see you are alone and weaponless. None of you possess magic. So, speak, why did you come to us?"

"We wish to be on the winning side of this conflict so maybe I can live in peace with the children and wife. These others wish the same." said one of the men. The others quickly agreed with the man that had spoken. Carlee lifted off and was about to leave when she slammed into the man who spoke and tore out his throat. "Let this be your answer. Feed the rest of the army with my leftovers."

The men fell to their knees begging for mercy as the creatures of the army arranged themselves and prepared for dinner. One man produced a small knife that he kept hidden about his person and was quickly disarmed and brought to the creatures who would be eating him.

The other just cried as the animals of the army of the dark lay into him. Before long there remained only the smallest slivers of bone to show that they had existed. A Bearman reached down and grabbed one of the slivers and began to clean his teeth. They were eating well as of late. Carlee was indeed a great second in command.

Carlee led from their stomachs. Almedda ruled through terror. The later proved to be more effective than the first but both won loyalty. The human was prone to using the men before she slaughtered them and sent them to the creatures. The creatures enjoyed the tearing apart and eating the meals. Especially the spiders. Morreal was to bring out the army once more at order of the Queen. The guard she had with her were the only soldiers not to go this time. The army of the light would be destroyed this time.

Morreal saw the weapons masters leaving and headed for Landsdale, she smiled. The best of the soldiers with her were going to kill the people of Landsdale. She could pass on the city of steel. There were bigger and more important targets for her to destroy.

It was just after noon when the army was in sight of the city of Metra. The surrounding lands had seen them coming obviously as the city was ready for the coming siege. Morreal ordered the spiders and Naga to go up the walls and destroy the archers. She had her archers set and ready to fire. They were just out of enemy bow range but her bows were better and magically enhanced. They could send an arrow further and higher than the light's elven bows.

The spiders were the first to try and take the walls as the Naga remained behind the giant animals. Slowly the spiders climbed the walls and soon they were getting close to the rim. Hot oil and arrows of flame rained down on the spiders and Naga. The Naga fell back and tried to avoid being doused with the oil. They almost succeeded, but the defenders were on point.

The first wave had fallen and Morreal was looking on with glee. It was the archers turn and then the drow. She had managed to summon all of them from their underground lairs and were now ready to take Metra for their own.

The archers fired up into the city and soon the arrows stopped falling. The defenders had either abandoned their posts or had been killed to the man. Since the people of the light were cowards, they had fled before the archers' arrows.

The archers moved closer and a wall of arrows flew from the direction of the city. Looking at them they realized they were their arrows flying back at them. They searched the city rim for archers and found none, just two men peaked out from the battlements. The gates of the city slowly opened and the horse of the enemy came rushing out of the city.

Morreal had her cavalry way too far back for them to help in this part of the battle. She had misread the enemy and that could cause problems. As the horse broke up the drow and archers, the enemy's infantry had come to bear on the back side of the horse. Now the army of the light had committed their whole army, so it was time to wipe it out. She sent out two thirds of each discipline of her army toward the front. It easily dwarfed the forces of the enemy. The army of the Dark would prevail.

The army of the light had seen the coming army from the wood line and despair came from the lips of the defenders. There was no way they would make it through this. Torlin and Garath used their powers to protect from missile weapons but that was the best they could do. Torlin collected the missiles and Garath fired them back to the enemy army.

The more they killed though the more that attacked. They were near their end when the horn sounded and the enemy roared. The Dark Queen was coming. Looking around they saw no entry of the dark host, but the shining armor and horse of Landsdale. They did not have many but they were well led by Garren and Gardell. The pair had the two hundred horses at their rear charging into the army again and again. The army felt the route and turned to face the new threat when the archers and infantry of Landsdale arrived.

Once more the enemy from Landsdale was not the largest force but the timing of each assault and the backing of each discipline had made a great impact on the enemy army. The city's defenders came to the aid of the new comer help after it was starting to be beat up and pushed back. Just utter numbers of the enemy were enough to push the army back.

By the time the defenders had arrived to spare the Landsdale forces a small wall had been erected with the dead and dying of the Dark

Land's troops. Again, Morreal had underestimated the forces of the light. As she saw several spiders leaving the battlefield, she called for the retreat. She would gather her troops once more and assault them in the darkness later today.

Landsdale' forces entered the city as heroes. The whole city lined the main thoroughfare and cheered the returning troops and people reached out to touch the soldiers of Landsdale. Their quick assistance was enough to save the city.

The people of Landsdale had come to the city two days before. Garren had a plan and it worked to a tee. But unfortunately, it would only work once. The city had sent out messengers, human and raven, but they had all been killed or severely injured that they could barely return to the city. None had gotten through. The enemy had massive numbers of troops and cavalry. Both human as well as spiders, snakes, giants, and undead.

The town of Landsdale had a contingent of troops to watch and protect their city. It was under the care of Mayor Flatfeet. The man had proven himself in the first war for Metra. Now the second was beginning and again the brave dwarf had once more taken on the challenges of command.

He was pleased with the arrangement of Garren and Gardell as the head of Landsdale. The city had grown dramatically since the walls of steel had been seen and people came from miles around to live behind them. It had even grown up a town around the walls that would come into the city as danger approached. It was all wood and easily set to fire to chase off the enemy. The buildings had little in them and the items the town dwellers possessed went with them inside the city.

Garren was fair and reasonable so that was a good thing. Gardell was a little skittish about being a princess, but Garren had warned her of some of the perils of being his wife. She did not care a lick and learned quickly the etiquette of being a princess. She would often bring fresh apples or bread out to the youngsters in the courtyard. She left none out. The children of the wealthy pushed and cut the line to be first. But Gardell would always have the poorest come to her first. The wealthy already had food and drink.

All would have their fill as she usually came with a wagon load. The apples and bread were sure fire winners. The cider she shared was received graciously. At first the princess made the cider herself, and none of the children wanted to disappoint the princess. But she realized that it was horrible, and switched to the palace cook's rendition of the drink.

These children loved the royals and followed them as they would tour the city. Every once and again, Garren would slip some of the poorer children of the city sweets he had stolen from the palace kitchens. This made him a super star amongst the children.

The royal couple was walking about Metra after the successful defense of the city, when the two-swordsman approached. Each had the tabard of the heron marked, and they leaned on either side of the road the couple was walking down. Both men had their weapons ready and leaned upon them.

Garren knew the heron marked men in the city and did not recognize these two. He called out to them and asked their names. "It is not important governor. Not important at all." said the closest sword master.

"I think he believes he knows us. Do you think he knows us?" asked the second.

"I believe he may believe that, do you know us, sir?" said the first.

"No, I believe that I do not know you. But you are blocking our way by accident and we need to get by." said Garren.

"We do not block the road by accident, sire. It is done quite on purpose. Now we will give you a fighting chance to save yourself. Draw your weapons and see how you fare." said the second man.

Garren and Gardell both drew weapons and prepared for the onslaught. The first few attacks and feints were blocked easily and the reciprocated blows also easily blocked. The four danced to the song of the blades for a short time until Garren and Gardell were showing wear from the nicks and cuts received from the master blades men.

Gardell fell to one knee and the more experienced Blades man went to finish her when the children grabbed the swords men's limbs and waists. Little hands pounded and struck the men over and over. Garren came to the first man who had been finally wrestled to the ground. "I should leave you to the heron marks but I fear they may be too harsh on you. They are not exactly the elven rangers, but they do come through in pinch. They are the best back up I have ever seen. Right darling?"

"Indeed. Who needs rangers when you have these young strapping men and women?" said Gardell as she ruffled the hair of one of their saviors.

"Ahh. We just had numbers and surprise on our side. Look here come the real heron marked these guys will get it for pretending to be heron marked." said one of the little ruffians.

"Ah hah. This is where the sounds of combat were coming from. These two were expelled from the heron marked. Great weapons masters but awful temperament. Believed they should rule. But now we have them in custody and they will answer our questions well or see the hangman's noose. Do you two understand?" said the Sergeant of the Heron Marked.

Garren and Gardell followed until they reached the heron marked guild house. None but members were permitted beyond the outer portal. Garren walked around the building and saw a druid in black robes looking in a window. He heard the sounds of questions being asked inside and saw the druid suddenly lift his hands to start a spell. Without thinking Garren drew his sword and removed the hands of the druid in one fell sweep.

The druid cried out in pain as Garren returned the sword to it scabbard. Looking down on the man he was about to ask what the druid was casting when another druid showed up and cast a spell toward the now stunned Garren. He watched the deadly spell come closer and then it dispelled as the other druid fell to his knees and then onto his face. Gardell's blade deep in his back.

"Can't turn my back on you for a minute without you getting in a fight." Laughed Gardell.

"You're telling me." replied Garren with a smile.

The herons were out a moment later and collected the cut druid and brought him in for questioning with the two swords men.

CHAPTER FIFTY-FIVE

THE BEST

The verdict from the herons came later the next day. One of the swords men had died under questioning. He had a massive skull melt down. The heron marked warrior said that the questions were the same for the second man and yet had no ill effect. The druid had bled out by the time they had finished with number two. Each of the men had all said the same thing though. The evil Queen had a tower and castle in the Dark Lands. She is known to be there by the flaming pillar that rises from the building she is in.

"We now have number two guarded by seven Heron Marked warriors. They are not going to let anything happen to him. They are the best of us guarding them. No one is getting to him, this time." said the yellow tabard heron marked warrior. He had just finished his report when the bells rang at the heron marked lair.

Tanis led the charge followed quickly after by the heron marked warrior. The boys were in the back and Gardell was a close third. They arrived at the house to see nothing amiss outside. Inside it was a different story.

Inside the remains of the guard at their door was found strewn around the room. Tanis quickly pulled the corpse back together in a pile, in the side of the room and they pushed open the door to the dungeon. Tanis tore back the curtain and saw that five of the swords man were dead. The second man had been killed dramatically. The other two swordsman were nowhere to be found. He looked around to find the bodies of the two dead men were gone. The space reeked of a magical entry.

Only the Dark Queen could have conjured it. The butcher's work was done by an orc with several daggers. The place was bloody indicating that most of the cutting began while they were still alive. The foot prints showed that she had been dancing while they cut.

The last of the herons looked like he had been picked up and squeezed magically. Wrung out well with a twisting motion. This must have been excruciating for that man. The Queen seemed to enjoy the suffering of the man and took pleasure in it.

The doors had been blown open by the magical entry and the guards at the inner doors were apparently killed instantly. The Queen was clever and yet killing needlessly. She had cut off the passages that could have been used for escape. But why did she risk coming to the capitol? Why do we take the chance?

Inside the mess on the floor a neat row of letters said "Dad, Come to me…." The rest of the message was obliterated by booted feet walking through the words. It looked like she had written more but only a few letters came through the wreckage of the floor. The floor looked like:

Dad Come to me … …. A… . . .il. a…e Y……

a.. ..u c.. fi….nall. d… .

The reference to dad caught his attention. Tanis looked closely to try and discern the rest of the message but was unable to. The message was too destroyed. Druids and Swordsmen continued to trample over the message, and soon it was totally obliterated. Better no one else knew of the message until he puzzled out the dad reference.

Artitous came into the blood-soaked house and looked at the swordsmen trying not to lose the contents of their stomachs. Some did while others had to retire to the rear of the house to get some air. Artitous waved his hand and the blood and body parts flew across the house and settled in the respective buckets. The cleaning took only moments but many still looked a little green around the gills.

Artitous looked at the remains and at the residue on the walls. "This was done from the inside. I believe we may have a traitor amongst the magical folk. They let the Dark Queen come in here and she herself did all of the damage you see here. As her strength grows so will her bloodlust. She is using more and more of the grimoire and we need to find and destroy that tome. It did not originally pose a threat to us but now that all the pieces are reunited it will be the death of us."

"I have a confession, Artitous. I stole a single page from the center of the grimoire. I put it aside for a rainy day. I believe it looks like a storm is brewing. And now we tip our hands a touch." said Tanis, watching to see who may be using the power to send a message or anyone leaving quickly. No one stood put so the traitor must have left already.

Word would get out and the Dark Queen would learn of it. Swordsmen and druids drink together and eat together and talk to each other. At mess they are very conversational. The Queen would know soon.

Artitous nearly jumped from his skin. "Give it to me let me review it. Where is it?"

"No worries, my old friend. I have it on my person at all times. So here let me show you the page." Tanis said pulling out a piece of parchment. "It is definitely the genuine article. Wouldn't you say Artitous?" asked Tanis.

Artitous looked at the document and saw what the page said.

We are setting a trap for the Dark Queen and her followers. We will have Christof and you guarding me for the time being. Do not let anyone know that this is a fake.

"I see," said Artitous as he read the paper again. "I see indeed." Artitous gave him back the paper and he went to the remaining Heron marked and asked them what they had learned from the two traitors and the druid.

"As I said one died quickly his head exploding as he tried to answer our questions. Young Garren saved the second man that fate. Apparently, there is a group of magical folks that come and go from here and they monitor prisoners and questioning. If the prisoner tries to talk, they are killed in the most dramatic way possible. The druid told of only two people he knew. They claim only to know two other members of the Dark Lands' fighters. This was in case someone was able to talk they could reveal only two others. There is only one left of the group that they knew of and that was Barrish. All the others are either gone or dead." said the swordsman.

"You have done well. We know one more piece of her puzzle. We have to watch closely our people and be careful to whom you speak. No one outside this room is to mention that we had gotten any information from these prisoners. We have only each other to rely upon." said Tanis. He walked from the room.

Artitous talked to Tanis in a low whisper as they left. "Are you mad? Those men will get a belly full of ale and start talking to anyone that will listen. Why would you let them report in front of all those people?"

Tanis smiled and looked at the arch druid, "I am pulling a page from Perrick Alon. The enemy you know becomes your agent. I am hoping that the dark side of this war finds out that we know how to interrogate these prisoners now. I also hope they will lower the number of spies that they send to us. If we know they come in trios, which is an enormous advantage to us do you not agree?"

"But the Dark Queen has other spies to learn from. I have two druids set to rat duty. They have been seen way too much to be a normal infestation. Crows circle constantly, not to mention the people we do not know about." said Artitous.

"It turns out that there is a circle of black druids out there. It is also plain that there is a bit of defection from our ranks. I must have Lord Nargus search the dormitories and watch shacks for anything that may be of a dark magic nature." said Tanis.

Lord Nargus had just walked up to Tanis and Artitous with his bow-legged stance. "I have to report I believe I have a traitor amongst my guard. What should I do with him?"

"Bring him to us at the palace wine room. I will explain later." said Tanis, "And while I have you, please conduct a search for dark magical items amongst your magical and non-magical folk. Inform me of any finds, do not move them just report them to us. Understand?"

"Right. Search discretely and report what is found without taking it form the objects into custody. Right." said Nargus. "I wish I was still leader of Cavalry."

"What and miss all this fun?" asked Tanis as the man rolled his eyes and walked away with is bowed legs from years on horseback. Tanis had offered to heal him of being bow legged. He had refused saying that he would not be able to stand or walk since he had been like this since he was thirteen when he enlisted in the horsemen regiments.

Tanis learned not to force others to his view of things as it had cost him many people and friends. Now he lets them tell him their views and then gives them his opinion, not before it was asked for. He had become a better ruler that way.

"Forcing your will on others will kill you in the end." said Tanis.

THE NUMBER THREE

The human spies and animal eyes and ears had sent all the same report, they knew she could travel magically. They also knew that she was merciless. The latter was a good thing. They also knew of her triplets. Again, a good thing. They will be searching all of their people without trying to find her or her main army that had yet to be engaged. Those were getting restless. She assured them that the time would come to attack.

She looked at the grimoire and looked for the missing page. He somehow still had a page of the grimoire. Should she send someone to steal the page or should she go herself. Her gut told her to send a trintator. A trintator was a thief of great skill, they could fade from one shadow to another close shadow, they could move undetected, almost indefinitely, and could steal just about anything. The only problem was that they had sold their souls in exchange for the powers. The trintators were not quite dead but not quite living either. They seemed to be in a limbo that caused them suffering and pain that they choose to inflict on others. They were Almedda's special pets.

The power of the grimoire was almost uncontainable, but she still was managing to control it verses the alternative. The more she used it the more it learned to obey her. The powers supplied by the grimoire were intoxicating. Why did they not study half dark and half-light? The dark was more intoxicating than the light and she could do anything she chose with the dark side. She could not fathom why they had forbidden it. If they just used death row inmates or spies, they would have no moral objection.

She chooses to use any human she captured. The animals all bend to her will with nothing but a talk and a wave. Animals had always fascinated her so she took extra care of them. But again, they frowned of experimentation with them.

She was working on a project that would blend a human male with a large bull. The Minotaurs she would build would have the same strength as a bull, but the intelligence of a man. That would be a sight. Let them battle and kill them. She had a lot of success with them but held them with the others in her army. The powers-that-be on the light side will never know what hit them.

The trintators left early the next day for Thalinburg. Their orders simple. Get the page of the grimoire and kill those that surround it. The soulless eyes looking at her blinked and then they bowed and turned fading in and out of the few shadows in the throne room. She loved to see them come and go. A few of her rivals had sent them to her shortly after she had gained the throne. She quickly gained control of the creatures and then sent them to retrieve the ones that had sent them after her.

She had enjoyed the turning of the nobles to petty thieves. Such petty people, losing it all for a slight chance to take her throne. She almost felt sorry for them. She had taken all of the noble's family and turned them all into Trintators and Mardocks. The children she held until they were old enough and then did the same thing to them.

She had turned a young man of about eleven years old to be a trintator and made a child a Mardock just to see how they would work. So far, they had been her most effective weapons. People just loved to help young children. She would make them regret that motivation.

Soon she would release the army on Metra as it was hidden nicely by a shield of dark magic close to the city. They would have no idea what had happened until her creatures and men had taken the gates and the walls and destroyed the city once more.

She just had to keep Tanis, Artitous and, Christof from finding out about the army by visiting their family in Metra. This was about to be accomplished as the brothers and families headed for home.

CHAPTER FIFTY-SEVEN

A HIDDEN ENEMY

Garren had set up for escorts from the Landsdale cavalry for the guests of Tanis Thalin to protect them. Garren arrived back in Landsdale within a few hours and the others not much later. Torlin was feeling strange things close by. He could not seem to shake the feelings that there were creatures near the city. The watch reported nothing, but he still felt it.

Torlin went strolling on the wall and finally grew weary of the feeling only in this area. He slowly cast a spell toward the hidden army and faint outlines appeared. Torlin was amazed. A large group of dark side warriors were hidden near the city.

Torlin turned to let the rest of the city know to sound the alarms, when he ran into Sir Monreal DuPont. See Torlin in such a hurry he asked Torlin, "Why do you move so quickly? Is something wrong?"

"Get your horse men ready. We are being watched and prepared for an attack. They have quite the army out there. We need to get everyone in and the gates sealed immediately." said Torlin.

"My Queen had said that you were too weak to see them from here. I see she underestimated your abilities." said Sir DuPont.

"Your Queen? What are you talking about? My God man, you did not buy into her recruitment, did you? It leads only to death. Do not think of reaching for your sword or dagger. You are not fast enough." said Torlin.

"I am more than fast enough to kill you. I am sorry but you die now. No one can know of what you have found." said Monreal.

As he reached for his dagger, he felt the pain of a sword piercing his back and cutting through his chest. "You did not listen. He said you were not fast enough for me not to kill you if you tried." said Roanda as she walked up behind the men. "Do you ever go for a quiet walk? What was that all about? I went looking for you to find out if you had heard from our scouts in the third quarter?"

"The Dark Queen has set up a massive army at our gates practically. We need to prepare for the attack. Our poor rangers may have stumbled upon their shielded forms." said Torlin. "And we had a quiet walk, once. In Landsdale." Smiled Torlin.

Garren's troops went south and the bells started chiming. The commander ordered his horsemen to return to Metra and sent a pigeon with a note on its leg to Landsdale. The note was simple:

They Come.

The horsemen made it back just as the large gates of Metra started to close. They were welcomed like heroes as the people realized that they were in fact there to help save them. Watch fires were lit and watches were set. The whole city was on alert that the bells ringing meant it was time for action. The army to the gates and walls, the tradesmen and women hidden deep within the bedrock of the city well protected.

Torlin watched as his people had begun to come into the middle plaza of the city. The palace looked out over this plaza and he realized they wanted to hear from him.

He walked out on the parapet and he spoke slowly and with much thought. "My people and my friends. We are being watched by an army of the enemy like nothing we have ever seen before. Their numbers are great, I will not lie to you. But the lack the morale and the benefit we take for granted. That benefit is we have something worth fighting for. Do not go out there when they come and fight for yourselves. Fight for the children hidden beneath our feet. Fight for those who were too old to join us. Fight for those tradesmen that may have to rebuild after us. But do not look to each other. We fight for those that cannot fight. We fight for those who will know tomorrow because we have a cause worth fighting for today. So, my brothers- and sisters-in-arms, be ready for the call for it will come soon."

The people exploded into a roar so loud that it shook some of the buildings in the plaza. Swords shook on shields. Spears beat against bucklers, and those with bows and arrows yelled out and clapped hands. His army was ready for war.

Roanda joined Torlin on the balcony and they watched the people of Torlin's army move as he had directed earlier. They would move to the walls, archer going up and remaining in the towers until the bell rang. The foot and horse would wait behind the gate and portcullis for the enemy to break through.

Torlin pulled no punches. They were going to breach the city walls. It was what we would do once the city was breached. Fighting street to street would give them the advantage, but just barely. The narrow roads and alleys caused bottle necks to even the odds. Thomas had insisted that they work that into their plans. Thomas was indeed a tactical genius. Torlin wished for just a moment that he was there.

Torlin did not reveal the army nor did he act as if he knew they were there. He would carefully monitor the situation and let them know when to sound the alarm. He ordered his troops to be at ease but be ready to go at any moment.

Torlin watched the other army when a raven appeared from Landsdale. The message was clear. The horsemen they had sent had to be all the aide they could give as they also had shadow armies outside their city.

Torlin was wondering how he knew that they were in trouble, when the leader of the horsemen of Landsdale came to him. "I took the liberty of requesting aid from your brother Garren at Landsdale. Has he sent his reply?" asked the horseman.

"Just got the response. We are both in dire straits. I sent the raven to Tetra and Thalinburg with warnings of hidden armies and I fear we all have one building, or already at the gates. Thank you for your initiative. I have a post that just opened up for the time being how would you like to fill it?" asked Torlin.

"However, I can serve the Royal Family, Sire. What is this post?" asked the horseman.

"The post is the head of the horse of Metra. What is your name young man?" replied Torlin.

"Callig Lowery, Sire. And I would be pleased to take this post until a proper lord can take the job." said Callig.

"It is yours until you no longer want it. You are the lord that will take the spot." said Torlin. "We younger men have to get involved in leadership; don't you agree?"

"I am honored, Sire, but I am no lord. I will hold the job that's all." said Callig objecting for the second time.

"Kneel Callig Lowery." Torlin instructed the man and produced a magical sword of energy. Tapping him on each shoulder and the top of his head. He said, "Arise Sir Callig Lowery. The head of the horse of Metra. And Lord of the land."

The man sputtered as he arose and shook the hand of Torlin. He was still trying to find his words when Torlin exclaimed, "See! I can still leave someone speechless!"

The crowd that had gathered laughed and cheered the new head of the horse and many a horseman came to congratulate the young lord. Even some of the old sergeants came over and shook the hand of the new made lord of horse.

The party was short lived as the army of the Dark Lands revealed itself. The enemy sent out its giant ants and spiders first. The beasts tried to climb walls of Metra but they were made by the Metradon with a precision that made hand holds and places for the spiders impossible to climb. The spiders would get only so far up the wall before falling back to the bottom. The ants followed after the very fast spiders and began to take small chucks out of the walls for hand holds and spider legs to catch.

Torlin held the archers who were now very anxious to get out there and shoot down the insects, but Torlin again held them back. Soon the ants were also falling down the walls. This time aided by blasts of air from the druids and wizards that called Metra home. Again, none below saw what caused the animals to fall. The rest of the Dark Queen's army had moved closer. Confidence was building in the enemy army and Torlin was waiting for it. Telling the archers to refrain from going out on the walls.

Crossbow men and their helpers came running up to the tower and they too were put on hold. The Queen of the drow came out of the army holding a grimoire. Torlin used magic to see the book and her closer. It was a grimoire but not the one they had hoped would come. This one was also in arachfra, the language of the spider and other insects.

The Spider Queen, Morreal, moved close to the wall whispering a spell. A young archer left the tower and fired an arrow down at the Drow. The arrow hit is mark and penetrated her heart. They had the druids perform the rites to make their arrows deadly to the other side. The Drow Queen let out a scream that could pierce eardrums. She tried to shift from a human to a spider but the change would not come.

She attempted to shift to a human and again, nothing. She let out one more wail and her limp form hit the road right in front of the gates. The spiders leapt upon her fallen body and began to tear it apart. The handlers had lost all control of the creatures as if the death of the Drow Queen released them from some kind of spell.

Looking down they saw the spiders attacking the enemy soldiers around them and the enemy trying in vain to get them back under control. Before too long though half the enemy lay dead or dying from their spiders and the spiders all lay dead. Torlin ordered the archers to the walls and had them use fire arrows to rain down upon the heads and bodies of the confused army at the foot of the wall.

Torlin used magic to rain down water to keep the fires down as the archers used the flaming arrows. The first to break was the ants. They had suffered the greatest loss to the spiders and the ants had lost the stomach for combat. Their handlers pushed and the ants turned on them as well. The ants tried to escape the fighting by climbing the walls and found only the arrows of the city folk raining down upon them.

Soon all that remained of the enemy were a few large demons and a few orcs and men that had survived the animal onslaught. These few were easily picked up or killed by Torlin's army led by the new head of the horse. Overall, the battle took half an hour that felt like a century to the city folk.

CHAPTER FIFTY-EIGHT

DEAD ALLIES

The evil Queen was shocked when the spiders she had living with her in her rooms had turned on her. The first one had knocked her off her large reading chair and had been burned to a cinder for its trouble. The other two attacked as she tried to rise and again, she fought back with the power. The two guards that followed her around constantly were already dead with their throats torn out.

She would probably try to dance for them later. If she survived this attack. She was wondering what had happened and realized that Morreal must have perished in battle. Waving her hand she sent all biological life, including her vase of flowers, blowing away in a fine dust.

The old crone was dead. Now she would be the sole ruler of her people. Looking over at the now heavy fighting going on in the palace and Carlee was hovering over the Queen. "Hey Carlee, you should see what I just learned. Stay above me. You may regret coming down if you do."

With that she raised her arms and sent the same spell she used to kill the spiders in her room down throughout the tower and palace. The sounds of the battle disappeared and soon all was quiet. Carlee flew down to the Dark Queen and exclaimed, "What have you done? You destroyed the enemy and our own in the same breath. What are we supposed to do now?"

"Do not worry. I am the Queen and I will get the different towns and groups out in my lands to send me soldiers. Even Tyris. My new palace staff will far exceed the prowess of my old staff. Send thirty of our riders to collect the people and supply each with a wagon. They would collect the best of everything for her.

Who could resist their Queen after all? She was getting better with her impulse control. She had only evaporated three hundred of the orcs and three Ogier. She had hoped that this was to happen and she would be able to replace the whole staff. Carlee came back a few minutes after the riders had reached the first village and they were met with hostile resistance from the people. Almedda/ Elizarade screamed and told Carlee, "They will join us or be killed and the village destroyed. After they have given up and allowed them to be culled, have the troops destroy them anyway."

"It will be as you say, Your Majesty." said Carlee flying to meet with the soldiers who were now warily watching the surrounding area. Carlee went into the air and saw a pack of the spiders headed for the forests of the borderland. This may make things a little more difficult. She turned to the soldiers and relayed the orders. She also let them know there were no unexpected visitors coming so continue as instructed.

Almedda smiled as she savored the thought of the town burned to the ground with every man, woman, and child left inside. These people and orcs and such needed to learn respect. She was confused. She had left the message on the floor of the palace in Thalinburg. Why has he not come trying to save her? These questions confused her.

She was sure that her brothers and father would have figured out who the Dark Queen was by now. If they had not, well, it was their problem. A Noom came into the room and bowed low. He announced the arrival of a guest. Almedda/Elizarade was surprised to say the least. No one came to see her. She rushed to the throne room to find the palace had just about been refitted with orcs and people working and picking up after the earlier fighting.

Sitting on the throne of bones from her previous enemies, she allowed the guest to be brought before her. A prisoner was brought to her with his head covered and hands and feet bound. Almedda began licking her lips, it had been a while since someone had visited. Looking down, she told the guards to remove the sack. A young man looked up at Almedda and a look of amazement came to his face. Here was the boy she had kissed behind the garden fence for so long. Looking him in the face, the man said, "Almedda! Run with me and we can get out of this place. My prowess with a sword and yours with the magic will see us free."

"My dear Marcus. What shall I do with thee? Come up here to me. I do not need to be saved from the Dark Queen. You see, I am the Dark Queen. I am in need of a permanent mate. You should do just fine. Join me on the dais and be my king. What say you Marcus Sandou, or do we just execute you now?" said Almedda.

"You do not need to execute me. I will accept your proposal. After all, how many days do you get asked to become a king? I whole heartedly agree." said Marcus. He hoped he would not have to prove his loyalty as that could become something very seriously deadly.

Almedda looked down for a moment and smiled. "Let it be known there is now a Dark King to go with the Dark Queen. We shall conquer all in our path. With his prowess in combat and mine in magical things, we should be able to overcome any obstacle to our total victory."

"I am yours to command, my Queen." said Marcus, kneeling at her feet.

"Very good to hear, Dear King." said Almedda.

"Send the trintators to the city of Metra and have them look for that missing page. Kill the entire royal family if necessary. After tearing the city apart, if they do not find their objective, have them continue to Tetra and repeat until they find the page. They should also do the same to Thalinburg. No royal survivors." said Almedda. "Also send my Minotaurs to the front lines. It is time we won this stupid little annoyance of a war."

CHAPTER FIFTY-NINE

WEIRD CREATURES

The day was starting out wonderfully in Metra as the remnants of the enemy army regrouped and found most of them wounded or cluttered together in small groups around the field. The horsemen did their jobs perfectly and lost but one man and that was to friendly fire from the walls.

It was an accident, but the druids and wizards had to make a full investigation. This was the third or fourth friendly fire incident they had since the horse came in from Landsdale. Someone needed to confirm they did not have a traitor amongst them. They had found almost too late the Mardocks attacking the wizards and druids of the city. There had been two of them killed and it was soon confirmed as they went after Torlin.

Many of these assassins had perished that day. Now they had people asking about his father and the supposed page of the grimoire. He had thought that the city had forgotten the royal family outside Metra. He was walking down the aisle in the palace when the Trintators moved in to attack.

Torlin immediately attacked from front and back trying to bring down his assailants. He had fireballs all around him that had not left an impression with the enemy. In fact, most of them walked right through the fire unscathed. Torlin looked for anything to hurl and found nothing. Then to his surprise as the first of the enemy reached him a sword blade showed up through the man. In a few moments the enemy all lay dead at the prince's feet.

"I really need to pay more attention in sword class, huh, Callig?" said Torlin.

"Yes Sire, you certainly do need to work on your sword work," said Callig and as he spoke, he fell to one knee. Torlin looked at the man and asked if something was wrong. Looking down a small puddle of blood was forming beneath him. Torlin quickly cast the slim amount of healing that he could. It had no effect so he called for the druids and went looking for the one who had hurt the knight and ran. He hurried down the hall and finally caught up with a man walking down the hallway like he had all of the time in the world.

"Halt, who are you?" asked Torlin.

"Do you not know me? We fought together earlier today and yesterday." said the figure turning slowly, "It is I, Chappel Eisner. I swear to you that I did not kill your knight or I would have fled. I sensed a dark creature this way and I went searching for it. So far, I have found nothing." Torlin stretched out his senses and soon felt the same evil.

"This way! It is coming toward us." said Torlin. He turned down a corridor and stopped at what was before him. It was one of the Minotaurs. The still dripping blade in his hand had proved the elf's story was true. Torlin fired a fireball right into the center of the bull man's chest. He bellowed in rage and swung his sword at the wizard that had caused it such discomfort. It was met by elven steel and deflected.

The elf cut the creature across its now exposed chest and the blade left a long wound across the burn.

Billowing again the creature began to swing wildly trying to hit both persons at the same time. The wild swing cut off the head of another trintator as it came to assist the beast in killing the two men. This again raised a cry from the Minotaur and a wild swing. Chappel stepped into the beast and stabbed it in the chest as Torlin blinded the beast with a fireball to the face.

The creature gave a sigh then fell to the earth. Chappel leaned on his sword as Torlin sat down to catch their breath. The assault had lasted only a few moments but it still was a hard-fought win for the two men.

As they rested a soldier Torlin did not recognize came into sight. The soldier came closer and as he looked the man before him seemed to shift. He seemed to grow larger as they watched. The man sprouted legs and a bulbous abdomen and rear section. He remained half human and half spider. The drow spoke, "I am looking for the one that killed Morreal. He has much to answer for. I am nothing more than a creature of intelligence that wishes to have a trial for the man for the fortunate dispatching of the Dark Queen."

"My dear sir, are you saying the Dark Queen lies dead on that field out there?" asked Torlin. "Surely, she continues to reside in the Dark Lands somewhere?"

"The Queen lies dead outside your walls. Of this I assure you. The spiders and the drow will not trouble you further. I will even ask that the trial be held here with a group to decide the young man's fault and his gains or sentence." said the drow male.

"Do you have a group of people, and I use the term loosely, keep in mind? I can find some to join it so there is equal numbers of drow and humans. The elves and dwarves will also have their representatives. Does this satisfy your need for justice?" said Torlin.

"That is more than I expected. We were always told that the concept of a public trial was above you. The people of the lands of the light seem to be reasonable and intelligent. We were always taught that men and elves would kill us on sight. I appreciate your candor and you speaking to me." said the drow.

"Please give me time to find the young man who fired that dread arrow. I will make sure that all the evidence will be there for your inspection. It is all I can do." said Torlin.

"I know the place the arrow came from. Let us get moving so that the enemy does not accidently find us and we must fight again." said Chappel.

"Sounds good, let us all go so that there are no incidences. My good friend drow, what is your name? I wish to address you properly." asked Torlin.

"I am called Romi. We do not have two names amongst us. We are called our name and then identified by our father's name, and his before him, and his before him, etc. Some of our kings and leaders have very long introductions. I will suffice to say that my introduction is not quite that long. Nor will I bore you with it." said Romi.

"Well, Romi, let us get this thing settled." said Torlin.

CHAPTER SIXTY

THE ARCHER

Torlin made it to the walls without incident as the rest of the soldiers were killing the assassins that had come for him. As he hit the street a young man of thirteen was being bounced around the upswept arms of the crowd. Torlin asked one of the groups what was the matter and the soldier said, "This is the young man that stopped the fighting before it began with a solid shot to the Queen's heart. We are thinking of changing his name to Cupid."

"We need to speak to the young man if you do not mind." said Torlin.

"Who are you to demand a talk with the young man? You are not but an aimless wizard." said the soldier.

"I am Torlin, lord of this city, and I demand to speak to the young man." said Torlin.

As Torlin spoke the crowd immediately dropped the boy. He was a little above the heads of the people then he was on the ground. A couple of people helped him to his feet and pushed him to the prince. Once more the young man fell over in front of Torlin. Getting slowly to his feet he saw Torlin and fell to his knees. "My Lord, do not kill me. I did not even know that my bow could fire the arrow. It had never done so before. I left it up in the tower. Please allow me to retrieve it and show you."

"No one is going to harm you. Go and retrieve your weapon and come back here immediately. Romi go get your people and we can get to this messy business." said Torlin. The crowd started to boo and threaten until it was explained that it was merely and inquiry to what had happened out in the battle.

The people renewed their cheers and caterwauling as the boy returned to the prince holding an elm branch with a string tied to it on both ends. He held it up so Torlin could see it and Torlin chuckled. Taking the bow from his hands he looked at it carefully, handing it around to the people standing around them.

Romi looked at the bow and laughed so hard that he nearly fell to the ground laughing. "So, this is the Queen slayer. Hold this bow well young man and it will always be an icon to at least one kingdom. You will all probably forget the events of this day but our city state in the Dark Lands will never forget."

"Then you may have it with my compliments." said the boy.

"It will be placed in the royal museum and tended to until it is no more due to age and not by destruction." said Romi.

"There was a reward for this woman's demise. It was set by my father almost forty years ago. Let me get you your prize, young man." said Torlin as he reached into his pouch. He took out a large handful of gold coins. It was more money than little Terrell Piken had ever seen. Torlin took out a small pouch and started putting coins into it. When the bag was full of gold coins, Torlin tied the bag and handed it to the young man. "If you do not feel that is enough come to the palace and we will discuss it."

The boy cried as the prince handed him the pouch of gold. "Now you can buy yourself a proper bow." Laughed Torlin. The boy was grinning up at the prince as he realized that the money was his. "Yes, my lord. I will purchase a very nice ash bow, I think. So, I can help on the walls." said Terrell.

"What is your name, young man? And how old are you?" said Torlin.

"I am thirteen and am called Terrell Piken. Thank you so much, my lord. I do not know what to say." said Terrell.

"Then say nothing and continue your heroic ways." said Torlin.

Looking at Chappel, Torlin looked at the bow that was resting behind the elf on the shop window. Chappel looked at it and handed it to the young man. "This is Marrowood. It is found only deep in the elven lands and only a few alive have one. This one came from the northern regions. You can tell from the narrow grain. The southern have a larger grain structure and make lesser bows. This one should be in the hands of an elf but the owner of it is dead now and the bow is without a host. I think it will like you. You see the bow is magical and will assist you in your pull to release and aim." said Chappel, "But it will be magically connected to you as long as you live and will help you in the healing of your wounds."

"But does it require you to be an elf to bond to you? And if it does not bond to me what happens? Please tell me." said Terrell.

"Well, if it does not bond to you, it will eventually kill you. But that is only in rare cases. They are usually pretty good at bonding to one person until that person is dead. Then it will move on. After your heroics today it should have no problem bonding to you." said Chappel.

"If you say so. So how does this work? Do I say a magic word or do I wave a hand over it? What do I do?" said the young man.

"Take off your gloves and grasp the bow. If it is to bond to you, you will know very quickly." said Chappel.

Terrell gingerly removed his gloves and grasped the grip of the bow with his ungloved hand. A slow tingle began to go up his arm and the bow seemed to grow red from the grip until it reached either end. The boy also seemed to turn red as the bow grew red. When both were red the bow suddenly went a blood red and the boy came back to normal. Chappel let out a sigh as the boy asked what happened. He claimed that he only felt a tingle then it was done.

"The bow chose you. If it had not it would have been just a nice bow or it would have turned black. If it turns black it would not have allowed your hand to be removed from it until it ate every piece of you. Congratulations. Now try it out." said Chappel.

"Wow, it worked? Well, where do I shoot and what do I shoot? Try the fence post and just draw the bow." said Chappel.

As the boy drew the string to his ears, and magical flaming arrow appeared on the bow. Startled, the boy let loose without looking. The arrow left the bow and sunk deep into the fence post. Trying again he aimed at the fence post and let loose. Once more it hit its target and the fence post began to burn.

Torlin waved a hand and it blew out the post. No signs of an arrow remained on the post but its damage was evident. Terrell looked around looking for the owner of the post, offering to replace it for him. The owner refused and sent the bow with the wizard and ranger. "What happens now? I have a fancy bow and a bag of gold, but no skills and nowhere to go. So, what do I do now?" asked Terrell.

"Why, you become an apprentice to the blacksmith and when the archers are called to the walls, you will come leading the residential archers' reserve. She will surely take you as apprentice." said Torlin.

Terrell head out to the smithy where he found Arlette working hard on swords and arrows. "Need a quiver of arrows, there archer?" asked Arlette.

"No ma'am. I am to be your apprentice. Torlin Thalin sent me." said Terrell looking at the floor.

"He did, did he? Well then let's have a look at you. Well nice looking, clothes need replacing. I have a little house in back that has two rooms. I will be happy to put you up there. By the way, I am Arlette Thalin. Granddaughter of Tanis Thalin and daughter to Torlin Thalin and Roanda Thalin. So, what do I call you?" asked Arlette.

"I am Terrell Piken. My dad was no mage and my grandfather not so grand a personage but they were good men before the wars. Afterwards they just left. First Grandpa left us to go to Heaven and then my dad. I have been alone ever since." Explained Terrell.

Arlette came closer to the young man and wrapped him in one of her signature bear hugs. The young man objected immediately and then let out a squeak as she squeezed harder and harder. As soon as it started it was over. Arlette stood away from him and looked down at her feet shifting ever so slightly with her foot. A blush covered her face.

"My dad is trying to play matchmaker again. He has been trying all year to find me someone. Well, there is an apron there. Put it on and come join me at the forge." Instructed Arlette.

Torlin watched and smiled as the two entered the forge. He would probably be vetting him for being a good enough man for her soon. Until then, let them work together and learn each other's ways. You never know.

CHAPTER SIXTY-ONE

FRUSTRATION

None of the assassins had been fortunate enough to kill a Thalin. Almedda was getting annoyed. She had sent bounty hunters and magical assassins. She had sent a plague upon them and they still stood tall. She would look into the grimoire for a better way to kill those infuriating people. Yes, they were family but enough is enough. She should rule.

An idea came to her mind as she sat and read the book. She called for a messenger. She needed to get a message to someone who should be able to dispose of those people in a rush. Especially if they come to each other's aid.

Her army had not attacked the city of Tetra or Landsdale by her order. They would be last. She sent another messenger to the army commander at Thalinburg. Destroy the walls and take down the royal family. She almost giggled in delight thinking of the carnage she was about to cause. True she no longer had the spiders but she still had plenty at her disposal.

Her husband came in as she was settling on her throne. She had made him stand next to her. He had no throne nor would he have one until Almedda declared that he could. She would have one built like hers for him but he just wanted a plain throne. The swords surrounding her were an intimidation to the man but he also knew she did not need those weapons. Her powers were growing more and more. She would be unstoppable soon.

He was to be the army's commander-in-chief. He was leaving to lead the army in Thalinburg. The journey would be long but she said she could make it much more pleasant for him. He excused himself and went to pack his bag for the journey and the battle. His bag seemed to have a person in it. The legs of his armor sticking out the arms and the helmet sitting on top. Even Almedda laughed as she cast spell and a hole formed in time and space and the army lay before him.

"Go ahead it is safe. Bring me the heads of the royal family or do not return at all." said Almedda as Marcus stepped through the portal.

He was amazed that the army camp was right in front of him and soldiers were taking him and his gear to the tent he would call home for a long while. The dark wizard that met him at his tent looked at the armor and had him take out the armor and weapons. The wizard then began casting his magic over the shining steel armor. As the wizard worked the shiny steel became black shiny armor. His weapons took a reddish hue. The sigil of the Dark Queen sat on his breast plate in deep red. He almost missed it on the black.

"The sword will be as Warmonger is. Thalin will have his unbeatable sword and now so shall you. The armor and shield have the sigil of your wife on them and will protect you from harm. I suggest you put on the armor and weapons as we got word, she wants the slaughter to commence. We would not want you to be late on your first day, now, would we?" said the wizard as he walked from the tent.

Ehrich, the wizard, listened in to hear the king's plans. He would be near impossible to harm with that armor. He would not soil Ehrich's work. He would bring down the princes and the rest of the royal family.

The king called for the wizard and the generals that were there. They were to look at the situation and see what they had to do. They had two of the greatest warriors on Dracos, but they were only two. Artitous and Tanis Thalin would be a challenge. One that we would bring home and feed to the greater demons.

There were no demons at the battlefield so they would have to use what they had. The engineers told them they could not burrow beneath the walls as the walls went down to the bed rock. A tunnel would take years to create. They could build the siege towers and siege equipment. Marcus smiled he started giving orders and designs for them to work on.

He had the head of the smith's make him a certain designed item. Again, it was a secret between the two of them. He then called for the alchemists and gave them yet another special project. He may not be magical but he was going to put on a show.

The wizards were told to wait until the signal was given to attack the city. The archers were to begin their assault now. The arrows should keep the walls empty. He ordered the bulk of the army to head toward the gates. That was where they would make their real assault. He had the army remain as they were ordered beyond bowshot at the gates.

They were still cloaked and he needed that for now. He saw two figures on the walls and gave a curse. "The two of them are going to ruin our surprises. Archers aim at the two men and do not stop until they are dead or gone. And do so for anyone else on the walls or tower. Understand? This needs an element of surprise."

Marcus was still fuming when the engineers came in and said his orders were done and working. His mood started to lighten as the alchemists and the smiths came with a report of readiness as well. His major surprise would enlighten all of the people of Thalinburg and his army. He went out and the three groups had assembled the project and had covered it with a cloth.

He looked under the cloth and smiled like a Cheshire cat. This was going to make all the difference. He had the soldiers near him push the device to the gates. The cloth still in place. He ordered the soldiers to fall back and he went under the cloth and sounds began to come from under the cloth.

Guards of the gate heard the sounds and tried to mount the watch tower over the gate to fire oil and arrows down upon him. He once more smiled as his archers lived up to their reputation. The gate guards fell quickly to well-placed shots. Marcus flipped some switches and then left the cloth. He told the archers to fall back and he ran with the archers beside him from the gate.

The guards did just as he hoped they would have. They pulled the cloth from the device and all of a sudden, the machine made a huge noise and a bright light.

CHAPTER SIXTY-TWO

THE DARK KING

Tanis was nervous as the clothed item was left at the gate. There was no magical threat but the Noom did not have a magical trap on their rooms either. Tanis asked that the guardsmen do not go to the device without Perrick going with them. They apparently only got a portion of the instructions because they went out with shields ahead of them.

Romi looked down and saw his own people waiting for battle with the city and he froze. They did not know of the peace treaty. He feared that the explosion would be considered an act of war. He had seen a device similar to that when he was training his troops in the daylight in the Dark Lands.

Many of his people that had come to fight came due to the compulsion of the Drow Queen. He was pleased that the old rule was over. A new better race of drow could now be born that would seek peace with the surface rather than wanting to destroy it. The old guard would slowly die off and no one would remember the hatred.

The drow called down to his people and to the guardsmen, "Run. Run quickly. Then drow come to the gates for great news." said Romi. The drow took off running on eight or two legs depending on how they had come to the battle. Of course, the majority showed their half spider form. It was probably an intimidation factor. Romi smiled as they got far enough from the blast that was to come. Romi said it was an exploding cabinet. And the range was rather small but it was very powerful. He said that the device probably had a triggering device connected to the cloth. Tanis called out to his people to get back inside the city and close the gates. But curiosity got the better of the dwarven guardsmen and they pulled the cloth.

Marcus saw the cloth being pulled and smiled the trigger would be activated and the device would blow up sending arrows and bolts and stones and caltrops flying all over the place. He would kill some his own but he would do damage to the gates and that was the idea. They would have to hold the gates with troops and he had plenty more of them then did the defenders.

One of his advisors said that the narrow passage to the gate and the gate itself would negate their numbers advantage. The defenders also had the elven ranger assault teams that would do a large amount of damage to their army.

Marcus disagreed at first and then realized his mistake. If those units came out to defend the city the army could very well be decimated. He would send in the drow first. They could be the cannon fodder. Marcus gave the orders and they all waited as the guardsmen came out to investigate the device.

The guardsmen looked at the device and saw the rope tied to the device and the sheet. Perrick Alon cut the cord and looked inside. Tanis had come as well and sent a strong beam of light up through the device so Perrick could see the inner workings.

"This would do a lot of damage to the surrounding area if there were people around it. That clicking is the line I cut spinning around inside. It is raveled so it is of no danger of exploding until a spark hit that middle sphere. Then boom. My boy could have built a better bomb. Well, I say we give it back to the people who sent it with a burning taper inside. Let them see what the device is about." said Perrick.

Marcus saw the blast of light and was about to order the assault when he noticed that nothing had exploded. He set everything himself. It should have worked. He looked over at the soldier sitting next to him and sent his head flying with a swipe of his sword. Another soldier grabbed the fallen man and yet another filled in the space left open. Marcus eyed him and decided not to swing again. Putting his sword away he was contemplating giving the wizard a formal position at court. He would be a savior of the wars.

As he watched the device slowly rose into the air. Marcus watched as it started to fly toward the army and Marcus ordered an arrow of flame shot at the sphere in the middle. An archer came forward and fired the arrow right into the sphere. The device exploded with a blast and he saw that his people had received the devastation as the bomb had gone three dimensionally instead of out to the sides. The enemy was unaffected. Marcus screamed and pulled out his sword and ordered the drow forward to attack.

The drow drew their weapons and marched forward and stopped at the gates. Romi came out and spoke to the drow leadership of which he was the head and a cheer went up through the drow army. The drow army lost the spider look and marched in the gates looking like dark elves. Many were waiting inside with drums going and people banging on pots and pans. The welcome made most of them blush.

The elves gave the drow a wide berth but the rest of the people tried to touch or see the passing soldiers. The people felt that every soldier was important, not just the ones inside the gates but the ones everywhere. The gates closed after the drow, sealing them into the city. Romi came and led the army to the barracks in the shadow district. It was so named because the walls prevented light from the sun to penetrate into it at any point in the day.

The drow accepted the barracks quickly and without objection. The light was starting to affect some of the drow. They had never been out of their mines and tunnels this long before. The shadowed barracks was perfect and reminded them of home. The drow lingered in the barracks appreciative of the foresight of the Thalin Family.

Marcus watched as the drow entered the city with a hero's welcome. They had betrayed the Dark Queen and thus deserved to die. He sent the Ogier next to attack the gates and had the men ready to attack as soon as the gates opened. It was only a few steps before the Ogier stopped and ran away from the field. Something had spooked them. Marcus moved forward to see what the Ogier feared so much. The sight he revealed to himself was breathtaking. It also made sense why they quit the field.

The faerimouth flew in from the north lands and landed before the gates of Thalinburg. They had put themselves into the statue form of their people and Ruark came into the city. He was met at the gates by Tanis and the two embraced briefly and the pair walked away from the inner city and headed to the palace district. Tanis did not like to live in the palace but Athinina told him that a leader needs to show prosperity and the palace did just that.

Ruark looked at Tanis and smiled, "My father would be proud of what we have accomplished between our people. We are now scattered to the important buildings in different cities and in the Capitol so that we can assist at a moment's notice when needed. We have all grown prosperous since our alliance has been made."

"We have had quite a bit of excitement since you had left. But we have come through ok. I still miss my elven father. But it is better off this way. After we finish the armies around the border cities, then we can regroup the elves and Faerimouth. Then we are protected in the north. The dragons are out of it until Marious shows his dirty face here again. He and the young ones have taken a lot of prizes from the Dark Queen. Mastol has been searching skies and dens all over to find him and has yet to find hide nor hair of any of the rebelling dragons. The dragons search still for them." said Tanis. "They have used the death dragons but we can take them down as soon as we see them. But again, we have seen nothing from them. It is like their holding something back. I just don't understand. With most of their powerhouse weapons and soldiers they could decimate this and the other cities. They have something brewing or they are just stupid. I have not figured it out yet."

"Looks like you have determined that their leadership is indeed that stupid. And soon they will prove it by moving on my army outside the gates. Let us retire and eat for a bit and then return to the walls. After all we have the alarm bells in case we are needed." said Ruark as he walked with a big smile on his face, "I am famished after that flight."

Both laughed as they entered the palace.

CHAPTER SIXTY-THREE

STATUES

Marcus could not believe that these small statues of three foot of stone scared away the mighty Ogier. These things were also so poorly carved that he just wanted to start breaking heads off of them. He ordered his war hammer be delivered to him so he could destroy these statues, and get the Ogier here to get these gates open. Marcus looked back and got his hammer. Looking back, it was strange. He thought he had brought more men than that. Lifting his hammer, he heard a sound that distracted him he looked back and saw fewer still people missing.

"We are all my people, Gaitlyn? Gaitlyn?" Marcus said as he looked around himself and saw only the statues. He started to leave the scene the statues forgotten. He almost made it out when Ruark arrived in front of the small army of stone. Looking at the faerimouth in the eye, Marcus drew his sword.

"Big mistake good sir. Drop the weapon and he may not kill you. But then he has a mind of his own. So do as I say and you will be unharmed." said Tanis from behind Marcus.

Marcus raised his sword and turned to attack Tanis. As he did the world around him went dark and he fell into the dark abyss.

"Can't say I didn't warn him. Ah well. Let's get your people inside, shall we?" asked Tanis. "He seemed to hold himself up like he was someone important. Who was he?" asked Tanis.

A drow came up to the group and shook the faerimouth's large claws. Ruark looked at him and asked why he shook his hand. "You have eaten the dark king. He was sent by the Dark Queen to finish this city and all the rest of them." said the drow.

"The dark king? I did not realize the Dark Queen had taken a mate. Well, hopefully we have seen the end of that army. Let us celebrate our brief victory." said Ruark.

Their attempt at a meal would come to an abrupt end as the alarm bells began to ring throughout the city. Tanis, Ruark, and Romi ran to the walls and looked down as the now leaderless units attacking at random. The city's defenders were raining arrows down on the enemy. At the top of the tower was young Terrell Piken firing down with his new bow. A smile passed his lips as he fired every shot. He found that he could not miss. He just hoped no one would be able to climb the walls and tower. The army of the light, now including drow and faerimouth, lined up at the gates awaiting orders.

Tanis looked down for a moment and smiled that he had grown his army that much. It appeared that they were all aiding each other and weapons were being passed out. Swords, shields, and bits of armor were given to every soldier and the young ones were delivering arrows to the walls and to the rangers. The rangers were anxious to get out of the confines of the large city and get back into the wilderness they loved so well.

Tanis was about to give the attack order but the gates remained shut even after the attacks with magic and a battering ram. The doors resounded loudly and clearly like a bell every time the ram hit the bronze gates. It did not take long for the men delivering the ram to the gates to give up. It was being shot at through the cover of the ram and it was not making any headway against the giant gates.

The armies of the enemy were still leaderless and they were being picked apart easily. Several tried to take command but were rapidly killed. The enemy army began to turn on each other as they swirled below trying to figure out who the enemy was. After what seemed like an eternity standing on the walls the enemy killed themselves. The people watching through the murder holes were cheering the victory as the last of the enemy was seen running and fighting each other, rather than face the evil elves and dwarves and men of Thalinburg. All Tanis said as they left was, "The Dark Queen is not going to like this."

CHAPTER SIXTY-FOUR

BAD NEWS

Almedda walked to the walls of her city. She inspected the troops daily. Especially since the Andromeda spiders had gone crazy and had gone back to their usual instincts and started killing everyone. There had apparently been another attack as two of her guard were hanging from the walls in webs. No use opening the cocoons. They were already dead. She checked the rest of her guard and they were all right this time. She would have to double the guard. This was one of the great spiders doing. It could only be worse if it was a Chimera.

She looked down at the scorpion men lining up beneath the city. Her guard now had three of the creatures as they demanded the right to have equal share in protecting the Dark Queen. That could be a dangerous position. A crow flew to Almedda's shoulder and whispered in her ears. Almedda responded, "What do you mean he is dead? He was surrounded with his army. How is he dead? I knew I should have gone there myself and gotten things rolling. Carlee! Carlee! I need your advice, dear friend." said Almedda.

The phoenix landed on the unoccupied shoulder and said, "What do you wish of me, my lady?"

"This animal spoke to me and I think I translated wrong. I need you to take her report and tell me what you think." said Almedda.

Almedda and Carlee sat and listened as the crow told its tale once more. Carlee laughed and said to Almedda, "You are a widow, my Queen. Eaten by a faerimouth of all things. Had he ever seen one before? That would explain the rest of your army going crazy and killing each other. We have one of the survivors just getting into the palace now. I spoke to him as he headed here. He said the slaughter was from our own troops."

The man walked into the presence of the Queen and she asked him for a report, "Well, my Queen, it is like this. The king went to look at the tiny statues on the ground near their gates. No one was shooting down at us so we decided to destroy the things so we could get by. King Marcus called for his war hammer and went to break the first of them and the thing looked like it came to life and wrapped the king in its wings. Well, the statue sat down and the wings opened revealing only a bent crown. If I am lying, I am dying. And then the creatures and drow turned on each other like tigers and the drow left and entered the city. They were not fighting the defenders; they were aiding them. Well about that time everything by us was ripping each other limb from limb, killing for the blood sport far as I could tell. I ran at the death of the king and decided to report what I had witnessed."

"So, they were torn limb from limb? Why are you not? They were killed with cuts and bruises, yet none on you, why? I am not sure I understand. Only a few escaped? How many?" asked Almedda. Waving for the man to come closer.

"There was four with me so a total of five. Yes, they utterly destroyed each other. We left as soon as the fighting started. Everything was out of control." said the man.

"So, you and your four friends, Ahh here they come, decided to run instead of face the horror that was unfolding in front of you. Let me describe the scene if I can," said the Queen as she lifted the second man into the air, "torn asunder like this?" she said as she tore the poor man's arms and legs from his body magically.

"Or maybe it was the cuts and bruises, like this?" she asked as she lifted the third man in line and proceed to beat him to death with her hands and magically. "Oh, this is fun. Now the three of you here. How should we deal with you? Oh, I know. I will give you to the scorpion men for dinner. If you're lucky they will kill you with their stingers before they begin to eat you. It has been a lovely time but you do not want to be late for dinner. Good bye to you, survivors."

The men begged and pleaded as they were dragged from the throne room. "A little hard on them, weren't you?" cooed the phoenix.

"They will stand as an example of what happens to deserters." said Almedda. "We must find a way to get around the faerimouth. They are impervious to most things and deadlier than most of the creatures of this world. We must get them to join our little country's army. We need officers as they ate the last set. What reports from Metra? Please say that Morreal is at least doing well." asked Almedda.

"Oh, I forgot she was dead already and that force has been destroyed. Do we still have the demons at Tetra? Did Barrish make it there?" asked Almedda.

"Barrish is at Tetra and is preparing the assault. As they have no magical folk in Tetra we will be coming in as a surprise. The city will be the first to fall and then we send the demons after the rest of them." said Carlee. She seemed to perk up with the prospect.

"Wonderful. We can make this even more interesting. If we can get the returning troops together and add them to the ones at Tetra, we could really hand out a major beating to Tetra. Thomas will never know what hit him." She giggled. "My nephew is still too young to understand the cloak removal spell and Thomas does not allow any other magical folk in Tetra. This should work just fine. Prepare my wagon and chariot. We will see the Queen at the fore of her army to destroy the good and great of our land."

CHAPTER SIXTY-FIVE

A STORY OF GATES

Tetra had not received any of the food stuffs and weapons from the other cities yet. Thomas was not worried but Meka was very worried. Pan Thor was there as a guest at the order of the Queen of Dracos. He was helping with the plans to defeat the army that was cloaked a little more than a mile from the city. She had sent a message to Thalinburg and Metra to please send the aid to the Eastern gate and not the Southern gate. The city had two gates the well-known southern gate and the obscure very hard to find Eastern gate. The aide headed to the city by that gate was not arriving and the armed forces being sent had the same problem. The Southern gate had the tall towers and great gates of heavy wood and iron. The Eastern Gate was a secret gate and had nothing drawing the eye to it. It also had a narrowing that a large force would be forced to compact itself long and narrow to face the defenders.

Opening that front gate was easily done by one man but it could hold against the largest of battle rams. And once inside the enemy had to traverse a maze of such complexity that if you did not know the city, you would never be able to get past the first set of lesser walls throughout the city. The many towers in the city allowed for arrows to rain down on enemies from all sides no matter where in the city they were. The barrage would break most enemies as soon as they entered the city proper.

Meka was watching for the clouds of dust that would indicate a supply chain and it was not long before she saw it. They approached the east gate and she rushed down to meet it with two companies of troops, one Tyris the other rangers, and opened the Eastern Gate. They fanned out around the supply wagons and the men driving jumped down and claimed they were stretching their legs.

Meka was concerned because she had seen what the Dark Queen was capable of. She sent for Paul Alon, the son of Perrick Alon and friend of the family, the thief to check out the wagons. She did not trust closed tight wagons in summer weather.

Paul came running as usual. She had told him he did not have to run everywhere but that was what he did. Paul reached the first wagon and looked at the seat first. He went deeper under the wagon looking for traps or surprises. They had stopped the wagons about a quarter mile from the gate. Anything goes wrong it won't harm the city.

Paul slid from under the wagon and checked the flaps. He peeked inside and drew his sword. He thrust it deep into the wagon and the sound of a man falling from the stab wound and Paul running back to the rangers gave away the trap. Meka had the troops surround the wagons just for this purpose. The two drivers of the first wagon drew swords and raced toward Meka.

Meka hefted a spear that had been left by one of the troops and killed the first driver. The second slowed down a little but too late. The spear pierced his abdomen and he too fell. The rest of the drivers had entered the fray, but were pick off by her troops. Three rangers came to escort her back to the city. She waved them away and drew her sword. The rangers fought alongside the Princess as she waded into combat. The rangers sent to protect her soon had their backs to the princess and the four killed their way around the wagons. The Tyris with their phoenix and swords had slaughtered most of the enemy secreted inside the wagons.

After the brief battle, the warriors of the light standing in victory were surprised to see Thomas coming to the field with a company of horsemen.

"You didn't leave me any. Where's the rest of them?" asked Thomas.

"They are all dead, you're late as usual. The wagons were headed to the secret gate. We have out in that army someone who know this city. I fear this was a ploy to shut down this gate so that they could get troops into the city. I fear the main attack is upon us. We had better be ready." said Meka.

"Sorry I was late do know many knights had not put on their armor this morning. More are coming to follow. As for ready we are and their little siege will not hurt us at all." said Thomas.

"You told us the rest of the horse are coming? Cancel the order, send them back. We set off an ambush. We must return to the city quickly and use this information to our advantage." said Meka.

Thomas pulled Meka onto his horse and they flew to the city. The horse and the two companies of troops returned to the city to see the first arrows fly off the walls down into the enemy below. Several orcs had made it to the top of the walls and a young man with a dagger was killing them as they reached the top.

The raid lasted only a few minutes. They were testing the defenders. Meka sent the Tyris and their companions to the wall.

She had found her companion phoenix in her room. She had introduced herself as Avery and the two had hit it off quickly. That was ten years ago when the phoenix had come to them. Now they could almost read each other's mind. Avery flew to the wall and kept watch for the enemy as Meka was taken to the palace by Thomas.

"If you do not wish a dagger in your ribs, you will put me down. I am going to the walls to give support and morale to our troops and present this sword I took from one of the soldiers in the east gate ambush and give it to that young man holding the dagger." said Meka. "And not one word about the mytan nor that I am not to be in combat any more. If you try and stop me, I will give you that dagger."

"I would not even attempt to stop you from going. I am not a fool. Besides, I believe you will do it. Ask your Tyris to take the east gate, and I will put the rangers to the Southern gate. There will probably be assaults at each." said Thomas.

Meka ran to the southern gate and found the young man who was holding the dagger. Taking the cloth, she was carrying the blade in she handed it to the young man. The man looked at it and grinned. "In all my life I never seen a sword as pretty as this. I am thirteen now and this is beautiful." He took the hilt and he swayed a bit.

"Are you ok?" asked Meka.

"I am a bit light headed. I think I will sit and set this blade to the side." said the young man and when he tried to set down the blade, it would not let him. The people around him, his eyes and mouth seemed to glow with blue fire. The boy just complained of pain in the arm and tingling in his head. As fast as the ailment hit him it receded and the blade settled down to the ground next to the chair the boy had tried to rest upon. The boy sat down hard and looked down at the blade. "Wow. That was a different experience. What happened?"

"It appears you are the proud owner of one of the dragon swords. When you grasped its hilt, it passed its power to you. You will now have a flaming sword regardless of the blade you possess. I think my brother made those but I may be mistaken. He is always doing things like having a sword pick its owner. Does the blade inside have a mark on it? That will tell us true." said Thomas as he climbed to the walls.

"Where did you find this? They are extremely rare." Thomas asked as the blade revealed the dragon running down its length. The boy was alarmed that the prince may try to take the blade from him and Thomas smiled. "Be calm. I have my own. Made by my brother and he showed only one other and she is dead. So, my brother must have made this one. But where was it that you found it."

"I found it on a dead mercenary in one of the wagons. I saw him fighting with just a dagger. So, I grabbed the blade from the first body I came to. And then I gave it to him. You know the rest. The sword chose him. So, what next?" asked Meka.

"Are the Tyris at the Eastern Gate? The danger is going to be there and we need a Special Forces army over there I believe. You lead them there, my dear." said Thomas.

"You're lucky that I like you or else, right to the moon with you. I am going on my way, the Tyris should be there already. I just had to drop that off." said Meka.

Meka was just arriving at the Eastern gate when the alarm bells started to ring. She looked over the edge of the wall to see the army of the Dark Lands moving past toward the Southern gate. Arrows harassed the army as it strode toward the gate, the fear in the soldiers' eyes told the story. They were being forced to this and were tired and completely without a shred of morale.

Meka almost felt sorry for them. She brought over a party of fifty Tyris to the town center and the militia man asked, "Is that all the soldiers you brought? Fifty? We have a few hundred."

"What is your profession, good sir?" Meka asked a man whose armor was too small for his girth.

"An Innkeeper." said the man. She asked several times the professions of the gathered troops and received many answers. From potters to politicians to bakers and innkeepers.

Meka said to the Tyris, "What is your profession, Tyris?"

As one unit they responded, "War."

Meka smiled at the militia man as the Tyris went to make traps throughout the square, "See I brought more soldiers. Now let's get going and prepare for the coming assaults."

The crowd was smiling and laughing as Meka went to assist in the defensive plans. They laid more traps and some pit falls and finally got the city ready for the siege. Everyone who was not going to be fighting was taken down into the caves and dungeons beneath their feet to protect them. Though some objected, they all did as they were told. A grizzled veteran argued that he needed to be up there with his old unit and Meka said to him, "You have served faithfully. Now it is time for some other to gain the glory and honor that you possess. Now I also need you and your fellows to guard these caves and let no one or nothing enter until I arrive to tell you they can come back to the city."

The old man grumbled but picked up a pike and called out to several others to do the same. They placed themselves against the rock faces and set the pikes to cross each other and Meka walked away. They would be well protected there.

Meka was heading away from the caves when Avery caught up to Meka. "Go back. The caves are compromised. The enemy doubled back and are heading right here. We need to hold until the rest of the army arrives to aid in the defense of those defenseless people."

Meka turned back to see the pike men at the cave mouth were already prepared. She ran to them and had the men set traps further up the cave entrances. She and Avery settled into an easily defended piece of the cave mouth, and hunkered down waiting for the worst. Avery squawked as the old men arrived beside her. "Good men. I need you back at the caves shaft. Not out here. I need you to be there to defend if I should fail. How did you know there was trouble?"

"Your bird talks awful loudly, and we are needed here. One woman will not stop the flood of the coming enemy, even if she is a Tyris. So, my lady, we stand or fall here. We have twenty men and yourself. I think at this point we may have the advantage." said the grizzled veteran she had set to watch the caves.

"You are good men sirs and we should not be fighting alone for long. Help comes quickly." said Meka. *I hope* she thought.

"My Lady, you are a poor liar. We know it will take time for the rest of the army arrive and even after they arrive, they have to fight to us. It may be a bleak day for most of us." said the man.

"Oh, I know. I have never been good at it. So. Now then let us hope they come quickly." said Meka as she hefted her sword and shield and prepared for the rapidly approaching army.

CHAPTER SIXTY-SIX

CAVES

Barrish was looking forward to the promise of defeating the Thalins from the hidden cave network. He knew he would have to face Thomas here and Christof, but one was young and inexperienced and the other old and cautious. He should be able to defeat them easily. He called for his scorpion men to move into position at the front of the cave. He would kill the innocents and then kill their men folk.

Barrish gave the order for the company of scorpion men to go into the caves and report what they see. The Dark Queen had given them the location of these caves. She seemed to know a lot about the Thalins and the cities. Her power was beyond anything he had ever seen over her enemies. It was like she knew the family personally.

Barrish waited for a minute then two then more until thirty minutes had passed. The scorpion men patrol had not returned the main army of the lands of the light were approaching from the rear and he wanted those caves before they arrived. He called out to the scorpion men in the cave and received no reply. They may have started without them.

Ordering in another patrol, he waited with baited breath as the scorpion men passed them. How long could it take to go in and send a man up with the news they were ready to kill? It was unreal how long it was taking. The man was not patient and sent another patrol out into the caves just men this time. Barrish saw two horrified men come out of the cave shaking and the rest remained below.

Barrish went to them and asked what the ordeal was. The scared men stuttered to answer, "They have slain the scorpion men, and their heads are lining the walls as we entered the cave. Then all of a sudden, they were on us. I and my friend here were lucky to escape."

"So, you deserted your friends to come up here and tell us what has happened? We have a way of dealing with deserters here, now don't we. Give them to the scorpion men and let them have their fun with them. You may get lucky and they will sting you to death before they eat you." said Barrish.

After hearing the report, the armies of the light had guards on their elderly and children. How quaint. They needed a proper send off. Looking at the demons, he ordered the lesser demons to go down the caves and deal with all of the people down there and come back when they were finished. They could destroy everything down there just get the job done.

Down in the caves the scene was much calmer and restful. The scorpion men were expected. They were an underground being and they were at home here. They had gotten a little lax as they walked down the path into the caves. At the narrows the scorpion men were surprised by the pikes coming into them from all sides. The whole lot was dead in a few moments and the bodies dragged away. The men took the heads and lined them up on the wall toward the entrance of the cave. Meka could not believe the skills these men still possessed.

They were admiring their handwork when the second group of scorpion men descended into the caves. They came on slowly and hesitantly seeing the heads of their comrades on the walls. They were so busy watching the heads that they did not realize they were under attack until it was again too late.

The men worked quickly and deadly when it came to dispatching the scorpions and soon, they were dragged away from the fight and their heads hung on the walls at the entrances to the caves. The group of men who came down were scared. If the scorpions could not survive down here, how could they? The men continued until they too were attacked. This time two men ran and were chased to almost the surface. The men went back to the hall and waited for the next attack and they did not have to wait long. Down the pipe came the Naga. The half human, half snake people of the sea were moving slowly down the pipe to the place where their comrades had fallen. They could see the events that had caused the end of their fellows and stopped shy of the narrowed entrance.

Preparing a slew of spells, the Naga moved forward. They turned to the walls quickly to find no one there. From behind the Naga heard a cough and flipped around to find themselves again killed before they could get themselves ready.

Meka thought they were done with patrols when suddenly she was hoisted into the air. The demon holding her was a big red demon called a furlac. She was being squeezed to death when a sword went under her arm and into the demon. More and more swords appeared in the monster and it released its grip, ever so slowly. As her head went below the demon's, a sword came and lopped off the monster's head.

Meka looked around to see who her saviors were. The old veterans and many of the young and the women folk stood holding weapons that had been dropped by the fallen enemies in the tunnel. Meka was amazed to see the youngsters and women attacking other demons and several demons phasing out in fear. As soon as it all began the fighting was over. No more units entered the caves and Meka sat down and cooled herself.

"I am proud to have you all in our city." said Meka.

"The pleasure is all ours, My Lady." said a young woman who walked up with a bloody sword in her hands. "I am one of the butchers in the city. There are several of us in the city and we specialize in different meats. Lord Thomas has been good to all of us, so we felt we could not let his Queen die at the hands of a demon."

"Of this, I am eternally grateful." Smiled Meka, "Of this I am thankful."

HAPPY REINFORCEMENTS

The scene above the caves was chaos. Barrish was trying hard to keep the demons and other creatures in line. He felt like he was herding cats as he chased first one group then another to the proper set off positions. He finally raised his hands and froze all of the soldiers in his army. He unfroze the officers to move their soldiers where they were supposed to be.

After what seemed an eternity, he removed the spell from the army and they looked at the tunnels down to the caves and realized that even the demons were not coming back to the surface. He looked at the larzod demons and nodded to them. They slowly headed for the caves when the horsemen from the city slammed into the side of them. The army started to join in on the horsemen until all of a sudden Thomas's rangers and infantry arrived behind the army and started to fire arrows and draw pikes.

The whole area around the army was surrounded with Thomas's infernal soldiers and they were raining death from above as Thomas attacked the demons headed for the young and old civilians. Barrish got a group of troops around the back of the horsemen and were charging to the attack when the very people he was trying to kill came out and broke the troops on their very weapons. All but a few pikes belonged to his army and they had stolen them.

The horsemen saw the sneak attack and the people with Meka defending their rear, the horsemen made a run at the main body of the army. Thomas's horsemen seemed to cut a path like a sword through fabric as they moved through the massed soldiers that were now way too tightly bunched together to defend themselves. To avoid the charging horsemen, they began to kill each other to escape. The creatures of his army were trying with all their might to get away from the armies of Thomas and Tetra.

Even the squad headed by Meka were chasing the army of the Dark Lands troops as they tried to escape. Barrish thought, *this is just not my day,* as he called for the retreat. The army slowly began to retreat toward the southeast and he saw the cloud of an army headed southeast. Expecting a confrontation, he ordered the warriors of his army to make ready to fight the new comer enemy.

The closer the army came the better view he had of their banners and sigils. The army was that of the king. The King's banner was held back and lowered to a staff down from the rest. From that he presumed the King was dead. Riding up to the other army the two clashed in a great grind. It took them several minutes to realize they were on the same side but by that time most of the king's army was destroyed and the rest assimilated into Barrish's. Evil plans were brewing in his head. He could make this work to his advantage.

The army had progressed a mile or so further down the road, when Barrish saw the dust of another army moving toward the south. Barrish once more called his troops to be ready and he pushed them hard to catch the other army. They caught them and again a quick battle that cost both sides a large quantity of their men and beasts ensued. Barrish once more reigned supreme and the now combined armies of the dark returned quickly to the dark land and set up camp outside the palace of the Dark Queen.

Almedda looked out the windows and saw the small force that surrounded her palace and smiled. Someone was going to die. Looking for a sigil she saw her husband's sigil and Morreal's. The sigil for Barrish was actually above the rest. So, he thought highly of himself. She called down to the tents and soldiers, "Whom do you serve?"

"Why we serve the Lord Barrish, My Lady. He brought us here." said one group of the soldiers. Several other inquiries gave the same answer. Her blood began to boil and she let out a laugh.

"Do you know whom he serves?" asked the Dark Queen.

"Why no, my lady. We are not privy to that kind of information." replied one of the soldiers.

"Have your master come to the castle, then I will explain who he serves." said Almedda.

"Why he won't do that until he gets the chance to call for a coup. Says the old Queen needs to be replaced with a strong King. And he will be that dark King." replied the soldiers.

A coup. Well, he really did think highly of himself. She would have to take a short trip down to the enemy encampment and see who knows who she is. She has been hidden away for a long time. The rank and file do not fear her, nor do the officers. The only one who does not want me to be here is the command staff. She will see to them herself.

She walked through camp without fanfare or attack so she was quickly to the well-guarded command tent. She dispatched the guards with a wave of her hand. Blowing the tent away revealed several men bent over a map. Barrish lashed out magically and it hit Almedda's shield and caused no harm to her. "So, my humble servants return. No chance of blaming everything you are doing on Morreal or Marcus. I know they both died for our cause. But you, you come here to have a rebellion. Barrish, how should I destroy you and your commanders here? Shall I take you all to the soldiers you so generously brought home to me. Let them have at you? Or maybe I take you to the dragons? That would be interesting to see you burned to death or otherwise killed there. Tell me how do you want to die?"

"My lady," began Barrish, "These troops will not follow you. They were saved from certain death by myself and the gentlemen here. Nothing you say or do will turn these idiots from us. They follow like a bunch of sheep. You have finally met your match. You knew we would rise up one day and destroy you. Now you will die." said Barrish as he sent spell after spell after the Queen. She stood silently as the barrage continued. After a while the smoke covered the entire body area of the Queen and the magical people looked at the smoke as meaning she was dead.

Barrish gave one last spell and stood there laughing. He had won that easily. How was that possible? But it was done. Barrish was just about to turn his back when the Queen emerged from the smoke and ashes. She threw a fireball into each of the generals at the table and they burned to ash almost instantly. She grabbed up Barrish with a flow of power around his neck. She slowly raised his body by the neck into the air. A very afraid Barrish looked the Queen in the eye.

"Surely, there has been an error here. I thought you might be losing your touch." said the druid

"Are you meaning to say you thought I was a pushover?" said Almedda. "You can admit it. I will not hold it against you. The coup on the other hand, well we must do something about that, now don't we? Let us see what I can come up with." She said with a little laugh in her voice as she took the terrified druid with her into the palace.

CHAPTER SIXTY-EIGHT

VIRGIL AND NEW FRIENDS

It seemed like an eternity, but peace was finally restored to the area around the three cities and the town of Landsdale. The enemy had attacked that town as well and found the steel wall an obstacle they could not overcome. Garren and his new bride showed themselves capable leaders and the enemy was routed quickly. Gardell was the new belle of the ball in the town. The town folk tried to build them a palace, but Gardell and Garren forbid it. The town folk still built them a manor house twice the size they needed.

Garren had received and urgent raven messenger. The dragons were coming. The enemy had about thirty of the younger dragons on their side, and they had been causing chaos around the town's area. The dragons on their side were a day or two away. Mastol had received a raven as well and was making what speed the dragons could make.

Garren grabbed the sword and armor his father had given him and Gardell put on her mytan and grabbed a long spear and mace and the town's militia followed the pair toward the area being attacked. They had made it about half a mile from the town when they were attacked by a group of noom. The dwarves quickly dispatched them and the procession continued.

The procession ran into groups of orcs and goblins. They attacked hard and it was a dear victory for Garren and Gardell as they lost five of their people and wounded were at least ten. They left some warriors there to monitor the dead and wounded until they returned to assist them home.

The procession could see the dragons as they finally got to the six miles from town mark. Getting their armor and weapons ready the procession waded into the dragons. A large male landed in front of Garren and tried to attack with his jaws. Garren drew his sword and swung with all his might as the dragon came in for his bite. Garren felt the sword hit flesh and looked down at the dragon's head on the ground. The rest of the creature fell to the earth and Garren turned to the militia and Gardell and smiled. Calls of Dragon slayer flew through the procession of dwarves. Garren would earn that title three more times that day and Gardell won one battle. The militia fired all of the weapons they had and helped kill at least two more.

Marious was seen flying over the chaos his people were creating and fired down balls of flame. He never came within bow range or weapon range sending his younger colleagues down to attack.

The first day saw the dragons leave the area. Garren and Gardell were considered heroes in the town of Riverton. They slept there with an honor guard from both cities' militia. It was about six o'clock in the morning when the pair was awakened with word that the dragons had returned with even more numbers.

Marious was lined up with his small army of dragons and the townspeople looked on in fear as the two heroes from the day before came out and stood before the already lined up militia. Garren seemed to shine like the morning sun verse the darkness before him. The dragon seemed more than there was supposed to be. There were more than twenty dragons there and his small forces would not be able to chase this group off.

"We are looking at the end for many if not all of us. We stand now alone before the dragon horde and I say that it was an honor to die alongside you all in defense of this town. May those that come behind us find more luck than we have drawn today." said Garren.

The army of Landsdale and Riverton moved forward and headed right at the dragons and as they started to run into their line the dragons took to the air and ran.

"There is no way that should have worked." Garren said. "We have the day!" He exclaimed. Looking toward the retreating dragons he let out a whoop and spun around and stopped mid turn. Behind him and his army sat the elders of the dragons with their horde of dragons. Mastol looked down at him and smiled. "Little one, thanks for the encouragement. What do we have here?" said the great wyrm as he looked down at Gardell.

"I am Garren's wife. And who are you?" said Gardell.

"He is an old friend. Sorry Mastol, should have made the introductions. Lady Gardell Thalin, Mastol the dragon. He is one of the elders of the dragon race and a close family friend." said Garren. "Please excuse her. It has been a long couple of days."

"Garren Thalin. You will not apologize for me. I am a grown woman and I say what I mean. Now Mastol, tell me all about the boy as he grew up." Smiled Gardell.

"Hey there, don't be going there. Not here at least. Let us return to Landsdale and give these dragons a proper welcome." Garren said quickly as he headed toward the town. They had traveled on foot because there were not enough horses for everyone. Garren regretted not having the horses now.

Mastol offered him and Gardell a ride but they both politely declined. They would not fly when their army was walking. "Are there not a flood of dragons about. People mount up on a dragon. We travel in style today." said Mastol. The other dragons looked at him with concern in their eyes but did as they were told.   The short flight held the warriors in awe. The arrival of the dragons made the town cheer and celebrate. They would be protected for a little while. The troops told the story of the first dragon slain and how Garren had not even flinched in the face of the dragon. He was truly the Dragon Slayer.

Mastol looked at him and raised an eye brow. "Dragon slayer? Do please tell." said Mastol. Garren was spared having to tell the tale by the eager troops that had been there. Each put in details the other forgot and still the other added more to the tale and it grew larger the more it was told.

Mastol was laughing as Garren tried to escape the scene and return to the manor house. He was bumped and shimmied by the dwarves as he headed back to his home and he suddenly felt the stab of a sharp object into his arm. Looking down at his left arm he noticed it would not move. Slowly his other limbs refused to cooperate and the druid was there his wife standing worriedly over him.

The druid looked at the wound and drew out a vial and tube. He wrapped the tube until a small pocket was surrounding the tip. He heated the air in the vial with a small taper and set the tube over the lip of the container as the taper burned. Within seconds the taper had burned out all the oxygen in the container and a vacuum occurred on the cup side against the wound.

The poison was sucked from the wound, at least enough to identify the culprit. The druid kept it there for a minute until the blood flowed red. Then he pulled the tube from the wound and gave the sickly prince a piece of honey bread. "Eat this. It will help. Get this man a beer to wash this down. He needs to build his strength again." said the druid.

"What is your name, good druid? I want to thank you for saving my husband." said Gardell as Garren sat in the center of the ground where he fell. He was feeling better.

"Virgil, My Lady, Virgil Jarvis. Your husband was poisoned with frog venom. It is normally a problem with dogs as they try to chew the frogs. The wound could only have come from a small dagger or a large cork screw. One or the other. Someone wanted your husband to die slowly and painfully." said the man.

"Who would know of these things? Whom should we be looking for?" asked the worried Gardell.

"Anyone with a dagger is suspect and as for who would know the tree frog venom, well that would be a wizard or a druid. Your husband does better now. See the food and drink helped. Up you go Garren. Now let us get you to your rooms." said Virgil.

The royal couple walked over to the manor house and opened the door and saw eight eyes staring back at them, Closing the door quickly, Virgil asked the crowd, "Anyone ready for a short fight?"

"What is wrong? I will take care of it." said Gardell as she headed for the door.

"Anyone not royalty please come forward. Ahh, yes good man, come. Come. It is just a large spider that needs disposing of. A very large spider." said Virgil. The dwarf came forward and Virgil placed the dwarf in front of the door. "You can fight when I tell you. Understand?"

"Yes sire, let's do this." said the dwarf. A small band of warriors had surrounded the dwarf and the royals and Virgil was waving for them to draw swords and bows.

"Ready to open the door? Shall we all begin?" said Virgil as the dwarf stepped forward and opened the door. Virgil pulled him back with a flow of air and the spider went after him. Behind the beast came the scorpion man. Apparently, they had gotten trapped when their army was defeated. Arrows and swords attacked the beast and the scorpion man until they were unidentifiable. The people looked warily at the two deceased enemies and called for a cleaning crew.

Garren had developed that as a way for non-combatants to feel like they had a job to do. He had, in fact, created teams for just about all the jobs needed in the town. They worked hard and the enemy was repelled faster due to it. The people loved him for making them all feel needed, a feat that his elder brothers had yet to master.

The cities had more people in them but he caused the town to be a happy community and he had people coming in from Riverton and Lyonsdale to settle here as well as come to see the town. The people looked at the steel wall with amazement. Several engineers surveyed it to see if similar could be done in their own towns.

Of course, they wanted to do it bigger and better. They would have their magical folks melt the steel and affix it to the wooden walls. They drew up plans and talked into the night as to how it should be done. Garren told them that he would only be speculating as it was his brother who created them.

The engineers left the next day headed to Metra. Torlin would enjoy talking shop with them. He was still weak from the poison attack when the assassin tried again. This time his lack of visibility was compromised by his movement through the tree next to the royals. Seeing the dagger, Gardell grabbed the man's wrist and pulled him into the light.

The creature began to scream and seemed to melt in the bright sunshine. Garren had a cover put over him and the screaming and melting stopped but he attempted to kill Garren once more. Garren ordered him to be bound and seated on the ground under the cover.

Gardell whispered in his ear and looked at the man. Sure enough, he was a Mardock, but with he looked like he had intelligence so he asked the creature its name. It did not reply but lay there and look pitiful. The Mardock was to be transported to the dungeons when the young man came from the crowd and stabbed the Mardock in the chest.

People reached to grab the young man but he seemed to fade away before their eyes. Gardell noticed the movement in the corner of her eye and struck with her sword down on the edge of the movement and the young man once more was visible as he was injured. The young Mardock lay on the ground clutching his now severed hand. His screams of pain brought the druids and they attempted to heal him when they noticed that he too was a Mardock. They covered the young man and still he screamed. The wound was not bleeding as the young man was already dead, but still he screamed. The Mardocks that had attacked the royals in the town were now either captured or dead.

They looked at the boy at their feet and said, "My God, she made a Mardock of a teenager. What kind of horrors is she capable of?"

"Let's hope this is the extent of her horrors." Prayed Garren as he shook his head and watched the executioner finish the undead assassin.

CHAPTER SIXTY-NINE

PLANS

The world was quiet for a few months as the royal family planned for the course of action Tanis was proposing. He was telling the others that they should bring the battle to her. She had been forcing them to her tune by forcing the battle to be fought her way. But if they came to her, she would have little time to prepare and return their attack.

Thomas was all for it. He had lost a great number of his rangers and troops to the Dark Queen and his horse wanted a shot at the royal caravan. Meka was on board with Thomas but Christof had doubts. "Mom, this is too easy. From an enemy that has been so forceful and so powerful, to being a wounded cat licking its wounds. I do not think so."

Thomas looked at the boy and shook his head. He was a good soldier but lacked real intelligence. The boy was good in battle but he still had so much to learn. Meka was coddling the boy. He needed to learn real battle. Not just a siege.

The army from Tetra met the armies of Thalinburg at the statue commemorating the First War of Power. The armies of Metra would be there shortly as would the armies of Landsdale. They had farther to travel. Tanis erected a command tent and waited for the missing brothers.

The armies of Metra arrived shortly after the tent was finished and the camp tables and maps were laid out. Discussion had started as to who had the most troops and where they would be best placed. The day turned to two and then three and the army of Landsdale did not show. Tanis was getting concerned and sent a runner to check on them.

The runner came back in an hour. The army was coming and they brought dragons. They had an assassination attempt and it almost worked. Two of the assassins were dead and Garren was recovering but ready to go to work.

Tanis was concerned, "What about number three? Garren how bad was the assault. Where was your injury? How deep? I need to know these answers."

"Father, my wound was superficial. It was tainted with frog venom but Virgil caught the poison and was able to remove the majority. The rest would have to work through my system. As for number three, there was no number three." replied Garren sitting down in the only chair in the tent. Gardell stood behind him and the whole family together filled the tent leaving little room for the work at hand.

Torlin seeing the space shortage waved his hands with a spell and the tent shot up into the air and when it came down was erected and much larger. The family still filled the tent but was not completely full. The youngest children remained in Metra; save Christof whose father wanted him to be blooded in a real war. Meka disagreed but was finally convinced by Thomas.

The young man was concerned as expected but he was acting strange. He said he had feelings from the Dark Lands. These feelings were only about certain areas. "I swear that my feelings are coming to me through the power. They are like a warning to avoid certain areas. Grandfather, listen. We must go east for another mile. I fear that there is a trap waiting for us here."

"If there is trouble there, then we will clear it," remarked Thomas.

Artitous piped up after a moment "Christof is the most powerful magical individual alive, save the Dark Queen. If he senses their forces, we should listen. He was born with unheard of ability and many talents, like detecting evil."

"How bad is the feeling here?" asked Tanis. Looking down at the map. Looking for another place to hide their massive army.

"Bad enough, Grandfather. But it is very clear one mile east. Cutting through the plains we may see some centaurs, maybe some of those spiders. But I think that they would be passive as they are non-combatants. This also gives us a staging area that is not on the enemies' radar. Barrish and the Dark Queen are all that we know are still alive after the loss at the cities. Things can go seriously wrong very quickly if either of them appears." said Christof, looking from side to side as if expecting a horde of enemies coming at him. "The evil is strongest near the center of the Dark Lands. It is there that the Queen and Barrish will be found. I can sense their evil no more. Sorry I can be of no more help."

"Your gift is worth a thousand men. Horsemen, one hundred go to the border of the Dark Lands and have whatever is there come here after you." said Tanis. "That should clear our way don't you think."

"Make ready. they are coming this way. I can sense them nearby." said Christof.

"Yeah, I can see them. Ugly buggers too. Draw weapons men of Tetra and attack the coming scorpions. Go, move. Christof, we have to move, now." said Thomas as he drew his sword. Christof shook off the feelings he was experiencing and created his magical sword. His father just shook his head and ran to confront the enemy head on.

"Mine does not go dull or break, Father." said Christof as Thomas swung his sword decapitating a scorpion man. Christof swung his sword and cut two of them through the middle and then finished them with a coup de gras, severing the two scorpion men's heart and lungs in one swing.

"Show off." said Thomas as he suddenly found himself and Christof surrounded by the creatures. He swung and swung as Christof worked the rear with strategical precision. The dead enemies piled around Thomas and Christof was growing and both men showed signs of fatigue. Their wounds were superficial but would require a healer's touch.

Without thinking first Christof swung right at is father. Thomas screamed at the boy as dived out of the way and then saw what he had missed. A severed hand fell to the earth and then the creature's head. Christof stood ready looking for more enemies to find the field empty save the bodies of men, elves, dwarves, and scorpion men. A few orcs and goblins died there as well but it was small number. Tanis looked amongst the dead and dying until he found what he was looking for. Leaning over he took Warmonger from the ground and put it back in his sheath.

The blade had killed two before they realized that it was a trap. They avoided the area quickly. But at least it worked a couple of times. Tanis realized now that Christof was right about his senses. The test had produced a result, just one larger than expected. The royals all met in the command tent. The thing that had amazed all present was that every one of them had survived.

"Put a pin in the areas you sense evil. We want no more surprises such as the last one. Christof, I know you are very tired but we need you to show us the way. Ignore your father. Use your abilities." said Tanis.

Christof looked at his grandfather and reached out with his eyes closed. "We need to leave soon. The party that we attacked was not alone and are returning with reinforcements. We have to go soon or be attacked again harder than before." said Christof. He looked at the map and magically marked every placement that he had felt. The mark faded until it was touched by one of the royals. "I could not key it in to the other commanders, just royal blood. Sorry." said a very upset Christof.

"Don't worry about that, boy. These marks need to be linked to the family only. Torlin, you and Christof get into the wagon. I want you two to create a weapon that will bring down the Dark Queen. It must also be able to destroy the grimoire. For that will be a thorn in all of our sides as long as it exists. And if you say move, we move." said Tanis. Tanis did not reveal that he did not trust the community of lords and ladies. They were not invited into the command tent it was the royals that gave the word for all of their activities. The lords just enforced the orders and apparently planned coups.

The order was given to move the camp to the dark land's fields. It would be there that they formed for the battle and to see if they could reveal and destroy the Dark Queen. Christof formed a blade of magic that he used and thrust it at his grandfather. Tanis twisted out of the way and came face to face with a minotaur. The beast was falling from Christof's blade and Tanis looked down at the blade in Christof's hands. "That is twice today I nearly lost a family member. You two really need to pay better attention." Laughed Christof as they packed the tent magically and started the march to the dark fields.

CHAPTER SEVENTY

READY FOR ACTION

The army of the light lands headed to the plains that filled both the human, elf, and dwarf people's lands. They did not even realize they were into the enemy territory until they saw the centaur's homes and them working and clearing land for food and work areas. They were friendly to the people of the light and none raised weapons. It was very nice to see the people of the Dark Lands being not much different than them. It made them wonder.

Christof twice warned them off a path or road due to the large amounts of evil he felt. The funny thing was that the villages and towns were not being felt as evil. They were so much like the lands to the north that the human army felt right at home.

They left the villages and towns unharmed as they headed deeper into the Dark Lands. The first small city they approached had a regiment of wolf riding tree folk. They attacked briefly and then rode back to the city. The humans defended themselves but did not pursue the enemy. After about half an hour or so, two of the tree folks rode out to the head of the column. Tanis and the royals sat with them and they realized that they were not there to harm their people.

The treelings were grateful. The Dark Queen had been sending raids of men, orcs, and goblins to steal their youth and press them into the army. They offered to aid the army of light if they would try to bring home their people. They said that they were all wizards and capable of assisting in healing and sieges.

They found the same kind of reception at several other towns and cities. They all were concerned about the army harming them. When it was explained that they were not there to harm the people of the Dark Lands. They were there to liberate and destroy the evil that has been ruling them for most of their existence.

The town folks were helpful and encouraging of the army and some even joined their ranks. It was as this was happening the first cloud of dust approached the army. It was heavy calvary of Ogiers and men. The leader of the calvary raised his lance toward the sky and him and two Ogier guards went to meet them halfway between the two armies.

Tanis approached with swords loose in the scabbard. Torlin had spells ready and Thomas and Christof had weapons ready by their sides. The group edged forward to the three warriors before them and drew up and dismounted. "Good men and Ogier, please let us have a talk. We are not here to destroy or harm your peoples and lands. We pass peacefully in search of the Dark Queen. Then we will give her battle, and those that choose to protect her." said Tanis.

"Then we will join your army. It is a constricted army you see here and now we can regain our own will and join you. Let us find and destroy Elizarade." said one of the Ogier.

"So, the Queen has taken the name of the necromancer. This is foul news to be sure. Does anyone know who she was before she became the necromancer?" asked Tanis.

"Does it really matter?" asked Thomas.

"It could be a way to return her to herself if we know." said Artitous.

"She is a mass murderer and a warlord. She is evil incarnate and this Queen appears to be stronger than any that has ever lived. I vote we just put an arrow through her." said Gardell.

"The Dark Queen once had the name Almedda. She never revealed any other name. She enjoys the pain she inflicts totally and completely. She dances in the blood of the fallen. She was evil even before the grimoire took hold of her. No amount of coercion will separate her from the grimoire. And she has made her life's work to kill all of the royal family. So, I fear you walked into a trap. But at least we die free." said the man.

"Almedda as in Almedda Thalin?" asked Christof.

"I doubt that. She would be about twenty-three now. The Dark Queen is about what thirty or forty?" said Tanis.

"But how do we know? It may be her. After all, she was the most powerful of the four of us. And that grimoire gives her even more power. How do we know?" said Christof.

Tanis waved his hand at the boy and walked toward the command tent. He was deep in thought. *Could the most dangerous enemy they had ever faced really be my daughter?* Thought Tanis. This could mean a major change of strategy. The Dark Queen is coming for the royal family. It was a question for later. If it was Almedda, why does she hide herself and why the cloak and dagger? Things were getting bad again. The rise of the Dark Queen makes lots of enemies and shows some's true character.

The next morning the plans that they discussed during the night were put into play. Tanis led the main column, with Torlin and Christof incase the Queen showed up. Artitous also remained with his old student. Thomas was sent south and west, while Garren and his wife went north and west. If one column was destroyed the other two may survive and complete the mission.

Gardell still tried to convince the elders that they should just get a few Tyris and rangers out for an assassination attempt. Then they could mop up the remaining troops. It would be simple. Garren was in agreement. How could they do anything else? The orders were handed out and Garren groaned softly.

The marches would culminate at the palace of the Dark Queen. The time to split was quite there, but Garren saw a small platoon of rangers leave under special orders by his grandfather and Martin. They were going to attempt an assassination. Garren prayed that they were successful.

Gardell saw the rangers leaving and asked her husband what was going on. The Tyris amongst them spoke of a curse on the castle in the Dark Lands. It was said that the castle was once a shining beacon to the world of Dracos. But an ancient Tyris Queen spoke to and sided with an evil necromancer, named Elizarade. The two were transformed into the two darkest people that had lived to this day. They were cruel and wicked toward the people. The people looked for a hero and could find none amongst them so they went hunting. The people first went to McCryden and the lands of the men. But no one was capable of defeating the Dark Queen. The longer that the two lived together in that castle, the more the castle was cursed. Their very spirit alone was all that was necessary. No spells, no sacrifices and it just started. The grimoire was written a few months before and the lands around the palace felt the effects. It became dark and giant insects and birds and dragons began to come from the land. The people went to the dwarves and still there was no hero. Finally, they went to their sworn enemy, the elves. The elven king met them and the discussion lasted long into the night They needed to find a hero. The king of the elves was a wise man. He knew that they would find no such hero.

The elven king recommended that instead of looking for the perfect warrior, why not combine the powers of all of the people with a small party of elf, dwarf, man, noom, and the Lochlyn trees. One each of each race. They would be warriors and mages, rangers and thieves. It would guarantee that they would at least make it to the chambers of the Dark Queen and her aide. The legend went on to say that the party found darkness covered the Dark Lands and was spreading. They finally made it to the palace to find the Queen was expecting them. They killed her guards and slay her herself with the loss of their poor ally, the Lochlyn tree fell to the Dark Queen's sword. Elizarade was nowhere to be found. But they looked at the great book that sat in the desk. The elf wizard looked down at the book and she grinned as the magic seeped into her. Turning she killed her companions and became the new ruler of the Dark Lands. She was later killed by a stray arrow, but the story gave the conclusion, to kill the Dark Queen's emergence ever again, they must destroy the grimoire without a magical person laying hands upon it.

Obviously, that had never happened but the book had been captured and separated several times. The pieces would call to each other and almost always returned to the Dark Queen. This time the Tyris hoped that a new woman would not fall to the ways of the book.

After they told of the beginnings of the Dark Queens and Elizarade, they came up with a plan to destroy the grimoire. It was just unknown how to destroy the book. There were rumors that Elizarade was the only one who could destroy the book. And that did not sit well with the men and women following. He started to ride for the wizard's tower and forgot it had not yet been finished. Almedda killed all of the people in that tower.

It could not have been his daughter. She was a little competitive, but she would never do the things that this Queen did. The Queen was a bully and she despised bullies. Tanis deep down though, knew it was her. How she became this despot he did not know but he was going to find a way to remove it from her.

Thomas was going to grab the book and Torlin destroy it with magic. Easy. They were still younger men and could do so as nimbly as Tanis, who was needed for the army out front of the palace. Should the grimoire get into the wrong hands, it would be devastating.

Almedda had known of the army moving into her lands as soon as they did. They were safely put away already. Carlee was watching from the air as often as she could without being seen. Almedda had been reading deep into the book. She knew how to destroy the phoenix, but she came in handy at times. The phoenix sometimes looked at her as if she were thinking the same thing. They were definitely a matched set.

Almedda called for her generals. They agreed that action should be taken but the deep question was what. They had several of the people from the Dark Lands following them so no conscripts could come from those towns and cities. That severely cut down on the number of soldiers they had to fight in the armies of the light. Several of the generals had argued that the Queen should move deeper into the deep dark. She was too valuable to the people to be captured or even killed.

A shadowy figure entered the room and everyone but Queen Almedda turned to see and had a shiver come over them. The creature kept his hood up and spoke briefly. "I need chimera and Griffiths to dispose of the main threat. Otherwise, the army follows Tanis Thalin like a child follows its parent. They would do anything he asks. I fear they are not as soft as we first expected. It could be a problem later."

"Very good, my friend. Very good indeed." said Almedda.

"Did you not hear what he just said? They trail him like a puppy dog and will allow no harm to befall him. How is this good?" asked the general standing beside the Queen.

"The way it stands I only have to kill one man to set the enemy up for complete failure. The kids would fall quickly once the father is dead. And the younger members of the family will perish even easier. Are your soldiers ready to fight or are they going to stay out of phase forever?" asked Almedda. "Gentlemen, allow me to introduce the Almeck demons. The leader of which has informed me that they can get to the King of the lands of the light and see him dead forever. A king for a king."

The creature showed white glistening fangs and a mouth full of sharp teeth to the generals. One of the generals asked how the demons would get past the Holy Avenger. His question was met with ridicule. Even the Queen was laughing at the inquiry. The demons must have a strategy but many of them could fall to that blade before he be overrun by the demons. That would really detour the talks with the demons.

The general quietly left the meeting looking like he was embarrassed by his question. He would show them. He did not see the half-phased demon follow behind him as he left.

DEMON HUNTER

Several hours after dark, a rider entered the camp of the Army of Light. The guards stopped him as he entered the camp, seeking identification. The man simply said, "I will speak only with Tanis Thalin. I come at great risk. If my Queen knew I was here I would also die by her henchmen. So, open the command tent and let me in before I am seen and slaughtered."

Tanis came out of the tent and ushered the man into the map room. The tents were large enough to have canvas rooms and the man looked impressed by their ingenuity but feared it would be lost after they were gone.

As they looked at the map, the man finally spoke, "I came here at great risk to my life to tell you that the Dark Queen has a treaty with phase demons called…." He fell were he once stood his blood flowing from a gash across the back of his throat. The demon moved quickly to the patriarch of the family and rammed his blade deep within the immortal man.

Tanis fell to the ground as Christof leapt to his grandfather's defense and grabbed the Holy Avenger and sliced at the demon. Unfortunately, by the time he had drawn and was able to swing the blade the demon had phased. Christof ran to his grandfather's prone body and felt for signs of life. The man who had come to warn them had died before he had hit the ground but Tanis still held on.

Christof used what little healing he knew to help knit the wound closed. The problem occurred that the wound would not knit. No matter if it was Artitous or Christof, the wound would not close. Christof watched the wound and he noticed the hilt of the knife phase in and out of existence. When it once more came into existence Christof went to grab the hilt and was stopped by Artitous. "That is demon wrought steel. Touching it can cause you to lose your mind or worse turn into one of them. Use your abilities the next time it is visible and take it that way."

Christof readied his spell and the dagger once more came into being. Grabbing it with the power he slammed it into the post in the middle of the room. As soon as it hit the hard wood, it stopped phasing. Christof then melted the knife to a puddle on the floor. The demon had returned while they were tending to the dagger and Tanis and he whispered into Christof's ear as he was about to plunge yet another knife into the now very wary young man. The demon phased into being and was about to stab the young man when the Holy Avenger plunged deep into the demon's heart. Looking back, he saw his grandfather sitting up and holding the sword and then falling back to the earth.

Christof tried to heal the wound again and again the wound refused to heal. Artitous leaned over the boy and made a poultice to put into the wound. He took a minute to bandage the injury and stood back. Christof had a deep, serious face on and he asked if his grandfather was going to make it. Artitous levitated Tanis and carried him to his bed. "It is hard to say. That was a demon blade and it was in deep. It depends upon how hard he is willing to fight. "

"Then he will fight with all of his might." said Christof as he watched his grandfather slowly close his eyes and fall asleep. Christof picked up the Holy Avenger and its scabbard and put it on his back. A man went to pick up the Warmonger with a blanket and Christof grabbed it before he could get it. The man watched and waited for the boy to be cut and amazement filled the man's face.

He pointed to the Warmonger and Artitous smiled. The weapon was staying within the family if Tanis falls. Christof placed the Warmonger across the Holy Avenger and he walked from the tent with both swords. Legend said that the Warmonger would erupt into red flames of wrath against an enemy, but his grandfather had never seen it happen. Maybe it was dormant. His thought kept coming back to the legendary sword of his grandfather's. He had it for more that forty years. Still, he lived up to the legend of the sword as it had never lost in combat. It had never broken, chipped or rolled its edge. The thing was so endowed with magic that it cut anyone but his grandfather who had ever carried it. It had killed many of them. Just as he was thinking about that he realized that it sat upon his back. He pulled the blade free and the blade sung. He looked down the blade and he saw the reflection of himself in it. It did not try to twist, turn, or otherwise try to cut him. He once more looked into the blade and he saw a flame begin to come from the blade as he saw the phase demon coming into being behind him.

Pretending he did not see the creature he stood and thrust the Warmonger under his arm and it cleaved the demon in half. Red flames traveled the length of the blade as more of the demons came into this world from theirs. Christof fought them like a legend of old as he would kill first one then another of the beasts, until none remained. As the last one fell, the blade went from red flame to plain steel once more. He went to clean the blade before the demon blood etched the blade and saw it was clean.

He tried again and again to swing the Warmonger and again and again no harm came to him. The grooms watching were terrified that the blade would somehow sever his head from his shoulders. They were impressed with the dead demons but were quite afraid for the boy's safety. Several times the men came with the blankets so as to not touch the deadly blade. Christof was playing all sorts of sword-based skills in his hands with the sword, making the poor men go nuts trying to get the blade away from him. As they had moved to a place to grab it, they realized that he was not harmed. He had held it and moved it longer than any one of them had without wound or scratch. Maybe the sword did follow him. And if he could wield the Warmonger and the Holy Avenger than maybe he was worth following.

Some of them ran and told others while, some ran to tell Artitous. Others went to the mages and told them of what had occurred and some to the soldiers. Soon the entire camp was sitting waiting for the boy to give the commands. They sat expectantly at the feet of the boy as he fiddled with the sword in his hand. Artitous looked at the boy and whispered in his ear. "They await your orders. You can wield the Avenger and Warmonger. In their eyes, that makes you the new head of this army. Let your instincts guide you. They will show you right. Now what do you think should happen?"

"You three there. Come to the royal tents and bring your wagon. You and half a platoon of Tyris will get Tanis to Thalinburg and with the Queen. His care will be done there were he will be safe. The buildings and city of Thalinburg are immune to demons and other underworld creatures. That and all the druids and mages in the city will give them second thoughts of entering. As for the rest of us, we wait here. I am not quite ready to venture deeper into the Dark Lands quite yet." Ordered Christof. The three men that he had selected jumped to their feet and he asked one of the elven healers to travel with the party.

He was amazed that the people were so eager to follow him. "Uncle Arty, why is this so? I can hold the Warmonger, so. I can wield the Holy Avenger, big deal. I am a mage and a warrior. I have no experience to nor any desire to rule. I could get people needlessly killed."

Artitous replied, "You are a symbol of power now. You wield the unwieldable blades. Your grandmother would be proud to have you lead this army. Tanis will eventually heal but it will take some time. For now, we have demons to hunt."

Christof marked the point by shoving a blade through the face of one of the grooms passing by. He went rigid then fell. The illusion it was wearing fell and the demon showed on the ground. As the demon fell others of its breed came and tried to grab Tanis. Christof and Artitous fought side by side defending the fallen leader while at the same time trying to make sure that people were only fighting demons, and no other men. Christof killed another demon and he called for everyone to cease their fighting. "I believe the demons have left. Three of those who can scry for demons and I will head out to follow the demons' home. Remember some of the mages and druids can sense the demons so be on your toes and be ready for more attacks by the demons."

Thomas came out of the tent and asked, "Who died and left him in charge?"

Meka grabbed his arm and told him, "Your father. He wields the great swords."

"So, I can wield them, boy give me the Warmonger so I can show these people that I can handle it just as well as you can." Screamed Thomas. As he grasped it, it cut him deeply on the shins. He lifted it high and tried to swing it. This time it almost took his head, had Christof had not grabbed the blade in time. Thomas fretted and fumed and went back into the tent to be treated for his wounds.

"We are both proud to follow you, son. Lead us well." said Meka.

Christof took Martin and Artitous with him. The Phoenix's Hand had automatically moved to Christof as soon as Tanis had been injured. Half accompanied the fallen Tanis to the city of Thalinburg. The remainder insisted on accompanying the young prince on his demon hunt. Christof watched his grandfather's wagon until he could no longer see it. Tears came to his eyes as he watched and he looked next to him and saw his father, tears in his eyes as well.

"I thought you believed him an imposter?" said Christof.

Thomas wiped his eyes and looked down at his son, once more with the bravado in place, "Sometimes people are wrong. Lead well." As he spoke, he walked away. He headed back to the tents of the royals and disappeared. Christof smiled. There was hope yet.

The next morning the army set up small camps surrounded with magical and physical walls. No one would enter or leave without everyone knowing. He did the outbound so he could identify spies. It did not make a racket, it just let him know who had left and returned in cover of night or by daylight. It was a useful tool.

The first day of the demon hunts found them looking for smoke. For no demons appeared and all they saw were puffs of smoke. It was proof that they had come this way. As they continued their hunt, the second day brought the first attack from the demons.

Christof had awakened. One of the magical seals he had set went off. It was an outbound person. But as he tried to figure who it was the demons descended upon the young man. These were the more common Javan demons. They were quickly dealt with by the Hand before he could get his sword free. These were not that smart for a demon. Watching the area around the camp showed him what he was concerned about. Furlac demons were headed toward them.

Christof was ready this time though with Warmonger in one hand and the Holy Avenger in the other. When the demons finally got to them, Christof killed the lead demon with two swipes of the sword. A large demon smacked hi and sent him flying. Martin put an arrow through its eye and it still came at them looking for Christof. Christof did not disappoint as he came into the battle in a rage and cut the legs of the demon out from under it.

A quick coupe de gras, and Christof was after the next one. The Hand had lost at least two to the demons so far and Christof was not going to allow them anymore. He swung his swords with the determination of a sword master. Avery, his mother's phoenix, came and joined the fight, saving Christof from a death blow by the largest of the Furlac. She was almost caught by the demon when Christof slashed it down its middle with the Avenger. Screaming in rage the demon turned and swung it axe at the pair now facing it. The phoenix flew higher while firing a blast of fire down on the demon. Christof rolled into the strike and forced the Warmonger into its neck and stabbed it through the heart with the Avenger. Bellowing once more it tried to turn and face the man and bird that were killing it but the turn only went half way as the demon fell to the earth. Christof pulled his blades from the demon and the flames came unbidden to the Warmonger once more.

Turning toward the trees he saw a mixture of the four types of demons they had seen, and they were a large group. He had lost quite a few men and women. Tired and angry, He set the remaining warriors and magical folk he had left in a battle line formation and took the middle spot expecting this to be the end of him. The demons had just about reached them when the elven infantry and the human calvary arrived and slammed into the demons. Christof was swept up onto a horse behind his mother and her phoenix landed on her shoulder.

Thomas came in with the horse and smiled. "You may make a warrior yet. Just next time try not to fall into a well-placed trap. Good thing that we were in the neighborhood or who knows what would have happened."

"Yes father, good thing that you were in the area. Right mother?" said Christof smiling at his parents.

"But of course, my boy" said Meka as she sheathed her sword and the groups were carried by horse back to the camps. Meka's bay was not even winded when they returned to camp. Christof got down and still brushed the horse and cooled him down. Even though the horse was not sweating he still treated the horse as if he had run for hours. The horse nuzzled into him and shook its nose. It was looking for its accustomed apple. Christof smiled at the horse and took out an orange. The horse looked at the fruit and at first refused to take it. When Christof had offered it again, the horse took it. After a little chewing the horse was nuzzling Christof again. Apparently, the horse liked the orange.

"One a day, you. Don't want to get you fat." said Christof as he patted the horse's nose. The horse pulled away and went to the end of the corral and nuzzled the female piebald horse in the corner. She was paying him attention.

Christof laughed as the female bit him on the nose. The bay just backed off and went to the hay trough. Advances for another day. Christof made his way to the command tent as the rangers began choosing the new members of the Hand of the Phoenix. Christof had other important duties to tend to.

The cook waited in the tent as Christof came in. "Sire, we have bad potatoes for baking. These are just no good for baking. What should I do?"

"Dear sir, what are they good for?" asked Christof.

"Why I guess they would do well stewed or mashed, My Lord," said the chef.

"Then do that. Anyone else have anything pressing I need to tend to right this moment?" asked Christof. He was about to turn when sheaves of paper were shoved at him with suggestions and requisitions. Everything from horseshoe nails to wagons were being asked for and borrowed and used for the war effort. He looked at his mother who was smiling from ear to ear. "Laugh it up, mother. How does father handle this? He has to have someone to help him with this."

"People feel that they need your opinion because you are in power. Hire a clerk. Your father has six. They will assist with the day-to-day operation of your kingdom. Important things will be brought to you for your approval. Welcome to the dirty side of royalty." Giggled Meka.

"Now where to find me some clerks." Smiled Christof as he slipped from the tent and went for a walk. The Hand of the Phoenix stayed a discrete distance but were ready at a moment's notice to move. It felt like having a pride of hunting lions following him all the time. He was afraid to put a toe out of line.

He nearly tripped over the young woman before he saw her. Steadying himself and the woman at the same time, he tried to speak, "I am sorry. I did not mean... are you ok? … Did I harm you?... Gosh, I did not intend…."

"You did not harm me, my lord." She smiled at him. "I was going to see your mother. I am Annissa. Annissa Pixton. I come from the village your people have liberated. I was looking for a job as a maid or something. I am afraid though that I am a poor maid. I am better at tending numbers and machines than a lady I am afraid."

"Annissa Pixton. Come with me. You have a job now. You will be my clerk and work closely with me every day to run this army and kingdom. I like your dress, if I may be so bold." said Christof.

"Thank you. How do you know that you can trust me? You just met me. I have never even met a prince before let alone let him take me home. What are your intentions?" said Annissa as she was dragged toward the royal tents.

"You will be second only to me. And I would make us equal if I could, but that I am afraid I cannot do." said Christof.

"You could marry me. That would make us equal." said Annissa. As she spoke, he dropped her hand and went ridged.

"I like you, yes, I do. But marry? Who said that? Maybe in a year or two but now?" Christof sputtered.

"It was just a theory, my lord. You have many young women to court you do not have time nor the want of a young no one like me." said Annissa as he looked at her with his eyes on the floor.

"I mean, you are very pretty. And you seem to be very funny and smart. What more can a man want. Even a prince may find you interesting or even fall in love. But we are speaking only in hypotheticals, right?" said Christof as he once more took her hand and led her on.

She smiled and blushed as he led her to the tent. All thoughts of bad things and evil royals left her head as Christof introduced her to his mother.

CHAPTER
SEVENTY-TWO

FINDING TROUBLE

The pair worked out wonderfully. Christof forgot about his wounded grandfather and his ill-mannered father. He spent a large amount of time with Annissa Pixton. She was a very capable clerk and soon the army was running smooth once more. Torlin's army had run into the phase demons and had sent them running without much harm.

Torlin asked after his father to see if there had been word from the capitol. He was surprised that Tanis had left Christof in charge, but admitted that it was a good choice. It would restart Thomas's old feud if he had chosen either of them. And Christof was unbiased even though his father would try to wrest control from the boy.

Annissa was always beside Christof ready if he needed anything. The first things she had suggested and he had done was hire more clerks. Each had a specialty, one handled the weapons, one the food, and still another the other equipment. Annissa had an assistant that fawned over her and made Christof jealous though she did not return his infatuation.

The clerks knew their places and any major questions went to Annissa and from her to Christoff. He looked at the women clerks and

Annissa would also get a bit jealous. One day Christof was talking to a lady clerk from his office. Annissa saw this and asked the clerk to return to work, then poured the contents of her tea cup onto Christof's head.

Christof sputtered then apologized. The girl just squeezed the prince and handed him a cloth to clean himself off. She walked away smiling as he tried to get the tea out of his shirt and trousers. Christof had caught her talking to the young assistant that she had and again he nearly turned beet red. He moved closer to the pair and Annissa shot up and sent him on an errand as Christof came forward. He just looked at her and walked away.

Annissa and Christoff continued like this for about six months and the girl found herself more and more in love with the young prince. She was just unable to tell him how she felt. Christof for his part was head over heels for the girl but again he was an awkward and ungainly thing. The two pretended they just liked working together as they continued their jealous tantrums.

Garren had come to report that he had engaged with the phase demons as well and saw the banter and jealousy. He watched them until one day they had their heads together. They both felt hands on the back of their necks that pushed their faces together, their lips coming together in a kiss.

"You will thank me later." said Garren as he prepared to leave to report back to his army.

Christof was apologizing and making all kinds of noises until Annissa grabbed him and kissed him again. This time the awkward boy kissed her back, and the two were like that for what seemed like forever. Christof looked at her and smiled, "How are you with a sword?"

"Why do you ask, my lord?" she smiled as she spoke.

"Because everyone in my family is a warrior." said Christof, smiling like a dog with a bone.

"I can learn quick, I assure you." said Annissa. "With the right teacher, that is. I wonder if Martin is available?"

Christof's jaw dropped as she laughed at his reaction. "Shall we go and study?" she asked the stunned Christof. "I was kidding."

The two were inseparable from that day on. Christof started the three armies marching once more. It was said that Christof had found trouble the day he found the young clerk. Annissa was told she was just getting a child with facial hair. He had allowed his beard and mustache grow after meeting the young woman to seem older. She was often heard with her girlfriend, that she had made in the camp, that he would be sheared after the wedding. Both laughed at the joke.

Christof did not realize that he had made a wonderful choice for a clerk and wife, but it would be short lived. She had finally realized that Christof was waiting for her to ask him to marry her as was her mother's people's custom. Annissa worked hard with his mother to figure out how to ask him. Meka asked her, "Have you seen him naked yet? If not, you must make arrangements to meet him in his bath. Then you can make the proper proposal."

"Why do the women in your culture ask the men?" asked the curious and now very interested Annissa.

"Do you expect us to allow a man to perform so important a thing." asked Meka and Annissa erupted into laughter.

"I suppose not. So how should I go about making the perfect proposal?" asked Annissa believing her previous question was just a joke she moved on.

"Well, have you?" asked Meka very seriously.

"Why no ma'am. That would be improper." said Annissa.

"If you don't, how do you know you will want him?" asked Meka very seriously.

"I guess that makes sense. But how do I go about it? Just charge in and sit down?" asked Annissa, suddenly blushing.

"What is wrong? Why are you blushing?" asked Meka.

"Does that mean I will have to strip too?" asked the girl.

"Of course not. You will have to arrange a visit in your bath." said Meka in a matter-of-fact manner.

"You are kidding, aren't you?" asked Annissa. "I am much too timid for that."

"It is tradition in our family. I am a Tyris and I have a good mind for how things should be done, I will help you. Come on. Christof is in his bath. Perfect opportunity." said Meka as she caught the girl's wrist and dragged her to the bathing tent. Guards stood outside and looked at the girl with a little concern. Their concern was lifted by Meka as she ducked into the tent and dragged her behind her.

"Christof, I have brought your lady to discuss your wedding be a gentleman and speak to her." said Meka.

"Mother!" Squeaked Christof. "What are you doing? I know you do this kind of thing in your kingdom but Father may have a problem with this"

He continued to stutter until the girl walked up to the tub and sat down. "Don't tell me she has recruited you too. The Tyris are great people and great warriors but this is ridiculous. We will discuss details when I am not so wet and bare."

"I would like a large trellis with red roses over us. If we cannot then we will find an arch. Either way it will boost the morale of our people that you have once more stopped. They are anxious to get this thing done." said Annissa.

"I will leave you two to it. Have a good visit." said Meka.

"Mother!!!!" Squeaked the boy one more time. Meka just laughed and ducked out of the tent.

CHAPTER SEVENTY-THREE

WAR!

The three separate armies arrived at their designated places and prepared for the coming war. Many of the species that lived in the Dark Lands had come to follow the army of the light lands. So many races were present that the people of the army could not remember who came first. Christof was amazed at the bulk of the army now. He had promised Annissa that the wedding would happen after the war was over. It would only be a short time now. In the distance the wizard's tower of the Dark Queen was standing in stark contrast to the bright blue sky and sunshine.

As they moved closer the world seemed to go darker until it was only moveable with torches to light their way. They had anticipated this and had the torches ready. The armies looked like a river of fire approaching the tower. The palace guard came streaming from the tower and palace ready to fight when they saw the fire coming toward them.

Fear took the guard and they once more returned to the safety of the palace and tower. A voice like a banshee rang out from the tower. "You cannot win even with those traitors. You have missed me again, even if you take the tower. I have moved my capitol again. You can continue to search but you will not find me."

The species that had joined the army quivered in fear at the voice. They took strength from the stoutness and lack of fear from Christof. Christof knew it was pointless to respond but he did it anyway. "Do not keep running face me and let us get this thing over with. There is no ending where you come out on top. Let me help you. We will bring you back to the light. And you will be able to rule with kindness and strength. Let us discuss this." As he spoke a great wave of power came from the tower knocking down the entire army with the exception of Christof. Standing like an oak tree in the front of the army, he reached over and brushed the dirt from his armor. If she was ever there, she was gone now.

"Form up the army, Split in three once more. Now we hunt." Ordered Christof. The creatures and people of the army got themselves back to their feet and prepared to go once more after the elusive Queen. Christof sent rangers in to take the tower and palace. She would never return here.

It was not long before they were in ogre and orc country. The broken windows and lack of maintenance gave the town its truth. Goblins came storming the sides of the army to only be pushed back and either killed or captured. Christof had said to capture if possible but if you could not, then do what you must.

It was a strange time as women and the children of goblins were taken into custody. They were released to their homes and a squad of elven archers stayed in the town to help them fix and build their town, and to make sure none of them went running to the goblins that had escaped. They needed no assaults from the rear.

Christof led the army farther into the goblin and ogre territory. It seemed that they had to fight every step of the way. The ogre did not want to speak of peace as they traveled further into the Dark Lands. They would attack the army at all hours, as time seemed to hold lesser meaning the further, they descended into the country. The ogre was the more difficult of the enemies as they were large and strong and very intimidating to the smaller peoples of the army.

Yet they continued to wade into the fray with the ogres following Christof, who though small in stature, stood tall and forced his way through the advancing enemy. The warrior would wade into a group of goblins and ogre and work the Warmonger with one hand and the Holy Avenger with the other. The enemy would see the Warmonger go into its burn stage and would fall back terrified by the young man with the flaming sword. It had frightened them so badly they gave the boy a nickname, The Flaming Man.

The goblins would look to see if the boy was present before attacking the main column. If he was in fact there, they would attack one of the other columns. Christof did not care. They all would eventually have to be faced either going in or coming out. When the ogre saw the Flaming Man they would howl in rage. Screaming in frustration that would then be used in the attacks on the other columns. As the army moved, Annissa and Christof stood together for much of everything. His mother had her acting more and more like a Tyris. It was then that he had noticed her ears. She was a different species of man but apparently could cross breed. He noticed that her ears were slightly rounded and covered in a fur like hair. He had never noticed them before with her hair down. Now she showed her ears and face with pride. His mother was really rubbing off on the girl.

He had nearly swallowed his tongue when she had come out one day in the boots and mytan of the Tyris. "Your mother had a couple that where too small for her and saw that they would fit me so she gave them to me. Aren't they grand?"

"My mother is going to be the death of me. Now Annissa please tell me, when were you going to show me your ears? They are beautiful ears. I do not care that you have furry ears." said Christof.

"About the same time, I was going to show my tail. After we were married. But now you have seen them both." said Annissa "I will pack and leave, my lord"

"Why would you do that? I love the person inside not the person outside. And besides a tail could be fun." said Christof, a little tongue in cheek.

Annissa was blushing again and Christof stroked the mouse like tail. "That is getting awful familiar, sir. Do not make me get my husband-to-be to defend my honor."

Christof dropped her tail and she swung it back up under his nose. "You are right this could be fun indeed."

Annissa was fighting alongside Christof and she and her tail were doing amazing things on the battlefield. She would attack one creature while stopping an attack from behind. Christof decided to never anger her. He might not survive.

When the battle was over, she came and wrapped her mouse tail around him and pulled him in for a kiss. Christof would definitely like getting used to this. They were embracing and unaware of the world when tragedy struck.

The arrow was fired at Christof, but the two of them where spinning and having a good old time when the arrow hit. The arrow screamed at the back of Christof to only find it with Annissa facing them. The arrow went in under her arm and buried itself deep within her. Christof felt the hit and reached out with the power to find the archer. Whoever had fired the arrow was far from them now. It could have been anyone. He immediately went back to Annissa who lay still on the black earth. He reached for her hand and tried to heal her. He had healed his father before he was even aware of what he was doing. He could save her now.

He slowly pulled the arrow back to see that it was of his army's livery. Someone around them had tried to kill him and had caught Annissa instead. A reckoning would have to be had. He would find and destroy the man who had killed her. He kept trying to heal her until the druids arrived what seemed like years later instead of mere moments.

They took the girl from him and laid her on the bed of a wagon headed for Thalinburg to get supplies. Two druids jumped into the wagon with her and preceded to work on her until they were out of sight. Christof had never seen those druids before. He called out to his mother and asked about the two druids and the wagon.

"Well, we are closest to Thalinburg but we have had no reason for supplies in months thanks in part to you and Annissa. How bad is the injury? Can it be healed?" asked Meka.

"I do not know any of those answers. I just need to know if she is ok and if I can be strong enough to save her." said Christof "Wait. There was no wagon headed for Thalinburg? Calvary, mount up and follow that wagon and return my wife-to-be to me."

"Where did the wagon come from? All of ours were out collecting foodstuffs that the villages were happy to sell us. It is not one of ours as they should not be returning until late tomorrow." said Meka.

"Mother, you are just full of good news. She is going to die. I just know it." Cried Christof.

"They would not have stolen a body. They will make sure she lives so that she can be leverage on you later. They are probably getting her healed as we speak." said Meka.

"Leverage. That has to be it, but the horse will get her back. And she will be as happy and resourceful as ever." said Christof.

CHAPTER
SEVENTY-FOUR

THE LOST LANDS

The armies had stopped for a period to allow for the return of the calvary. Christof looked at the arrows that the elves had made to kill the ogre. The large head and barbed tip made it especially dangerous. Why had they used one on Annissa? Christof was thinking of the girl that had captured his heart and shook his head. First Pan Thor, now Annissa. A Catarel, cat person, and now a mouse person. He did not even know what her race called itself.

As if thinking of the cat pulled him to him, Pan Thor approached him with concern on his face. "Young one, we need to think of moving soon. These are called the Lost Lands. It is dangerous to linger here. Otherwise, dangerous things find and attack you. A dragon would not linger here. They are deathly afraid of what lies beneath these lands and I am sure that they know we are here. I would ask Mastol if we could use one or two of his friends a shift to help with the watch. If we choose to remain that is."

"We remain until my wife-to-be is found. Not a moment longer but also not leaving a moment sooner. They know where to find us here." said Christof. "Besides the horses need the rest and so do our people.

I will watch closely for signs of these creatures you warned me about. Any sign of them and all of the army will be brought to bear on them."

"As you say, young one. Just be careful. We have an assassin amongst us and they will continue to come for you. I will remain close for a while until I am sure that the threat from the assassin has been quelled. We are looking diligently." said Pan Thor.

"You mean that arrow was meant for me? My god I have killed the woman I love. They were after me. My god, what should I do if they find her well again? Do I send her away or do I keep her like a prized doll that none are allowed to get near?" asked Christof.

"Neither, she is her own woman and let her make up her mind. By the way, did anyone notice the tail? Or was I dreaming it." asked Meka

"Oh, she does have a beautiful tail. And nice fuzzy ears. I have not had the opportunity do see much else of her, but I am sure she has fur elsewhere as well. We shall see one day soon. I hope." said Christof.

"My mother-in-law is going to have kittens, no offense meant Pan Thor, just a second member of the royal family from a culture of mice people. What next?" asked Meka.

"Don't ask questions you do not want the answer to." replied Pan Thor. "No offense taken."

As Pan Thor predicted the rumbling from beneath the ground started a few days after the abduction of Annissa. The horse still had not returned and each passing day gave Christof less and less hope that she would be returned unharmed. No messengers from the calvary did not help either. It would have been thought that they would at least let them know if they had caught the wagon yet.

But no word was driving Christof mad. He would spend most days with a spyglass trained behind them looking for the returning Calvary. His vigilance had saved them from a few ambushes by the ogre and goblins. But it had not given them the results that he wanted. It was the last day of the meridian in Dracos when the horsemen returned. Wagon in tow. Christof ran to the wagon but was crestfallen when he saw the wagon was empty.

"What happened? Where is Annissa? Speak man. Tell me everything. I need to know what happened." said Christof.

"We found the wagon loaded with the druids that had gone to aid the young woman, but they were all dead. We saw hoof marks all the way down the road and half of us went after the men on horseback. They have a small lead but their horses will not take the punishment our horses can. So, we will find the whelps with your lady. It is only a matter of time." said the commander of the calvary, Lord Nargus.

Was there anything about the wagon seemed funny to you? Pieces from a healer's kit, the arrow shaft, anything?" begged Christof.

"We did have a couple of men seem to disappear in the wagon but it must have just been imagination. Surely there would be no traps in an old wagon full of corpses now would there." said the commander. Christof ran to the wagon and cast his dispel magic spell as he ran. Slowly the wagon seemed to twist and change. The resulting time trap with the two horsemen was revealed.

"This is what we call a time trap. You are literally taken out of time and space until the trap is released as I have just done. I was hoping that Annissa would be there, but the trap was probably set after they made their getaway." said Christof. "I would like a roll called of all of our army, and report anyone missing immediately."

"Yes sire. It is done every day, but we can do it again now." said the gathered generals.

It was as roll call was being done that the first of the great beasts of the Lost Lands decided it was time to come to the surface. At first, they believed it to be just a huge scorpion, but the other facets of the creature showed that it was a construct of a scorpion, dragon, and a huge worm looking thing. The worm section remained below ground as the rest of it fought the army of the light. Nothing seemed to stop the creature until it finally was attacked by several dragons. Even Warmonger seemed to not faze the creature. Christof had been in the front row of the attack and had nearly been swiped right off the map as the scorpion part of the thing swept its claws and cut several defenders in half. Even men that had seen everything wept at the creature. Looking at the worm body, Christof saw that it still moved. He roused the army to arms just as the other sections once more attacked the army. Christof made the comment that it was the worm body that needed attacking.

The army took Christof's advice and the attack was over as fast as it had begun. Except the creature did not stay away. Almost as soon as the creature went down into the ground once more it came up from the ground, this time with four more of the creatures. Christof was asked what they should do and he said, "Attack the area on the ground between the creatures. I believe this is a nasty creature, but we will find out soon enough." said Christof as he attacked the ground between the five creatures. After only a moment of attack, the ground rumbled and the great beast showed itself with a crash. Hundreds of the arms flung from around its head, and that is all it seemed to be, these creatures on the ends of its tentacles and a big eye. After a few minutes of attack, the creature screamed in pain and let loose with all its tentacles. The dragons came quickly to attack the eye of the creature. The entire army went after that eye and soon the creature slumped over in death. Looking at the devastation all around them, they carefully sheathed weapons and started to aid the wounded.

Tremors once more hit the ground around the army and they watched for another attack as they prepared to move. They would not survive another attack by one of those things. They would need to move. Christof feared that the calvary would be unable to locate them but the dawn proved that fear unfounded.

Into camp rode the knights that had set off after the horses. Their manner was somber as they brought themselves before Christof. "Sire, we over took the Cretans that took your lady. We worked hard to liberate her. But she was executed by the leader of the band as we were about to take him and her. We did our best and it was not enough, sire."

"You have done well. It was not your fault. I will see this bandit leader if you would sir." said Christof. His chest fallen and melancholy getting the better of him. The bandit leader was brought before Christof and he stared into the man's eyes and asked, "Why did you have to kill her?" His voice a gentle whisper. "You realize who she was?"

"Why yes, my lord. My orders were simple, kill you or kill her. I figured I could get a ransom instead. Aww well. I followed my orders as I was over taken by your brute squad there." said the bandit, shouting at the top of his lungs.

"You have made a grave error by following that order." Spoke Christof. Again, at a whisper. He drew the dagger he kept at his waist. His cousin had made it for him and he went nowhere without it. It was supposed to be similar to the Holy Avenger, but it turned out a kind of half and half blade. It seemed to favor both the avenger and Warmonger.

"Raise your head, and receive your sentence for the murder of my wife-to-be." Whispered Christof as he prepared to plunge the dagger into the man in front of him. A strong hand on his arm prevented him from plunging the dagger into the man's heart. Looking up, Christof saw Artitous staring down at him. "He deserves it. He murdered her."

"No, Christof. He murdered her out of fear for his own life. He knew it was either die by your hand or by the Dark Queen and he chose you. Now why would he do that? Surely, he knew you would be angry, upset, and sick with grief. But he still chose you. He figured he could get a fair hearing from you. Something others would not be willing to do. I know it is hard, but you must or you are no better than him and his people." said Artitous.

"But why did he have to kill her? Surely, there was another way?" asked Christof, raising his voice as tears entered into his eyes and cries entered his speech.

"He did, but it would have meant his instant execution by his subordinates if he had not. And now he offers knowledge of the Dark Queen and her whereabouts. It will probably end poorly for him, but at least he is willing to try." said Artitous.

"He killed her. So, let's have this information and see if it warranted a life." said Christof. He walked toward the prisoner and a magical fireball slammed into the man and killed him instantly. "No. He was supposed to tell us where the Dark Queen is. It is not right. No. No. No."

"Christof. He is gone. There is nothing we can do now. Are you sure you did not throw that fireball at him? Tell me true. It came from your direction." asked Artitous as he grabbed the young man and held him. The younger man breaking down into tears. With shivers of grief running through him. The older man just held him and spoke comforting sounds to the man and soon he quieted from his grief.

"Christof. Your grandfather had another wife before he met Athinina. She too was murdered and your grandfather's children as well. He grieved for a long time. But he finally came to see that a job needed to be done, and he did it. It took him time though and you will need time too." said Artitous.

"I will find and end the Dark Queen. She will know justice. Dealt by me or by another. She will know justice." said Christof.

"That is the spirit. Now let's do something about it." said Artitous as he led the boy to the marching grounds and they headed deeper into the Lost Lands. *Christof would bear watching.* Artitous thought.

CHAPTER
SEVENTY-FIVE

DEEPER INTO THE LOST LANDS

As the armies of the light progressed through the Dark Lands and Lost Lands, Almedda was getting concerned. She had taken one of the Thalin family, and emotionally crippled another. But still there were at least six more. Not to mention that Catarel, Pan Thor, and his other wife, Athinina. Why the boy was interested in the mouse girl was beyond her, but that was settled now. Christof would be off his game for a long time due to that one act.

Almedda summoned some of her personal guard. She had a special plan for the army that was slowly approaching her. She enjoyed watching the torches of the enemy advance through the constant dark. They looked like a snake when they moved, and like a great sea when stopped.

They had the worst yet to come. They had faced one of the creatures of the Lost Lands, and thought that that was the worst this land could produce. Wait until they ran into her reserve army near her palace. There were a little of every race of Dracos as the Dark Lands had sects from every species common or otherwise. Plus, she did have her soldiers that deserted the lands of the light and came to her in the Dark Lands. Deserters were not the best troops to add to her army for if they did it once they would do it again. But they made good fodder for the frontlines.

If for no other reason than to demoralize the enemy, she would keep the deserters. Seeing your own people staring back at you was definitely bad for moral. It also gave her plenty of playthings for her experiments. The lion minotaur was looking up as was the half man, half fire drake. She could not meld human and dragon unfortunately. The Dragon was just too big.

She did not like to experiment with her own people, it was bad for morale. The armies of the dark contained species only she knew and controlled. No had ever seen an intelligent Minotaur. Now they were commonplace. Intelligent scorpion men, harpies and ogre. She had made them all and now they were the rule instead of the exception. Her enemy had to work harder and harder the more of these creatures they met.

That caused a smile to cross her lips. It was costing them more and more the further they advanced. By the time they reached her, they would be ready for destruction. Either too weary to fight or too few. She hoped for both. This way there would be plenty of subjects for her experiments. They thought that leaving a skeleton force in the cities would be sufficient should an enemy come at them while they were gone. Her deal with the Metradon and the Tetradon would show them that was a false sense of security.

That deal had made a smile cross her lips. She paid attention, dear brother. She paid attention to it all. Even if she lost and the army of darkness was defeated. They still had no home to go to now. The thought made her laugh out loud. She had really planned for everything. No way they had enough people to fight at the cities and in this conscripted army that they had to add her people to. They would all fall before her secret weapons.

The Metradon and Tetradon would be easy to clean up after the army of the light was destroyed. They did not even see it coming. Almedda was most pleased with herself, as her army started to march toward the advancing river of fire. Her peoples were used to the darkness and needed no torches to see. They would be seen too late for the armies of the light to do anything about them.

She loved when a plan came together. The river of fire was not nearly as large as it was prior days. She watched it closely and knew when it was attacked. The harassing forces she had put out were doing the job given them. Her nephew was leading the army of the light. That was troubling. Tanis, himself, should be at the head of the army. She called for her spy in the headquarters and he explained about Tanis taking a severe injury. And the fact that Christof could wield the Warmonger. This amazed her. Her father showed her that blade whenever she had asked and it never turned in his hand. Now Christof can do the same thing. That was troubling. It must have something to do with the cave of glass. The power must have skipped a generation. She got her natural power, but she was not nearly as powerful as Christof.

But now with the grimoire she was the strongest magical person on Dracos. Christof will learn that lesson quickly. She had not heard word of Artitous, but assumed he traveled with the army. She was so intent on the main river of fire she missed the other two coming at her from the north and south. The westward travelers were her focus.

It would not be long until the two armies connected. She would come out victorious this time. No one could stop her. She thumbed through the grimoire and searched for a spell that would really put Christof down and out quickly at the beginning of the battle. She really could not believe that they had traveled this deeply in her realm with no support from the outside. Her creatures would end that.

The army of darkness had lined up in a "u" pattern. Leaving the opening facing the advancing army, the creatures of the night prepared to go to war. Weapons were loosened in their sheaths, teeth and claws flexed. These creatures were serious and ready for combat. The first of the torch being light army entered into the "u", the creatures of the army of the dark refrained from springing their trap. They wanted to split the army in half. More and more entered the opening until Christof himself entered the trap.

Her troops remained hidden as he examined the trees that had suddenly blocked their path. He cast a spell to see the trees better and then he cast one to move the trees. As he did, the trap was sprung. Her army attacked from three sides and the horse soldiers were totally made useless. Many had dismounted and attacked on foot. Others kept trying to get their horses to be able to move, but to no avail. Christof fought hard and used not only the Warmonger but also his sword of light that he created magically. He would attack targets with magic to keep the army together and tried to send the horse to the rear of the battle so that they could regroup.

Almedda from her tower sent devastating spells into the armies. The people of the light and the dark were being killed in mass waves of disintegration. She laughed as each wave hit and more and more people just ceased to be. Her power was that much like a god. She could command the heavens and hells themselves, if she so choose. She decided who down there lived or died. As she was contemplating that the second army found her tower. She had sent all of her troops out to the battle but she had an army they did not know about. She waved her arms and shouted a word of power and the suits of armor and statues of soldiers came to life. She had them line up around her apartments and protect her.

She attempted to snipe them from her windows, but they were more than she thought. She could not send her disintegration balls down on them due to arrows coming from the first army. Her army was actually deserting back to the tower and palace. She had definitely not expected that. This was most difficult. Her troops took to the walls and the arrows toward her ceased. She picked up the spent arrows with the power and rained them down onto the army of the light.

Christof had taken several small wounds that were slowly draining him of energy. He would be useless before too much longer. She fired off a fireball in his direction and it dissipated before it came near the prince. Either he or Artitous had dispelled her spell. It showed her though where the magical folk were and she attacked the areas there. Christof was the first to order the fall back and prepare to siege the city and the tower. He was sure she would break under the strain of the two armies laying siege on her city.

It was that morning that the last army arrived at the city, and they too added their might to the siege. She sent siege breakers out every other hour. Testing the waters before she sent her dragons. She called Marious to her and laid her plan to break the siege around the city and allow free commerce again. The dragon laughed at her plan but agreed that it had a great chance of success.

Mastol had kept the dragons back thus far. He was being conservative with his dragons. He knew the plans that he and Christof had made. He also suspected the trick of the Dark Queen. Christof's army was slowly pushing the enemy back to its stronghold. Mastol was concerned, it was too easy. Mastol removed further back and saw the approaching horde of dragons. They were twelve full grown dragons and several dozen young ones. The elders should know better.

Mastol let out a roar and the fighting stopped for just a moment. The dragons perked up at the roar and took to the air. Including Mastol. The dragon horde of Christof's army was consisting of thirty elders and countless young. The dragons named only the elders. The young were often given nick names until a formal name could be conceived for the new elder. The young perished too often to keep giving them formal names to remember in the roles of the dragons.

Mastol and the elders attacked the incoming dragons and realized that certain known turncoats from the horde were not present. Mastol left twelve veteran elders to keep the dragons to the rear occupied while Mastol went to the front and waited for the rest of the dragons. Marious had not shown himself yet, but he would be coming for Mastol. Mastol's eyes were capable of seeing deep into the dark as were all the dragons. Living in subterranean caves and such the eyes of the dragons got accustomed to the dark. The enemy dragons would not have the advantage.

Christof started throwing fire spears at the incoming dragons but he stopped as he became exhausted. The siege had begun and now he had to let Mastol handle the dragons. He had his generals watching for the possibility of siege busters as he himself went to lay down and recover his energy. He sat out the first alarm allowing the generals to handle the problem.

The second alarm came in and once more he was inclined to allow the generals to run the army. It was the third alarm in the hour that caused Christof to rise and find out what was the trouble. Christof walked out into a scene of chaos. He had his trumpeter announce that he was coming and the enemy stopped in their tracks. The army quickly started to form their formations as the stunned enemy began once more its attack, this time attacking toward Christof. He was once more the target. He could deal with that as far as was needed.

Christof stayed to the rear conserving his energies as much as he could. He saw the dragon battle continuing above him and to their rear. Right now, it was a pitched battle and seemed to mimic the battle happening below. As Christof's army kept pushing forward the dragons above and behind kept pushing forward. But as Christof was pushed back so too were the dragons. The strangeness of war, that was for sure.

All three battles were ending in stalemates as soldiers and dragons let fatigue get to them. The defenders at the camp had created a rotation for it and when the next battle arrived. The dragons did quite close to the same except the elders were not fatigued only the young were near exhaustion. Christof made the comment to Mastol, "You never seem to tire, my friend. It must be nice to be the king."

"You have not seen anything yet, young one. The best is yet to come." said Mastol. He was concerned about the attacks on each other. He knew these dragons and they knew him. Yet they followed the traitor that would destroy the progress they made with humans. The dragons were a stubborn race but an open civil war between them had never been seen by humans.

All of the peoples of Dracos feared the dragons. Now they had to worry about getting caught in the cross fire. This would set back relations by centuries. Mastol had asked for parley and the other side just jeered and laughed. These were some of the wisest and strongest of his people. They should have known better.

Mastol sat and watched the horizon. He had others watching the other horizons, but he watched the direction of the tower and city. That was where the renewed attack was going to come from. Jasper flew up to Mastol and lay flat at his feet. Some of the young still remembered their manners. "Well met, Jasper. How can I help you?"

"Elder Mastol, I have news from the rear guard. The dragons that had attacked from that direction have been subdued, and will be of no more threat to us." said Jasper.

"You can say the truth. Those dragons are dead. There were good friends in that attack. They were corrupted by Marious and his wild ideas. I would never have figured they would let it go this far. It is a sad day for dragons. Our numbers are small enough and to have to kill our own. This troubles me. They were against involvement in human affairs. I encouraged the return to the days of dragon riders. Maybe it was my fault after all, saving Tanis all those years ago." said Mastol.

"You cannot blame yourself for this terrible day. You did what you thought was right for dragon kind. The dragons are involved in matters of the planet now. We knew that the dragons living in the Dark Lands would go to the Dark Queen. They were little known to us, as we were to them. But any loss of dragon life is terrible. You saved many dragons from being slaughtered as monsters. People now know we do not eat virgins and kill for the joy of it. You did that. You have saved our people from destruction, at least immediate destruction. In the later years who knows? I know I do not. Maybe we will begin to prosper again. We have not bred ourselves out of living yet. We are still here. Thanks to you." Jasper said to the older dragon.

"You give me too much credit. I did what needed doing. I was not even concerned about the reactions. Yes, it was well received, but at what cost?" whined Mastol. He sighed and lowered his head. He would fix this. He had too. He was still unaware of who the Dark Queen was. She meets everyone through the veil of darkness. Her features are indistinguishable from any other woman. She was careful with her identity. Some said she was the daughter of the king. That she had faked her death all those years ago. Some the reincarnation of the necromancer Elizarade. Others still the incarnation of the Dark One's Daughter. Her actions made the woman a criminal, no matter who she was. But they still had to lay hands on her. That could prove difficult.

CHAPTER SEVENTY-SIX

IDEAS

Christof woke in the darkness as he did every day in this forsaken land. The creatures below were staying there and the siege breakers were slowing down. Maybe she was finally running out of troops. He was tempted to try and take the city, but caution stayed his hand. His father was saying the time was ripe. His Uncle Garren agreed with his father. The army of Torlin was content waiting on the word of Christof.

Torlin advised the young man only this, "When you make the decision to move. Move. Do not hesitate and do not doubt or we all will fall. No matter when we move there will be casualties. But be ready when we move."

So, Christof went and made the rounds that Annissa and he had while she lived. He found out who needed boots and who needed a new weapon. He made sure in triplicate that everyone was ready and outfitted with all of their gear. And he showed that he was rested and ready, despite his desire for revenge. He kept that hidden deep. Artitous knew about it but he did not comment on it. He knew young men needed no help in that department.

So, Christof went to the command tent and prepared his reports and records and looked at the newly made map of the evil capital. The generals and family of Christof came in and scoffed at the layout of the streets and the palace. A good man had died bringing them these maps. He died with enemy arrows deep within him. But at least they had gotten the intelligence and he did not die in vain. Christof looked at the maps and shuttered a moment or two. These were not accurate. He saw some of the city when the gates opened for the enemy, and it did not match the map. There were no straight runs anywhere. Especially to the palace. He told this to his generals but the men and women had said they were the real deal.

Christof thought that they had been altered and he was going with it. He ordered the rangers try and find and accurate telling of the city. *The layout will help us considerably,* thought Christof as he looked down at the perfectly straight lines on the map. The rangers arrived back with a very different map of the city. The map they had gotten from the man was obviously wrong now. The new map showed locations and names upon it.

It was then that Christof gave his ideas to the generals. They would launch their attacks at each of the gates and use magical rams instead of cutting trees. This way another magical user could protect them all from the flying arrows. They could also protect from falling anything. The city folk may try a large variety of weapons to stop the rams. Magical shields could take more damage than wooden ones.

Once inside they wanted to take the walls. The towers on the wall would provide cover from magical attacks. It also gave them quick access to the rest of the city and the palace. The maze of roads down below would take them forever to navigate. You would need guides to get through. From the towers It was quite a bit easier. The walls traveled into the inner city and also to the outer edge. They also led into the palace directly. They could also attack from above. The high grounds are definitely the important ways.

Once more the army was split and assigned different gates. They were about to begin their assault when the gates opened to them. They were wary of entering but they did and immediately went to the walls. Looking back at the gates showed people pulling open the gates and closing them.

The leader of those people waved and disappeared down one of the roads with his colleagues. The archers took their places along the walls and made ready to fire down into the soldiers coming to the wall. But surprisingly none came. No alarms sounded and no defenders met them. They found several bodies, but no living guards.

Someone in the city wanted her out of their city. The army of light was going to be their weapon. The army took the walls quietly and moved toward the quiet palace. They were just about to reach the palace proper when an alarm bell ran twice and was quickly silenced. Looking around at their surroundings they saw a guard slain at the bell and a couple of townsfolk protecting it. It was quite the scene as they passed each watch point. The watch points were being watched by the people of the town.

They encountered none of the soldiers that had fled to the city. This concerned Christof, and it did not settle with him that they had fought their way this far. A man came up to the top of the wall and looked at Christof. "Legend spoke of the armies from far away. Lead by the man with the flaming sword to liberate our city. We thought the prophecy was incorrect until we saw the blade in your leader's hands. A magical warrior. Who would have known? There have been no sounds nor lights visible inside the palace in three days. I fear that the army and Queen have somehow evaded you this time."

Christof answered the man, "I thank your people for making our entry easy and for keeping the guard from us until we were able to get this far. We will check the Tower and palace and see what is the problem. We hope that they have not learned to travel magically. If they have, we may be in for ambushes and attacks coming from anywhere. We do not know how to travel except by walking and riding. Do you know where she may have gone?"

"I was her head of house hold. She trusted us with all of her care when she first arrived with us. Then she began her experiments on the people of the city. She said she had a nasty prize waiting for the liberators of the city. So be wary in the palace. We will come with you to guide your way." He said as he turned and walked toward the palace.

The soldiers walked behind the man and entered the palace proper. As they entered a roar was heard down the hallway from them. Looking down the hallway they saw the minotaur coming toward them with flames surrounding him. The soldiers drew weapons and prepared for the attack. They were surprised by the attacks coming at them right that moment from the sides. They had fallen for a trap and the butler of the Queen stayed in the middle of the army shaking like a leaf on a tree.

"I did not do this." said the Butler as they finally destroyed the last of the bull men.

"Anything else she was experimenting with?" asked Christof.

"She has a thing for lions," said the man.

"Lions? What was she doing with lions?" asked Christof. As he asked the question, he turned to see what was breathing on the back of his neck. Slowly he turned to face whatever it was. He turned to find himself face to face with a Narasimha. Narasimha were creatures with the head of a lion and the body of a man. Grabbing Warmonger, he barely got the weapon raised before the cat man was on him. He swung at the hybrid and Warmonger went right through the creature coming at him. He turned around to see a pride of the creatures attacking his men. He waded into the fray and found men and Narasimha moving away from him. He roared and attacked a Narasimha standing there with fear painted across its face.

The creature fell as well to the Warmonger, then he realized that the armies on both sides were looking at him. He raised Warmonger and was about to attack again when Torlin and Artitous grabbed him and lay him down. His rage at the creatures and the inability to catch the Queen was frustrating him. He struggled with them to get to his feet and saw the hilt sticking from his body.

"Is it poisoned?" asked Christof as the sight of the knife caused him to faint as he spoke. Artitous and Torlin worked quickly and removed the blade from the boy's chest. He was fortunate that the wound missed all of his internal organs. It would have been almost incapable of healing had it been an eighth of an inch to the left or right. Christof was either the luckiest man alive right now or the assassin was a very good shot to appear it tried and failed to hit its target. Either way he was injured again and would need attention.

CHAPTER SEVENTY-SEVEN

THE SIEGE

The minotaur and Narasimha were attacking non-stop pushing the army from the palace. They would have to wait out the creatures. They were just too many and too strong for the force to handle. Plus, they had to find the assassin that had attempted to kill Christof.

Christof was growing impatient waiting for himself to heal. The druids had done a fine job of stitching and healing the wound. Now it just took time. Time, he feared, they did not have. Christof saw the hole in the air above him open and saw the arm lowering the large scorpion. Christof was looking at the magic and forgot about the scorpion until it landed on his chest. The creature was prepared to strike when it was picked up and put back through the hole in the air. Christof used another set of air flows to keep the hole from dropping any other surprises.

When the first hole was blocked another formed to his left-hand side and this time a dagger pressed through the hole looking for his side. Again, all it found was an air plug on the hole. Artitous had heard the sound of the scorpion and came in to see what was the matter. Seeing the holes in the air he tried to send fireballs up the holes to the originator of the holes. The plugs made those impossible too. The holes stood there open unable to do anything and each time one was sealed, another one came into appearance. There was definitely something else going on here as the two prepared to fire a fireball through the hole. The person on the other side tried hard to keep composure and return fire. Instead, the figure closed the hole and did not open another.

"Uncle Artitous. Did that woman look familiar to you? She could very well have past for the Almedda that I had vague memories of." said Christof.

"Yes, she did bear a stunning resemblance. But even if it was her, it would make no difference. She is so far corrupted by the power she would be unsavable. Not even with our considerable power. That creature was only capable of hate and death. We will see who is the deadlier then." said Artitous, preparing for another hole in the air. "She has discovered traveling. She could literally drop an army on us right now. She tilted her hand a little too much today."

"She showed this part of her abilities yesterday when I was stabbed. I had managed to keep the rest of her abilities at bay." said Christof. "I think I know her. She let her mirror drop for just a moment. It just can't be. That person I know to be dead."

"Well, who do you believe it to be? Surely, they cannot be that intimidating to you. They cannot come for you any harder than they already are. So, tell me who you believe it to be." said Artitous.

"I believe it to be Aunt Almedda. I know she is dead, but that is who I saw when she lowered her disguise for just a moment." said Christof. "Surely they had another mask on beneath the veil of disguise."

"I believe you may be right on your vision. It can very well be Almedda. It never sat well with me that a young woman who was brought up a druid and an outdoors person was to die from exposure to the elements. If for whatever reason she could not get home she would have known how to construct a shelter. And the animals would not have attacked her, not even in death, for she was a member of the druid clans. So, finding her nearly destroyed skeleton dressed in the clothes she was wearing when she went missing has always concerned me. I thought a murderer had gotten her." said Artitous.

"Well, if she is Almedda, who is the skeleton in her grave?" asked Christof. A voice from behind made him jump out of his skin.

"It is some poor lost child that she came across. Too bad for the child." said the voice. Turning around the Dark Queen stood there behind him. Artitous was frozen in place a spell moving on his lips. His guards also were petrified. He stood alone with the Dark Queen and found out that he could not use his powers she had blocked him before he turned to face her.

"Why did you murder the child? Surely, she was of no threat to you." said Christof slowly drawing the Warmonger from its sheath. Swinging hard at the head of Almedda, the person in front of him faded to smoke.

"You'll have to do better than that." She said as she faded into the darkness.

Artitous finished his spell and found no one to cast it at. "Where is she? She was here one moment and gone the next. We have serious trouble on our hands, I would say." His guards turned and looked into every crevice of the tent and found nothing.

"It is definitely Almedda. She murdered a child of her age all those years ago. The child should have her identity found and be properly buried. And Almedda in her own grave. She is already dead to us and her actions secure that idea. I will put that poor creature down." He picked up the Warmonger and put it back into the sheath as he spoke.

It may have hit home a little harder than he meant but everyone around him knew he was upset. The woman he loved dead and his lost Aunt now the Dark Queen that had ordered her death. He would have his revenge.

The palace was dark as reported by the leader of the townsfolk. The army sat at the gates and saw no one enter or exit. They were definitely aware that the army was there, so why did they just stay hidden? No one came to check the gates and no one came magically to attack them. Several large demons had come crashing through the army before they had been dispelled. The minotaur was not seen any more than the Nakashima. These creatures were mostly nocturnal so everyone in camp was asleep when they attacked.

The guard was getting better about keeping watchfires lit and burning. In this land of permanent darkness, the enemy had a great advantage as long as it was dark. The fires should keep the residents here at bay.

Christof heard the alarm bell and jumped to his feet. He had felt the attack coming an hour ago and was just waiting for it to begin. Christof ran out of his tent just as the bell was silenced. That should have had several guards on it. He rode to the bell to see Pan Thor and a troop of mouse people standing in the firelight. "Sorry for the alarm. It seems that we look like the enemy. No one was harmed but it was strange for a moment. These people have come to replace Annissa as your clerks. They want to do this because of the caring and love you showed for Annissa. They just need to be shown to the supply tents and administrative tent. I scrutinized them personally. They are good people."

"Thank you, Pan Thor, but I have it all in my hands now. I do not know how to deal with clerks it appears. I get them killed. So, thank you for coming and I hope you will not take offense as I say no thank you." said Christof.

"We came here for you. We knew the risks and we are ready to face them. You did not kill Annissa. She chose you as her potential mate, and that means a lot in our culture. You are a part of our family. And you need our help. That much is obvious. Let us help you." said an older lady mouse person.

"But I do not want anyone else hurt for me. Don't you understand?" said Christof.

The mouse woman looked around and smiled a tender smile at Christof. "You need us as much as we need you. I see that this place needs clerks to see to your day-to-day work. I would ask you give us a small trial. That way you may see if we are a burden or a blessing."

Christof tried to argue but nothing came out of his mouth. He looked at the mouse people before him and smiled. It would be nice to have these people around. Christof finally found his voice and said, "This way. We will show you our camp and get you up to date."

The mouse people cheered and went right to work. Soon the camp was ship shape and tight. The way it should be.

CHAPTER
SEVENTY-EIGHT

DAYBREAK

Christof was readying himself for the day when a beam of light hit his tent. It was small at first and slowly increased. The siege had gone on for almost three weeks in permanent darkness. Now a small beam of light hits his tent? This he had to see for himself. Walking out of his tent saw amazed soldiers looking at this small shaft of what appeared to be sunlight. He looked around and saw no one using magic, so there was indeed something happening.

Slowly the beam became larger and larger until the camp seemed to be in a spotlight. As it grew the locals that they could now see looked up in wonder. Then they looked at him. They all fell to knees and bellies screaming out for Christof to bless them. Christof finally found the person in charge or at least he thought he did and asked why they prostrated themselves so.

"There is a legend and a prophesy that the god of light would return us to light. That he would come as a young man with a burning sword. And that he would rid the land of the evil that was consuming it. We saw what you have done behind your army. Rebuilding our lands and our homes is something that is praise worthy on its own but bringing back the sun. That we will remember forever." said the older man.

"I am no god. I am magical but I had nothing to do with the light I assure you." said Christof.

"Yes, you did. You made the evil one leave. And that is definitely praise worthy. She has not been seen in our streets taking young people for her twisted experiments. She runs from you and hides. This is something worth praise. All this you did. And we are eternally grateful." replied the old man.

"Well then, a thank you is all I need. I have to find that Dark Queen. I just do not know where to start." said Christof.

"That is easy just follow the darkness. It is not stronger than light when the time actually comes." said the old man. "Even her monsters are gone. We will clean the palace and have it ready for you as your headquarters. That is the least we can do."

"I will follow the darkness. That is sage advice. Thank you." said Christof as he opened the door magically to avoid any traps or pitfalls that may have been placed on the door. "It looks safe. Rangers, examine the palace and ensure that it is safe. Then report back to me."

The rangers entered the building and returned after what seemed like an eternity. The sun was up now and the city and surrounding areas were bathed in light for the first time in a long time. People wore large brimmed hats to protect their eyes from the light as they went about their business of the day. Some stopped to offer prayers to the new light. Then they continued on their ways.

These people would adapt. Christof enjoyed the view from the palace. It showed the landscape and some pitfalls they almost ran into. The surrounding area looked like it had been attacked by a very powerful wizard. The very mountains had been drilled through with some kind of magic. The look was surreal and the people gave it no second looks. That was really amazing to him.

The people of the city explained about her experiments and how if you went in to the palace, you never returned. Christof made an effort to find the dungeon and release the missing people. Christof first walked the halls looking for stairs going down. He found some that were a backdoor to the stables. But on a cursory walk, he could find no entrances down. So, he once more walked the palace using a spell to reveal the hidden.

As he walked there were hidden doors everywhere. No wonder the creatures of the palace could attack with such unseen frequency. It would be good to keep in mind. He had Artitous with him as he walked and together, they tagged the hidden doors with a symbol for them to recognize the doors. After what seemed an all-day search, Christof finally found what he was looking for. Directly beneath the tower was a stairway hidden into the tower. They slowly moved down into the dungeon and went in. The cells were all filled with terrified men and women. They clutched small children to them as they entered the room. A guard came rumbling out from behind some torture equipment, ready to inflict harm on the incoming enemy. Christof froze him in place and had Artitous prepare a cell for him. Artitous got a cell emptied of its previous occupants and the jailor went in.

After being locked in, Christof released him from the spell. The creature looked like a half troll, half human creation but he was not going to sit still while the others in this dungeon grew more and more afraid. Christof made a flock of illusionary birds and he let the children chase them. They enjoyed the moments of being children as their parents watched on.

The birds were finally all caught, and the game over, Christof started asking questions of the prisoners. He wanted to know why they were taken and how. Why did they not fight when they came for them?

No one seemed to have an answer for him. They did not fight for sake of the children. The children were too afraid to run away. This amazed Christof because that is how people reacted in his lands. These were no different.

Christof brought the people from the dungeons and allowed them to return to their homes. When they reached the courtyard where the horse would be brought next to the tower, they savored the new light in their faces. They had been so long alone and with no light, and now even their homes were flooded with light. They were brought to tears with the beauty of it all. They cried as family led them home and returned to them their freedom.

A strange sight greeted Christof. A bird landed on the wall next to him as he watched the families reunite and go home. This bird was not a twisted bird with feathers as black as coal, like those they had encountered. It was a beautiful song bird and Christof was amazed. He saw some of the other animals travelling around the city and they slowly went from twisted and diseased creatures to their previous selves. They moved with vigor and excitement as they were released from the Dark Lands curse as the lands revealed more and more in the sun.

As the day wore on the sun slowly began to sink behind the mountains. The small group of people from the city came to them and inquired as to the pin pricks in the darkness. They had never seen this before in the darkness that had covered them for generations. Christof explained that the pin pricks were in fact stars far, far away. They shone at night to help them feel the light as they slept. Many stood in wonder in the streets looking at these strange phenomena, their faces shining at the lights and the moons as they rose to show a little lighter in the darkness. Christof notice the look on their faces, and was puzzled as he had seen this earlier on the faces of those in the dungeons.

"It's hope." said Artitous as one of the clerks came up to Christof for a signature. "They have finally found hope. And you gave it to them."

"Those clerks have everything running like a spinning top. No more misunderstandings, no more indecipherable orders, or poor requisitions. These mice people are really a great team to have around. Where has Pan Thor gone? I haven't seen him since we cleared the palace." said Christof.

"He is up in the tower. He and Torlin are up there looking for strongholds that we can liberate. I think it is more important to help other people experience this than it is to find and destroy Almedda." said Artitous.

"I am not sure, but I believe that this may be the fortress of the first Dark Queen. It matches the description and it definitely shines in the sun as it clears off all of the foliage of the dark lands. My mother would know." said Christof.

"It is indeed an impressive palace and city. But I feel the magic slipping away as it clears and grows back to its original glory. But let us focus on the Dark Queen."

"I think I agree, let me check with my clerks." Laughed Christof.

He finally felt that he was doing what it was that he was supposed to do. It is important to destroy the evil, but it more important to bring the others of this world together so we all can present a united front against the powers of the grimoire.

He was on the wall still looking into the sky as sunrise once more lit up the skies. It would be a great day.

TROUBLES

Almedda looked through the magical hole she created in the edge of the Dark Lands. She had a hard time seeing due to the light. So, he broke the curse from generations ago. That was a trick. He was now as powerful as the evil that had started all this. She had to find a better curse for those lands when she takes them back. Light was hope, and hope meant resistance. Bad enough she lost that fortress. She had moved to the south east once more. This time to a fortress by the sea. She saw the darkness over the waters and the people trying to harvest from the dark seas.

She saw that these people were used to the darkness now and they worked and moved without a bit of resistance in the dark. She also saw that they did not care who ruled from the tower by the sea. The city here was a great one. One of the great wonders that was believed to have been destroyed in one of the wars of power. There were so many and she was rapidly remembering all of them. The more she read the grimoire the more she remembered what the others who held that tome had remembered. She was definitely almost one with the grimoire.

Carlee had flown off to get something to eat, and Almedda was awaiting her meal. She was having a surprise from the kitchen. She called down a few times but she did not get an answer. She became more and more impatient the more time that lapsed.

The maid came in with her tray and Almedda called her over. Her teeth had started to sharpen into deathly fangs and as the maid came to her, she sunk her teeth into the poor woman's throat. With a snarl she ripped out the flesh of her throat. Blood splashed into her face and she let the warm flow hit her face as the woman died. She took several more bites from her before calling in another maid to clean the mess. These women were desensitized to the demise of the others. As long as they did not do anything to upset the Queen, they were safe. The Queen was sated by her appetizer and dinner. The woman was removed and the blood mopped up. A separate maid came to clean Almedda. Almedda let the maid do her job and soon she was once more the image of a Queen.

The people who came to end up serving in the palace each knew where to go to hide when the Queen approached. Even after being cleaned, she could have a desire to attack again. The maids were the biggest targets she would go for. She left the Ogier guards alone for they would turn on her and her powers would do nothing to the big brutes. They were immune to the power, and using it against them only angered them.

She smiled at the guards and got up from her throne of bones and skulls. It was the one thing she would insist came with them. Many of those transporting that throne had relatives in it. They were solemn as they moved it, and never did they attempt to retrieve their loved ones due to the anger of the Queen. Disrupt her games and whims and she would see the whole lot destroyed or added to the throne. The bones would grow brittle with time so she would take more people to replace the worn bone. Many were now not only marked by the knives that cleaned the bones, but some now had an array of teeth marks. This made people uneasy around her.

She chooses when people were permitted to enter her chambers and when it was the throne room. She had a fling with most of the young men of the palace and some were invited to her rooms. Those boys and young men found themselves to be in a world of pain and despair before the Queen would kill most of them. They were the lucky ones were the youth that she took to her rooms, most of them never came out speaking or being more than a shell of the person they were.

Her habits made her a very undesirable lover and all of the young men knew it. She was definitely a praying mantis. She would play games so vile and repugnant and either kill them or make them wish they were dead. She said she was looking for a king but thus far had not found one.

Barrish, she did not torture. He had some use yet and he was fun to scare. She asked him a few months after the first daybreak in the borderlands, what they should do? It was wrong to run but they had the larger army. The realms that they liberated were just the borders of the Dark Lands. She was concerned that they may do the same in the entire Dark Lands. She would destroy the entire Dark Lands before she let that happen. Barrish was not concerned about the army out there was just fishing right now. Light had been brought to small sections of the Dark Lands and she controlled most of the remainder.

Barrish had suggested that they lead the enemy to the land of the dark wyrms. See how well they deal with the dark dragons. Marious was gathering some of them, but the rest wanted to live by the code of non-involvement. She liked the idea. It was the perfect way to get the dragons to fight for them. An army arriving in their lands would definitely cause most of them to come to her. A few holdouts may go to the enemy, but she was sure they would become very angry at the newcomers.

Barrish set out the next day and had the army at his back. The Dark Queen's banner flew above Barrish's own. He hated that but she was watching. So, he behaved. It would not be long before he took control of the Dark Lands for himself. The assassins he hired to kill her would do the job soon enough. He was thinking of how he was going to use her hide to make a saddle. She would be with him, under him for the rest of his life. The idea made him smile.

He left the walls of the city, and he saw several of the palace guard on the walls. They threw several people off the wall and hung them by the feet. Barrish looked at them and saw that his coup was not going to happen. The bodies being displayed were the assassins he hired to kill her.

That may make things a little more difficult. He would have to come up with a ruse to get her off his scent. There were now enough of the noblemen and women there waiting for her every command. All the dark nobles were ready to kill to take power and she knew they would try, so he could lay the blame there.

He perked up again as they continued toward the stationary enemy. It would not take long to taunt them into following them, and then sending them into the dragons' lands. That was going to be fun but first he needed to draw them out.

CHAPTER EIGHTY

THE CHASE BEGINS

Christof started to think about moving on when scouts reported an army headed their way. Christof had all the generals and officers meet with him in the new command tent which was six times larger than the old one. It held them all and had room for clerks and other persons that needed to be there. Christof did not have a map of the area, so Thomas hired a clerk to create some. Christof was not aware of this until it was presented to him by his father.

The map was well made and went all the way back to the other liberated lands and had plenty of empty space to add to it as they progressed. Laying it out carefully he had the generals explaining how their particular units functioned in the light and the dark. It would be a trick to get the enemy to come into the new daylight that bathed the lands. But come they will. Christof decided to meet them where the darkness was just beginning to show signs of the light. It would make things a little difficult, but the previous battles had to be lit by fires and torches. It was nothing new to them.

Christof had the army get ready for combat as the enemy approached, then the enemy pulled away. The generals ordered the pursuit but Christof was hesitant. Something was off. They were meeting them on their turf. They should have attacked. But Christof allowed the pursuit. Thomas was convinced they were afraid of the army and was going back to some palace or other. He had seen the banners. Barrish was indeed with them and so too was potentially the Dark Queen.

Torlin had a bad feeling as well and told his nephew that he was concerned. He sensed something coming. A bad problem. The pursuit was losing sight of the enemy and Christof ordered a halt. He would not chase any army that was running that hard away from them. He gave the orders to prepare for a return to the palace. As they moved back, Torlin was casting spell after spell and he asked Christof to also cast protective spells to cover their return.

Christof set a large shield in place and the army returned to the palace where the pursuit began. He was more relaxed as they entered the light once more. Their new found community was ecstatic at their return. He had left a group of scouts out into the Lost Lands and keep watch for the army returning.

Barrish was proud of himself. The dragons would be scrambling to join them at any moment. The army was in pursuit and soon he would lead them to the border of the dragons' lands to cause an uproar. They would have no problem coming to the dark armies after that.

He entered the citadel that the Dark Queen had hung his assassins from and entered the palace proper. The Queen was waiting for him and he was quite pleased with himself and what he had accomplished. The Dark Queen was smiling as he came in and had him come stand beside her. "You forgot some people did you not? I was attacked by some of those invisible assassins of yours. They really become visible again when they are killed. Come closer. I want to see if you can explain this to me."

He stayed where he was standing and gave his report. "The enemy army should be pushing into the dragons' lands looking for us now. It won't be long before they decide to destroy this army and declare war on the lands of the light."

Almedda purred to him, "Please come beside me. I wish to whisper your orders into your ear."

Barrish slowly approached the woman and he leaned his ear to her. "I want you to die." As she spoke, she sunk her teeth into his neck. Tearing out a large portion of the right side of it, Barrish fell at her feet. He quickly put a cloth on his neck to try and stop the bleeding but he did not have enough time to save himself. As the man died, Almedda smiled. "No one betrays me. Understood?" she said as she addressed the other nobles. "Now who wants to take his place?"

She would not make the mistake of letting her guard down again. He was looking for the opportunity and saw it as he left. She watched him be hauled off and the nobles around her looked at her with fear. That would be acceptable for now. She chewed the piece of Barrish in her mouth then spit it to the ground. He was not tasty. And he was as tough as shoe leather.

Looking at the nobles she randomly chose one of her generals and told him the army was his. He reported to no one but her. She would see this done.

She had waited for three weeks then a month and still no dragons. She ordered scouts to see if the enemy had been destroyed. She waited again for two to three weeks and she still did not see dragons. The scouts returned and they reported that the army of the light still remained in the last palace in the light. The scouts were dismissed and her general called forward. "What do you say we should do?"

"I would give them another few weeks to attempt to find you. Then we will go after them. If we are lucky, they will hunt for you in straight lines and go right into the dragons' lands." said the general.

"Lucky? They have my nephew at the head of their army. He is not only very smart and powerful; he seems to be able to sense the evil of this land and confront it before it can attack him. We need to get someone close to him and kill him. It is the only way we can win this." said the Dark Queen. "I have been looking for a way to mask the army from his senses but the magic itself would give away the position of the army."

"What if we hid the army in the dark far from his feelings and had the mask lead them right to the dragons and us. He should fall for that." Smiled the general.

"Not worth that grin but it may work. Get things set up and we will begin the pursuit again." said Almedda. "Yes, that just might work."

CHAPTER EIGHTY-ONE

SOMETHING IS WRONG

Christof was on the wall when his senses came into focus. A magic shield of dark magic was coming closer. It was headed to the west of the Lost Lands and into the dark once more. Christof was not sure that it actually hid anything. All the generals in his army were trying to get him to order the pursuit. But it was wrong feeling. Like a trap. He explained it to Torlin who seemed to believe he may be sensing the shield and not the creatures because the shield is blocking the creatures.

It made sense but it still meant that a magical person and a small force at least was in the area. "Do not pursue. Keep in the Lands of the Light and do not go off after her army. I fear treachery afoot." said Christof. He hit the shield hard with a flow of powers waiting for it to crumble but it did not. Whomever cast it was still there maintaining it. Christof hit it several more times and still the same result. He began to wonder who held it.

"Barrish is not this strong, is he?" asked Christof.

"I do not believe it is one person. Not even the Dark Queen herself could withstand those strikes alone. She must have a full coven at her disposal." said Torlin.

"How many dark wizards and druids are there?" asked Christof.

"Unfortunately, too many." said Artitous as he walked up to the conversation. "We did not even know of dark druids until your birth drew them out. They hide well in plain sight."

"I will find a way to find and destroy just the dark wizards and druids. It will not be pleasant either." said Christof.

"And that would make you no better than they are. Remember your training and your sense of purpose. You are not them." said Meka, as she too came into the conversation.

"But they killed her. Now this army of theirs taunts me day and night. I can take no more! Mother, what should I do? Go after the army that may or may not be there, or remain here until we know more?" Begged Christof.

"Rest on it, boy. You make better decisions when rested. Ask your mother. She knows." said Thomas as he strode up. "Were we having a family meeting and I did not get invited?"

"Of course not, Father. Just venting." said Christof. "The secret meeting was an hour ago." Snickering as he spoke.

"Very funny, little man. Even with the Warmonger you are no match for me." said Thomas.

"It is just too easy. Father, I was picking on you. You are no fun." said Christof.

"Now Christof you know how your father is. Do not tease him so." said Meka with a laugh and a slap to Thomas's back. Thomas almost fell to his face before he caught himself and stood again.

"If I did not have to keep you two you would be so exiled from Tetra. Speaking of which when are we going home? We need to protect what we have, not just liberating other peoples." said Thomas. "These walls in the Dark Lands are enormous. Maybe I should increase the size of our walls."

Meka just gave him the look, and he stopped short. He knew that look and he knew he would just get himself into more trouble if he opened his mouth again. Meka took his hand and walked away with him. "Let Christof think. He has many decisions to come too. You can go to the parade grounds and have your men do their drills. You'll like that, right?"

Christof did not hear the response as he suddenly had a messenger come up to him. "My lord, bad news from home. The Metradon and Tetradon are on the move. They are approaching the fields of the Pheni from the Mountains of Doric. Your wisdom is asked for. I was to return as fast as I could with and answer."

"The Metradon and Tetradon? It is funny to see them cooperating. See if they split and then keep the siege going for as long as they can. We march as soon as possible for home." said Christof.

Christof called his clerks together and had them prepare all of the orders to get ready for the long march home. He was leaving a sampling from every people that joined with him and those he brought from home to defend the areas they had already liberated from attack. He left Pan Thor as the governor of the new lands and the people welcomed him with open arms. He was amazed by the outpouring of support.

They left the city early the next morning. It would take several weeks to a couple months to return home, or at least that was what everyone believed. As they began the march on the road they traveled to the city. It was a short road and now it seemed to go on forever. He did not realize that his clerks were really taking care of these people. All of his cities now had roads connecting one another. This was cutting the travel time in half or more. His army moved easily on flattened and paved roads than the previous dirt roads. Too many things went wrong on those roads.

The blacksmiths were driving their wagons instead of having their apprentices drive so they could work while they traveled. It was a relief to see them all working together and that the men had some free time. Of the large number of blacksmiths with them only Arlette was working with her young apprentice, Terrell Piken. Since Tanis had pushed them together, they were practically inseparable. If she was not his supervisor, she would have asked him to marry her, but propriety had to be observed.

She had told her mother of her intent and was told she should wait until after the war was over. She did not want to lose the helper nor did she want to lose the close friend. She was not ready to jump into bed with him quite yet, but it had come close a couple times. She needed to get away from him for a day or two. That would settle her down.

She was working again and he was at her side. She was embarrassed when he stole a kiss the first time. She did not know how to be seductive. She only knew metals and leather. Yet this guy found her dirty face and clothes attractive. She could not believe it. They would steal kisses every so often now, but she tried to play them off as nothing. She was strong but not that strong though. She found herself looking for alone time with him.

She shook her head and continued to hammer horse shoes and nails and wheels. She even made a sword for Terrell. The blade was of mytheral and the hilt of gold. She had saved for a long time to get the gold to make the hilt. And the mytheral she made was second to none. Not even the dwarves could craft the metal the way she could. The blade was strong and flexible, yet would not break no matter what you did. The blade was worth many thousands of coins but she gave it to him. He could not believe the workmanship in it and had used it twice to defend the smithy alongside Arlette.

He made the first move on this day in the open wagon. He helped her move the last of the shoes from the fire and then he stopped her and kissed her deeper than he had ever done before. He pulled out a ring and asked her to marry him. She had never been so insulted. It was the woman's place to ask. She was Tyris after all. Her mother saw what was going on and told the boy to wait a moment while she spoke to her daughter.

"You are not technically Tyris. You are a blacksmith. They are more revered in our culture. But they can be asked to marry without insult. You are young but it should be a good match. I look forward to the wedding. Go over there and accept his proposal and make him a partner in your smithy." Scolded Roanda. "You are like every other blacksmith, important and worthy of happiness. So, take it."

"Terrell, you'll mess up your new pants on your knees like that. Get up out of the ashes. I will marry you. But you will have a hammer put through you if attempt to take it back. Remember that." She laughed as she grabbed him into her arms and kissed him as deeply as she had always wanted to. She looked slyly toward the house side of the smithy and smiled widely. They started to move that way when her mother blocked their approach. "And where are you two going so stealthy? You can smooch all you want. But one in the bedroom is still the rule until you're wed." Roanda said with threat in her voice.

"Understood, Mother. Was just hoping for a preview." Giggled Arlette.

"Do not try my patience or I will have your father cast a spell to keep your husband-to-be incapable of your preview." said her mother without a giggle.

The army had reached the Plains of the Pheni in record time with even a road heading toward the horizon toward Metra and Tetra. The big road led toward Thalinburg. It was a wonderful sight. And the laborers building the roads were the prisoners of war that had been taken thus far. Even the magical folks amongst the prisoners worked to seal the road magically making it even smoother to travel.

The prisoners looked happy and many saluted as Christof passed. Something was wrong with this picture. Prisoners were always sour. He called over one of the guards and inquired why they were so happy. "Why sir, they are doing something to increase and help each other. Their own people benefit from their work. It makes them happy to work and happy to be here."

"Don't forget the beer, my lord." said one of the prisoners and the lot of them laughed.

"If beer keeps you happy then I will supply it." said Christof as he continued down the road laughing with the prisoners and guards.

Christof called for his clerk and ordered the beer be given to the prisoners working on the roads. He then asked who had done the roads.

"Why it was Annissa that started that, my lord. We are just finishing what she started." said the older mouse lady.

"Thank you, Harriet. As soon as the order is written, take the rest of the day off with the rest of the clerks." said Christof.

"It is our pleasure to assist and follow you, sire. We appreciate the time off. One of us will wait your orders, while the rest wait our turn and relax." said Harriet.

Christof feared he would be followed and he was sure they were following him. He had hoped that he had left enough behind to guard his new territory, but now he was not so sure. Something was wrong. The enemy did not pursue nor were there any attacks on the road. It was scary to say the least. It felt like the enemy was frustrated. No matter that. The enemy could remain frustrated.

Soon enough the cities were in sight and Christof ordered a halt. Each of the rulers of the cities would return to their respective cities and Christof would deal with Thalinburg and the other cities as soon as possible. He gave the order that he would come when he could. No one was to come to him demanding to be first.

As he made himself clear, his father sauntered up to him. He began asking about Tetra and Christof repeated himself about no one asking. Then he told him "This means you."

CHAPTER EIGHTY-TWO

HOME TO THE RESCUE

Torlin was the first to lead his armies back to Metra. He and Roanda had Arlette and Garath with them not knowing what they were walking into. Torlin remembered the first round with the Metradon. It had almost not turned out well until his father had arrived with the dragons. He did not even have the twins yet. But still he was worried about the end of the war. Now with the twins and his wife, he feared even more. How did he keep the Metradon away?

They came over the final ridge to a view of sheer madness and carnage. Both sides had given as well as they had received but the defenders were slowly weakening. They had very few arrows left and the beam weapons were wreaking havoc on the archers on the wall. The archers were slowly tiring and the beam weapons killing as fast as they could show their faces. The Metradon had set up a command tent and had messengers coming and going. They knew that the end was near even though they had lost more than half their soldiers. Their support people were being dragged onto the frontlines to fight. They were often fumbling weapons and feeling most uncomfortable.

Torlin saw the command tent and blew it across the space setup between the walls and the Metradon camp with a blast of wind. The commanders inside grabbed up weapons and turned to face what they thought was a small group and froze at the army coming toward them. They tried to turn their forces and managed to get a small number ready to face the new enemy, and were cut down. The craftsmen and camp followers that were pressed into combat surrendered willingly, while the warriors amongst the Metradon tried to kill both the humans they hated the Metradon people they saw as traitors.

Torlin protected both as well as he could and soon the attacking soldiers were subdued and bound or dead. They gave little choice sometime Metradon who had thrown down their weapons were brought into the city and allowed to restart the businesses they had before the stasis occurred. He could only imagine sleeping so long the world you knew no longer existed.

He made sure they understood that any act of treason would cost them their freedom if not their lives should they attempt to harm the city. Members of the resistance amongst the Metradon on the battlefield were welcomed like kings when they returned to the city, and prisoners into the deep dungeons that were originally built to contain them. Torlin had no compunction to using these cells as they had been put there by the Metradon when they took the city the first time.

Torlin hated the thought of how they had taken the city and held everyone inside guilty of treason and circled them and shot into the crowd. If not for Tanis they would all have perished. His father was still healing and would be unable to aid him. He had seen an end to the Metradon horde that was attacking the city. The rest would live in peace or they would be destroyed. No more games.

The Metradon were happy to comply. Soon the smithies were banging away and all of the production services that were in the city began to hum once more. The people were pleased and the Metradon proved great allies.

On the way to Tetra, Thomas had a bit of a problem. Were the Metradon were caught off guard the Tetradon were waiting for the army to arrive. They had runners watching for the army to approach and they quickly prepared an ambush. Christof once more proved to be the savior of the army. He slung about himself with magic and the Warmonger and soon the enemy lay dead at his feet.

Christof had seen carnage but nothing like the battlefield in front of Tetra. Thomas paused, just like the rest of the army did. People who defended the city lay dead mixed with Tetradon and other creatures from throughout Dracos. The scene was so graphic that some of the warriors had to excuse themselves to the back of the column to get air. The battle was already over, it would appear as the few Tetradon left standing were of the Resistance. They wore the red scarf to identify themselves. They would bear watching but they went around the field helping to carry the wounded and dead. The Tetradons were left were they fell. They would be dealt with when they could. The injured Tetradon were being tended and brought to the dungeons where all this had begun.

The leaders of the Tetradon lay dead. Three Horns lay still on the field. Three Horns was the new leader of the Tetradon. The trouble that one had started. His top lieutenants lay around him and the humans that had followed them. They all appeared to have been in the command tent when the battle started. Remnants of the cloth lay all around them.

Thomas picked up the dagger that Three Horns had in his hands. It was the one he had given Dagmar a long time ago. What seemed like another lifetime ago? Meka looked at the dagger and took it from Thomas and threw it to the ground. "That is the dagger that thing stabbed me with. May it rot with its owner." said Meka.

"It really is not a bad little dagger. Except for its history, my love. I always wondered what he had done with it. Now we know. As you have said. Let it rot." said Thomas.

A man from the city was going around and collecting fallen weapons and arrows. The cart he had overflowing with the weapons of war. He reached down to get the dagger and Thomas told him to leave it. It would not do to be on another person; human, elf, or dwarf. The man looked at it once more and moved on. He picked up the spent arrows almost in reverence. He gently put them into his cart in quivers that as he filled one moved to another. There had to be forty full quivers of arrows there. Yet he continued to collect the fallen equipment. Again, all of his charges were treated with reverence but the arrows above all. He gently placed daggers and knives into sheaths and swords into scabbards. Spears and pole arms stuck out above the cart tied in a bundle in the corner, while maces and war hammers and like weapons were placed with care in the center of his cart. The weapons were going home.

Thomas watched the man with admiration. It was a menial task below most people, but it was a task that needed doing and he was doing it. Thomas was amazed at the care he took with the weapons and other valuables found on the field. He collected armor into another cart as it was stripped from the fallen. A grisly job, but he did it with pride.

Behind him came the wagon for the bodies. They waited for him to do his job but many complained that he did it too slowly. Thomas looked at them and the haphazard way the bodies were in the wagon and Thomas said, "Maybe if you took the care for the fallen men and women of our army that he takes with the weapons and armor, we may be able to identify who goes with what parts."

The men looked at Thomas and jumped into the wagon wrapping bodies and their parts into the shrouds they carried. The wagon was rapidly looking like a funeral wagon than a meat wagon. Thomas just watched. The men with the bodies would probably go back to the way they were doing before when he looked away, but the man with the weapons and armor continued just as he had from the beginning. The funeral wagon went on to the next section the other man had finished with and they looked back at Thomas and placed the fallen into the shrouds and placed them on the wagon.

It was a shame. The people who cared were so few and far between. But he was to blame for that. He chased a lot of the people who cared away. Meka noticed his face and the lack of sneer or upset for the slow weapon man on it and asked him, "Are you well, my dear? You rarely look upon the remnants of a battle without a sneer or a mixed sense of joy and excitement. Yet this time you do not. Why is that my husband?"

Thomas spoke softly, "I had always seen this after it was collected and recycled for the next war or battle. The people who went and cleaned the battle fields never once came to mind. The funeral wagons were the ones without couth, while a simple task as picking up the lost and useful from the ground was treated with reverence. Maybe that is what I do wrong? Am I not appreciating the smallest jobs enough?"

"I think you have just started to, my husband. Keep this lesson in your mind, everything is important to our city, from the brick makers to the generals. It just does not seem to make a large difference to the world how many bricks are made until you are building, and a general is worthless until a battle looms. There is glory in every job that can be done. No one is unimportant." said Meka.

"I think that I am learning that lesson." said Thomas as he spurred his horse forward and headed for the city. He had much to ponder.

The scene before Thalinburg was by far the most unusual. The city of Landsdale was left unmolested, but the entire army of darkness seemed to be parked outside the capitol. Martin was leading as Christof had elected to go home with his parents. Martin saw the encamped enemy and called the army to a halt. The army of darkness would attack by night, and thus be most aware then. It was the middle of the day. Martin sent runners and scouts out to assassinate the enemy sentries. When they had returned, Martin sent them to run off their horses and other mounts. As they filtered back, the rest of the army was approaching unaware to the enemy.

Martin was beyond the first section of tents when he launched the attack. They fought from the inside out. The command tents were destroyed and the generals killed or taken prisoner. Martin was pleased at the capture but realized that they still had an entire army to fight.

The rangers were laying about themselves with swords and fighting knives. The enemy was numerous but with little skill. Many gave up in front of the rangers, and were sent to the outside of the camp to the rangers now fighting from the outside in.

The rangers within fought to those outside and they united into a solid front. But it was not necessary. The enemy had given up. Martin had the prisoners brought into Thalinburg and brought to the main dungeon where they were sorted into different cells. Martin found that many of the prisoners were conscribed to the army. They wanted nothing more than to go home. The generals that were captured went into another cell. These men were wicked as the came but gave up to be spared dying on that field. They would go to trial. Then their fate would be decided by Tanis and Athinina.

The regular army of the enemy was put in yet a third cell. These men would once more be tried and then marshalled by the order of the King and Queen. The men would be treated fairly, unlike the prisoners of the dark army, who were executed on the spot or taken for experiments by the Dark Queen.

Tanis was still wounded and was still unable to attend nor preside over the trials, but Athinina went to him and asked his opinion on certain cases. Two of the generals had offered to reveal everything they knew about the Dark Queen. One by one they were brought into the hall and the generals looked around at the surrounding columns. Calm and completely empty except for the Queen and her aide.

The first man began to speak and all of a sudden, his throat began to seize up. He was choking on his own tongue and nothing they did or tried to could relieve him. They tried all kinds of resuscitation and found it all useless. They still had a mole in the palace. The second man was brought in the dead of the night and without warning. The man made it again to the throne room and the Queen asked him his name. The general was about to answer when a flow of fire went right through the man. Someone was watching them.

The first of the generals to be tried was not willing to say anything about anything not even in his own defense. Athinina ordered him sent to the headsman. The second general's trial was much like the first and he too was sent to the headsman. The last of the captured generals was brought before the Queen and she whispered at him in soft tones that could not be heard throughout the room. The man shook his head and strode back to the prisoners' box.

The regular army soldiers that were taken prisoner were no more talkative than the generals. They found their punishment was the same as that of the generals except these men were sent to the gallows. After all of the executions were done, the walls and towers were filled with the bodies of these men hanging like a cold, bitter fruit.

Athinina left them there for a while to be a warning to those who would attack the city. The men were magically disposed of after they had been there for a while and were starting to bring foul smells and illness to the city. Athinina spoke often to Tanis about the trials and the lack of remorse by enemy's regular troops. The conscribed army of the enemy was taken and brought back to the lands they were taken from. There they were released with the assurance if they return to any of the cities with violence in mind, they would be executed.

Garren and Gardell were home before any of the attacks on the larger cities. They watched the armies of the enemy pass and harassed them with side attacks. They winnowed down the numbers of the enemy until they were more than manageable to the cities they marched to. At Metra, they actually got involved in the battle. The phoenix of the Tyris were dispatching more of the enemy than the weapons the women of the Tyris and men of Metra did. It was definitely a shock when the men and women quit the field and the phoenix finished the enemy.

They spent a small amount of time with their comrades in Metra before they headed for the city of Tetra. The Tyris with them and the men and women of their army were in high spirits when they arrived at Tetra and saw the battle under way. The Tetradon were clearly wiping the city's defenders from the walls. Garren ordered the attack and the men and women of Landsdale were once more involved in a battle that turned out to be evenly matched until the city realized that help had come.

The city sent its troops into the fray and soon the battle was over. Gardell was walking the field looking for her husband. She found some of his body guard and saw others that had died at his spear. He would have to teach her how to handle a spear when she found him and returned to Landsdale. She continued to look and went into the city proper looking for him. She hunted everywhere he would go to and found no sign of him. She found some of the men that were assigned to him that day and asked them what had occurred.

"My lady, we tried to keep up with the man but he was so concerned by the Tetradon that he did not realize he was away from us. We fought to him and saw the terrible thing. My lady, please go to Artitous. He was the one working on him. I hope beyond hope that our assumptions are incorrect. Well, just go to Artitous." said one of the men.

"What happened? Tell me." said Gardell. "Please say you are not telling me what I fear most."

"My lady, I can give you no tidings. Go to Artitous." replied the man.

Gardell ran to the houses of healing and rushed into the back house reserved for royalty. "Where is Artitous? Where is my husband? Please someone tell me."

"I am here, Gardell. The news is not good. Go in and talk to him. He is so severely injured he may not have much time left. He took five or six of those blasts from the Tetradon before he fell. But he took a great many with him."

"Garren! Speak to me. Tell me you will be ok. Please tell me you will be ok." said Gardell.

Garren opened his eyes slowly and stopped half way. "My love, I am sorry. I think that I did more than I should have. I was trying to help clear an area and got ambushed." He stuttered.

"Keep still, be quiet and work at healing yourself. Don't speak. You will be wed. I have good news for you. We are to be parents. You will be a father." said Gardell.

"I fear you will have to tend them yourself. I am spent. I have no more strength in me. I love you more than life its self. You will be a great ruler and mother." Whispered Garren as he closed his eyes for the last time and slowly slipped away.

"You cannot go. I need you. I cannot do this alone. Please wake and tell me you are ok. I cannot go on without you." Cried Gardell.

Artitous clung to the falling woman and led her from the rooms. "It is not good to dwell on his passing. Remember him the way he was with you. Are you truly pregnant? I will tend you myself if you are. The Thalins will mourn his passing greatly. As I know you will. His child or children will be your solace now."

"I cannot believe he is gone does anyone know how? What was he doing wrong? I was hiding because of my condition. I rode into combat with him and hid. I should have been at his back." Gardell said.

"No, you should not have been there!" said Artitous. "You were where you were needed. He chose to fight; he could have stayed clear. No one would have judged him. He died saving you and your family and his family. He would want it no other way. If you were there you would have died too. The man who brought him in said he was betrayed by one of the guards. He moved to give the Tetradon a clear angle to shoot. And he made sure that Garren was injured beyond healing. There were stab wounds as well as hits by those things. They are not all bad, but they are not all good either. And we still have a traitor amongst us."

"We will find his killer. We will execute the man who did this. He or she will have nowhere to go. I will make them pay." said Gardell. "I will make them pay."

C H A P T E R
E I G H T Y - T H R E E

A FUNERAL FOR THE PRINCE

Gardell had arrived with Garren's body at the mausoleum that had been built to house the bodies' of Garren and Gardell and their children. It seemed colder than she remembered. The marble worked as only the dwarves could and steel work that was unmatched by his niece, Arlette. The leaves upon the steel gates looked like they could flutter to the ground in a strong breeze.

It was fall again and the leaves were changing colors. She could remember the two of them looking at them on the path through town looking at the change of colors. They had enjoyed those times.

The royal family was coming to pay their respects and to inter Garren. It was supposed to be a private ceremony, but already people he had affected in one way or another was filtering into town. His body was hidden to avoid grave robbers and other treacherous deeds be done to the body. Several people were taken into custody for trying to break into the palace. The Tyris-in-charge was watching very closely and told one of the would-be robbers that it was a lot easier to get into the palace then it was to get out.

Thomas and Meka arrived first and immediately went to the palace. Thomas was making demands as he walked into the quiet palace and Meka was trying to quiet him down. Torlin and Roanda and Arlette and Garath arrived next. Sasha traveled with Garath and was received with open arms. The two were bound for the wedding hall, but not for a while. Let their wounds heal. Athinina arrived without Tanis. She gave his regrets to the rest of the family but his injuries prevented him coming to the funeral.

Athinina asked if everyone was here. The rolls of the royals found that Christof was missing. Thomas and Meka thought that he was with them when they left but they had not seen him.

Well-wishers and those who saw Garren as a hero came streaming into the growing town. They were all demanding a public service and Athinina went to Gardell, "I believe the service had better be public. We can have a private one later. Where is Pan Thor and Artitous. They were supposed to be here, too. It is up to you though Gardell. He was your husband."

As if speaking his name was a beacon in walked Artitous and Pan Thor. The two were very rarely not together, they were always talking magic or some other thing. Torlin would get jealous as the cat did not show him anything.

"Don't worry kitten. I will teach you when you are ready." Was all he would say to Torlin when he asked.

The two went into the building housing the royal family and the body. They could not let the battle injured body be put into state, so Artitous had the local sculpturer produce a statue of Garren for the town square. The funeral, it was decided would wait on the statue.

The family announced this to the crowds and they seemed satisfied by their solution. They also announced that the family would inter the body due to damage to it privately. Again, this seemed to be taken well.

Athinina led the procession with Gardell as they approached the crypt. The older woman embraced the younger and made soothing sounds. They went into the crypt and the boys Garath and Christof carried the body into the crypt. Athinina offered up the prayers for the dead and they left the crypt.

Christof moved over the doors and magically sealed them so none would get in. He fashioned twelve rings that would allow access to the crypt and gave them to the royal family present. Gardell spoke to Athinina, "I guess I am no longer a royal. So, I will pack and return to the Tyris camps."

"Why my child would you do that? You became a royal the day you married my stepson. That does not go away with the death of your spouse. This is your place to rule still and you may mourn for a time but the day-to-day matters of state will have to be returned to. For now, though, mourn. "

The sculpturer was finished twenty days after the commission of the statue. He hauled piece of marble he had worked into the middle of the town's square. They had it placed just in front of the avenue to the palace. There was room to add more as they became needed.

Gardell revealed the statue the next day. She tried to stay strong but his likeness was uncanny. She broke into tears and had to have his stepmother offer up the traditional prayers for the dead. The crowd pressed forward slowly trying to touch the statue and get a rubbing of the name upon it.

At Gardell's insistence the statue had listed all of the names of those who had fallen in the battle with Garren. His was first and center, but the rest were there for the families. Garren the dragon slayer was what people called out to the four winds as they looked at the statue and the podium with all the names listed. The town square was to be a place of reverence after the ceremonies. Garren's statue would eventually be joined by those of his immediate family.

The family once more split off back to their respective cities and as they left a cloud opened above the town. "I have taken two. How many more will you lose before the game is over?" came the voice from the hole in the sky. The townsfolk were on their knees fearing it was a god displeased with them until the magical folk launched fireballs and lightning at the hole.

Laughter sounded as the hole in the air closed. Gardell tried to get her bow before the hole closed but she could not. Hetrick was flying low over Gardell protecting her master. She let off a fireball as well but again it missed.

Christof came from where ever it was he was hiding and brought out one of the guards floating and trussed up like a turkey. "Gardell. I have found the man that killed your husband out right at the order of the Dark Queen. Apparently, she still targets us. It is your town, Gardell. You pass judgement."

"Thank you, Christof. But I am sick to death of bloodshed and death, so I will allow a trial by his peers. The people of the town will decide his guilt and what should be his sentence. I cannot right now." said Gardell.

"Very wise of you," said the now tied up man. "Yes, let them decide. I may walk away yet."

"Trust me you will not walk away without a sentence of some kind or I will impose one. Do we understand each other?" asked Gardell.

"Yes, I know. I have a chance to live and escape to freedom." said the villain.

Gardell dragged the man to the center of the town square and stood him upon the pedestal there. Lifting him up for her was surprisingly easy. Looking at the man he smiled down at her like he knew something they did not. She looked at him and demanded to know why he smiled. "Oh, my lady, I smile because I am happy. They will not execute me."

"People of Landsdale, how should we treat this traitor? He caused many a death, including that of Garren Dragon Slayer. How do you find him? Guilty or not guilty." Shouted Gardell.

"Guilty!" came the roar from the crowd. "String him up on the hanging tree."

"They cannot mean that ask again." said the villain but people were already making way for the executioner. He walked deliberately to the stand with a noose in his hand. "Good lady, surely, we can have a recount?"

"They all said the same thing. You are to die. Now." said Gardell. As she turned her back the villain drew a dagger, he had secreted about him, and jumped onto the back of Gardell. Before he could bring it down on her though several rangers shot him full of arrows.

"The villain is dead now. Disperse knowing that he will not harm us again." said Gardell. She marched toward the palace her eyes filling with tears. Thomas came up to her and said "He was a bit young for the front lines, I think. He was always braver than he should have been. He had good taste in women though. If I were not married, I would come for you."

Meka elbowed the man in the ribs and he looked at her with a confused look on his face. "He is just picking on you. Trying to raise your spirits. He did not mean anything by it." Apologized Meka. "That vile man really tried to kill a Tyris with a dagger. Gardell, you have kept up with your weapon skills have you not? It is good for the child or children. They may even grow to be kind and smart like their father."

"Yes, it would be nice. I wish for health. I know I should pray for women that I can train to be strong, but a little boy in his honor would be great. I could call him after his father." said Gardell, a smile appeared briefly on her face as she held her stomach protectively. "This child or children will be honored by their father's strong passing. His spirit will protect his children."

"Remember that life ends in death just to be born again. We are in an endless circle. From now forever forward." said Meka.

"I just wish he were still here at my side." said Gardell.

They turned from the square when chaos broke out. The royals did not look as the guards tried to keep order. They took a few more steps and then a man grabbed Thomas's arm. He turned to confront the man only to see that he had no head. The body fell and the royals ran back to the square. The sight that greeted them was definitely a massacre. The faerimouth were back in the square as well as the guards who were on one side, and on the other was Gaitlyn of the forest elves. He had helped Thomas and Meka what seemed a lifetime ago. He looked at Thomas and Meka with contempt. At his side was an army of trolls. People in between were being assisted away, the guard and the trolls tried to prevent it.

The guards removed the last person and the archers opened up. Gaitlyn had archers of his own but Christof put up a shield to protect the small army of guards and royals. The arrows seemed to dissolve in front of the trolls and dark elves. They must also have a magical person. Christof sent a magical blast at the enemy and their shield fell. The archers of Landsdale fired into the trolls and elves set against them and their arrows struck true. An arrow flew right for Thomas's heart, when a flow of air knocked it away.

Thomas looked at his son who was busy fighting, and then looked around himself. The young wizard saved his life then attacked the trolls. The woman in the robes looked familiar but he could not see through the hood. And some kind of spell kept her quite unseeable. Her curves and her body she had no problem showing but her face she hid in the cowl of her cape.

The enemy was all but routed and archers dispatched to finish those who escaped, including Gaitlyn. "He is quite charming and a really good warrior is he not?" asked the woman that had saved Thomas. "He reminds me of you, Thomas. And how I want to kill you. But not today. You have earned a reprieve since Garren died. Next time we meet, the arrow will find its home where it was aimed."

He drew his sword to kill the wizard and she faded away. Artitous and Christof tried in vain to close her escape route but were unable. "That was the Dark Queen. She came here to see the funeral. I wonder why she did that. If she came around, we must check the crypt and make sure the body had not been tampered with." said Christof.

They reached the crypt just as the sun was setting. Christof lit the way with a ball of light above his head that made the darkness move from him. He made it to the sepulcher and waved in front of the steel gates with the ring he had made. It opened slowly for the prince and he rushed inside. The light followed behind with his parents. They opened the crypt and the body was still inside. Everyone breathed a sigh of relief until he saw several bite marks that were not on the body before burial.

The Dark Queen had come into the crypt to rip a few pieces of meat from a body? It made no sense. Christof closed the grave and they all left the crypt. Christof once more waved the pattern in front of the door and it locked again. No one would be able to get in without powerful magic again. The royals had theirs with the rings. Anyone else would be unable to enter. Christof saw to it.

CHAPTER EIGHTY-FOUR

A VISITOR IN THALINBURG

Each of the royal family had left for their respective cities. Christof even left for the city in the Lost Lands. They had to find out its name. The others made it home and Artitous stayed behind in Landsdale. He spent many a day looking in on the princess there. Looking for signs of the kind of deep distress that could cause her problems.

She knew what he was looking for and assured him that she was not going to harm anyone. Including herself. She was showing as the season changed from fall to winter and winter to spring. It would not be long until the child came into the world. As the days of her pregnancy came to an end, she was invited to Thalinburg to have the child.

She took the first wagon out and arrived to meet the Queen of Dracos at the gates of the city and rode together on the way to the palace. Tanis had taken a turn for the worse lately after hearing of his son's death. He seemed to give up wanting to live.

Athinina was concerned but Artitous would snap him out of it. He always did. She was feeling better as the child made itself known. It was a mover and she was quite comforted by the babe's motions within her. Athinina smiled at her and the two rode in silence for a time. As they entered the palace, Gardell was walking gingerly. The Queen called for Artitous and found that she was not yet into the labor. The babe was just trying to stretch its legs.

The midwife that had delivered Torlin and Thomas looked at the young lady and said, "Gee my lady. Twins run in the family hard, don't they?"

Gardell mouthed the words and said, "No, no. There is no way it is twins."

Athinina laughed and said "Do not doubt this woman's words. She has predicted twins on three of our family and it has come to pass. She is elderly now but she still likes to hang around for you youngsters."

"Twins would mean having someone to help corral them. I am not ready for that." said Gardell.

"It's called a nanny, silly. You forget you are royalty. They will come out of the wood work to help care for the babes. Twins are a good thing; I think so anyway. They keep each other occupied." said Athinina.

"Don't you start too. I am not having twins." said Gardell. "See, only one pushes the womb. If there were more in there I would know."

"You will see, Gardell. You will see." Laughed the Queen.

It would be a couple of weeks as spring wore on before the labor was complete. Gardell had been trying to pick out names while waiting for the child. She refused to believe there was more than one. The midwife came in every so often to make sure she was comfortable. She was sitting in a big, comfy chair when the first wave of contractions hit. She called out and the guard, Thomas, looked in and said "Not again."

He called for the midwife and stood a bit away from her. He was fearful of the pregnant royals. Athinina had almost crushed his hand through his gauntlet. He still had the scars on his hand from the steel. Gardell waved the man over and asked him to help her to the bed. The contraction hit her when they were half way to the bed and she squeezed the poor man's hand so hard the steel bent on his gauntlet.

Looking down he saw it was not too damaged but he had to get his hand back. He was helping her into her bed when the next contraction hit. Holding the woman half in the bed half out he pushed her up into the bed and quickly took back his hand. It was too late she had done the same as the queen all those years ago. He walked to the healers and they laughed as he reported how he was injured.

"You really know how to charm the royals don't you?" joked one of the druids.

"Laugh it up. One of you will be going in there without a gauntlet." Smiled Thomas the guard.

The midwife arrived after what seemed like an eternity. Gardell was still in denial. There was no way it could be twins. He would not have produced twins. She was so confused that she missed the words from the midwife. The midwife laid her down and checked to see if the child was right.

"So far so good, my lady. Just get ready to push. There will be a small amount of pain. So be ready. Here bite down on this. It will help." Instructed the midwife. The next contraction hit and the princess nearly broke the wood and leather bite stick. It would be necessary to change that it seemed.

The family had come to see the child come into the world, and Arlette was in the room with her calling her name and ushering her on. Hetrick was asleep on the headboard of the bed and opened an eye as

Gardell let out a yell. The midwife continued to put the stick back in her mouth and she continued to spit it out.

The child was coming now she could feel it and one more push brought the babe into the world. The little boy was perfect and shining. He would be like his father. She was about to take the child to her breast when the contractions started again. "This is not a child; it is the after birth." said Gardell. She was hoping beyond hope anyway.

The labor produced another child this one with a raspberry stain on his face from the chin up the left side of his face. This child scared his mother but she quickly smiled. "Is he ok? Is it over? Can I hold them now? I had better not have another one in there or I will raise my husband from the dead just so I can murder him myself."

Everyone laughed at the joke and she was given the children. They both were hungry for little ones. This was good they will survive. She closed her eyes and let the children eat when her head began to swim. She told the midwife and she checked the womb. "My god, my lady. How do you withstand the pain? There is a major tear in the uterus and we must do something about it immediately or we may lose the mother."

The druids offered her fruits and meat to eat while the midwife made a salve and applied it. The pain nearly made her jump but it was done quick. The midwife looked concerned as she watched the mother. She seemed to be in good spirits, but she did not know that she could still perish. Any kind of hard pressure and she could completely bleed out from the womb. She saw Gardell trying to move and helped her adjust her position. She munched happily as the babies were taken to be cleaned.

The midwife went to the Queen. "She will not be able to move for at least a few weeks. The tear may grow if she travels and then there will be nothing I can do. She left Mayor Flatfeet in charge. But he may be in charge forever. She teeters on the border of life and death, yet she is happy. Why is that so?"

"She will of course remain here. She will be kept as non-mobile as possible. Until you give us the word, she is well. She was happy because her husband and she would be reunited, or she would get to be with his children. Either way works for her. If she dies, she gets him. If she lives, she gets his children. There is no lose for her." said the Queen.

"Just make sure she is well tended and I will check on her every few hours. I hope the salve works but I cannot tell until the morning keep her still until then." said the midwife as she walked away. The children would not be left parentless. The babes would be better off with the lady without children who approached her yesterday. She said she was a friend of the royal family and that she would take the young men if the need arose. The need is arising. She must use the charm she gave her.

She blew over the surface of the medallion as she was instructed and the dust came up and she breathed it in. She suddenly became woozy and disoriented. A few moments later she was dead and the lady came from the closet. She looked at the woman and then took her uniform and got into it. She was not cut out for this but the need is there and she will do her best with both boys.

She walked into the room to see the mother looking at her offspring. She saw the woman enter and she knew there was to be trouble. She called a guard that the woman had dispatched before entering. Gardell knew in that moment when the guard did not come that she was about to die. She reached for her husband's spear and the weapon was taken away from her. She felt the wound inside her open again and she drew the last resort she had. She drew the silver sword of Arlette's making. She said that it was good against the vampires and were creatures. It would not do well against a person but she had to try.

Screaming for help, no one came. Slowly the woman took the weapon from Gardell and she pushed her head back. "I would have normally just cut your throat, but your body is going to do it for me. Enjoy what life you have left."

She walked over to the cradles and lifted both children with a flow of air and walked from the room. Gardell continued to scream and soon they grew fainter and fainter. Eventually, she heard them stop. She was dead. These two were orphans now and she would raise them right. Oh yes, she would.

CHAPTER EIGHTY-FIVE

ORPHANS

The search began immediately for the babies and the murderer that had killed their mother. Garren's spear was deep within her. She did not even have a chance to name her the children. Athinina would do that as soon as the traitor or traitors were found and executed and the babies back in the royal palace were they belonged. They had a funeral for her that was just as well attended as that of her husband. The statue was put next to that of her husband in the town square. They would live on immortalized in stone.

Mayor Flatfeet was named as the regional governor to govern the city until the children were old enough to do the job for him. Athinina and Governor Flatfeet agreed that this would be best. In other words, nothing was going to change.

They followed the woman's trail for days and seemed to come no closer to capturing the fugitive. The babies should be slowing them down. The wagon or sled or whatever kind of transport they were using was not slowing down and it was headed toward the Mountains of Doric. A powerful witch lived in those mountains, long ago giving the orders that she was not to be disturbed. The trail headed south as they reached the foothills. The trail was a false one.

"Lose something?" said a voice from above. The search party looked up to see the Dark Queen looking down at them through a hole in the air. The magical folk tried to fire into it, but their spells had no effect. Martin who was leading the search fired into the hole with his bow and again the arrow fell to the ground. "Better watch where you put your valuables. You will never know who is lurking."

The search party turned south and away from the mountains toward the lost lands. A bird was sent to alert Christof that they were on their way. They would need assistance in the hunt.

Christof met them at the border with several hundred archers. "You may need more rangers. The terrain is dark and forbidding but use your torches and you should be ok."

"Thank you, my lord." said Martin. "Has anyone passed this way with children? Two babies. I need to find those babes."

"Well, if the Dark Queen has them, you know they are already dead. If not, you stand a fighting chance. Are you sure they came this way?" asked Christof.

"I am sure of nothing. One woman is dead and one guard. She was tying up loose ends it would appear. We do not know if she went north, south, east, or west. The trail is so faint that she must have been barely touching the ground." said Martin. His anger was apparent. "Was really hoping your watch towers had seen something."

"Not yet but it is early yet. I know how it feels to lose people close to you, I feel your pain as I too have lost someone close to me." said Christof.

"You do not understand what it is to lose two parents and the be kidnapped and forced to be someone they are not to protect them. God, I pray she has them. Because if she does have them, they are already with their parents. I fear though that we travel in the wrong direction. Something pulls me another way." said Martin.

"Well, I have not even seen the children but I felt their birth. It must have been felt all over the world. It was no secret that the children were born. Every magical person on Dracos must have felt it. Let your magical folk lead your search. They should be able to feel the twins and lead you true." said Christof.

"I hope you are right." said Martin as he walked from the throne room.

Christof had a feeling something would be a foot. After all, the family is being hunted and executed. Garren was a kind man and very loving to his wife and the whole family. He also had the people of Landsdale in his sway. The Tetradon had killed a great man. He knew about the dagger wounds but he tried not to think about it. It troubled him that an assassin had made it that close to one of the royal family. The two children born to them need to be in a safe place.

From the way they felt the children being born they were definitely magical. It would not do to have them learn the dark arts. They would be a valuable weapon for the Dark Queen. But he sensed them vaguely when he stretched out his magic, but even he could only go so far. As far as he stretched that he felt them that strongly tells him they are as powerful as he is, probably together, but he would love to find out.

He called Martin to return to him and when the ranger came, he told them to hunt in the Mountains of Doric. Martin and his group of rangers as well as a druid he picked up at the city left that morning. The saddled up as Christof had given them all horses to make the journey faster and more comfortable.

Martin let the druid lead the way. He seemed competent and eager so he let him take the point. He rode beside the druid and another ranger rode on his other side. If he was on point, he would be protected. So, the three-rode side by side and the druid reached out to feel the twins. The druid asked questions about the twin's parents if they were both magical, who their grandparents were. After a while Martin began to geta bit nervous. The man asked too many questions. Especially about their linage.

"Suffice it to say they are of the royal family and must be found." said Martin after growing annoyed with the questions halfway to the mountains. The druid still led them straight toward the mountains, surely it would be more aimed the closer they came. Martin had asked one of his rangers to go and fetch a second magical person to assist in finding the children. The extra three months lost going to the Lost Lands gave the kidnapper a large lead. He would close that gap.

The new wizard came up and Martin saw them before the rest and ordered a stop and rode to the pair before they could break cover. He told the wizard to wear ranger garments and weapons. For now, the druid did not need to know he was being double checked on his directions. Martin suspected that the druid needed their assistance into the mountains and after he used them to get close an accident would occur and kill the rangers. The wizard was a shield from that.

The three people rode to the middle of the pack of rangers with the new ranger sitting by himself on his horse in the middle of two other rangers that were watching everywhere and nowhere at once. They seemed relaxed, but the truth was they would spring to action in a heartbeat and attack with full strength and vigor. A ranger at rest was as deadly as a warrior in full armor and with weapons drawn.

The rangers rode for many more days the journey much like the day before with little interaction with the locals that left them be and the rangers left them be. Uneventful day past every uneventful day. The druid always claimed that they were getting closer. Martin's hidden wizard confirmed that they were indeed closing in on the children.

So, they continued to follow the druid and continued to go on an uneventful journey. They lost track of the many miles that they had traveled by the time the mountains began to rise up ahead of them. The days had past to almost five months. They had to give the horses a rest after the ride took them through the Fields of the Pheni. The heat had caused excessive sweating and they brought them to the well and washed them down. Since recovering the swords, the water was now pure.

The horses took the water and were re-energized and the ride resumed. Soon they were on the foothills of the Mountains of Doric. The larger mountains were still far away but the druid called for a slowdown. The horses would be of no use soon enough but for now they could continue. The druid led them higher into the foothills where all of a sudden, they were being attacked by different creatures that infested the local area.

The sword spiders were there but they were much smaller than those that had been brought to the capitol. They were aggressive but soon they had given up attacking the party. The druid led them down a path and a shed had been seen far below them. The druid looked at the rangers and smiled he waved his hands and disappeared. The horse was dismounted as the weight coming off of it made the horse wince.

The hidden man ran for all he was worth, he did not want the rangers to be anywhere near him. He needed to get in that shed and kill all of the occupants or the Dark Queen would kill him and his family. He had signed up with the hope of immortality and now had to do this menial task that Christof had assigned him. The boy was too trusting and should have realized he was too eager for the assignment.

He continued down the path and was so focused on the shed he did not hear the creatures behind him. AS the first attacked him he assaulted them with loud magical attacks and it drew the rangers but he was not going to get this far without those children. The creatures attacked once more and again he rebuffed them with magic but they were getting closer and closer so he could not use his magical attacks. He tried to back away and found his path there blocked as well. The last thought through his head was that he was supposed to live forever.

The rangers allowed the wizard to show himself and they approached the shed going the same way the druid had taken. They saw the sword spiders feasting on something and killed the lair of them. The druid had not gotten far it seemed. The magic attacks were evident around the area. The druid had tried to cut his way through with his dagger. He had succeeded in only angering the hive. They would have fed on him until he was gone, had the rangers not killed them all.

The only one they did not find was the queen and they kept close watch for her. It would be unfortunate to get this close to die by the spiders. They traveled toward the shed, getting closer as the hours past. The path to the shed was winding and took them forward and back. They moved forward and the wizard found several illusionary traps. "The wizard that set them was very powerful," he said, "and they should call on Christof or Artitous to assist them."

Martin just had him disassemble the traps. They needed to get to that shed. Martin called out, "Hurry down toward the shed now brothers surround it and prepare for the final assault to retrieve the babes."

"My house is not a shed," said a mysterious voice. "It is small but comfortable. You cannot have the children and there is no use in fighting for it. You may come in and see that they are safe and well-tended. They grow strong and I am slowly teaching them the great arts. They are twin boys, young and getting stronger by the day. They will won't plateau like Christof and Tanis have. They have to learn how to control the magic now before it kills them and all of us."

"You cannot have the children they belong with their family." Martin called out to the voice.

"You may see them this once but by tomorrow we will be gone elsewhere. Do not follow this time or I will be forced to do things I have no desire to do." said the voice. "I will keep my traps locked up tight so that you can arrive unharmed. The boys now have names. You can tell the rest of the royal family. This way they will know what to call them when it is safe for me to return them home. They are called Dunmar and Danson. Danson is afflicted with a strawberry stain on half of his face. I am the wizard, Raylene, and I will get them where they need to be. You will just have to trust me."

"But we do not even know you? How can we trust you? Please just return the children. They will be taught by the great wizards and druids of this world, Tanis, Torlin, and Christof Thalin. They will have the tutorage of Pan Thor and Artitous. What more can we do?" asked Martin.

"They must learn neutrality. That is something that the Thalins and their brood there have yet to learn." said Raylene. "Good bye rangers. You have lost your chance. We leave now."

As she spoke her shed moved as the dragon below it raised up its head and prepared to take to the skies. The rangers tried in vain to keep the dragon from taking off but they were unsuccessful. The dragon took off and flew high toward the mountains.

"Can you still feel the children?" Martin asked the wizard.

"Unfortunately, not. She has shielded them from our senses. She did not think she had to, but now she knew she would need it. Not much we can do, sir. Nothing, in fact. I am sorry. Winter comes early here. We should move quickly to the flat lands again, and come up with a new strategy." said the wizard.

"Then we return to Thalinburg and recoup and strategize. I appreciate your coming to our aid. It was a close thing, but the druid got what he deserved." said Martin.

"Let us return then," said the wizard, mounting his horse and heading back toward the cities.

CHAPTER EIGHTY-SIX

ONCE MORE INTO THE BREECH

Martin arrived at Thalinburg as winter started to touch the cities. The cold was refreshing to the ranger. He brought his horse into the stable yard and he headed to the Queen to give her the bad news. Christof and Torlin were there, though he himself did not know when he was arriving. They were both sharp as tacks. Christof had begun shaving it would appear. He was covered with salve that Torlin himself was quite familiar with.

Torlin was standing as Martin came in and bowed to the Queen. "You have lost the trail of the children. We know. We felt her raise the shield. We offer our condolences. You have found the approximate place of the Witch of the West, who I might add is not our enemy. Neither is the Dark Queen. She has played the mediator for many a war, because she has no allegiance to anyone. The children will be safe with her for a while. We can now search till we die and probably will not find her again."

"But I was within bow shot of her and did not fire, My Lords. I could have killed the dragon but I did not." said Martin as he once more settled to one knee.

"Gee, I think that Martin thinks he is infallible. Or at the least the source of the complete lore of the mountains. No one has because of the dangers of those mountains. Martin is supposed to be omnipotent. How do you live with such failure, sir?" said Christof. Looking down into the face of the older man that had been their head ranger for so long many have forgotten when he came to them. He was an elf and showing age so he had to be quite old. But he fought and defended the family as any of the younger men did.

"My Lord, I am none of those things. I just should have done more." said Martin.

"If you are none of those things then you must forgive yourself. No one could have guessed this turn of events. Did she say anything to you?" said Christof.

"I was told that the children were named Dunmar and Danson. Danson is suffered a strawberry stain on his right side of his face. The boys are healthy and their power already matches yours and Tanis. She says they will grow even stronger as their years progress. They are powerful each, but they can meld their powers and be three times stronger than either of them solo." said Martin. "She said their magic will continue to grow throughout their lives unlike you and Torlin where it kind of leveled out."

"That is troubling," said Torlin. "How is this possible? I wonder if the magic of the cave has grown as it goes from generation to generation. I was the strongest magical being on the world of Dracos, then came Christof who is even stronger than I am, now there are these children and they are stronger than either of us. We must hope they are neutral. Otherwise, we may have a problem with the Dark Queen tempting them to the dark side of magic. They are safe for now, but we will have to intervene at some point and bring them home."

Martin sat forgotten and they finally realized he was still there. "You are free to go, we will speak again less formally. We just have to figure this out." said Torlin.

The decision to go for the end of the war with the Dark Queen was made later that week. Once more the Army of Light was assembled again with Christof at its head. Tanis remained too ill to partake in battle. So, Christof led them back to the city in the lost lands. Christof finally revealed the name of the city, Glasburg.

They left for the city in the dark that Almedda had made her home. Christof had been able to scry for the demons that she employed to keep the peace in her city and lands. He would be still searching and scrying as they moved on. A large concentration of the demons indicated that was the place. Christof led them toward the demons.

They had started to run into resistance the closer they came to the Dark Queen. The demons were joined by mercenaries, dragons, and other creatures of nightmare. They attacked the Army of Light as they moved toward the Dark Queen. Slowing the army to near a crawl as these creatures continued to come at them. Christof set up three battle formations as they traveled. One tier was the fast-track horses and knights. The next tier was archers and crossbowmen. The final tier was the infantry and spearmen as well as the magical folk and Christof, Torlin, and Thomas. Meka and Roanda remained behind to ensure they were not left short in their cities.

The demons were dispensed with by the magical folk. The magical folk were protected by the third-tier foot soldiers. The horse stayed away from the front until the demons were taken care of. They then came to attack the remaining troops attacking the army. It seemed that she was creating more and more creatures as the resistance increased as they moved forward. It took three weeks to cover the last two miles to the city as the resistance was pushing hard at the army.

They finally fell back to the city when it was within site of the army. The darkness was deep. They had no lights in the city but the city teemed with creatures of nightmare and legend. Christof fired off a flare of magic above the city. The light caused a mad dash for the walls and into shelter as the light hurt their eyes. It was dispelled quickly, but Christof had already seen the lay of the city.

It was not a difficult assault once they were in the city. The problem was the place was like an ant hill. And his light had stirred it. They were mounting the walls and crawling down the walls headed toward the army. Second tier warriors, the missile weapons cleaned up most of the approaching creatures. The Dark Queen showed herself on the walls and an archer took a shot at her. The arrow went through her shoulder but she did lean on the wall. She was really there.

Christof went to the gates and blew them from their hinges. He moved with his rangers toward the palace while the Queen was distracted. He quickly made the palace and grabbed their greatest of dangers, the grimoire. They quickly went to the wall and found the Dark Queen trying to heal herself of the wound. Christof had a druid step toward her and heal her. Christof grabbed her up with flows of air so she could not attack them or the druid healing her. She screamed and yelled as they healed then carried her to the magical holding cell that they had created for her. She was still screaming as she saw the last of her demons fall.

She spoke a series of sounds and then smiled. Christof looked back and saw the largest demon he had ever seen rise up before him. "I am Gedamel." said the creature. "I am to destroy all of the Thalin clan. I guess I will start with you, Christof. Your pain in the heart is admirable, but makes you vulnerable." He said as he made images of his Annissa appear before him. Christof lost his focus for one moment and then he regained his composure but it was too late as the demon swung his great mace into him. Christof flew aside as the mace hit, and he was shocked and hurting. He stood up facing the demon and said, "Deception is your way and now I know it. What will you try now?"

The demon made an image of an angry Tanis facing him and the young man attacked once again at the demon. His swords met the side of the mace. A smiling demon moved down and swung his mace and whip. Each met with a sword and neither did any damage. Christof struck and hit the side of the demon's leg with the Holy Avenger. It left a gash that would have been a lot less damage had it been Warmonger or any other blade.

Christof attacked again being encouraged with the first shot. Christof over reached and the mace once more swept him to the side of the army. The young man moved quickly back to face the demon. Once more he attacked the distracted demon and a gash came deep into its whip arm. Archers finally attempted to aid Christof with volleys of arrows fired into the demon. The demon laughed and swung the mace into the archers. As he lined up for another strike Christof got into position and took off the demon's hand off just past its wrist. Mace and hand dropped as the demon finished his swing. He looked confused at the stump at the end of its arm and looked down to see the hand and mace on the ground.

Turning back to Christof, the demon struck the happy Christof with the whip. Spinning the young man in a circle and cutting his face. Christof launched a barrage of fireballs at the demon and attacked again, as the fireballs hit, with the Avenger. Christof hit the demon across the belly and the demon fell. It tried to rise but was quickly decapitated by the young man. Christof took the head to the Dark Queen. "I guess your vengeance had a bit of a problem. Take her back to Glasburg where we can have her trial and subsequent execution." He said as he threw the head of the demon into the cage with the Dark Queen.

The army moved back toward the city of Glasburg and they travelled singing songs of the bravery of Christof. Christof asked them to sing of Garren and Annissa. They were the true heroes of this war. Together with Gardell and Tanis. Too many to name were killed in the name of the Dark Queen and the Army of Light and the Thalins. And so many more were injured permanently. He said that those are who deserved the songs not the lucky ones who made it. The men sung of them and of Christof. The songs embarrassed him but Thomas remarked that was the cost of being a hero.

"I am no hero. I survived. That is all that makes me a hero." Stammered Christof.

"Boy, you saved many more lives from her potential harm by what you did. That demon alone was a danger that could have cost all of us our lives. It is not how you did it or who you did it for, it is the deed itself. You are going to end up a statue on the Fields of the Pheni. Right beside your grandfather. I will be there but on the other side along with Torlin and Meka and Roanda. But the people will consider it proper that you reside next to your grandfather's statue showing that you were the hero of this war. You brought in the Dark Queen and ended her reign of terror. You are a hero. Enjoy it. It will not last forever." said Thomas as they rode.

They rode for a mile when a large cloud came over the horizon and two groups of dragons fought with demons assisting one side. The army stopped and several men including Christof went to aid the dragons that were being assaulted by the demons. He raised his sword when alarm bells struck up on the other side of the army. Christof was about to return to the army when both groups of dragons and the demons attacked the small party. Christof did not see how the army fared but he was injured and covered by the body of a ranger.

Horns blew and the knights of Glasburg that had not come to the battle with the Dark Queen attacked the enemy attacking the now nearly depleted Army of Light. It took another hour but the land was saturated with the blood of men and all the races of Dracos intermingling on the ground. Even the blood of dragons and demons mixed with the other's blood.

Bodies were laying everywhere, the good guys and the bad guys. A woman danced for a while in the distance as the defenders of Glasburg came to assist the army. The woman disappeared as they arrived a large book in her hands. She would try again another day.

The army started to search for survivors in amongst the fallen. Thomas moved himself from under the body of the demon he had killed. Torlin was still tangling with a small demon and Thomas assisted him in dispatching the beast. The rescue army was now pulling the dead when they found Christof. They quickly wrapped him in linen and brought him to the druids. Christof woke to find himself in Glasburg with the druids working on him healing the wounds that he had had inflicted on him during the battle.

"Am I dead?" asked Christof.

"Not yet, my son. But it was a near thing. I return to Tetra in the morning and Torlin returns to Metra. The Dark Queen escaped and recovered the grimoire. We all did this for nothing. So many men lost." said Thomas.

"It was not for nothing. We have taken from her the greatest strength she possessed. She must now rebuild and she has nowhere to go but deeper into the Lost Lands. The people will regroup and fight without us now. Look Father, the sun rises above the Lost lands. No more shadows in the distance. The Lost Lands are no longer Lost. That is what we accomplished here." said Christof.

"Wise beyond his years it would seem." said Torlin as he pushed Christof down onto his back. Rest for the next adventure. Your wounds are not yet mended and you need to regain your strength. Sleep well, Demon slayer." said Torlin as he closed the light.

The end of Book Two of the Saga of Dracos

EPILOGUE

TIME TO COME

It would be a long time coming. Christof moved from his city into the newest palace they had just acquired. He had his feelers out and would know where and what she was up to. He knew she was out there but so too were many other new magical folks being born. He found out that she used to single out magical children and would drain their essence from them. It was an abomination.

But the war would come again. Both sides would have increased the numbers of soldiers they hired on. Better to be ready for the worst and hope for the best. The feelers felt the Dark Queen on one morning and it seemed to be she was in the palace throne room. Running quickly drawing his weapons, he entered the door of the throne room. Almedda sat there lounging like she was on a lounge chair, draped across both handles.

"You won this round. Do not try to find me. I will find you when this conflict will be ready for round two. Have a nice rest. You earned it and I need to rebuild my empire. Do not try it. I am leaving now. Just wanted to tell you I will be back." said the Dark Queen.

Christof slammed his swords back into their scabbards and sat in the throne that was now empty. He would be ready next time they met. He would be ready.

The End.

GLOSSARY OF NAMES

Name	Last Name	Definition
Artitous		Druid teaching the boys and girl
Bearman		A werewolf kind of bear/man black colored.
Dagmar		Ruler of the Tetradon
Faerimouth		Gargoyle like creatures
Furlac		Big red demons very strong.
Gedamel		Great demon that nearly killed Christof
Harriet		Mouse person who runs the clerks for Christof.
Mardocks		Undead Wizard killers
Martin		Head of Royal Rangers and tutor to the boys, Garren and Thomas.
Mastol		Dragon friend of the family
Meka	Paron	Wife of Thomas Thalin
Metradon		Original inhabitants of Metra. In stasis for 10,000 years
Morreal		Charina's Mother/ Drow Queen.
Paul	Alon	Thief and ranger. Son of Perrick Alon friend of Thomas.
Paulen		Leader of the Metradon Resistance.

Perrick	Alon	Thief and advisor to the royal family. Governor of the dwarves of Thalinburg
Tanis	Thalin	Immortal father of the children. Powerful magically and physically
Terrell	Piken	Boy who slays Morreal.
Tetradon		Original inhabitants of Tetra. In stasis for 10,000 years
Thalinburg		Capital of Dracos
Thomas	Thalin	Evil twin of Torlin who rules Tetra
Torlin	Thalin	Son who is Magical. Wizard more than druid. Rules Metra
Two Horns		Leader of the Metradon
Almeck Demons		Demons that phase into and out of existence.
Almedda	Thalin	Twin in the second set of twins. Druid more than wizard. Dark Queen.
Andromeda Spiders		Defenders of the dark lands
Annissa	Pixton	Christof love interest and clerk
Arlette	Thalin	Daughter of Torlin and Roanda smith
Asher		Evil wizard that takes Metra.
Athinina	Thalin	Mother of Thomas and Torlin, ruler of the world of Dracos.
Avery		Phoenix that bonds to Meka.
Barrish		Evil Druid Running from Thalinburg.
Callig	Lowery	Horse man in charge of horse in Metra saves Torlin's life and dies in process. -Sir
Carlee		Phoenix that bonds with Almedda
Chappel	Eisner	Elven leader in Landsdale
Charina	Thalin	Tanis first wife deceased
Christoph	Thalin	Son of Meka and Thomas magical
Claire		Mother of Almedda and Garren
Danson	Thalin	Son of Garren twin to Dunmar magical strawberry stain on right side of face.
Drummond		Noom assassin boss

Dunmar	Thalin	Son of Garren, magical no strawberry stain.
Elizarade		
Gaitlyn		
Garath	Thalin	
Gardell	Carlin	
Garren	Thalin	
Glasburg		
Hetrick		
Janell		
Jasper		
Javan		
Landsdale		
Larzod		
Lyonsdale		
Marcus	Sandou	
Marious		
Marzioa		
Metra		
Minotaurs		
Mirren	Overmeyer	
Monreal	DuPont	
Naga		
Narasimha		
Nargus		
Nemeth		
Pan	Thor	
Paul	Thalin	
Pommel		
Raylene		
Rexon		
Ridley		
Roanda	Steelhand	
Roland	Pikeman	

Romi		
Ruark		
Sasha		
Saundera		
Talicia	Brewster	
Tamron	Flatfeet	
Tetra		
Tobin	Masters	
Trintator		
Virgil	Jarvis	
Yangzom